The Sea
of
Tears

Raglam
*of the World*

• Ironpass

Northern Guardians

High
Fastness

• Northwarden

• Dencamp-on-the-Teeth

Cutter's Gap

• Kenting Rush

The Blackwood

EASTERN
KINGDOMS

• Highcastle

WOLD   • Wolfram

• Cavell Keep

Prank's Stone

The
KINGDOM

• Dolth

Rodez

Ran

The Straits of
Ilthros

Romney

Tiburn

Buyer

Sloop

THE
KINGDOM
OF
ROLDEM    • Roldem

Lyton

Bas-Tyra

• Sadara

Malac's Cross   • Silden   Cheam

Saladoor

Rillanon

The Sea of
Kingdoms

• Timons

*The Grey Range*

• Dean Taunton

• Mallow Haven

The Green Reaches

*The Peaks of Tranquility*

Pointer's Head

Peaks
of
the
Quor

• Jonril

GREAT KESH

• Kampari

Ishlang

Min

Ithra

Spires
of
Light

Mother
of
Waters   • Dosra

Ishap's Deep

Khattara

Caralién

Zacara

DARK
HAVEN

Kesh

Hattaresh

Sunnom

Wasra

Overn Deep

Kimri

*Grimstone Mountains*

• Tupa   Jalóme

Queral

The
Great
Sea

The Guardians

• Ahar

Hansulé

Ashunta •

The Girdle of Kesh

Brijané

Dong
Tai

Teléman

The
Clasp

THE
DRAHALI
KAPUR
DESERT

DRAGON MERE

*The Belt*

LESSER KESH
[KESHIAN CONFEDERACY]

Peaks
of
Torment

R.M. Askren 2007

# RIDES A DREAD LEGION

## ALSO BY RAYMOND E. FEIST

# RIDES A
# DREAD LEGION

BOOK ONE OF THE DEMONWAR SAGA

## Raymond E. Feist

*An Imprint of* HarperCollins*Publishers*

HarperCollins books may be purchased for educational, business, or sales promotional use. For information please write: Special Markets Department, HarperCollins Publishers, 10 East 53rd Street, New York, NY 10022.

FIRST EDITION

*Designed by Joy O'Meara*
*Map designed by Ralph M. Askren, D.V.M.*

Library of Congress Cataloging-in-Publication Data has been applied for.

ISBN 978-0-06-146836-0

09 10 11 12 13   OV/RRD   10 9 8 7 6 5 4 3 2 1

*Another one for my mom,*
*who is still my biggest fan after all these years*

# CONTENTS

# ACKNOWLEDGMENTS

As always, I am in debt to those who created Midkemia so many years ago, where paper, pencils, funnylooking dice, and cheap beer were excuses to hang out and develop lifelong friendships. We may not always be in touch as we used to be, but each time I tell a story in this world I'm reminded of some wonderful times.

To my editors—Jane Johnson, Jennifer Brehl, Katherine Nintzel, and Emma Coode—who helped with a difficult project, many thanks. I rarely ask for help but when I do you're there with great suggestions. You make me look good.

Thanks to Jonathan Matson, as always, for being far more than a business associate but a real friend who brings value to my life.

And to the many readers, old friends and new, who take the time to let me know you're enjoying the work; without you, I'd be doing something else.

*Raymond E. Feist*
*San Diego, California 2008*

# RIDES A DREAD LEGION

# CHAPTER 1

## WARLOCK

The demon howled its outrage.

Amirantha, Warlock of the Satumbria, reeled back from the explosion of mystic energies unexpectedly hurled at him. Had his protective wards not been firmly established, he would have instantly died; the demon was powerful enough to send sufficient force through the barrier to slam the magic-user hard against the cave wall behind him. The blow he took on the back of the head was going to raise a nasty bump in quick order.

Demons always brought with them a large amount of mystic energies, enough to destroy any unprepared mortal standing nearby as they entered this plane of reality. It was one of the reasons for erecting wards, beyond merely confining the demon to a specific location.

This one had arrived with a much more impressive explosion than the Warlock anticipated, and that surprised him.

Amirantha incanted a single word, a collection of otherwise meaningless syllables that together formed a key, a word of power that activated a much more complicated enchantment. It was a trick taught him years before, which often had been the difference between effective control of a summoned demon or dismemberment at his hands. This word strengthened the ward spell that confined the creature.

Amirantha regained his feet as the demon continued to howl at discovering himself summoned to this realm and confined. Experience had taught the Warlock that demons rarely objected to being summoned, as they found this world easily plundered. They just hated being confined and controlled. It was the one thing that made Amirantha's chosen area of study problematic: that which he studied kept trying to kill him.

Amirantha took a deep breath to calm himself and studied the enraged conjuration. The demon was not one he recognized; this was obviously a battle demon of some sort. Amirantha knew more, perhaps, than any man living on Midkemia about demons and their nature, but he knew only a tenth of what he wished to know. This particular one was new to him—though he conceded he hardly had an exhaustive knowledge of every demon in the Fifth Circle. He recognized the basic type: massive upper torso, roughly human in build, with a bull's head, or at least something that resembled a bovine. Long horns arched down and forward, giving weight to the Minotaurlike appearance. Absently, while beginning to conjure a spell designed to immobilize the demon, Amirantha wondered if such a monster had been the basis for the ancient myth of the Minotaur.

The legs were, if anything, goatlike, and there anything remotely familiar about the creature ended. The eyes burned like hot coals, and the body was covered in something like black fur up to the waist, though it was not wool, hair, or fur as Amirantha recognized such. The upper body was black leather, but slicker, shinier, as if leather had been tanned, dyed, and polished, and his horns were blood-red. Amirantha also observed from the howls shaking the cave that the demon's disposition was getting nastier by the second.

More to the point, the demon looked on the verge of rending his way through wards that should be impenetrable. Amirantha knew better than to ever place too much stock in the word "should" when a demon was involved.

He finished strengthening his spell of confinement and saw the demon step back a moment, shudder, then return to his attempt to rend the wards, accompanying his effort with an even louder bellow.

Amirantha's eyes widened slightly, his only outward concession to surprise. The demon just shrugged off a spell designed to immobilize any conjured entity. Or at least Amirantha's idea of "any" until this very moment.

Looking at the railing demon, Amirantha, Warlock of the Satumbria, stroked his chin whiskers as he considered what he observed. A vain man by any measure, he affected purple robes with silver needlework at the collar and sleeves and had his servant trim his beard and hair weekly, knowing exactly how it should look each time. His receding hairline had caused him to let his dark hair fall to his shoulders, and his dark brows and pointed chin beard gave him a look to match his calling in life: a summoner of demons. Or at least look the part to those who were willing to pay gold for the summoning or banishment of demons.

He muttered a very reliable invocation and watched. The demon should have instantly knelt before his master in abject obedience, but he could sense the summoned creature's rage growing at the command. Amirantha sighed in a mixture of frustration and confusion, and wondered what he had conjured this time.

Ignoring the ringing in his ears, the Warlock reached into a large belt pouch. He had personally sewn this pouch years ago, patiently weaving magic into the threads as he labored under the supervision of a master artificer named Leychona, in the great City of the Serpent River, his one and only attempt at fabricating magic cloth. He had been pleased with the results, this confining bag that let him gather together many stones of power without disastrous consequences. He was especially proud of the needle-work, but found the entire process so tedious and exasperating he now paid artificers and tailors to fashion what he needed in exchange for his own skills or his gold.

His finger rubbed lightly against a series of embroidered knots inside, which indicated each pocket he had fashioned. He found the one he sought in less time than it took to think on it and withdrew a stone prepared against a time such as this. Hold-ing it aloft, he incanted a spell that drew power stored in the stone and he directed it to the hastily reinforced barrier. He felt, almost physically, the shock reverberating through the ward as the demon hurled himself against the mystic defense.

Then the creature paused, looking at the space in the air where the barrier stood, *as if he could see it,* and pulled back his massive right fist. He unleashed a blow that might shatter a bull-hide shield, and Amirantha could swear he felt the shock from it travel through the air to strike him. At least that's what he told himself when he flinched.

Then the demon struck even harder, and Amirantha raised his hand to reinforce the barrier with more energy. To his aston-ishment, this time he did feel the energy translated into a blow that ran up his arm, as if he had struck a massive boulder with a sword or scythe. He stepped back, until he stood hard against the wall. "What do I do now?" he muttered absently.

Again the demon hurled himself at the barrier and Amiran-tha, Warlock of the Satumbria, knew he was going to get through. Pushing aside a sudden urge to laugh—the unexpected and dangerous often affected him this way—he drew out another object from his large belt pouch and smashed it on the floor.

A noxious gas erupted from it and Amirantha fled from the deep cave in which he had conjured the monster. It was a sum-moning area he had especially prepared for this ritual, protected by multiple wards and other safeguards he had erected against such a mishap. He hurried along a narrow tunnel, muttering, "What next?"

Reaching a larger open area closer to the entrance of the

cave warren, he cursed himself for a fool. All his real items of power were still in the cave where he had summoned the demon. He had been so surprised by the unexpected conjuration, he had left them on the floor. He had thought himself ready for any eventuality with the demons he usually summoned; it never occurred to him one he hadn't summoned might appear unexpectedly.

Shaking his head at his own stupidity, he stopped. At least he had left another lantern here, more to indicate which way he needed to go rather than any anticipation he might be fleeing this way for his life, having abandoned his other lantern. Muttering to himself, he said, "Sometimes I wish I was as clever as I claim to be."

He turned toward the tunnel through which he had just passed, realizing that if he didn't stop the demon here, the creature was free to choose another exit from the caves. Not only would that be bad for anyone living within the demon's reach, say ten thousand people by last census, it would also be disastrous for Amirantha's reputation.

The Governor of Lanada was waiting near a particular cave mouth, with a fairly sizeable retinue of soldiers but nothing that could stop this monster should it come their way, and not only would the Maharaja's Court look with disfavor upon any itinerant Warlock getting one of their regional governors disemboweled, he was almost certainly not going to be paid for banishing this demon.

He readied himself, pulling a long wand of ash from his belt. The device had been a commission made by the finest wandmaker in the Kingdom of Muboya, and was capable of seven very effective theatrical effects, each designed to elicit "oohs" and "aahs" of wonder from onlookers. But it also had four really powerful enchantments that could inflict significant damage if the need arose. Amirantha was fairly certain the need had arisen.

He was greeted by the stench of the gas he had released; designed to weaken and finally incapacitate demons, it was not all that pleasant for humans to inhale. He knew that meant the demon was through the wards and coming toward him. Then Amirantha winced.

It wasn't the odor that made him shudder but the cave-rattling sound, a combination of tones and vibrations that made his heart jump at the same instant he felt the need to cringe. It was a shriek of anger that made his skin crawl, as if he were listening to a smith sharpen a sword on a turning wheel—there were moments when the scream of metal sounded just like that. If nothing else, the Governor of Lanada was getting a better performance than the one Amirantha had originally planned.

Then the demon was coming straight at him.

A voice from behind said, "Need help?"

"It would be appreciated," the Warlock said to Brandos. His companion had been outside the cave mouth, reinforcement for just such a moment as this, ensuring the Governor didn't get curious and send in some guards to "help" the Warlock banish the demon.

Amirantha pulled out his ornately carved wooden wand and spoke a single word in a language known to very few living men. A searing burst of heat washed over the two men as a massive ball of fire exploded through the tunnel, sweeping over the demon, forcing him back a dozen steps.

"I'm going to need a few moments to banish it."

The old fighter was still powerful, though nearing fifty years of age, and had more experience than he wished to have confronting demonic opponents. This one looked to be the most dangerous so far. "Where are the rest of your toys?"

"Back in the summoning cave."

"In the cave?"

"Yes," said Amirantha quietly. "I realized that myself, just a moment ago."

"Well, then, we'll have to do this the difficult way, won't we?" He had a buckler, a small round shield, on his left arm, and he pulled a broadsword from its scabbard. "It's times like this I wish I had taken up baking."

Brandos knew he did not need to defeat the demon, only delay it long enough for Amirantha to banish it back to the demon realm. It was only a matter of a minute or two, but the experienced old fighter knew that even a few seconds could be a very long time. "Let's go in before he gets here. I don't welcome trying to keep him from those side tunnels. Best to keep him confined."

Amirantha took up a close position behind his friend, and Brandos moved forward a few yards, up the tunnel from where the demon had retreated from the flames. The stench of the gas filling the cave was nearly overwhelming, but it had the desired effect. The demon approached down the tunnel cautiously, halted, then stood motionless a moment, regarding the two humans.

The demon opened his mouth, and sounds issued, not the inarticulate sounds of rage and anger but something meaningful, with rhythm and distinct pronunciation.

Brandos said, "Is he casting a spell?"

Amirantha hesitated, his curiosity overcoming his need to rid this realm of the demonic visitor, and with haste. He spent only an instant listening before he realized Brandos was correct: the demon was a spellcaster!

"We should interrupt that, I think," said Amirantha. He hastily uttered a single word, another cantrip release that he had prepared against such encounters. The single word acted as a mystic placeholder for a long, involved spell, and instantly the full force of the enchantment was released. The result was rendering the raging demon suddenly unable to speak. The efficacy of the spell was dependent on several things; most important, how powerful a magic-user the target was compared to Amirantha. The average village enchanter would remain silent until Amirantha lifted the spell. A powerful magician would be silenced only for a minute or two. A more powerful magician would shrug the spell off with little effort. This demon was an unknown quantity.

Amirantha began the spell of banishment and was halfway through the incantation when the demon again found his voice, resuming his own incantation.

"Bloody hell," muttered Brandos, as he darted forward, starting a slow looping overhand blow at the demon's head, then, at the last moment, moved his blade aside as he knelt and unleashed an efficient and punishing blow at the demon's left leg. Shock ran up his arm as if he had struck a trunk of a massive tree, but the demon howled in pain and retreated back up the tunnel, his spell-casting interrupted. The demon was injured, as often is the case with cold metal, especially iron or steel, and knelt for a moment, nursing the injured leg. Beyond that, years before Amirantha had the old fighter's sword enchanted by a magician down in Maharta to inflict additional pain on demons. Now he wished he had paid the man for the spell to cause injury instead of mere distraction.

Amirantha finished his own spell and the air seemed to come alive with hissing energies. The demon screamed defiance, and then the very stones beneath their feet vibrated for a moment.

"He's still here," observed Brandos.

"I can see that," countered the Warlock. "He's using his own magic to remain here."

"What next?" asked Brandos.

"A more powerful spell of banishment, obviously. But we're going to have to wear him out."

"Wonderful," said Brandos, shaking his head. "So I bleed and you chatter."

"Try not to bleed too much."

"I'll see what I can do," said Brandos as Amirantha withdrew a large, gem-like object and smashed it on the floor.

A curtain of hazy ruby energy sprang up, bisecting the tunnel. "Back through the wards!" commanded Amirantha, and Brandos did not hesitate. He had been through too many of these confrontations to ignore the Warlock's instructions.

The magic-user had a deep voice, which resonated even more in the narrow confines of this tunnel, and as he quickly went through a cantrip to strengthen the new wards, he reached into his pouch once more. A tiny point of light pulsed on the palm of his hand as he held it out, cradling it, quickly growing into an orb of throbbing crimson light. He threw the orb at the demon as the creature moved purposely toward the two men.

Instantly the demon was engulfed in a scintillating web of crimson threads, exploding in tiny lights of white heat as they touched his skin. He howled and the stones of the tunnel shook from the sound, dislodging fine soil and rocks, which fell on Amirantha and Brandos. Brandos took a quick look above and behind, as if checking whether the entire hillside was about to come down on them. Seeing things were relatively stable, he returned his attention to the enraged demon.

"I think it's annoyed," Brandos said dryly.

"What was the first thing that made you notice?" asked the Warlock.

Brandos swung again as the creature advanced, giving Amirantha a moment longer to begin the complex spell of banishment. As a safeguard, he quickly placed another set of wards behind the first, as an emergency measure. Over the years enough mishaps with summoned creatures had given him reason to establish a series of increasingly powerful magical barriers at need.

The demon recoiled from the blow, but Brandos wasn't trying to attack it, only slow it down. "Back!" commanded Amirantha, and the old fighter was back across the next invisible threshold.

The Warlock uttered an invoking word and a wall of pulsing violet-colored energy sprang up from floor to ceiling, encircling the demon in the tunnel. It was a sizzling cylinder of light shot through with rose and golden colors, and the demon struck and recoiled, as if he had hit a wall of stone. Smoke coiled from his flesh and he exhibited charred wounds.

Brandos had fought enough demons to know that they expended energy to heal themselves; they were weakened each time they were injured. Demons had an exasperating ability to feed off other sources of energy, given the chance, so it was better to weaken them as fast as possible so the summoner could banish them back to the demonic realm. "Do I need to hit him a few more times?"

"Wouldn't be a bad notion," said the Warlock as he readied another set of wards.

9

Brandos feigned high and outside, causing the demon to raise his hands above his head; then the fighter crouched and thrust, taking the creature's left leg out from under him again. With another stone rattling bellow, the huge monster fell back, crashing onto the floor with almost black blood spurting into the air. It smoked and emitted a foul stench of burning sulfur when it splashed onto the stones, and Brandos pulled back.

"That was a good strike," observed the Warlock.

"I try for the greatest result from the least effort; I'm getting old, you know," said the fighter as he retreated back to where Amirantha had erected the next confounding wards. Taking a deep breath, as perspiration flowed down his face, he added, "One of these days you're going to get one of us killed."

"More than likely," agreed the Warlock.

"Or both of us," added Brandos, raising his buckler and holding his sword ready against any new, unexpected problem.

The demon healed the latest wound, slowly, and both men took that as a good sign. Healing required time without distractions, and the more he needed to heal, the more time he required. Lacking time, he devoured his own magic essence to heal injury, leaving less magic to use against Amirantha and Brandos.

"We're wearing him down," observed Brandos.

"Good," said Amirantha, "because he's wearing us down, too."

"Can you banish him?"

"A minute more, perhaps two."

"Very well," said Brandos, and he stepped forward, reading the boundary of the ward, striking hard at the demon. It was an easily anticipated blow, and the creature raised his hand to sweep Brandos's blade aside. Brandos had expected such a move. Demons were, if anything, predictable when it came to non-magical combat. In their realm, the bigger, stronger demon almost always won combat by simply overpowering the smaller, weaker opponent. Rarely did demons of the same stature confront one another. In this realm, their physical strength and savage nature gave them a decided advantage against any but the most powerful creatures. A greater dragon would make short work of such a foe, but anything smaller would be in for a severe test. For a single human swordsman, intelligence would have to overcome brute power. Brandos turned his wrist at the last instant as the demon tried to brush aside the blow, and let his blade slide along the upraised left arm of the demon, inflicting a scraping series of cuts that caused the demon to retreat a half-step. Then he lashed out with his uninjured right arm, almost dislocating Brandos's shoulder from the blow taken on his buckler.

Brandos retreated across the threshold of the wards again and braced for an onslaught. The demon hesitated only a moment, then charged Brandos. As he crossed the barrier of the ward, he shrieked in agony, but still came toward Brandos and Amirantha. It was three strides to where the fighter stood ready, and the demon paused to gather magic. Amirantha felt a spell of some consequence begin to manifest.

"Damn," said the old fighter. "More magic." He lowered his shoulder and charged.

The demon's spellcasting was interrupted by Brandos's heavy charge. He drew his buckler up against his left shoulder and rammed it into the demon's chest. It felt like hitting a stone wall, but it threw the demon backward a few feet and allowed Brandos just enough time to pull away before a massive clawed hand would have decapitated him.

Brandos lashed out with his sword, striking the demon's exposed arm. As he expected, the touch of magically enchanted steel caused another smoking wound and the demon again cried out in rage. As he pulled back to stand before Amirantha, Brandos shouted, "He's a first-time visitor to Midkemia; no protection spell in place to prevent harm from cold metal."

With a practiced move, fluid in its execution, Brandos let go of the hand grip on his buckler, letting it dangle off his arm. He flipped his sword from his right hand to his left, catching it with his now free hand while he drew out a dagger from his right hip. He threw the dagger with as much force as possible, impaling the demon's right foot, pinning it to the dirt floor. Black smoke and a sulfurous stench filled the cave, and the conjured creature screamed in pain. Then it fell silent, regarding the two humans with a demonic stare of glowing red eyes, and, with a calmer tone, resumed his incantation.

"Now would be a good time to finish," said Brandos, flipping his sword back into his right hand as he slipped his left back into the strap on his buckler. "This fellow is bloody determined!"

In a fraction of a moment, Amirantha had to make a choice, to continue his spell of banishment and risk Brandos being struck with a potentially lethal blast of magic, or abandon it and employ a spell prepared against such dangers.

His affection for his friend overcame his desire to finish this business in an orderly fashion, and he ceased his conjuration of banishment, shouting, "Close your eyes!"

Brandos did not need to be told more than once. He hunkered down as much as he could behind the small protection of his buckler, closing his eyes tightly.

Amirantha closed his eyes as he incanted a five-syllable word that had no meaning in any language known to humanity but which unleashed a very powerful and destructive bolt of energy. The Warlock knew from painful experience that a crimson bolt now flew out of his upraised hand to strike the demon. The energy would pour into the creature through his skin, causing him to light up from within.

A sudden flash of searing heat, lasting mere seconds but hot enough to scorch the hair on Brandos's arm, and the stench of something foul cooking filled the tunnel. Then it was silent.

Brandos let his arms drop to his side as he let out a long sigh. "I wish you didn't have to do that."

"So do I," returned Amirantha. "An orderly banishment is so much less taxing—"

"—and painful—" inserted the fighter, inspecting his singed arm.

"—and painful," agreed Amirantha, "than destroying the demon."

Shaking his head and again letting out a long sigh, Brandos said, "Have you ever considered this conjuration of demons so you can banish them for a fee might not be the best use of your talents?"

Smiling ruefully, Amirantha said, "Occasionally, but how else can I earn the coin necessary to broaden my knowledge of the demon realm? I've already learned as much as I could from those creatures we're familiar with."

"Speaking of which, why didn't one of them show up?"

Amirantha shrugged. "I don't know. I was seeking to conjure Kreegrom—he's almost a pet now."

Brandos nodded. "Ugly as sin. Have him chase you a bit back toward where the Governor's men can see him. Let him follow you back inside, give him a treat, and send him back." He nodded. "Good plan." Then he fixed his friend with a scowl. "If only it had worked!"

"I didn't think the creature I was conjuring was going to be a battle demon."

"A magic-using battle demon," corrected Brandos, as he sheathed his sword.

"A magic-using battle demon," echoed Amirantha. He looked into the tunnel, now filled with a noxious, oily black smoke. Remnants of charred demon flesh decorated the walls and floor of the tunnel and the stench was enough to make a battle-tested veteran vomit. Almost the entire left leg of the creature lay on the floor a few feet away. "Let us collect our fee from the Governor, remove ourselves from this quaint province, and return home."

"Home?" asked Brandos. "I thought we'd head north a bit, first."

"No," said Amirantha. "There's something here that is both familiar and troubling, something I need to ponder in my own study, with my own volumes to reference. And it's the safest place for us to be right now."

"Since when did you concern yourself with safety?" asked the old fighter.

"Since I recognized that familiar . . . presence behind this demon."

Brandos closed his eyes a long moment, as if weighing what he had just heard. "I'm not going to like this next part, am I?"

"Probably not," said Amirantha, inspecting the contents of

his belt bag, seeing what would have to be replaced. "When I let loose that final bolt of energy, and the demon exploded, a series of magic . . . call them signatures, hallmarks of spell craft, tumbled away. All of them were my own, the wards and spells I had fashioned, save two. One was the demon, which I expected, alien and unfamiliar, nothing out of the ordinary, but the last was another player." He was silent a moment, then said, "A player familiar to me. A magic signature as familiar to me as my own."

Brandos had been with Amirantha for most of his life and had heard many stories from the Warlock. He could anticipate what was coming next. Softly, almost as if sighing, Brandos asked, "Belasco?"

Amirantha nodded. "Belasco."

"Bloody hell," said the old fighter softly. His face was a map of sun-browned leather, showing years of privation and struggle. Hair once golden blond had been grey for more than two decades, but his startling blue eyes were still youthful. Shaking his head, he said, "Still, one thing about traveling with you, Amirantha, is things are always interesting."

"You find the oddest things interesting," said Amirantha.

"Comes from the company I keep," said Brandos.

Amirantha could only nod slightly. He had found Brandos as a street urchin in the City of Khaipur, nearly forty-two years ago. Despite being countless years older than his companion, the Warlock looked to be twenty years his junior. Both men knew that magic-user would outlive the fighter by a generation, yet they never spoke of it, except upon occasion Brandos quipping that Amirantha's proclivities would end up getting the old fighter killed before his time. Despite the unlikely appearance of the two men, Brandos looked upon Amirantha as a son looked upon a father.

How a practitioner of what could only be considered a particularly dark form of magic had come to play the role of foster father to an illiterate street boy was still a bit of a mystery to Amirantha, but Brandos had somehow insinuated his way into the magic-user's affections and they had been together since.

Amirantha led Brandos past the charred remains of the

demon to the summoning cave, and picked up two large leather bags, handing one to the fighter. Both men shouldered their burdens. Looking around the cave, the overturned ward stones, the burning pots of incense, and the other accoutrements of demon-summoning, the Warlock said, "Not that I'm criticizing, but what brought you to the cave?"

"You were taking a bit longer than normal and the Governor was getting restless. Then all that noise erupted and I thought I'd best see what had gone awry."

Shaking his head slightly, the Warlock said, "Good thing you did."

They exited the cave, a deep recess in the hillside a few miles away from the village of Kencheta. Waiting astride his ornately saddled horse was the Governor of Lanada, who said, "Is the demon dead?"

Raising his hand in an indifferent salute to the ruler of the region, Amirantha said, "Most efficiently dead, Your Excellency. You can find his remains somewhat scattered around the tunnel about a hundred yards within."

The Governor nodded once, signaled to one of his junior officers: "See that it is so."

Amirantha and Brandos exchanged glances. Local rulers were usually content with the promise of relief from whatever plagued their domains. On the other hand, Amirantha said to himself, they usually caught a glimpse or two of the demon, not just howls and bellowing from within a dark cave.

A short time later, the young officer returned, his face pale and covered with perspiration. Amirantha said, "I should have mentioned that peculiar stench—"

"You should have," agreed Brandos.

"—takes some getting used to."

"Well?" asked the Governor.

Nodding, the officer said, "It is so, Your Excellency. Most of the creature was strewn around the tunnels, bits here and there, but one leg was intact, and it was . . . nothing of this world."

"Bring it to me," instructed the Governor.

Again Brandos and Amirantha exchanged questioning looks.

This time the officer motioned to two of his older soldiers and said, "You heard the Governor. Go get the demon's leg."

A short time later the two soldiers emerged, carrying the huge charred leg between them. The smell caused even the most seasoned veteran to go pale, and the Governor backed his mount off slightly, holding up his hand. "Stay," he instructed.

From his vantage point, he looked over the leg, from the top of a thigh covered in burned hair down to a foot with three massive toes ending in razor-sharp claws. Whatever it might be, it was nothing of this world, and at last the Governor nodded. "We had word from the Maharaja's Court that charlatans promising to rid outlying villages of demons, dark spirits, and other malefactions were preying on the gullible. Had you been such, we would have hanged you from that tree," he said, pointing to a stout elm a few yards away. "As this is certainly what can only be a demonic limb, I am convinced your arrival so soon after word of this demon's appearance in the hills is but a lucky coincidence, and shall convey such to my lords and masters in the City of Maharta."

Amirantha bowed his most courtly bow, and Brandos followed suit only an instant after. "We thank His Excellency," said the Warlock.

As the Governor began to turn his mount, Amirantha said, "Excellency, as to the matter of payment?"

Over his shoulder, the Governor said, "Come to my palace and see my seneschal. He will pay you." With that, he rode off, followed closely by his men-at-arms.

Amirantha and Brandos were left alone and the Warlock said, "Well, at least it's on the way home."

Shrugging, the warrior picked up his friend's shoulder bag and said, "There are times one must settle for small benefits. At least this time we get paid.

"Maybe it was a good thing that demon showed up. Kreegrom is fairly hideous until you get used to how he looks, and the smell takes even longer, but for a demon he's about as menacing as a big, stupid puppy. If that Governor caught wind that he was playing 'chase me' with you and not really trying to kill you, well, I don't particularly relish ending my days hanging from an elm." He glanced at the indicated tree as they walked past it. "Though I will confess it's a handsome enough tree from which to be hanged."

"You do always see the good in a situation, don't you?"

"Someone around here must," said Brandos. "Given the usual nature of our trade."

"There is that," agreed Amirantha as they started down the road that would take them to the Governor's Palace in Lanada, then on to their distant home.

The village had been the closest thing to a home Amirantha had known in the last thirty years. His tower was atop an ancient hill, Gashen Tor, highest of the hills overlooking a village called Talumba, two days ride east of the city of Maharta. He resided there for four or five months a year. The rest of the time he and Brandos would travel.

The farming community had come to appreciate the presence of such a powerful user of magic close at hand, even if his chosen area of mastery was one considered dark and bordering on evil by most people. The Warlock had wandered from another land, they said, and had come to this lonely hillock to avoid persecution. He had built the single tower in which he resided, using demons as labor, it had been said, and he had placed wards about the tor to prevent invaders from troubling him.

The truth was far more prosaic, as Amirantha had used magic, but not his own, to build the simple tower. A pair of magicians, masters of geomancy, had used their arts to move rocks and place them in such a fashion that when they were done, Amirantha had only to have a local carpenter from the city install two wooden floors, hang doors inside, and build some furniture, including the large table before the magician, and the heavy chair in which he sat.

He studied some old texts he had written nearly a century before, letting out a long sigh of regret as he pushed them aside. He looked out the window of his study, at the village below, now in the reddish glow of sunset, and considered how more or less idyllic his life had become for the last twenty years—if you didn't put too much emphasis on the occasional mishap such as the one three days before up near Lanada.

He remembered when he had first come here, with the young Brandos, and how he had decided, almost at whim, to take up residence. He looked above the village at the distant sunset and wondered how much of his decision came from his affection for these sunsets. It was, he thought, an odd thing to become fixated on, but then so much of his life was a series of choices that looked arbitrary, even capricious, at times. Such as giving a home to an uncouth street boy who had tried to rob him more than forty years before.

This village was as much a home as any he had known since his own childhood, a time so distant he often had to stop and concentrate to remember much about it. The villages had at first been awed by, even frightened of, the Warlock on the Hill, as they called him, but he had prevented the raping of the village by marauders on more than one occasion, and had even kept the army of the ambitious Maharaja of Muboya from occupying the village when they had annexed this region into their burgeoning nation. He took pride in having done so with ruse and guile and no loss of life. While absent many of the concerns over right and wrong common to most people he knew, Amirantha did scruple over crossing certain boundaries.

Some of his concerns were simply practical in nature: dabbling in what were considered the blacker arts brought scrutiny that could lead to persecution. Most of his concerns, however, were for his own well-being; he had seen too many times that traveling down a certain very dark road to knowledge cost the magician far more than the approval of others. Not a pious man, the Warlock still wished to face Lims-Kragma as every man must some day, certain he had no major stains on his escutcheon, though he could accept having to explain a minor blemish here and there. He might not be considered a good man by some, simply because of his chosen art, but he had his principles.

Besides, he had seen better men than himself fall prey to the lure of the dark arts. It was a drug to most magicians.

He moved slightly in his seat and determined, as he had every day for the last two years, that he needed to take a trip to the city and purchase new cushions. He glanced around his study. The fire burned as it always did during the cold weather, casting a warm glow across the room. The sleeping quarters below were often drafty in the winter, and the magician often slept upstairs, next to the fire. He was convinced it had something to do with the way the chimney was fashioned, but never could find the time to have anyone look at it, so for three months a year he endured blankets on the floor.

Brandos entered the room, trudging heavily up the stairs from below, circular stone steps that hugged the interior of the round building. "What did you find?" he asked without preamble.

"What I feared," said the magician, standing up. With a wave of his hand he indicated the old tomes on the table. "I think we need to undertake a journey."

"Going shopping in Maharta, are we?"

Amirantha regarded his oldest friend. At nearly fifty years of age, the warrior was still a powerful-looking man, even if his hair was now completely grey bordering on white. His sun-worn, leathery face spoke of years campaigning, and he bore an impressive number of scars. "Well, yes, for I do need a new seat cushion, but that will have to wait." He glanced to his old tomes and said, "Something very bad is happening, I think, and we need to speak to someone about it."

Brandos pulled out another chair and sat. "Anyone specific in mind?"

"Tell me about this Kaspar."

Brandos smiled and nodded. He sat down on a small stool near the fire and said, "Here's what I know:

"About a month or so after General Alenburga disappeared ten years ago, this Kaspar of Olasko arrived in the Maharaja's court along with a small army of soldiers from the Tsurani world. The young ruler of Muboya gave Kaspar the title of General of the Army, announced that Alenburga had retired to some distant place, and turned his attention to consolidating his holdings while getting ready to conquer some more.

"But this is where it gets interesting. Kaspar seems to have earned the Maharaja's trust, and has come up with two diplomatic solutions to conflicts—set up a very difficult relationship with some of the Clans ruling the City of the Serpent River and annexed two city-states to the north without bloodshed. He's also gotten Okanala allied with Muboya after a long war, through a couple of well-crafted royal marriages, effectively ensuring that the Maharaja's grandchildren and the King of Okanala's will eventually end up ruling a combined empire. He helped Okanala put down two rebellions, and now Okanala and Muboya unite to move against those murderous little dwarves who live in the Grasslands to the west."

"A prodigious list of accomplishments for so short a period of time." Amirantha tapped his chin with his right index finger, a nervous gesture Brandos had seen since childhood. "Now, what else?"

"Speculation and rumor. Kaspar is an outlander, from far across the sea to the northwest, a nation called Olasko, so I have been told. He was a ruler there before being deposed, and for some years has been absent. Somehow he became close to General Alenburga and little is known of that. It is also rumored he vanishes for a week or so from view in Muboya's new capital city of Maharta, simply to show up again as if he had always been there."

"Magic," said Amirantha. "He goes somewhere, but no one sees him leave or return."

"Or he enjoys very long naps in the privacy of his quarters," quipped the old fighter. "Perhaps with friends; he's reputed to have quite the eye for the ladies."

Tapping his chin as he weighed his options, Amirantha was silent a long while. Brandos knew his foster father preferred silence when he was reflecting, so the old fighter got up and left the study, trudging down the stairs.

The tower was a simple cylindrical keep, with three levels, the middle consisting of two large rooms, one for the Warlock and one for Brandos and his wife, Samantha. Brandos crossed the short distance down the tiny hallway separating the two sleeping rooms and moved down the stairs to the bottom floor, where the kitchen, storage room, and garderobe were housed. The kitchen smelled of fresh-baked bread and something bubbling in a cauldron by the fire—Samantha's well-regarded chicken stew, if Brandos knew his wife's cooking, and he did.

Brandos paused a moment to observe his wife, a stout woman who still could spark a fire in her husband with a whispered suggestion in his ear. The years had taken their toll on the former tavern girl from the Eastlands. She was wearing a simple green dress, with a blue cloth wrap fashioned into a head-covering, in the manner of the people of the Eastlands. Brandos had met her in the huge tavern at Shingazi's Landing, on the Serpent River where it bends near the Eastern Coast, less than a mile west of the Great Cliffs, overlooking the Blue Sea. With the aid of a lot of flirtation, and a lot of good wine, she had agreed to come to his bed.

But rather than forget her, as he had so many before her, he kept thinking of the pleasant-looking, somewhat plump young woman from the Eastlands. After Brandos had spent months mooning over her, Amirantha gave his foster son leave to go visit her.

He returned a month later with his new wife in tow. Despite Amirantha's original reservations, he had come to understand that Brandos had found something rare in his tavern wench from the Eastlands. A fact Brandos knew the Warlock envied, even if he had never spoken a word.

Brandos knew his foster father better than any man alive knew him, and he knew that only once in his life had the old magic-user succumbed to a woman's guiles. The entire encounter still amused him; if it weren't for the fact of Amirantha's genuine pain at how that liaison turned out, it would have been the stuff of a comic bard's ribald tale.

Samantha looked up at her husband and smiled. "Ready to eat?"

"Yes," he said, returning the smile.

As he sat at the table, her expression turned to a frown. "Very well, when are you two leaving?"

Brandos shook his head and smiled ruefully. She could read him like a broadside posted on a wall in the city square. "Soon, I think. Amirantha is very troubled by what happened up in Lanada."

She only nodded. One of her knacks was ignoring how her husband and his foster father made their living: by contriving to summon demons in distant lands then banishing them for a fee. Yes, they occasionally did do real work, dangerous work, for those willing to pay, but those were rare callings, and the rest of the time the two were little better than a pair of confidence tricksters.

Still, there were things she and Brandos were willing to argue about, and things left unspoken; it's why their marriage had lasted for twenty-three years.

"Is there any point to me asking why?" she said coolly. "It's not like it was when the children were here." She stopped and looked at her husband almost accusingly. "Bethan is out at sea, sailing who knows where? Meg is living with her husband up in Khaipur."

"Donal is down in the village with the grandchildren. You can walk down to visit any time," he quickly countered. He knew where this was heading.

"And his wife just loves having me around," she said archly.

"What is it about two women under the same roof?" asked Brandos rhetorically.

"She'll come around when the baby is born and she needs another pair of hands, but until then, she sees me as an intruder." As he was about to speak, she cut him off, her vivid blue eyes fixed on him as she absently pushed back a strand of grey hair trying to escape from under her head covering. "It's lonely here, Brandos. With just myself, and you gone for weeks, even months at a time . . ." She let out a theatrical sigh. "When you returned early, I can't tell you how happy that made me.

"When are you going to stop all this traveling? I know how wealthy we are. You don't need to do this anymore."

"That would be true if Amirantha wasn't always worried about what he might have to spend someday to buy one of his . . .

devices, or an old libram of spells, or whatever else he might take a fancy to," countered her husband. "Besides, it is his wealth, isn't it?"

"Yours, too," she shot back. "It's not as if you were sitting around doing nothing."

He knew there was no avoiding the subject. "Look, most times I would be arguing on your side, agreeing with what you're saying. We just got home, we've been gone over a month, but this time, well, we have to go."

"Why?"

Samantha put her hands on her hips and repeated, "Why?" Her tone was defiant and bordering on angry, and Brandos knew for the sake of his peace of mind he must tell her.

"It's Amirantha's brother."

She looked stunned. She blinked and then asked, "Belasco?"

He nodded once.

She said, "I'll prepare a travel bag. Enough food to take you to the city. You can buy the rest as you go."

Her sudden change in mood and manner were entirely understandable. Over the more than two decades they had been together, she had heard the same stories Brandos had, as Amirantha chatted over supper. And she knew two facts without being told: Belasco was a magician of mighty arts, easily Amirantha's equal, and he had been trying to kill Amirantha since before Brandos or Samantha had been alive.

# CHAPTER 2

## KNIGHT-ADAMANT

Sandreena sat motionless.

She focused her mind on the seemingly impossible task of thinking of nothing. For seven years she had practiced this ritual, whenever conditions permitted, yet she never reached that total vacancy of thought that was the goal of the Sha'tar Ritual.

Despite her eyes being closed, she could describe the room around her in precise detail. And that was her problem. Her mind wanted to be active, not floating blankly. She resisted the urge to sigh.

On her best days in the temples, she found something close to nothingness, or at least when the ritual ended she had no memory of anything and felt very relaxed. She was still not entirely convinced that not remembering what she had thought about and having no thoughts were the same thing. That concern always caused Father-Bishop Creegan some amusement, and the fact she was thinking of the Father-Bishop was another reminder that today she was far from her goal of floating consciousness.

She was aware of every single thing in the room around her. Without opening her eyes, she could recount every detail in the room; her ability to notice detail and recall it without flaw was a natural skill honed and refined since joining the Shield of the Weak. Her vows required her to protect those unable to protect themselves, a task far more complex than first apparent. Often in disputes, there was little time to ascertain the justice of a claim, or the right and wrong of an issue, so it took quick judgment in deciding where and how to intervene. Attention to detail often gave her an advantage in not making things worse, even if she couldn't make them better.

The smell of the wooden walls and floor, rich with age, and the faint pungency of oils used daily to replenish them and keep them sealed against the moisture tantalized her, recalling memories of other visits to this and other temples. She could hear the faint hissing of water on hot rocks as the acolytes almost silently moved through the room, bringing in hot rocks from a furnace outside, managing to carry an iron basket with the glowing balsa, placing them quietly on the floor, then ladling water over the surface, a sprinkling that caused steam to rise with very little sound. She remembered her days as an acolyte, concentrating with all her willpower to move through a room much like this one without disturbing the monks, priests, and occasionally a knight like herself. It had been her first step on the path toward serving the Goddess. As many as a dozen men and women would sit silently, their clothing folded neatly on benches along the rear wall, and her job had been to ensure the tranquility of the room remained undisturbed. Like others silently treading around her now, she had worked mightily to discharge her tasks yet not become a distraction for those meditating. At that time, she had wondered if there could be a more difficult task; now she knew the acolytes had the simple role, and those seeking floating consciousness the more rigorous challenge.

She felt perspiration dripping down her naked back, almost but not quite enough of an itch to make her wish to scratch. She willed her mind away from the sensations of her own flesh. She was sitting with feet crossed, eyes closed, her hands resting palms-up on her knees; nothing was supposed to distract her from seeking floating consciousness; yet that drip of perspiration was almost as if she were being touched. She felt her annoyance at being annoyed by it begin a cycle she knew well. Soon she would be as far removed from a floating consciousness as she would be in combat or taking a lover. She found a spark of irony, because in both those cases, she might even be closer to floating consciousness; other parts of her mind seemed to predominate when fighting or loving, not every questioning, every critical part that made her difficult for most people to be with.

Like all members of her order, Sandreena was always welcome at any Temple of Dala, the Patron Goddess of those who swore oath to the Order of the Shield of the Weak. Being a member of an errant order, she wandered where the Goddess directed, often being the only authority or protection for small villages, tiny caravans, or isolated abbeys. She often adjudicated disputes and dispensed equity by reason, but she was well equipped to do so by force of arms if necessary.

She turned her mind into the sensation of that drop of perspiration that was now reaching the top of her tailbone, and as it pooled there for a moment, she metaphorically dove into it, seeking to float within it. She took slow, deep breaths, enjoying the almost sybaritic pleasure she took from the hot steam, the silence, and the total absence of threat as she found her quiet place within that drop on her spine. A light breeze outside made some brass wind-chimes ring softly, heightening the calming experience. Then she caught a hint of something unwelcome, a musky male odor so slight it was almost unnoticeable. It hit her like a physical slap.

She knew the ritual was over. This was not the first time since joining the order her presence in the sanctuary brought unwelcome results. There were two other women partaking in the ritual, neither young nor attractive by common measure. Such considerations should be of little consequence in the service of the Goddess, but human beings were by nature imperfect, and often those considerations became important. Sandreena shifted her weight, feeling each muscle tense and relax in turn as she ended her meditation. Now she was very aware of her nakedness, the perspiration running down her back and between her breasts, and her hair matted to her head. One young acolyte waited near the door to the bathing room, with a towel of coarse weave for her use.

She stood, one fluid motion, like the dancer she had been once in another life, and, without looking behind, knew one of the young Brothers was watching her depart, examining every movement as she quietly left the room. She knew what he saw: a young woman of exceptional beauty, with sun-colored hair cut at the shoulders and a pair of heroic battle scars, but no other obvious flaw. She knew there were many flaws, but they were all within. And she saw her own beauty as a curse.

Long legs, strong buttocks, narrow hips and waist, and a little broad in the shoulders, she was at the height of her physical power. But nothing could change her face, the straight, almost perfect nose, the set of her pale blue eyes, slightly upswept—almost exotic—a full mouth, and chin bordering on the delicate. She was stunning when she smiled, though that was a rare occurrence. Even in the armor of her order, men still turned to watch her pass.

She resisted the temptation to turn and see which of the young Brothers had been aroused by her presence; that was his burden to bear and if he was wise in the teachings of the Goddess, he would know it was his weakness to overcome, a lesson put before him to instruct and make him stronger.

She just hated the idea of being someone else's lesson.

Sandreena took the towel and entered the bathing room, sitting on a bench before a bucket of cold water. She picked up the bucket and inverted it over her head, embracing the sudden shock of cold and the clarity of thought it brought. She used a towel to dry herself off and reveled in the quiet of being alone in the bathing room. In her lifetime she had experienced very little solitude. Perhaps above anything else her calling had brought her, those times alone on the road or in camp, when all she heard were what nature provided—the wind in the branches, birdcalls, and animal sounds—those were the moments she prized the most.

After that came her time here, in the Temple in Krondor. It was, as much as any place, what she thought of as "home." She had been raised in the streets by a mother addicted to every drug known, favoring Dream, the white powder that, when smoked, reduced one's consciousness to a day or more of intoxicated images and experiences, more vivid than life itself. Her mother had protected her, as much as her weaknesses permitted, until she began to become a woman. What Sandreena considered her curse, a body that took away the breath of foolish men, came early in her eleventh year, and by the thirteenth Banapis celebration she had become a beauty. Her mother had shown her tricks: keeping dirty, cutting her hair short, binding up her breasts to look boyish. That had kept her daughter safe until the age of fourteen, when one of the bashers had caught a glimpse of her and saw through the disguise.

The Mockers of Krondor were a loosely run organization under the control of the Upright Man, but not so tightly controlled that the well-being of one street girl was of any consequence. The basher took her while her mother was unconscious in the throes of delirium induced by a gift of a vial of Bliss. After that he had come looking for her on a regular basis. He always brought Bliss, or Dream, or one of the other narcotics sold by the Brotherhood of Thieves, which was all her mother cared about.

Sandreena finished drying off and went to the dressing room. Her armor was being tended by the monks detailed to care for visiting Sisters and Brothers of the Shield. She quickly donned her preferred raiment: baggy trousers and a loose-fitting tunic, both of unbleached linen cloth; heavy boots; and her belt. As she dressed, she reflected her first man actually hadn't been such a bad fellow. At the end he professed love for her, and she remembered his taking her as being almost gentle in a clumsy, fumbling way. It was the men after him who taught her what it was to be cruel.

She was fifteen years old when she got word her mother was dead. Too much of a drug, or a bad drug, or a man taking out his anger on her; no one knew the cause, save she was found floating in the bay near the Fisher's Dock at the south end of the harbor. It was strange she was that far from her usual haunts, but not strange enough for the Upright Man or any of his lieutenants to look into the mater; what concern had they over the death of another addict whore? Besides, she had given the Mockers a daughter who was a better value than the mother had been. This girl was a true beauty, with a face to make men turn and a body to make them stay. After she had been taken from a particular bruiser's crib and installed in one of the city's finer brothels, she began earning real gold. For a while, Sandreena had learned what it was to wear silks and gems, have her hair clean every day, and be given good food. She had become expert in the use of unguents, oils, scents, and all manner of makeup. She could look as innocent as a child or as wicked as a Keshian courtesan, depending on the client's need. She was schooled on how to comport herself and how to speak, learning the languages of Kesh and Queg, but more important, how to speak like a well-born lady. For teaching her language, reading and writing, and how to learn, she forgave her captors enough to not hunt them down, each and every one, and deliver a harsh punishment. The Goddess taught forgiveness. But she vowed never to forget.

What she hadn't forgiven her captors for was an appetite for things that were better avoided—too much wine, many of the same drugs her mother craved, fine clothing and jewelry, and, most of all, the company of men. Sandreena had left her previous profession with one profound ambivalence: she craved the touch of men she despised, and hated herself for that desire. Only the discipline of the Order kept that conflict from destroying her otherwise strong mind. And the experience she had with two men in her life.

Sandreena left the dressing room and found a young acolyte waiting for her. "Father-Bishop would like a word with you, Sister."

"At once," she responded. "I know the way."

Dismissed, the boy hurried along on another errand, and Sandreena let out a barely audible sigh. The Father-Bishop had managed to give her two full days of rest before finding something for her to do. As she started toward his office, she amended that thought: something dangerous that only a lunatic would agree to do.

She reached a corner of the temple and looked out a vaulted window. To her left she could see the Prince's palace, hard by the royal docks and dominating the entire city. To the right were two of the other major temples close at hand, in what was called Temple Square: the home of the Order of Sung and the Temple of Kahooli. The other major faiths had their temples close by as well, but those two were especially close. She wondered, not for the first time, what her life would have been like had Brother Mathias been in a different order.

He had been the first member of the order she had encountered, and the first of the two men in her life for whom her feelings were not dark; she loved Brother Mathias as a daughter loved a father. After three years in the elegant brothel, one of them lost to the very drugs that had taken her mother, she had been sold by the Mockers to a Keshian trader of enormous wealth; he had become so enamored with Sandreena he had insisted on buying her and taking her back to his home in the Keshian city of Shamata. As he was as active in illegal trading as he was in honest trading, the Mockers considered him a valuable associate, and while not in the habit of selling girls—slavery was not permitted in the Kingdom of the Isles—they gladly vended her services for an unspecified duration to him, in exchange for a prodigious sum of gold.

It had been Brother Mathias who had saved her life and changed it. She could not remember that first encounter without becoming overwhelmed with feelings, and now was not the time to show them—not before the Father-Bishop, in any case. She turned her mind from memory and to the matter at hand.

She reached the modest office wherein worked the single most powerful man in the Order of the Shield of the Weak. In the Order, only the Grand Master in Rillanon ranked higher. As the Grand Master's age had robbed him of the ability to carry out any but ceremonial responsibilities, most of the Order's business was directed by the seven Father-Bishops. The most persistent rumor was that Father-Bishop Creegan was the most likely prelate to become the next leader of the Order when the Grand Master's health finally failed him.

To the surprise of nearly everyone who came to see the Father-Bishop, his office contained no anteroom, no clerk or monk waited outside, and the door was always open. Everyone who resided in the Temple in Krondor knew the reason: the Father-Bishop's door was always open to anyone who needed to speak with him, but for the sake of the Goddess's mercy, one's reasons for disturbing his work had better be good ones.

She stood outside the door, waiting to be bidden enter. She remembered the first time she had been here, having come fresh from her training at the Temple in Kesh. She had returned to Krondor with a mixture of anticipation and fear, for she had not been back to the city for five years, since being sold to the Keshian. One minute in the presence of the Father-Bishop, and every concern she had about returning to the Kingdom's Western capital had vanished. If ever a man lived who could be simultaneously in the moment and constantly planning the future, it was the Father-Bishop.

He noticed her standing there and waved her in. "I have something that needs investigating, Sandreena."

He didn't indicate she should sit in one of the four chairs placed around the room, so she continued to stand. His desk was simple, little more than a table with a single stack of open baskets nearby in which to place documents for his staff to dispose of, and he kept them busy.

He would be considered a handsome man, Sandreena conceded, not for the first time, but there was something in his manner that was off-putting, a quality that might be considered arrogant if he wasn't always right. Still, he had been instrumental in helping the former whore from this city find a meaningful way through life, and for that she would always be grateful. Besides, she considered, he always found the most interesting tasks for her, so long as they didn't get her killed.

"I am ready, Father-Bishop."

He glanced up, then smiled, and again she felt a strong sense of pleasure at even the hint of his approval. "Yes, you always are," he acknowledged.

He sat back, waving her over to a chair. She knew that meant a long discussion, or at least a very complex set of instructions. "You look well," he observed. "How have you been since last we spoke?"

She knew he already knew exactly what she had been doing in the year and a month since she had last been in his office. She had investigated a report of interference with lawful temple practices in the Free City of Natal—false—then on to the far Duchy of Crydee, where an isolated village was suspected of harboring a long sought-after evil magician by name Sidi—also false. But she had encountered a mad sorcerer who had attempted too much investigation into what were called the Dark Arts, and had to save the population of a village from his depredations. His small band of dark spirits had completely sacked the village, leaving those surviving without means to endure the coming winter. She interceded with the younger son of the Duke of Crydee, who agreed to send aid to the village—his father and elder brother had been away from the Castle at Crydee, and the boy had easily ordered the Castle's reeve to send help quickly. In all, it had been a very prosaic but important burden, once the mad magician had been disposed of. The Duke's younger son, a boy of no more than fifteen, by name of Henry, the same as his father, had impressed Sandreena. He was called Hal, and had shown both maturity and decisiveness in acting as interlocutor between his father's surrogate and the itinerant Knight-Adamant of the Temple of Dala. Often the outlying villages seemed more a burden than a benefit to the local nobles, producing little in the way of income from the land but often requiring a disproportionate degree of protection from marauding bands of renegades, raiding goblins or dark elves, or whatever other menace inhabited those regions, and there appeared to be quite a few.

She had spent the better part of the past year there, and had left only once she saw the village back on a firm footing. Along the way back to Krondor she had intervened in a half-dozen minor conflicts, always taking the side of the outnumbered, besieged, or beleaguered, as was the calling of her order, attempting to restore a balance and work out a peaceful solution, mediating where she could. And she was often struck by the irony of just how much violence needed to be employed to achieve a nonviolent outcome.

"What are your orders, Father-Bishop?"

He furrowed his brow slightly. "No time for pleasantries? Very well, then. To your task. What do you know of the Peaks of the Quor?"

Sandreena paused a moment before answering. The Father-Bishop had little time and less patience for attempts to impress him, so she finally said, "Little that is germane to what you wish me to know, I suspect."

He smiled. "What do you know?"

"It is a region of Kesh, south of Roldem, yet despite that isolated and sparsely populated. Rumor has it smugglers put in there from time to time, seeking their way past Roldem and Kesh's revenue ships, but more than that I do not know."

"There is a race of beings there, the Quor. Hence the name. They are in turn protected, if that is indeed the correct term, by a band of elves."

At that she raised an eyebrow in surprise. To the best of her knowledge, elves resided in the lands north of Crydee.

"We have a little information beyond that, but not much. This is why I have decided to send someone down there."

"Me, Father-Bishop?"

"Yes," he replied. "There is a village on the eastern side of the peninsula, by the name Akrakon, the inhabitants being descendants of one of the more annoying tribes of the region, but long ago subjugated by Kesh. They more or less mind their manners, but lately they've been troubled by marauding pirates." The Father-Bishop's tone changed, as if he were being reflective. "We've had word of these pirates before, for over ten years. We have no idea who they are, and why they would trouble villages like those along that coast . . ." He shrugged. "All we know is they seem to have an affinity for sporting black headgear: hats, scarves, and the like. Where they come from, what they want, whom they serve . . ." Again he shrugged. "Be cautious; occasionally they number a magic-user or two in their crew. Our first report of them involved a demon, as well."

She nodded. Now she knew why she was chosen. She had faced down more than one demon in her short tenure with the order.

"As Kesh's Imperial Court is occupied by far weightier concerns, it is fallen to us to investigate this injustice."

"And if I should also happen to discover more about these people in the mountains above, the Quor, all the better."

"All the better," he agreed. "But be cautious, for there is another complication."

Dryly, she said, "There always is."

"Apparently, very powerful people are also interested in these Quor and those elves who serve or protect them. People who have influence, even reach, into very high offices." He sat back and said, "The magicians."

She didn't need to ask whom he meant. The Magicians of Stardock had for a very long time been mistrusted and looked on with deep suspicion by the various temples in the Kingdom and Kesh. Magic was the special province of the gods, granted to their faithful servants to do the work the gods intended. Magicians were seen as expropriators of powers intended for only a chosen few, and as such suspect at best, untrustworthy at worst. Many magic-users were seduced by the darker arts, several being marked for death by the Temple's leadership due to past wrongs.

Sandreena had had several encounters with magic-users over the years, most with unhappy outcomes, and those that weren't

were still difficult. The sad truth was even the most depraved of
them had some reason that justified their behavior. She recalled
one particularly ugly encounter with a group of necromancers,
a trio of maniacs who had become so overcome by madness
there had been no alternative for the Holy Knight but to see
them dead. She still carried a puckered scar on her left thigh as
a reminder that some people are incapable of reason. One of the
dying magicians had thrown some mystic dark-magic bolt at her,
and while the initial injury had been minor, the wound would
not heal, festering and growing more putrid by the day. It had
taken a prodigious amount of work by healers in the temple to
keep Sandreena from losing her leg, or worse, and she had been
abed for nearly a month from it.

"I'll be alert to any sign the magicians have a hand in this,
Father-Bishop."

"Before you go, have you paid a courtesy visit to the High
Priestess?"

Sandreena smiled. No matter how devoted the members of
the Order might be, there was always politics. "Had you not
summoned me from my meditation and cleansing, I would have
paid that call first, Father-Bishop."

Creegan smiled ruefully. "Ah, just when I thought things
were going smoothly, I cause a fuss."

"That fuss was caused long before today, Father-Bishop."

He shrugged slightly. "The High Priestess is . . . steadfast
in her devotion, and among those who are not pleased to see
their brightest students choose the Adamant Way. You would
have risen high in the Order as a priestess, we both agree. Still,
it is not for us to question the path upon which the Goddess has
placed you."

Sandreena's smile broadened. "Perhaps not to question, but
apparently it is permitted to demand a certain level of clarifica-
tion."

Father-Bishop Creegan laughed, which he rarely did. "I miss
your wit, girl."

She resisted the urge to reflexively sigh at the word. He only
called her girl in their more private conversations, and there had

been a time when their mentor and protégé roles had come very close to becoming something far more personal. The Orders of Dala were not celibate; though, like in most clerical orders, the demands of the calling made marriage and family a rare thing, liaisons did occasionally occur. Still, for a man of his rank and stature to become intimate with an acolyte, or even a Squire-Adamant, would have been inappropriate or at least awkward. Moreover, her natural suspicion of and aversion toward all men until she'd met Brother Mathias had made it difficult for her to be clear enough in her own feelings to trust what she perceived as a more personal interest in her by the Father-Bishop. So they had never confronted the tension between them. Still, both were painfully aware of the attraction. Forcing down disturbing feelings, Sandreena said, "If there's nothing else, Father-Bishop?"

"No, Daughter," he said formally, apparently recognizing his own previous choice of words. "May the Goddess look over you and guide you."

"May she guide you as well, Father-Bishop," said Sandreena. She quickly departed and made her way down the long corridor that dominated the south side of the huge temple. Directly to the north was the huge central temple yard, with the worshipers' court and several shrines around the edge. Unlike other temples, there were few causes for public worship of Dala, but there were many occasions when suppliants came to offer votive prayers and thanks for the Goddess's intercession. So there was a constant coming and going through the main gates of the temple, at all hours of the day and night.

As a result, most business within the temple took place in the offices along this one corridor. Residences and guest quarters, servants' quarters, and all the requisite function rooms, kitchen, pantry, laundry, as well as the baths and meditation gardens were on either side of the great courtyard. Sleeping quarters for the clergy and those, like herself, of the martial orders, were in a basement hall, below the one she now walked.

At the opposite end of the hallway was the office of the High Priestess. The fact that the offices of the two leaders of the temple were as far from one another as physically possible was not lost on many. Unlike the informality of the Father-Bishop's office, the High Priestess had an antechamber, in which sat one of the Priestesses of the Temple, the High Priestess's personal secretary. She looked up as Sandreena entered the room. If she recognized Sandreena from previous visits, she didn't show it.

"Sister," she said softly, in even tones. "How may I assist you?"

Fighting off a sudden urge to turn and walk out, she said, "I am Sandreena, Knight-Adamant of the Order of the Shield. I am paying a courtesy call upon the High Priestess."

The woman, slender and of middle years, stood up, and made the motion look almost regal. She wore the plain robes of the Order, a brown homespun bleached to a soft off-white tan. Around her neck she displayed the sign of the Order, a simple shield hanging from a chain, but it was not lost on Sandreena that they were made from gold and of fine craftsmanship. A gift from the High Priestess, no doubt. "I will see if the High Priestess has a moment for you."

Sandreena quietly prayed a moment was all she had, for she knew that an invitation to sit and "chat" meant a long and tedious inquisition. A moment later Sandreena's worst fears were justified when she was ushered into the High Priestess's chambers and found two chairs flanking a table with a fresh pot of tea.

High Priestess Seldon was a robust-looking, stout woman in her fifties. She had cheeks that could only be called rosy and hair so light grey as to border on white. Which made her sable-dark eyes all the more dramatic and penetrating when she fixed her gaze upon Sandreena, as they had on more than one occasion. "Ah, Sister," she said while beckoning Sandreena to take the empty chair. The High Priestess was an ample woman, who seemed to grow in girth each time Sandreena met with her—or the Knight-Adamant simply couldn't recall just how large a woman she was.

"What brings you to Krondor, child?" she asked. Sandreena almost winced. If "girl" meant the Father-Bishop was putting aside his authority, "child" meant the High Priestess was asserting hers. Despite the fact that Sandreena had served for four years as a Squire-Adamant in the temple and trained in every weapon blessed for use by the Order, and that for three years since she had been allowed to wander the Kingdom and Northern Kesh as a weapon of the Goddess, the High Priestess was ensuring that Sandreena remembered who was in authority in Krondor and that she was the traitorous girl who had given up the path of the Priestess and had taken up arms better to bludgeon the unworthy into seeing the error of their ways.

Just as Sandreena was about to answer, the High Priestess said, "Tea?" Without waiting for her guest to answer, the High Priestess began to pour the hot liquid into fine porcelain cups. Sandreena examined the cup handed her by the High Priestess and said, "Tsurani?"

Her hostess shook her head and said, "From LaMut. But it is of Tsurani fashion. Real Tsurani porcelain is far too dear in cost for us to use here. The Goddess provides, but not to excess, child."

Even that tiny explanation felt like a reproach to Sandreena.

"So, again, why are you in Krondor?"

Sandreena knew she owed no explanation to anyone to visit any temple of the Goddess. She could claim it was mere happenstance that brought her to the capital of the Western Realm of the Kingdom of the Isles. She also knew with certainty the High Priestess would already know of her being summoned to the Father-Bishop's office. Why believe in coincidence when a conspiracy is possible?

"I was in Port Vykor, High Priestess."

"Visiting Brother Mathias?"

Sandreena nodded. He had been the one to first bring her to the Mother Temple in Kesh, where she had been tutored with the expectation she would become a priestess. He had come into her life again, when after coming to Krondor, she had changed her calling from that of a novitiate in the Priesthood to a Squire-Adamant in the Order of the Shield of the Weak. Mathias had stepped in to take her as his squire when the debate between the High Priestess and Father-Bishop

Creegan had grown contentious. After years of visiting Krondor, Sandreena knew that to Creegan she was a useful tool,
and whatever personal affection—or desire—he might possess
for her aside, that was how he saw her. High Priestess Seldon
saw her as something taken, a setback in her seemingly endless
struggle with the Order and those associated with it, especially
the Father-Bishop. His office had nothing to do with the Order,
but he was formerly a member. It was rare that one rose from
the martial orders to a position of authority within the Temple
proper, but Creegan was a rare man.

"He is . . . content," said Sandreena slowly. "The illness that
takes his memories has not lessened his pleasures in most things.
He's content to fish when allowed, or to walk the gardens. He
sometimes remembers me, sometimes not."

"He is well otherwise, then?" asked High Priestess Seldon
and, for a brief moment, Sandreena saw a hint of genuine concern and affection. Brother Mathias had refused rank and position over the years, but had gained great respect and reputation
in the Temple.

"The healers at the retreat say he is healthy and will abide for
years. It's just difficult . . . to not be remembered."

"He was like a father to you," said the High Priestess in a
flat, almost dismissive tone, and whatever spark of humanity
Sandreena had glimpsed was again gone. Sandreena was Creegan's creature, and the High Priestess would never forget that,
or forgive what she saw as a betrayal. Sandreena knew much of
the friction between the High Priestess and the Father-Bishop
stemmed from the High Priestess's view that Creegan had
usurped too much of the authority in Krondor—as much as
from losing a talented novitiate priestess to the Order, which she
took as a personal slight. It was rumored the High Priestess saw
herself as a viable candidate for the most holy office in the Temple when the current Grand Master's health failed. And Creegan
would be her biggest obstacle to the office of Grand Mistress.

Sandreena resisted the temptation to remind the High Priestess that she had no idea what a father was like, given her mother
had no idea who the girl's father had been, and from what she

had seen of other fathers growing up, they were a poor lot at best, and drunk, abusive, womanizing, brutal monsters at worst. No, Brother Mathias had been something closer to a saint. He had become, and remained to this day, the only man she trusted without reservation. Even Father-Bishop Creegan was a man she viewed with a small bit of reservation, because his needs always trumped hers or anyone else's. She just nodded and made non-committal noises.

"So, what is next for you, my child?"

Sandreena knew it was best not to equivocate. The High Priestess would have her own sources in the Temple. Yet, she didn't have to tell the complete truth. "Word has reached the Order that there are pirates troubling a village down along the coast of Kesh. It seems the Keshian Court is too busy to be bothered, so as I am the closest Knight-Adamant to that village, I'm to go." Using her title reminded the High Priestess that despite her rank and former position of authority over Sandreena, the girl was here as a courtesy, nothing more. Draining her tea cup, she rose and said, "And I should be on my way, High Priestess. Thank you for taking time from your very busy day to see me."

She stood waiting for a formal acknowledgment, as was her right, and after an awkward moment, the older woman inclined her head in consent. She could demand any priestess or novice remain until dismissed, but not a Knight of the Order. As Sandreena reached the door, the High Priestess said, "It is a shame, really."

Sandreena hesitated, then turned and said, "What is a shame, High Priestess?"

"I can't help but feel that despite the work you do for the Goddess, you've somehow been turned from the proper path of serving her."

Sandreena instantly thought of a dozen possible replies, all of them unkind and scathing, but her training with Brother Mathias made her pause before speaking. Calmly she replied, "I always seek the path intended for me, High Priestess, and pray daily to the Goddess she keeps my feet on it."

Without another word, she turned and left, and as she strode down the long hall, she wished right now for something to hit—a brigand or goblin would do nicely. Lacking one close at hand, she decided it was time to go to the training yard and take her mace to a pell, and see how fast she could reduce the thick wooden post to splinters.

Sandreena stood panting, having taken out her bad temper on a pell for nearly an hour. Her right arm ached from the repeated bashing she gave the immovable wooden target. Like all members of her Order, she carried a mace as her weapon of choice. The tradition of not using edged weapons was ancient, lost in time, and believed to be part of her Order's doctrine, to establish a balance: those she was fighting were given every opportunity to yield, even to the point of death. Edged weapons spilled blood that could not be given back. On more than one occasion she wondered if the original proponent of that tradition had ever seen how much damage to a body was done by a well-handled mace. Having one's skull broken open was as fatal as bleeding out.

An acolyte approached, a girl wearing the garb of the Order, someone's Squire, or perhaps a Page in training. Given that she was very pretty, for a moment Sandreena dryly considered she might be part of the Father-Bishop's personal staff. Sandreena nodded a greeting. "Sister."

The young girl was holding a small, black wooden box. "The Father-Bishop asked me to give this to you. He said you would understand."

Sandreena laughed. She was on his staff.

The girl looked slightly confused and Sandreena said, "Sorry, just an idle thought after a long practice. Are you training for the Order Adamant?"

The girl shook her head. "I am a scribe and cleric," she answered. "I serve in the Temple library."

"Ah," said Sandreena. The Father-Bishop had one of his little spies where she could monitor all the comings and goings of the Temple; beyond being the repository for all the Order's valuable volumes, librams, tomes, and scrolls, the library was where the scribes all did their superiors' bidding. She took the box. "Thank you."

She watched the slender girl walk purposely away and for a fleeting moment wondered what her life story had been before coming here; did she have a loving father, and a mother who had wished for grandchildren? Was she a fugitive from a harsh and uncaring world? Putting aside those thoughts as pointless, she opened the box.

Indeed, she understood what the contents of the box heralded. A single stone of dull pearl-white was set within simple metal clamps, and that in turn hung from a leather thong. She took out the stone with a sigh of resignation. It was a soul-gate. Before she departed, Sandreena would have to endure a very long and difficult session with one of the more powerful Brothers of the Order, preparing her stone so that in the event of her death, her spirit could be recalled here in the Temple, and questioned by those with the magic to speak to the departed. Moreover, if the magic used was strong enough, she would be resurrected in the Temple. This was among the most powerful magic available to the Temple, rare in the extreme, and most difficult to execute. She absently wondered if her scars would come with her in the event she was resurrected; the scar on her thigh had the habit of itching at the most inconvenient moments. Then she considered the stone.

It meant whatever she was being sent to discover was important. Important to the point that even if she didn't survive, the discovery must be reported to the Temple, even if that report came from her ghost, kept from Lims-Kragma's Hall for a few additional hours. Or, if Lims-Kragma was willing, she might escape death entirely, should the need be great.

Despite the heat of the day and her exertion, she felt a chill and the need to be clean.

From a window high above the marshaling yard behind the Temple, Father-Bishop Creegan watched the girl regarding the soul-gate he had sent to her, and said, "She's young."

The man standing at his shoulder said, "Yes, but she's as

tough as any Knight-Adamant in the Order. If Mathias was still sound, or Kendall still alive, I'd say either of them would do, but right now she's the best mix of skill, strength, and purpose you have."

Creegan turned to face his companion, a man he had known for most of his life, though known well only over the last three years. He was dressed in the garb of a commoner, and a rather dirty one at that, his hair left scruffy and his chin beard surrounded by days of unshaved stubble. Even his fingernails were dirty, but the Father-Bishop of the Order of the Shield of the Weak knew well Jim Dasher was but one of several guises employed by James Dasher Jamison.

"Are you acting on behalf of the Crown?"

"In a manner," said the most dangerous man in the Kingdom—from Creegan's point of view. Not only was he the grandson of the most important Duke in the Kingdom of the Isles, he was also reputed to be the mastermind behind the Kingdom's intelligence services, and even, according to some, in control of the criminal brotherhood known as the Mockers.

Jim Dasher looked out the window a moment longer, then said, "An impossibly beautiful woman, that one."

"As dangerous as she is lovely," said Creegan.

Jim Dasher looked at the cleric and said, "You two . . . ?"

"No," said the prelate. "Not that the thought hadn't crossed my mind a time or two." He waved his guest to a small table with two chairs. "If I have a flaw, it's my love of beautiful women." The room was not utilized for any specific reason, but Creegan long ago had claimed it for clandestine meetings, other moments when he felt the need for privacy from the army of those working for the High Priestess, or when he wanted a few undisturbed minutes to think.

"I knew her," said Jim, "when she was a whore."

"You?" asked Creegan.

Jim Dasher laughed, a single bark of embarrassed humor. "No. Not that way. I may not be the first name on her list of people she would wish dead, but I am high on that list, no doubt."

"Really?"

Dasher nodded. "I'm the one who sold her to the Keshian trader."

Creegan let out a long sigh, slightly shaking his head. "The things we do in the name of the greater good." Then he cocked his head slightly, and asked, "But it was you who arranged for Brother Mathias to intercede and rescue her from the Keshian, wasn't it?"

"I wish I could claim such," said Jim. He looked out the window, into the distance, and said, "My plan was to have her endure the company of that fat monster for a month, then make contact with her and turn her to my cause; I was going to promise her a safe passage back to the Kingdom from Shamata and enough wealth to start up a life without fear, if she provided me with certain documents that were in the merchant's possession."

"I never knew that," said Creegan. "I always thought, somehow, it was all some elaborate plot to rid yourself of a Keshian spy and Mathias just happened to recognize the girl's quality."

Jim barked out another laugh. "Zacanos Martias was as much a Keshian spy as you are. What he was, however, was a choke point for certain . . ." He paused. "Let's say since his demise it's been easier for me to get certain things in and out of Kesh. I now deal directly with certain providers who before were cut off from me by Zacanos." He drummed his fingers absently on the chair arm. "Still, I wish I had been able to get those documents from him. By the time my people got to his home in Shamata, someone else had been through his effects, leaving nothing of importance."

"Who, I wonder?" asked the Father-Bishop.

"The Imperial Keshian Intelligence Service," said Dasher. "Which, of course, doesn't exist."

"What?"

Jim waved his hand. "Old family joke." He sighed. "As long as the Emperor is smart enough to leave his spies in the control of Ali Shek Azir Hazara-Khan, I have my work cut out for me." He sat forward, as if in discomfort. "That family has been responsible for more trouble between our two nations than any other single group of people."

"Why not simply have them removed?" asked Creegan.

"Well, to begin with, it would constitute an act of war, and we need an excuse to bloody our noses against Kesh's Dog Soldiers like a house fire needs a barrel of pitch. Secondly, it's not how things are done in the game of spies. Death is the last choice in all circumstances. And lastly, I really like Ali. He's very funny with some wonderful tales, and he's a very good gambler."

"Your world is one I barely understand," admitted the prelate.

"As is yours to me, but we can both agree that sometimes the greater good demands we trust one another."

"Obviously, else you wouldn't be here." The Father-Bishop stood. "I need to return to my office." As he walked his guest to the door, he said, "Still, if you didn't engineer that encounter between Brother Mathias and the Keshian merchant, who did?"

"You'd have to ask Sandreena about her recollection, but I honestly say if there was another player in the game, I have no idea who it might be."

"Perhaps it was the Goddess's divine plan," said Creegan and Jim saw he was not being facetious.

Jim said, "I've seen too many things in my life to hold anything involving the gods as out of the question."

Jim Dasher glanced out the door, out of habit, and said, "I'll try to be as inconspicuous on my way out as I was coming in."

"Then good-bye," said the Father-Bishop as Jim Dasher hurried down the short hallway that led to the southernmost stairs. Creegan knew from experience there was a good chance that, despite the Temple being thronged with the faithful, the agent of the Crown would manage somehow to get cleanly away with no one noticing the scruffy-looking commoner. He gave him a momentary start, so they wouldn't be seen leaving the tower door together.

Sighing at the feeling that things were becoming far too complex and the enormity of their undertaking was going to prove too much, even for the combined resources of the Crown and the

Temple, he put aside worry as best he could. There was no point in wasting time and thought on things outside his control. Better to trust the Goddess and move on to the day's needs.

He moved to follow Jim Dasher down the stairwell and, as he suspected, there was no sign of the man in the massive, open courtyard when Creegan reached the door.

# CHAPTER 3

## TAREDHEL

The air shimmered.

As heat rose off the warming rocks on the hillside, a light breeze blew across the valley as larks flew overhead. The afternoon sun bathed the grasses in a warm blanket as spring arrived in Novindus, chasing away the night's chill. A fox sunning herself raised her head in concern, for she smelled something unexpected. She sprang to her feet and turned her head first one way then another, seeking the source. Nothing could be seen. Curiosity gave way to caution and the vixen darted off, fleeing deep within shadowed woods in two bounds.

The cause of her fright, a solitary figure, made his way carefully through the thinning trees. At this altitude, the heavy woods below were giving way to alpine meadows and open reaches, providing easier transit.

Any observer would think him a man barely worth notice, a large floppy hat masking his features. His body appeared neither overly stout nor slender, and his garb was a simple traveler's robes, grey homespun or poor linen. He carried a sack around one shoulder, resting on the opposite hip, and used a gnarled black-oak stave for aid in difficult footing.

He paused and looked at the peaks to the north and south, noticing the bald crowns above the timberline. He put aside any possible appreciation of the majesty of those mounts, known by those who lived nearby as the Grey Towers, and rather considered them as a constituent element in a very complex evaluation of this valley's defensibility.

Once, a people lived here. Once, invaders came and drove those people out. Then the invaders departed, but the original inhabitants of this valley never returned. There were signs of their settlements scattered throughout this region, from a deep pass to the north, beyond which a large village of dwarves resided, all the way to the south, where the high ridges gave way to sloping hills that led to bluffs commanding the straits between two vast seas.

Like all those of his race, the traveler knew little of the dwarves to the north, or the seemingly numberless humans. Of those who had lived in this valley before, he knew much, but it was lore and legend. What little he had gleaned from those he had spoken with, what he had been able to piece together, provided him with many more questions than answers.

He had traveled this continent for three months, barely noticed by most he passed by, and even when seen or spoken to, barely remembered after; he was an unremarkable being, one who may have been tall, or perhaps not; a man of some circumstance, or perhaps of modest means. The color of the hair? Perhaps brown, then maybe sand, or black. It was part of the guile created by the arts that the traveler employed that made him difficult to notice or remember.

Looking around, to finalize his sense of the place as much

as to ensure he was unwatched, the traveler reached within a belt pouch and withdrew a crystal, something of no intrinsic value to anyone else but to him it was the most precious possession imaginable; it was his only means of returning to his people. He held tightly to the crystal and let his glamour slip, revealing his true appearance before his return. Had he created the portal and stepped through in his current guise, his death would be immediate. The traveler considered it odd, but while he knew there was no physical change—merely the cessation of an illusion so powerful only the most puissant of magicians might see through it—he felt as if he were casting off clothing that was too small. Without conscious thought, he took a moment to stretch his long arms before incanting the brief spell that activated the crystal.

Suddenly a sizzling sound, like a burst of lightning, followed a moment later by a rip in the air, looking like a tall curtain of heat shimmer, then, where the air rippled a moment before, a portal hung above the ground. Twelve feet in height, nine feet across, a grey oval of nothingness formed. An instant later the traveler stepped through it and vanished.

Up in the trees, a motionless figure observed the departure. It was by only the most strained of coincidence he was in this valley at all, for it was unoccupied by any being since the Riftwar with the Tsurani. But the game trails and pathways along the northern side of the south ridges gave faster access to his destination than the more frequently used routes along the roads through the Green Heart Forest to the south. And, like most of his kind, the notion of solitude or anticipation of danger didn't bother him, but an appreciation of swift passage was keen in the messenger. Of all the mortal races, only the elves had better woodcraft skills than the Rangers of Natal.

He was a tall man, rangy and burned dark by the sun, though his brown hair showed streaks of red and blond from that same sun. His eyes were dark and hooded, his high cheekbones and narrow, straight nose giving him an almost hawk-like stare. It was only when he smiled he lost his grim visage, something that rarely occurred outside the comfort of his home, in the company of family.

Alystan of the Rangers of Natal was undertaking a service for a consortium of traders in the Free Cities, in negotiation with the Earl of Carse, carrying a bundle of documents considered vital. His sun-darkened features were set in an expression of concentration, his dark eyes narrowed as if he was willing himself to see every detail. His dark hair was still free of grey, but he was no youth, having spent his life from boyhood serving his people with stealth, speed, and sword.

He had chanced upon the newcomer's trail an hour earlier, seeing fresh tracks in the spring damp soil. He had followed and at first thought little of a solitary man, perhaps a magician, from the look of him and his heavy staff. But his usually limited curiosity over a solitary man—even should he prove a magician—wandering the wilds of the Grey Towers, was piqued when he first glimpsed the traveler, or rather from the first moment he took his eyes off the man.

A trained tracker his entire life, Alystan could not recall the man's appearance from one moment to the next. Was his cloak grey or blue? Was he short or tall? He followed the man and three times took his eyes off him and could not recall the details of his look. That made it certain he was a magic-user, and moreover he was using some glamour to hide his true appearance. To his consternation, Alystan found it easier to follow the man's tracks than simply watch him. Something made him wish to turn his attention away, to be about other business, so he forced himself to stalk this mysterious figure.

Then he saw the change. At that instant, every detail of the creature's appearance was etched into the tracker's memory. The glamour had fled and now the Ranger of Natal knew the traveler's true look. And, upon witnessing the newcomer's departure, he knew this was now the more important task. The last time strangers appeared and disappeared through a rift in this valley, that arrival heralded the coming of a twelve-year-long, bloody war. And from the creature's appearance, it might be history was repeating itself.

To Alystan, it looked as if an unremarkable man had transformed himself into the tallest elf ever encountered. He wished he had been able to move closer, see more detail, but didn't want to risk revealing himself, and the traveler was too quickly gone from this world.

From what Alystan could see, he judged the creature stood nearly seven feet in height, with massive shoulders but a surprisingly narrow waist, giving his chest physique a startling V shape. The proportions of his legs were more like those of an elf, though powerfully muscled. His grey-shot red hair had been tied high atop his head in a decorative band, falling to spread down below his shoulders. But it was the color red that had startled him, for it wasn't the reddish-brown or even orange-tinged red seen among both humans and elves, it was as vivid a scarlet color as he had ever seen. And had the light not been playing tricks, Alystan would vow it was a true color, not the product of some dye, such as women in the Free Cities used to suit a whim or rid themselves of grey. The brows were the same vivid hue, and had been treated with a wax or other substance so they swept out and up, mimicking a butterfly's antennae as much as anything the Ranger could envision.

Alystan moved cautiously, against the possibility others of this creature's kind might be close by, though he doubted it. This valley had remained unoccupied in the century since the Riftwar, the dark elves who had once abided here being content to remain far to the north. And Alystan had only seen trail sign of one man. Or elf, he amended.

Alystan continued to review what he had seen as he made his way back up to the higher game trails. Like the other elves Alystan knew, the newcomer had shown an almost effortless movement, as he had stepped through the magic portal. But unlike those elves known to the Ranger, this one had trod with a heavy foot, as if lacking wood-lore or simply not caring. No elf of even modest experience would have left tracks so easily followed.

There was another thing about that creature. Alystan had only caught but the briefest glimpse of its face, as it peered upward, but it had been enough to note the eyes. They were deep-set and pale, blue so light it was almost a cloud color as the creature had stood regarding the landscape around. And there was something malevolent in that face. Alystan couldn't express how he knew, but he was certain this was no mere elf from another part of this world, unknown to the Rangers, but something else. Something intelligent enough to pass as human through magic arts, no mean feat for even the most powerful of magic-using creatures, the great dragons. Not only was this elf a magician of some fashion, but a very powerful one, Alystan judged.

And, for some reason, Alystan was most troubled by the creature's attire. Upon his brow, he wore a delicate circle of gold, with a heavy polished ruby set in the middle. Elves occasionally wore what passed for jewelry, but only at festivals, being content with the beauty of flower garlands or other natural adornments the rest of the time. And there was the manner of his clothing.

This elf wore finely made garb, and the circlet upon his head was of equally exceptional craftsmanship. While striking in countenance and massive in body, still the elf did not have the look of a warrior or hunter; given his guise as a human traveler, the creature apparently was intent upon stealth, not conflict. Alystan knew for certain this elf was some manner of magician, but his garb and magic illusion marked him nothing remotely like the Spellweavers of Elvandar, or the Loremasters of the Eldar. Their magic was as much a thing of nature as mind and will, and what served the elves of Elvandar, as well as the black arts used by the Moredhel, was all of a piece, as much as elven clothing or song. This conjuration of illusion, worn around the shoulders like a cloak, this was too much like dark human arts.

And this elf hailed from a people who enjoyed beautiful things as much as humans did, for his robes were of shimmering weave, pearl-white satin or silk perhaps, and the hems were decorated with threads of ruby and azure color. And the staff of oak, which before had seemed a simple walking stave, in the brief instant Alystan saw it, showed itself as obviously a thing of magic, adorned at the top by a large glass orb that glowed from within, even in the bright sunlight. Alystan was certain no human—certainly no Ranger—had encountered this elf's kin before.

As he picked up speed, Alystan wondered less what manner of elf was this and more why was he here. He knew that once he had finished in Carse, rather than return to Bordon, he must hie himself to the dwarves of the Grey Towers, in the village of Caldara, and take counsel with them. They knew more of elf lore than any others this side of Elvandar, and it was upon their borders this elf trod. Perhaps the dwarves would know why such a being was obviously scouting this region. And every experience he had over thirty years of running these mountains and the forests on both sides of the peaks caused him to know in the pit of his stomach that no one in the Free Cities or the Kingdom of the Isles would like the answer.

Demons howled in rage and pain as they assaulted the barricade. A shower of arrows rained down on them, striking dozens as they sought to climb the obstacle using the bodies of their fallen comrades as means to crest the defenses.

Undalyn, Regent Lord of the Clans of the Seven Stars pointed to a wave on the right, nearly able to reach the top of the barricade, and shouted, "There! Pitch!"

Two conjurers waited nearby, far enough behind the battlefront to be relatively safe, flanked by a dozen archers detailed to bring down any fliers who might target the magic-users. A massive cauldron of burning pitch waited atop a blazing mound of logs, and the two magicians acted in concert. Well practiced in their arts, they closed their eyes, needing no sight to manage their task.

The massive cauldron, placed atop the huge pyre by a dozen men and two draft animals, rose into the air, as if an invisible giant hand gently lifted it. It floated safely over the heads of the defenders and upended over the demons below.

Flaming death rained down on those nearest the top of the barricade, while the defenders below hung back a moment, as waves of heat washed over them, singeing hair and eyebrows.

The usual demon stench was made even more noxious by the odor of burning hair and flesh. The demons on the right fell back, but without looking, the Regent Lord knew they were still hard pressed in the center and on the left.

He turned away from the sight of the massive pile of writhing, flaming demons and assessed his position. His warriors fought valiantly, as had their fathers and grandfathers before them. For a hundred years the Clans of the Seven Stars had struggled against the Demon Legion and for a hundred years they had made them pay a dear price for every inch of ground gained, for every village sacked, and for every life sacrificed.

Still, he knew that his resources were dwindling and theirs seemed without limit. In the distance he saw a dark cloud on the horizon, yet he knew there was no rain in the air. Before he could speak, one of the lookouts on the tower above shouted, "Fliers!"

Knowing his command was gratuitous, as his magic-users were already conjuring their defense, he still felt the need to give the order. "Shields!"

Part of his nature was to be wary of ceding too much authority to others; this he knew could be a failing. But another part of his nature took pride in every serving warrior, priest, and magic-user knowing his task and answering need without hesitation. The more desperate the struggle for the survival of his people, the more filled with pride he became.

He was Undalyn, by lineage and law, leader of his people, Regent Lord of the Clans of the Seven Stars. He was the most powerful elf among his kind.

His features were typical of the people, though his skin tended toward a darker tone, due to his passion for hunting and years under the sun. His blue eyes were the color of the ocean, with flecks of green, and his brow was unlined, despite his more than three hundred years. Snow-white hair was tied high above his head in a noble's knot—white leather decorated with five perfect rubies placed in gold settings—to fall in a long cascade down below his shoulders. Handsome by the measure of his race, he nevertheless had a dark and dangerous aspect to his features that was revealed at odd moments, though he rarely raised his voice in anger. It was his eyes that hinted at the fury always contained within.

He was accorded the utmost respect by the People of the Seven Stars, the Taredhel in the old tongue, for it was his burden to guide them, as it had been his forefathers' before him. But no Regent before him had burdens such as his, and the wear on him was taking its toll. Dark circles under his eyes told of sleepless nights and endless worry, frustration, and ultimately a sense of doom.

He felt more than saw the energy barrier go up, as the remaining magic-users employed one of their more powerful spells. The demons had encountered this barrier before, yet they came and hurled themselves against it, time and again.

Archers waited against the possibility that one might rend the mystic defense, but so far it had failed to occur. Those on the walls dealing with the milling demons below could barely spare a glance toward the skies; they knew what would happen.

Archers on the wall peppered the retreating horde of demons, who appeared to be marshaling for one more assault on the wall should the fliers secure a breach. The Regent Lord took a deep breath and pulled out his sword, again to be ready should any flier breach the barrier. He glanced at his hands and saw they were free of blood. His shoulders ached and he felt as if he could sleep for a week, yet he had not struck one blow against the enemies of his people.

His soldiers had kept the demon horde at bay for another day, and he had been free to oversee the defense of the barrier and not put himself at risk. Other days he had not been so fortunate, and he had killed his share of demons with his own hands, returning to his palace at night covered in their evil black blood.

He watched without emotion as the fliers struck the barrier. The sky above scintillated in rainbows of color as the winged horrors of the Demon Legion literally bounced from the defensive barrier; the Regent Lord knew there must be some intelligence among these monsters, but those who assaulted his defenses every day seemed without any spark of intellect. Had the demons possessed half the elves' cleverness, they would have overwhelmed the Seven Clans years before. But even without anything remotely resembling organization, they were grinding the Clans of the Seven Stars to nothing. Worlds had been abandoned and now here on the home world—he shook his head, for this wasn't the true home world, but it was the capital of his nation—they were making a final stand. He knew what every elf among the Clans knew: no matter how valiant the struggle, eventually they would fall.

The fliers beat in fury against the barrier, but it held. Lately demons capable of some magic had appeared from time to time, costing the elves dearly, but for this day the victory would go to the Clans.

The demons withdrew and the Regent Lord surveyed the barrier. He was no more an expert than any other warrior but he was no less. As the fliers withdrew and the sun lowered in the west, he knew the battle for today was over.

He removed his helm and almost instantly an aide was at his side to take it. Another came and said, "My Lord, we have a report that the Conjurer Laromendis has returned."

The Regent Lord didn't ask what news he brought, for the Conjurer had been under strict instructions to divulge his findings to no one before reporting directly to the palace. He could not afford unfounded rumors racing through the capital until the truth was known. The fate of the Clans of the Seven Stars rested on certain knowledge, not hope.

"I will return to the palace at once."

"He is being transported to the palace, My Lord," said the aide, a youth who bore a striking resemblance to one of his sons lost years before. If there was a stirring inside for an instant, the Regent Lord pushed it aside; too many sons had been lost to too many fathers, and fathers lost to sons. They all shared in the tragedy that was this war.

With a dismissive wave of his hand, the Regent Lord shooed his aides to one side and alerted the portal guardian he was to return to the capital. The magician whose sole responsibility was to manage the portal nodded, and, with a simple spell, activated the portal. His job also was to destroy the gate should the demons breach the barrier, and give his life to keep them away from the capital a few days longer.

The Regent Lord stepped through the portal and suddenly he was in the marshaling yard of his palace. Two companies of warriors stood ready to answer the call should reinforcements be required. The Regent Lord motioned to the Officer of the Yard and said, "How go the other struggles?"

"Well, My Lord," he answered. The old elf was still robust-looking, though the Regent Lord knew he had sustained enough injuries that his fighting ability was severely diminished; but his mind was still as keen as ever and he was among those most trusted by the Regent Lord to act in his absence. Jaron by name, he was given full responsibility to decide where reinforcements were sent and when. Men lived or died on his orders, and that trust had been hard won over years of service. "They fall back along all fronts, and for another day we hold." Glancing around, he repeated, "Another day."

"We live another day," echoed the Regent Lord.

"Rumor has the Conjurer returning," said Jaron in a low voice.

"Best not to repeat that to anyone," said the Regent Lord, walking away without further comment. He knew he would reach his chambers before the magic-users would and he wanted a few moments to compose himself in private, lest the news the magic-user carried was ill. He also knew he needed to be composed should the news he carried be good. Walking silently toward the large doors into the palace, the Regent Lord of the Clans of the Seven Stars cursed hope.

The Regent Lord of the Clans of the Seven Stars sat quietly, waiting, trying to enjoy one moment of solitude in a day dominated by violence and noise. The enemy battered the Barrier Wall every minute of every day, yet here, in the heart of the capital, he could indulge in the illusion that his city was as it had been since he was a boy. Deep within, he knew he was weak to long for days past, gone beyond reclaim, but still, it calmed him and gave him hope that someday the People would find a haven as tranquil as this world once was.

Around the room, large open windows admitted the elements. The Meeting of the Regent Lord would always be in the open, so that the People and the Spirits of Ancestors might witness it. Such was the law. The only adornments to the room were the battle standards of the Host of the Clans, each hanging from the ceiling, providing a constantly moving reminder of the People's history as they stirred in the wind.

The tall warrior rested on a simple wooden chair that had been his nation's seat of power since myth was left behind and memory began.

The people, his race, were dying and there was nothing he could do to save them as long as they remained here.

Despite the heat of the day, his shoulders were covered in white fur, the mark of his rank, the pelt of a snow bear he had killed during his manhood rite high in the mountains of Madrona. He rested his hand upon the hilt of his father's sword, Shadowbane, absently caressing it as he might his wife's body.

Below the mantle of fur he wore a light tunic and trousers of dark green cloth, simple but for the gold thread at the collar and cuffs; his feet clad in fine brown leather boots, still covered in dust from his morning walk inspecting the city's defenses. The same dust covered his nearly white hair, and he wished for time to bathe, but he knew much needed to be accomplished before a relaxing bath was possible.

He looked out the window at the blue sky and felt the warmth of the sun on his arms and face, felt the heat under his furry mantle, and he welcomed the sensation, trying to drive away a cold that gripped his very soul.

Then a scout, his hair tied up in a hunter's queue, entered. "He's here, My Lord."

Seeing the herald, he knew what was about to be said. Waving away the courtier, Undalyn spoke. In a deep voice, he commanded, "Show yourself, Conjurer!"

The magic-user strode into the throne room, his white robes free of stain, his staff aglow with power. He bowed and said, "I am here, my lord."

"Show me," commanded the Regent Lord.

Raising his staff, the magic-user slowly moved it through the air, and as he did a scene appeared, images forming as if painted on an invisible wall, but they were moving and alive, and when the shimmering ceased, it was as if the Regent Lord viewed a scene through a magic window. But while the window in this chamber overlooked the sun-baked table lands of Andcardia, this magic window showed a completely different landscape.

The Regent Lord scanned the scene before him. It appeared they stood on a hill ridge—late afternoon, from the angle of the sun behind them. Across a vast valley he could see more peaks. Everywhere he looked he saw abundance. The trees were old, heavy growth, and from this one vantage point he could see two large meadows in the distance below. White clouds floated above, pregnant with rain, and the wind carried exotic scents mixed in with those familiar to him: balsam, pine, fir, and cedar. The sounds were of the forest rich with game and in the trees birds sang without concern. "This seems a hospitable land," observed the Regent Lord. Fixing his gaze on the magic-user, he asked, "Is it Home?"

Knowing that his life—and his brother's life—probably hung on his answer, Laromendis, Supreme Conjurer of the Circle of Light, hesitated, then said, "I must speak with the Loremasters, m'lord." As the Regent Lord's expression darkened, he hastily added, "I'm being cautious, but yes, it is Home."

The Regent Lord's expression betrayed a tiny flicker of relief. If this was the ancestral homeland then there was still hope. "Tell me of it, the ancient home."

"It is a fair world, my lord, though not without problems." He moved the staff and the scene disappeared.

"Problems," repeated the leader of the Clans of the Seven Stars. "Is there a day in a life without problems, on any world?"

The Conjurer said nothing at the rhetoric.

"Name them," said the Regent Lord as another figure came through the rift, his hand on his sword. He was a warrior nearly equal to the Regent Lord in stature, and he seemed on the verge of speaking until he saw the Regent Lord raise a gauntlet-garbed hand indicating he wanted silence.

"This world is rich in game, crops, and metals. But it is home to others."

"Others?"

"Dwarves," he almost spat.

"Dwarves," said Undalyn. "Is there a world we have found without those grubbers-in-the-mud?"

"I fear not," said the Conjurer. He had located several worlds without dwarves in the last ten years, but they were not habitable; this was not the time to engage in petty debate over the fine points. Since the discovery of the translocation magic and the search for the homeland, all hopes for the survival of the People had turned to locating the mythical Home, which the Conjurer had felt was futile. Finding a world to which they could flee, any homeland, new or ancient, that was the key for a race now reduced to a relative handful by thirty years of battle with the Demon Legion.

His discovery of the Home was a happy accident, nothing more, or at least that's how he saw it; his vanity nearly equaled the Regent Lord's and to admit someone without a hint of knowledge in the arts might be right would be unthinkable. Laromendis, Master of the Arts of the Unseen, would settle for the Regent Lord being lucky.

And lucky for himself and his brother, too, he quickly amended.

"Humans. They thrive there like flies on dung. Their cities are ant hives, with thousands in residence."

"Our people? Do they abide?"

"Yes. But they have . . . fallen."

"What do you mean?" asked the Regent Lord.

As if needing to emphasize a point, Laromendis moved to stand before the northernmost window, providing a vista of the city outside. Tarendamar, Starhome, capital of the Clans of the Seven Stars, and for generations a monument to the majesty that was the People. The Regent Lord came to stand beside the red-haired magician and looked down. Still untouched by the brutal war to the north, the city remained much as it had when Undalyn had been a boy. The Hall of the Regent's Meeting was a short walk from the Regent's demesne, a palace by any other name, and this very hall, ancient and honored, had been among Undalyn's earliest memories, as his father had ensured the next Regent Lord would understand the responsibilities of his heritage.

He knew this precinct well, as he had played in every alleyway and garden, swam in every pool and brook, climbed the holy trees to the outrage of the priestesses, and had come to love this city as if it were a living being; it was a living being; it was the heart of the Clans of the Seven Stars.

Built of elven magic and sweat, this city was the crown jewel of the elven people. The seven great trees formed a massive ring around the heart of the city, one mystic tree for each of the sacred stars in the heavens. Even in the harsh light of Andcardia's sun, the deep shadows within the bowers glimmered with fey light.

It was from those seven trees—the "Seven Stars," as they had been called from the start—that all the power of the Taredhel was drawn; each tree had been grown from a sapling carried from Home to this world, the first refuge of the Taredhel, the "people of the stars," as they called themselves.

They had fled from their birth world, ages before, and found refuge on this inhospitable world. Dry, with small oceans and lakes, scorching hot save for the middle of a short winter, the world had grudgingly yielded to the magic of the original Spellweavers, and those original seven magic trees, the "stars" carried from Home, had been the anchor to this world that had allowed them to survive. The survival of those trees had been paid for by the very blood of the Taredhel, and if the Clans of the Seven Stars had a world in which their soul resided more than in Andcardia, it could only be Home.

When the trees began to flourish, so did the Taredhel, the

trees providing them with magic they called Home Magic. They had taken that Home Magic and at first used it to bludgeon this Andcardia into submission, then they had refined it, blending it with the natural harmonies, until a magic native to both the Taredhel and this planet emerged, and over the following centuries, it had changed both the world and the elves.

Now lush forests hugged the mountainsides, still halted in the lowlands by blistering hot table lands and vast deserts. Yet even they were slowly retreating as the Water Gatherers found ways to use the translocation magic to bring water from other worlds. In his lifetime, Undalyn had seen the sea level gradually rise and lakes expand. Where his grandfather once had hunted the great scaly lizards of the Rocky Flats, now an orchard of redfruit trees sheltered the melon vines, and streams ran through the heart of the flats all the way to the sea.

Undalyn was impatient for Laromendis to continue, but he still had the patience of an elf. He knew the Conjurer was trying to make a point. Finally the magic-user spoke. "They have nothing like this."

The Regent Lord inclined his head and said, "No cities?"

"Only the darkest among our kind, the lore speaks of them as the Forgotten."

The Regent Lord glanced around, seeing that only one servant waited near the door and he was out of earshot. What the Conjurer spoke of was approaching heresy. Lowering his voice, he said, "Those . . ."

"They are called Moredhel on the home world."

"The dark people." The Regent Lord nodded. "They have a city?"

"A rumor." Laromendis moved away from the window as he gathered his thoughts. "In the north, in slavish imitation of the Masters, a city fashioned as a twin of the city of lore. Called Armengar by the humans, it was destroyed, according to the tales. Our people's name for it I did not discover, but I've heard the tale enough times to judge some truth to it.

"I spent most of my time with the humans, for it is easier to gull them. The humans thrive, so many of them. In some ways they are like us, but they are inferior, like the other short-lived races. And like the others, they breed like mice. They are everywhere. So I disguised myself as one and lived among them for months. What they know of our people borders on myth and legend, or, at the very best, rumor.

"I traveled from where I appeared across one of their larger nations, learning the language as I traveled—fortunately, there are many nations and languages, so someone who spoke oddly barely brought notice.

"We know so little of these creatures, these humans . . . I found it fascinating."

The Regent Lord looked at the magic-user with a narrowing gaze. While the ancient Spellweavers were venerated and honored for their work in transforming this harsh world, those like Laromendis and his brother Gulamendis were viewed with caution approaching fear. The so-called dark arts, anything the conjurers and demon masters found "fascinating" was likely to be viewed with suspicion. "Why?"

"Too many reasons to list, m'lord. But first-most is their magic. It is varied to the point of being beyond calculating. So many approaches to seizing the power of the world and bending it to their will, it staggers the mind.

"There are those who use arts so very much like our own I wondered at first had elves been their first teachers, but there are others . . . called Greater Path magicians, who have no subtlety, no . . . grace, in their craft, yet who possess vast power. It is difficult to explain to one not given to magic."

The Regent Lord nodded. By nature elves were at one with the natural magic of their race, but circumstances had forced the People to adapt, to change their ways. Among the Taredhel were those like the two brothers, who hungered after power like a starving man after a meal. And like the Regent Lord, there were those who gave up any understanding of the arts so they might best bend their will to serving the People.

"Tell me of the humans later," said the leader of the Clans of the Seven Stars. "Tell me more of our people. You say The . . . Forgotten exist?"

"So it would seem," said the magic-user. "Humans know little of our kind, but there were enough rumors, as well as a few facts, that I could piece together some understanding of how our brethren fare on the Home.

"Humans call the Forgotten 'The Brotherhood of the Dark Path.'"

The Regent Lord nodded. "An apt name if the secret lore is true . . ." He hesitated, realizing he had inadvertently uttered a blasphemy.

The magic-user chose to ignore the remark. "There have been many debates among the Farseeing if the secret lore is literally true or metaphor." With that observation, he signaled the Regent Lord he understood the comment and would make no issue of it. Given the current situation among the People, any hint of blasphemy brought swift and harsh responses; it was why his brother currently languished in a dark cell. Then again, Laromendis's younger brother always did have a tendency to speak first and think second. A bad trait in one who submersed himself in demon lore at a time when demons were threatening to obliterate the People.

"What did you learn of the Forgotten?"

"Little; to the humans the Brotherhood is almost a myth, though I did encounter a traveler from the city of Yabon, far to the north of a realm known as 'the Kingdom,' and he did swear that he had once seen those . . . unspeakable beings.

"Our people war among themselves, the Forgotten against those more like us," said the Conjurer with a hint of mixed emotion, anger and disgust. "I walked the land, posing as a human traveler, listening to tales, gossip in taverns, buying drinks for sailors, speaking with priests and anyone who might know ancient lore. In one place did I find an abbey of some god, but their wards were too strong for my guise to endure, so I could not enter. But I did encounter one of their members on the road and did confine him and question him. He was a monk and his mind was disciplined but eventually yielded most of what I learned of their ancient lore, which I now share with you."

"Did you kill him after?"

"Of course," said the Conjurer. "He was merely a human, after all."

"No dishonor," agreed the Regent Lord. Killing a prisoner would be dishonorable if it were a warrior of the People or an equal race.

"The Forgotten war against those most like us, who abide in a grove they name Elvandar."

At the utterance of that word, the Regent Lord's eyes grew shiny with emotion. He said the name softly, "Elvandar." It simply meant "Home of the People," but it echoed with a deeper meaning.

In ages past, the People served a dread race, the Valheru, and endured slavery and degradation. Then came a great upheaval, a war in which the very fabric of time and space was rent and chaos reigned.

The ancestors of the Taredhel were among the mightiest of the servants of the Valheru, called, in their own tongue, Eldar. They were the Spellweavers, the masters of the groves, the keepers of the land, and the librarians of their masters' power. Many of those who had served with their masters on other worlds had perished, though some rumors abided that a few had escaped and sought refuge. It was that faint hope that there were others like them out among the stars that had driven a band of Eldar to escape through one of the tears in space and time.

To Andcardia they had come, a band of no more than two thousand magic-users, hunters, and their families. It was a harsh land, but eventually they made it their own. As centuries passed, they grew to prosper, and now they dominated this world, numbering in millions.

In the past few centuries, they had learned the secrets of the translocation magic, opening up tears in the fabric of the universe. No fewer than a dozen magic-users died in mastering the arts, but now they could open stable tears between worlds. And find new worlds they did.

Some were inhospitable, others barely able to support life. A few showed promise and upon them the Clans of the Seven Stars established colonies. Some of those colonies had grown and were flourishing.

The People thrived, and when they encountered others, they tolerated them as long as they did not oppose the will of the People. If they did, they were crushed. All was glorious, until they found the world of demons.

"Those in Elvandar served a queen . . ." continued the Conjurer.

The Regent Lord's eyes went wide. "She dares!"

"She outlives her king," said the Conjurer quickly. "He . . . may have been of the line."

The remark hit the Regent Lord like a physical blow. His eyes grew even more shiny with emotion. Among the most ancient, sacred lore of the Taredhel was the story of the first king and queen of the People, a couple who shepherded the people through the early chaos of that horrible war that drove the Taredhel from the Home.

Little was known, save their names, which would never be mentioned aloud, lest their spirits be disturbed, but they had been read in the annals, by every Lorekeeper and Regent Lord. "Her name?"

"They say it is Aglaranna."

" 'The Gift,' " said the Regent Lord.

The Conjurer said, "It also is 'Bright Moon,' for the largest of the three moons is also known by that name, 'the Gift.' "

The Regent Lord shouted, "Send for the Loremaster!" To the Conjurer, he said, "Continue, but speak not of this or of the Forgotten until I summon the Meeting.

"What of these humans who number like mice? Have they one ruler?"

"The humans live in many nations, with many rulers. They war among themselves on a regular basis, it seems."

"That is good," said the Regent Lord calmly. "What else?"

"The dwarves live at peace with their neighbors and are content to do so as long as they are untroubled. There are also goblins and other like creatures."

"Goblins?"

"Lea Orcha," said Laromendis.

Shaking his head in near disbelief, Undalyn said, "My father raised me to be a pious man, like all of our line, yet I will confess to having been guilty of doubt." Lea Orcha, or Goblins, as they were named in various tongues, were nightmare creatures, conjured as bedtime stories to frighten children into being obedient.

"They worship ancient dark gods and spill blood in sacrifice. They consort with trolls and other inferior races."

"Goblins . . . how have they never been exterminated?"

The magic-user shrugged, a human gesture he had picked up and which caused the Regent Lord to frown. "I don't know," he said softly. "There is so much discord and warfare among the human tribes, they hardly seem to have time to deal with goblins." The Regent Lord indicated he should continue.

"This world is known by several names in different tongues, but most commonly is called Midkemia, a human word.

"The land I showed you in my vision is a valley in mountains called the Grey Towers. This valley was once home to the Forgotten. A human tribe called Tsurani drove them northward, and to this valley the Forgotten have never returned. To the south live dwarves, but there are natural barriers between that valley and the dwarves' own; some ancient mines link them, but they are abandoned and are easily defended; to the north there are paths and trails leading up into those northlands where our evil kin abide.

"Once established in this valley, we may range far and wide. To the east, the humans live in a federation called the Free Cities. They are poorly organized and ripe for conquest.

"It is to the west that danger lies, for there is the outpost region of one of the mighty human nations—" He stopped speaking as the Regent Lord raised his hand.

An elderly male in robes entered the room, carrying an ancient tome, in which all history of the People had been recorded since the Time Before. His eyes were dim with age and behind him strode a younger male, his heir, who when not assisting the Loremaster was studying every scribble, every note, preparing himself for the day he would assume the responsibility of that office.

Both bowed before the Regent Lord, who said, "Midkemia. Do we know that world?"

The Loremaster paused a moment, but his assistant leaned over to whisper something. "Speak aloud!" demanded the Regent Lord. "No one dares hide a word from me in my court."

The younger male looked abashed, and said, "I beg My Lord's forgiveness. I meant no slight. It is just a case that I have studied some of the earlier passages more recently and recall seeing that name."

The Loremaster waved away the apology. "His name is Tanderae, Regent Lord. He is young, and perhaps a little rash, but his memory is as mine was in the prime of my youth." The older historian's face was wan and his eyes watered. "Soon this office shall be his, and I recommend him to you."

The younger historian bowed low before his master and the Regent Lord.

"Very well," Undalyn said to the younger historian. "What of this world?"

"May my student speak, my lord?" said the old Loremaster.

"Yes," responded the Regent Lord.

"In the time before time," began Tanderae, using the ritual words signaling they were speaking of the most ancient of myths, "before fleeing the Wrath, the people abided.

"Slaves were we in our Home, ruled by the cruel masters, the Lords of Power, the Dragonriders.

"Then came the Wrath, and the skies were torn, and the Dragonriders rose to contest a great war. Many of the People perished, and many were lost among the stars, left behind when our masters returned to the Home to struggle with the Wrath.

"As the struggle continued," said the young Lorekeeper closing his eyes as if reading from the ancient text in his memory, "many came to the Home. Dakan Soketa, Dena Orcha, and Dostan Shuli, those lesser beings, came across a golden bridge, feeling the Wrath as it descended on the world."

He stopped and said, "'Midkemia' is a word used by the

Dakan Soketa, my lord, which is the ancient word of our people for humans. And the humans called the home world 'Midkemia.'"

The Regent Lord closed his eyes, as if silently giving a prayer. Then he said, "It is Home!" To Laromendis, he said, "Tell us of this valley, the one you showed me."

The magic-user nodded. "To the west are the westernmost garrisons of that nation I spoke of, 'the Kingdom.' The humans there have three small cities, barely more than large towns: Tulan, Carse, and Crydee. They are well-fortified. We can isolate them by land, but they have a vast navy and can reinforce by sea. We shall need a quick strike at all three fortresses to seize them."

"At the right time," said Undalyn. "But first we need a secure bridgehead on the Home world. We must devise a plan to give us time." He thought of the great Barrier Spell, the sphere that held in check the advancing Demon Legion, weakening to the north. It had been breached three times in the last ten years, and at last report had failed to the far west for a time. The fighting had been brutal and many of the People had paid the ultimate sacrifice while the magicians repaired the breach. It would fail, eventually, so time was not a commodity in abundance. Guile and wit would have to serve until force could be brought to bear. Looking at Laromendis, he said, "The plan for conquest will be considered, and perhaps an accommodation with those already in residence upon Home is in order. But that is for others to consider. Upon you I place different burdens."

"I serve, my lord," answered the magic-user.

"We are hard-pressed. Our enemies have driven us out of Thandar Keep, so Modaria has fallen."

The Conjurer said nothing, but the slight tension around his eyes told the Regent Lord what the unasked question was. "No one survived," he said softly.

Modaria was the last of the outpost worlds, so now the entirety of the People remained on Andcardia. "We made them pay, dearly, but as it has always been, for each of them we spent three warriors." His deep voice took on an almost plaintive tone as he said, "We need safe haven, Conjurer. Is this such a place?"

There was a moment's hesitation, and the Regent Lord demanded, "Speak! Is this a safe haven?"

"There are demon signs. Not recent, but . . . demons have been there."

The Regent Lord threw back his head in a gesture of rage and torment and let forth a howl of pure barbaric anger and pain. "Is there no refuge?"

"Signs, my lord," said the magician. "But no demons."

"How can that be?" said the Regent Lord as he fixed his dark gaze on the magician.

"In my travels I saw many lands, heard many stories. In brief, a century ago, a demon lord reached this land, but without a battle host. He took the guise of a woman, a queen of the humans, and conquered a third of that world before he was finally defeated.

"A magician of vast power, aided by other magicians, and as stout a human army as can be imagined, defeated the demon and threw him down."

The Regent Lord sat back, his head cocked to one side as he listened, and he shook his head slightly as he said, "Just one. That is unusual." He was silent a moment, then said, "But even one means more may be coming."

"I bring hope, my lord. For there are hints and suggestions in the stories that this demon did not come to this realm by conjuration, but rather through . . . a gate."

"The Demon Gate!" spat the Regent Lord. "That tale grows old, Conjurer. It is a fantasy to explain free demons among the mortals and absolve those like your brother of blame. Every master of lore since the time before time has avowed no demon can come to this realm unbidden! I will hear no more of this blasphemy, lest you wish to end up with the same fate as your brother!"

At the mention of his brother, the Conjurer's face went rigid.

Lowering his voice, the Regent Lord's expression turned to acceptance. "He still lives."

"In your dungeon, my lord?"

The Regent Lord actually smiled. "He had to content himself with a cage I had placed in a small courtyard. I thought the dungeon overly deleterious to his health, with no sunlight. I wanted him still alive if you returned, as you have. It does get a little uncomfortable in the afternoon heat, but otherwise he is well enough."

A slight flicker of expression crossed the magician's face, but he remained silent.

The Regent Lord said, "Your brother's continued survival depends on your obedience, Conjurer."

The magician inclined his head. "Gulamendis and I serve at your pleasure, my lord. Thus it has always been."

The Regent Lord's mood darkened. "Be not glib with me, Conjurer." He pointed to the west. "The Plains of Delth-Aran are covered with the bodies of warriors who 'served at my pleasure,' and I count each loss as an affront to our people. There are children here in Tandamar who will never know their fathers' faces.

"Across five worlds we have battled the demon legions, and each world we leave behind is littered with valiant fighters who 'served at my pleasure.' And their females and their young." Behind the anger in the Regent Lord's eyes, the Conjurer could see the genuine pain. "My grandfather, and his father before, all stood defiant and with resolve, and each warrior serving 'at their pleasure' gave full measure and left us lesser for that sacrifice.

"I would not dishonor their memories by forgiving those responsible for this horror visited upon the People. Now they are here, on the World of the Seven Stars, and we have nowhere left to go." Then his voice went soft and he almost whispered, "Except Home."

The Conjurer said nothing. It was an old argument, one that he had many times before. Laromendis and his brother were practitioners of the mystic arts, a barely tolerated calling under the best of times, and this was hardly the best of times. Laromendis was a master of illusion, a conjurer, who could kill a warrior with his own belief and imagination, conjuring up an illusion so real to the fighter that an imaginary killing blow would end his life. Gulamendis was a Master of Demons, and like the others of his calling, he was blamed for the terrors visited upon the People. Laro and his brother had been raised in a remote village by a mother who knew they were inheritors of a great and terrible gift, the ability to use magic.

The Regent Lord said, "Now, is this world safe?"

"I think so, my lord." Laromendis paused as if organizing his thoughts. "As I have said, the story I have pieced together tells me this world has powerful protectors, men and women who serve to stem the comings of those with whom we battle." He paused again, then carefully said, "We may have found allies."

"Allies!" shouted the Regent Lord. "Dwarves, lesser elves, humans! Perhaps we should treat with the goblins? Would you have me be the first ruler of our people to treat with those we have warred against since the time before time? Would you have me seek succor from those who are fit only to be conquered and bent to our service?"

Laromendis said nothing. He knew this was an argument that would take weeks, even months of debate, by the leaders of the Regent Lord's Meet. And Laromendis knew that if he was to save his brother's life, he must make sure when the Regent Lord's Meeting was called, the Loremasters and priests were allied with his view: that the fate of the People hung in the balance, and to save what was left of the once proud race, it must come to making accommodations with those who had always been counted as enemies.

The Regent Lord asked questions for an hour, insightfully pulling out details needed for his next plan. Finally he said, "We shall move two clans into this valley, have them occupy the fortress at the north end." Laro nodded. The dark elves had left everything intact. While overgrown and falling apart after a hundred years, it still would provide a safer place from which to muster, and could quickly be reclaimed as a highly defensible position.

"Have the Solis and Matusic muster," the Regent Lord ordered, and the herald bowed and departed. Laromendis kept his face expressionless, but inside he smiled. The Solis were under the command of Seboltis, Undalyn's favorite surviving son. That unexpected decision would give Laromendis a tiny advantage when the time came, for the Regent Lord would be less inclined toward conquest as the only solution if the heir to his throne stood at risk. Like his brother, Laromendis knew the People must change to endure. The Regent Lord would seek conquest, to reclaim Midkemia as the rightful home of the Taredhel. He might reach an accommodation with those living in Elvandar, even acknowledge their queen as the true ruler, giving up his line's power—though Laromendis counted that unlikely. But he would insist she govern a people who ruled the Home, not shared it with lesser beings.

Laromendis knew that line of thinking had done nothing but destroy the lives of millions of the People over three generations. To survive, the People would need to put aside dreams of conquest and come to terms with the dwarves and humans, and that required planning and luck, for the two brothers were barely tolerated and hardly trusted, yet it came to them to change the mind of the Regent Lord.

A messenger appeared at the door, nearly breathless for the dash up the long flight of stairs from the stable yard below. As he fell to his knees before his ruler, he lowered his head and held out the scroll.

The Regent Lord appeared to know what was in the message before reading it, and his expression darkened as his worst fears were fulfilled. "Garjan-Dar has fallen. The demons are through the breach."

Laromendis knew two things: the demons would be repulsed, but at great cost, and the Barrier Spell would be reestablished again. But how many more times could the breach be repaired, for warriors needed to hold ground while magic-users spent their lives to maintain the spell? Once more, twice perhaps, but eventually the Barrier Spell would fail, and soon after this city as well would be besieged. And against the Demon

Legion, the walls of this city would prove little obstacle. A week or two, perhaps a month, would the master arts of masonry and magic keep them at bay, then, at last, the city would fall. And with it, the heart of the Seven Stars.

The Regent Lord stood, put his boot against the shoulder of the kneeling messenger and pushed him away. "Get out!" he shouted, and the messenger appeared glad to obey, obviously relieved the Regent Lord's wrath had been limited to an impolite kick. In days past, his head might have adorned a pike at the entrance to the keep.

The Regent Lord moved toward the window and stared out. He took a deep breath, then he asked, "Which is your birth world, Conjurer?"

Laromendis said, "This one, my lord. Far to the north in the snowlands, at the foot of the Iron Mountains."

The Regent Lord said, "I was born here, as well, but my eldest son was born on Utameer." The Conjurer knew this, but if the Regent Lord felt the need to belabor the obvious, the magician was not fool enough to interrupt. "When he was but ten seasons, I took him hunting bovak and longhorn greensnouts in table lands to the east of the city of Akar. It was hot, all day, every day. Rain came rarely in those lands, and when it did it thundered and came down in a deluge. Children and small animals were sometimes washed away in flash floods. Lightning would rip the sky as if the gods themselves were at war." He turned to look at the magic-user. "We are going to lose this world, Conjurer, as we lost Utameer." He leaned against the window's edge, staring off into the distance. "As we lost Katanjara, and Shinbol, and the others.

"In my grandfather's grandfather's time, we conquered across the stars, we the People. The Clans of the Seven Stars ruled worlds!" Sadly he added, "Now we come to the end of our reign. Now we must become refugees."

Turning away from the Loremasters and the magician, he moved back to the chair and said, "We must return Home. It is our only salvation."

Turning to Laromendis, he said, "Eat, rest, then return at

first light. You shall conduct our battlemaster and a company of scouts to Home. We will begin preparing the way." He glanced at Laromendis and said, "Go!"

The Conjurer bowed, turned, and hurried from the hall. He had a great deal to do between now and the morning, and had no illusions he would get any rest. It took a great deal of energy to plot treason.

# CHAPTER 4

## HARBINGER

The rider raced up the hillside.

Alystan had paused in Carse only long enough to deliver his messages and eat a hot meal, sleep in a warm bed, then leave again at first light. It had taken him three days of hard running to reach the Keep at Carse and deliver the merchants' replies to the Earl's request. As the negotiations had ended on good terms, nothing more needed to be said, and the merchants could wait for another to return with the Earl's agreement.

The Ranger kept his own counsel on the matter of the elf, not wishing to involve the Kingdom in any of this unless it became necessary. At this moment the only evidence he had was what he had seen and nothing more, and there might be some explanation that would remove his foreboding. Yet there was something in the manner of that elf, the way he carried himself for the brief moment that Alystan saw him, something that communicated menace. If he was anything, he was dangerous.

Alystan bid farewell to the Earl and his household that night, for early the next day he was out the gate of the Keep as dawn approached. He accepted the loan of a sturdy gelding from the Earl and promised he would return it on his way home.

The quickest route to the dwarven stronghold at Caldara was through the Green Heart, the thick woodlands dominating most of the Duchy of Crydee. For ten miles or more from the sea inland, the coastline was dotted with small hamlets and solitary farms, trails and roads, and three towns of some size: Tulan, Carse, and Crydee. Light woods occupied some of the land between them, but once a traveler moved farther inland, heavy forest was all one encountered.

The Rangers of Natal were second only to the elves in their ability to move swiftly and quietly through the heavy woods, but when it came to the open road, they had no difficulty in letting a horse carry them swiftly. The Rangers were a close-knit society, the inheritors of a unique birthright. Their ancestors had been Imperial Keshian Guides, the elite scouts of the Empire's army, men who had come to the region when the Empire of Great Kesh had expanded northward. Like Kesh's dog soldiers, they were apart from the mainstream of Keshian society, living by themselves when not on duty. When Kesh withdrew from the northlands, leaving their colonies abandoned, the Guides had become the de facto intelligence and scouting arm of the local militia. Cities had become autonomous and had bound together in a loose confederation, the Free Cities of Natal. And the Guides became the Rangers.

Rangers still lived apart, though from time to time a Ranger might wed a town girl. Mostly they lived in large camps, moving as it suited them, always vigilant for any threat to the Cities. They felt kinship with the elves of the north more than the citizens of the cities they protected, and their only equals in their own eyes were the Keshian Guides and the Krondorian Pathfinders, also descended from the original Guides. The three groups had a traditional greeting—"Our grandfathers were brothers"—which was, to them, a bond.

But during the Tsurani invasion, many Rangers had died beside soldiers from the Kingdom and the Free Cities, and because their numbers had been small, it had taken a devastating toll. Now Alystan feared another threat of that magnitude was approaching, and remembering his grandfather's stories of the Riftwar, he knew another such invasion might mean the end of the Rangers.

Alystan was newly wed, and as he rode through the dark pathways of the Green Heart, he thought of his young wife, staying with his own mother and father as they broke winter camp down near Bordon and prepared to move up into the mountains for spring and summer. They had spoken of having their own child someday, and while they had yet to conceive one, Alystan now felt the fear that he might never see that child should his worst suspicions prove true.

The Ranger rode through the first day without incident, as the patrols from Carse eastward had kept the King's Road clear of bandits and other troublemakers. He had seen game sign, bear and elk, so he knew few hunters were nearby.

In years past, the Moredhel, the Brotherhood of the Dark Path, inhabited these woods and up into the Grey Tower Mountains, and such a ride would have been suicide without a company of soldiers to escort him. Now times were more peaceful and the worst a lone traveler might face was a small band of poachers or the occasional outlaw. Still, goblins roamed the Green Heart from time to time, and more than three or four could prove dangerous to a solitary rider.

Alystan made a cold camp the first night, not wishing to draw attention to his presence with a fire. He staked out his horse and moved some distance away so should the animal draw unwanted attention, he would not be close by. He risked losing the horse that way but gained the advantage of not being surprised in the night.

The night passed without incident.

Alystan quickly saddled his horse after inspecting it to ensure it was sound. The animal was one of the best the garrison at Carse had to offer, a solid gelding, well-trained and fit. Not the fastest mount available, but one capable of long journeys at good pace. With luck he would reach the dwarven stronghold at Caldara within three more days. He mounted and returned to the road.

Three days later a nearly exhausted rider and horse approached a gap in the mountains, across which a large wooden palisade had been erected. Two dwarves stood on either side of the road, dutifully taking their turn at watch, though for years it had hardly been necessary. They waved him through, recognizing him from previous visits, and Alystan entered Caldara.

The village was lovely in the morning light, nestled in a cozy valley with trails leading up to the high alpine meadows that were used for summer grazing, and down to lower valleys where the cattle and sheep were kept during the winter. Alystan knew that to the east were well-tended fields and a small stand of apple trees in an orchard that marked the eastern boundary of the holding.

The buildings were all of a kind, heavy thatched roofs atop wooden structures plastered over to keep out winter's cold. All were pristine white and shined in the morning sun, save the massive longhouse that dominated the community. Here lived the King and his retainers, as well as a large part of the local population on any given day. The longhouse was the hub of dwarven activity and on any given night any member of the community might be found sleeping on the floor of the great room before the huge fire as much as he would be back in his own bed. Unlike the plastered walls, this building had been constructed in the old way: huge boles of trees stacked in cradles, forming outer walls that would defy both the elements and attacking enemies.

The floors were stone upon the earth, flattened and smoothed so one could barely feel the joints between them when walking over them. But they were as impenetrable by sappers digging up from below as the walls were by those above the ground. The dwarves were miners and understood the uses of tunnels in warcraft as well as in mining.

Alystan pulled up before the entrance to the longhouse and dismounted. He unsaddled his gelding, and put the saddle over the hitching log, then quickly wiped down the animal with a rag from his saddle bags. It would have to do until he took it to the stables and tended to it. Dwarves were not horsemen, and the horses they did keep were draft animals, all of whom would be out in the fields this time of day, pulling plows as the dwarves readied the ground for the spring planting.

As he finished up, a dwarf emerged from the building. "Aly-stan of Natal!" he said with pleasure. "What brings you our way?"

"I come to see your grandfather, Hogni. Is he inside?"

The young dwarf's grin split his long black beard. The dwarves were small compared to humans, but still broad of shoulders and powerful of frame, averaging a little over five feet in height. Hogni was especially tall for his race, nearing five inches over five feet. He had a merry light in his eye as he said, "Grandfather refuses to take his rank seriously, as always. He says he's 'new to this King business' as it's 'only' been a 'little over a hundred years or so.'

"He's down in the fields plowing. Come along, I'll take you there."

As he moved away, he waved over a dwarven boy and said, "Toddy, take that horse to Grandfather's stable and see to him, will you?"

Alystan smiled as he took his longbow off his shoulder and returned it to the familiar grip of his left hand. His expression was dubious, as the boy barely reached three feet in height, topped with a shock of red-blond hair and an apple-cheeked grin, but if Hogni was confident in his ability to somehow reach the gelding's withers and clean him off, he wasn't going to argue. The horse had rendered stout service and deserved to be treated well. Only the urgency of his news kept him from properly tending to the mount before seeing the King.

They quickly made their way through the village to the eastern fields where a half-dozen draft horses pulled plows. Crossing carefully over the newly plowed rows, they approached a dwarf with a completely grey head of hair and beard. He was perspiring heavily as he wrestled the plow's iron blade through soil packed hard by a winter's weight of snow and the morning's frost. The horses, like their masters, were powerful but diminutive, looking like broad-chested ponies as much as true horses. Yet Alystan knew they were a special breed of true horse, used for this work by the dwarves for centuries.

Dolgan, King of the Dwarves and Warleader of Caldara, reined in the gelding who pulled his plow, and waved a greeting. "Alystan of Natal! Well met!"

"Greetings, King Dolgan. Have you no liegemen to plow your fields?"

"I do, but they're busy plowing their own at the moment, and it's in my nature to wish it done right the first time." He took a well-worn long briar pipe out of his pocket and quickly produced a contraption of flint and steel, a clever device fetched up from the Free Cities in trade. A big spark ignited the tobac in the pipe, and Dolgan took a long pull. He made a face and said, "This is a useful enough gadget, but that first taste of burning flint I can do without." He puffed again, looked contented, and asked, "What brings you to Caldara, Alystan?"

Alystan held his bow with the tip on the ground, a habit Dolgan knew meant the Ranger was being thoughtful at choosing his words. The gesture always gained him a moment to think. "I bring word of something strange, and troubling. I seek your wisdom and counsel."

"Well, that sounds serious enough." He tossed the reins to Hogni and said, "Finish up here boy, and then go help your father. I'll be in the longhouse with our guest."

"Yes, Grandfather," said the young dwarf with a resigned smile. The King might like to see the plowing done right the first time, but he also enjoyed chatting with travelers in the longhouse over a flagon of ale. The youth glanced upward and smiled. It was barely two hours past breakfast, hardly the time his mother would approve of her father-in-law tapping the ale keg, despite his being King. Putting the reins over his shoulders, Hogni flipped them and shouted, "Ha!" The horse threw one impatient

glance backward, as if asking if the young dwarf was really serious and did he have to return to his labors; another flick of the
reins told the animal it was indeed time, so he reluctantly returned to dragging the plow through the rich mountain soil.

Dolgan listened carefully as Alystan finished his narrative. The
old dwarf was silent for a very long time, then said, "This is troubling news."

"You recognize this newcomer?" asked the Ranger, before
taking a long pull on the marvelous dwarven ale the King's less
than pleased daughter-in-law provided. She seemed irritated
to the point of saying something, but held her silence before a
stranger.

Dolgan shook his head. "No, though I would not have recognized the so-called mad elves from north of the Teeth of the
World before they ventured down to Elvendar." He turned and
shouted, "Amyna!"

Hogni's mother appeared a moment later and said, "Yes, Father?"

"Send Toddy to find Malachi. Have him join us here,
please?"

She nodded once and departed.

Dolgan said, "Malachi is the oldest among us." He chuckled.
"He was old when I was a boy and I'm nearing three hundred
years, myself."

Alystan's expression was barely held in check. He knew the
dwarves to be a long-lived race, like the elves, but he had no idea
they lived that long, or stayed as robust as they apparently did.
Whatever consternation he had glimpsed in the Dwarf King vanished with the boy. The old dwarf seemed content to smoke his
pipe, drink his morning ale, and chat of inconsequential matters,
how fared his human acquaintances along the Far Coast and in
the Free Cities, what news from Krondor, or farther. It was clear
to the Ranger than Dolgan was keenly interested in matters outside his own small demesne, which, given the dwarves' history,
was understandable.

An independent people, the dwarves nevertheless found

their fortunes tied to those of the surrounding humans and, to a lesser degree, the elves to the north. Twice in the last hundred years, war had visited the west, first the Tsurani invaders in the very valley where Alystan had seen the stranger, and later by the armies of the Emerald Queen, from a land across the sea. The second struggle had involved the dwarves indirectly, but the repercussions had echoed through the land for a long time. Trade had been reduced to a trickle for years, the west nearly forgotten by the Kingdom for a decade, and banditry and piracy had risen. Things were nearly back to the way they had been before the coming of the Tsurani, Alystan's grandfather claimed; in fact, he insisted it was better, as the dark elves no longer hunted the Green Heart or the Grey Towers. Given the history of bloody warfare between the Rangers and the Moredhel, Alystan was inclined to grant his grandfather's view had merit.

Time passed, but Alystan was like all Rangers, possessing patience born of generations of woodcraft and hunting. A fidgeting hunter was a hungry one, his father had told him many years before, on his first hunt.

At last the boy Toddy returned, quietly and slowly escorting the oldest being the Ranger had ever encountered. The dwarf moved slowly, his steps tiny, as if he feared losing his balance. He appeared shrunken with age, so he was barely a head taller than the boy, and slight of frame. In contrast to the robust stature of the other dwarves the Ranger knew, this was startling. His skin was parchment-white and almost translucent, so the veins of his hands stood out over knuckles swollen with years of inflammation. He used a cane, and the boy held him firmly by his left arm. His hair receded, and fell to his shoulders, and whatever color may have once graced that ancient pate had fled, leaving snow-white wisps. Cheeks sunken with age were marked with small lesions and sores, and Alystan knew this was a being at the end of his days.

The old dwarf looked about the room, and the Ranger realized either he was blind or his vision so poor he might as well be sightless. He sat and those in the room remained silent.

Then he spoke. "So, what reason have you to rouse an old

man from his nap?" he demanded. His voice was surprisingly strong and deep for so frail a figure.

Dolgan said, "Malachi, this is Alystan of the Free Cities."

"I can see he's a Ranger, Dolgan," said the old man, and Alystan reassessed his judgment on Malachi's eyesight. "Well, you have something to say, else they wouldn't have required me to come here, so say it," instructed the ancient dwarf.

Alystan retold the tale of the traveler. Malachi said nothing the entire time, but he did lean forward slightly, as if paying closer attention, when the Ranger began describing the creature's true appearance.

When Alystan was finished, Malachi leaned back and let his chin drop, as if thinking. The room remained silent for several minutes, then the ancient dwarf said, "It's an old tale, told by my grandfather's grandfather, from the time of the Crossing."

Dolgan said nothing, but he glanced around the room at the other dwarves who had gathered there while Alystan had spoken. There were now perhaps twenty dwarves, most of whom Alystan recognized as being part of the King's Meet, Dolgan's council of advisors.

Malachi paused, then said, "At the end of my days I am, but I remember this tale as if it were told to me yesterday.

"My first raid was against the dark elves to the north, who had been troubling our herds in the lower meadows, when calving was under way. We had chased off a band and my father"—he pointed at Dolgan—"and your father, though he had not the title of King, but Warleader, decided we needed to carry chastisement to the miscreants and let them know there would be no stealing of calves from the dwarves of Caldara!" He took a breath, and said, "We followed the thieves through two days, and the night we camped before the raid, my father told me a story told him by his grandfather.

"He said before the Gods warred, dwarves lived on a distant world, and fought long and hard against the great goblin tribes, Lea Orcha, the Orcs, the great *wryms*, like our dragons, but stupid, yet cunning. They defended their crops and herds from gryphon and manticore and other creatures of myth. Father spoke of ancient legends, of great heroes and deeds, lost to even the Lorekeepers, for this was before the Crossing."

Alystan said, "The Crossing?"

The old dwarf nodded. "A madness consumed our world, a war visited upon us by beings of power beyond even our most puissant Lorekeeper's art. We know them as Dragon Lords."

"The Valheru," said Dolgan, thinking of his time spent with Lord Tomas, during the war against the Tsurani. He had learned much since then of Valheru lore, while he watched the boy from Crydee grow into a being of unimaginable power; but there was far more untold, he knew.

"Aye," said Malachi. "So the elves call their former masters. My father told me it was the very masters of this world who drove us here, by design or chance no one knows.

"But flee the home world we did. Great tears in the heavens above and earth below opened, swallowing up those nearby. Some, it is said, went to other worlds, by chance and happenstance, whim of the gods, or luck. But most of us hunkered down and resisted the forces of chaos on all sides.

"There were races of men on our home world, along with the Great Goblins and our people. It was they, these masters of magic, who constructed bridges to flee from the destruction visited upon us during the Chaos Wars.

"Much was lost, but this much remained: that in the ancient times many others ranged across these lands, kin to those we chased, but not those in Elvandar, with whom we were at peace. He told a tale of a time when the wars on the ancient birth-world forced dwarves, humans, even the magic-users of the Dena Orcha—"

"Orcs!" spat Dolgan, as if the very word was an insult.

The Ranger looked at the old man.

"Dena Orcha in the old tongue," said Malachi. "The true enemy of our blood. The Great Goblins. None live on this world."

"But they live in our memory," said the Dwarf King.

Malachi waved away the comment. "All the magic-users of many races banded together to save worlds in the time of the

Mad Gods and raging Dragon Riders. They formed the Golden Bridge and many of our ancestors came to Midkemia.

"But there were already living here the elves and some others, the serpent men and the tiger men, and we were met with war and magic.

"Fighting on both sides of the Golden Bridge went on for a time without time, for the very nature of the universe was twisted and fluid.

"Then it was over," said the ancient dwarf quietly. "In days after the Crossing, but before the line of Kings was named, in the dim mists of memory, this was told by the elves to our ancestors. Many of their people fled this world as we had fled our own, and to the elves they would be known as the Lost Elves."

The old dwarf sat silently for a minute and said, "I can only guess, but it may be one such as that has returned to this world, for never have I heard of such a one before. You'd best ask the elves, for this much I know: of elven magic many things can be said, but nothing I have heard in my long life speaks of illusion as guise." He said, "If I may leave, King?"

His tone left no doubt the request was only for form, as he turned and started to get up as the King waved permission.

As the old man was about to leave, Dolgan said, "Malachi, one question. Why did my father not speak of this to me?"

Malachi shrugged. "You would have to be able to ask him. Your father was a quiet, thoughtful leader. He spoke very little." Dolgan nodded. "My father liked to tell stories." Again Dolgan nodded.

"I remember one more thing," said Malachi. "Three great bridges were built, on our birth world, or so my father said his grandfather told him. Two were built by humans and dwarves, and one by the Orcs. One bridge led to the Tsurani world, or so I believe from what we learned from those Tsurani who came to our world. If any of our people crossed, no memory of them remains with the Tsurani. The other came here, and it was over that bridge that humans and dwarves came to Midkemia.

"The Orc bridge went to another world, and from the time of the Chaos Wars we have no longer been plagued by that ancient hate. Some humans and dwarves crossed with them, it is said. Perhaps," posed the old dwarf, "those Lost Elves built their own bridge to escape their masters?" Without waiting for an answer, Malachi left the hall.

Dolgan and the others remained silent for a long while, then Dolgan said, "What if the Lost Elves built their own bridge to escape their masters, indeed."

"But now one returns," said Alystan.

"Apparently," said Dolgan.

"Know this, welder of Tholin's hammer," said a voice from behind. Dolgan and the others turned to see Malachi returned from the hallway. "One last thing," he added, pointing a frail finger at the Dwarf King. "It was your ancestor who led our people here, making these mountains our home. It was his brothers who led other bands to Stone Mountain and Dorgin. But our people were once as numerous as the leaves on trees. Where one dwarf crossed the bridge from our home world, five remained to fight the madness that came to destroy our home.

"No one knows what that madness was, save it shattered worlds." The old dwarf seemed fatigued from telling his story. Then, as if catching his breath, he raised his voice. "If Lost Elves are coming to this world, you must call the Meet and counsel against the possibility of war! Since we've come to this world we've found enemies, Dolgan, King, and while these Lost Elves, if that is who they are, are kin to our friends in Elvandar, they are also kin to the dark elves." Malachi nodded to the boy Toddy to take Malachi back to his quarters.

As the boy led away the ancient dwarf, several of the dwarves in the room nodded, and Hogni, Dolgan's grandson, said, "When the Tsurani came, and we first heard of them that night in the cave where you and Father and Uncle Udell found Lord Borric huddled against the raiding goblins, Father told me he felt a cold in the pit of his stomach."

Dolgan nodded. "I, as well, and I feel it again."

The Ranger said, "I can only tell you what I saw. I could put no name to that creature until this very hour. I have never heard of these Lost Elves until this day."

Dolgan said, "It could be some type of coincidence. The creature might have been some other being that merely looks like our own elves. After all, don't the Tsurani look like other humans? Or perhaps it was a human you saw, and he put a magic guise on for whatever need he might have on the other side of the rift through which he traveled." He puffed on his pipe and was silent for a moment. "Still, if it is the return of an ancient race of elves . . ."

"Caution urges you prepare as if they are coming," said the Ranger. "I'm for Elvandar and the Queen and Lord Tomas."

Dolgan fixed the Ranger with a stare for a moment, then said, "And I'm with you. For if anyone has any memory of those days, it will be Tomas. He often doesn't recall his Dragon Lord past until prodded by events, and if there was a time for prodding, it's now."

"You'll ride?" asked the Ranger.

Dolgan grinned. "I'm old, but I'm not dead. It's thick woodlands between here and the River Crydee, and I've yet to see a horse I couldn't run down. I'll keep up, have no fear."

Hogni fidgeted and cleared his throat.

His grandfather fixed him with a barely hidden amused expression and said, "What is it, boy?"

"You said when next you went to Elvandar, I could come as well, Grandfather."

Dolgan feigned a scowl, then said, "That I did. Get ready. And tell your father he gets to play King for a while until I return. We leave in an hour."

Hogni grinned, and hurried to gather his travel gear. Dolgan sighed. To Alystan, he said, "He's young. Not quite forty years yet."

The Ranger, who was only a few years older, suppressed a chuckle. The moment of mirth passed, and the grim aspect of what they were facing returned. Despite the brisk fire nearby, the room seemed colder.

# CHAPTER 5

## EXODUS

Laromendis began his spell.

Across the vast courtyard sat a huge iron cage in which his brother rested, as best he could in the blistering afternoon heat. The guard who stood before the cage hadn't glanced at the Conjurer, so that when Laromendis finished his spell and approached, the guard saw two figures: the Conjurer and a guard captain.

The guard looked quizzically at the pair, unaware that one of them was a figment of his own imagination, and when they stopped before him, he heard the officer instruct him to draw away and give the brothers a moment of privacy. The guard nodded once, then moved away.

Gulamendis looked up at his brother and smiled,

though it obviously pained him to do such, his lips cracked and bleeding from the heat. "How fare you, Brother?"

Laromendis shook his head as he thrust a small water skin through the bars of the cage. "Drink slowly." He said, "I'm faring better than you, by all appearances. What happened?"

"Our master the Regent Lord became vexed by news we had lost the outpost at Starwell and turned his wrath upon me. As he already had me in the dungeon, and he couldn't rightly kill me and keep your service, he decided a little torment might serve to show his wrath." He glanced at the sun, which was now lowering toward the Keep. "In an hour the shadows will cover me and I'll be all right."

Pointing to the skin, Laromendis said, "Hide and nurse that. If you do, it should last for a few days." He glanced over his shoulder at the distant guard. "I don't think they'll completely forget to feed you and give you water, but they may decide to let you suffer a bit. It's the mood of the times."

"Not a lot of joy to be found," said the demon master. Gulamendis moved aside the stale straw that was his bedding and hid the remaining water. "I'm better than I look. I send Choyal into the kitchen at night to fetch me extra food and drink." He chuckled but it came out a dry, rasping sound. "But imps are so stupid. One night it will be a delicacy from the Regent Lord's own larder, another night it will be rotten vegetables."

"I'll do what I can to get you out." Laromendis paused, looked his brother in the eye, and said, "I found Home."

His brother's expression was fixed. The resemblance between them was staggering, as they were almost twins, but Gulamendis was slightly shorter, a little thinner, and had hair of a lighter, almost orange, red.

"What?" asked Laromendis.

"If you have found Home, what need has the Regent Lord for us?"

"There are problems," said Laromendis, standing. "I must leave, as the guard is returning and I can't be here if a true officer arrives. Just know that the Regent Lord needs me for a while longer, and because of that, you will be safe, if not comfortable.

"And I have a plan."

The younger brother smiled. "You always do."

"We need to get you to Home, because not only will you be safer there, the People will have need of your knowledge."

"Demons?"

"Perhaps; I can say no more. If you are questioned, ignorance is your ally."

He turned and hurried away from the cage, nodding once at the guard, who returned to watching over Gulamendis. As quickly as he could, he got out of the courtyard and made his way to the small quarters set aside for his use. The Regent Lord had grudgingly admitted to the Conjurer's usefulness by providing him with a modest suite of two rooms, one for sleeping and the other for study.

There was little of value here, save a volume of notes the Conjurer had prepared before departing on his latest exploration, the one that had taken him to Home. He sat for a moment on his bed and thumbed through the journal. When he got to the last page, he reached over to a small table, expecting to find his quill and ink there. He glanced over and recognized instantly they were out of place; someone had been in his quarters, reading his journal.

He withheld a smile, as he expected no less from the Regent Lord. He wrestled with what he had heard of his distant kin on Midkemia and what his own people had become. There was much to admire about the achievements of the Taredhel, but, in truth, there was much apparently lost.

A trapper from Yabon had told long stories about the elven forests to the west of his homeland, so long as Laromendis paid for the ale in the tavern in Hawk's Hollow. The stories he told painted a picture of a people at one with the forest, content if not happy with their lives, able to come and go effortlessly through the woodland. He spoke of elven magic, but what he said in hints and suggestions told Laromendis volumes.

The great Spellweavers and the older Eldar endured! That fact had been purposefully left out of his report to the Regent Lord, for two reasons. First, he had no proof that what the trapper had said was remotely accurate, even if he felt in his bones that it was. Second, he needed to discover for himself how many magic-users of the elves of Elvandar there were, and what capabilities they had. A great deal of the ancient lore had been lost with the crossing of the Starbridge, as his people called their route from Midkemia to this world.

So much of it had been rooted in their spiritual links to the very soil of that world, the energies that rose from the heart and soul of the planet, to be coaxed and finessed into serving the Edhel, the People. This world had different magic, and it had been a difficult blending of that which had been brought with them and that which they found already here. The seven great trees—the Seven Stars, as they were called—had been their anchor to the old magic from Home. But the soil had been alien soil, from a world with its own rules and nature, and from that blending had come the majestic force that the Taredhel had first struggled to control, then come to master.

The Taredhel Spellmasters were most likely the equals of all but the best the humans and elves had to offer on Midkemia, but there were so few of them left; many had paid for the survival of the People with their blood. They were honored and remembered in the annals, but each loss weakened the People beyond measure.

More students were sent to fight the Demon Legion every year, less ready, less practiced, and less able to withstand demon magic. If there had been any other way for the Regent Lord to find Home without utilizing rogue magic-users like Laromendis and Gulamendis, he would have put them to death years ago.

The relationship between magic-users in the Star Guild—the legatees of the original Spellweavers who fled from Home—and those outside that organization had always been strained at best, and outright hostile at worst. Wild magic, or broken magic, or any number of other terms had been used to describe those with the gifts who came into their power without the training of the Star Guild.

The Star Guild had labored for generations to tend the Seven Stars, to bring the wild magic of Andcardia under control, and to prevent the destruction of the People. Their labors had earned them a place at the tables of power and the most gifted among them, the Chief Magister of the Guild, sat second only to the Regent Lord in prestige and power.

In times past, those like Laromendis and his brother were hunted down and murdered, or captured and indentured to the Guild as "dirt magicians," or some other demeaning epithet. But now "dirt magicians" like Laromendis, and "demon lovers" like his brother, were too valuable a commodity to be squandered away by bigotry. This Regent Lord wasn't a great deal more forgiving of "deviant" practices than his forebears, but he was a great deal more pragmatic about using talent whatever its origins.

Laromendis put away his journal, certain it would be read as soon as he left the city and making sure nothing he had written would be inconsistent with what he had told the Regent Lord.

He stood up and looked out the window. He was unable to see that portion of the courtyard where his brother sat imprisoned, but knew that by now the shadows were covering the cage. Silently, he said, *Just a while longer, Little Brother. The Regent will be reading my journal within an hour after I depart, and no matter what he may think of us and our arts, he needs us. You will be free soon.*

Putting away his pen and ink, he placed the journal on the small table and sat back on the bed, thinking. He should rest, but his mind was racing.

So much he hadn't told the Regent Lord, so much he wished to share with Gulamendis. And a handful of others, for this world was Home and, moreover, he sensed down to the fiber of his being that somewhere to the north of that valley he had scouted, there lay all the answers the People sought. If they were but wise enough to recognize those answers.

He knew that he was working toward his own purposes, though he believed his purpose was as dedicated to saving the People as was the Regent Lord's. But he also knew that the Regent Lord suspected him of having a different agenda. So, glancing at the journal once again, he resisted the urge to smile; let the

Regent Lord and the Chief Magister and the other members of the Regent's Meeting suspect his purposes, even conclude what those purposes were, just as long as they didn't suspect what his real goals were. Let them think his ambitions were personal: power, glory, wealth, freedom for his brother; those were goals they understood. His real purpose and goals would be as alien to them as the nature of their terrible enemies to the north.

Sighing despite his iron resolve, Laromendis stood up and left his quarters. He must eat something, he knew, then be about his business, for by dawn tomorrow a thousand Taredhel warriors, magicians, and scholars would be moving through the translocation gate to that lovely valley long ago abandoned by the Forgotten, and once more the Clans of the Seven Stars would return to their ancient homeland on the world humans called Midkemia.

Laromendis stood next to his ruler, as the leader of the Clans of the Seven Stars surveyed the valley below. His face was a fixed mask, but the slight sheen in his eyes and the softening around them told the Conjurer all he needed to know; the trap was sprung. The thought of somehow saving Andcardia was gone, as the ruler of the Taredhel looked upon the ancient homeland of the race—Midkemia.

The Regent Lord waved his Warleader to his side and softly said, "Begin."

The Warleader, Kumal, stood for a moment beside his ruler, experiencing the emotions that struck every elf like a hammer's blow when they stepped through the translocation portal. This was Home!

He nodded once, turned, and walked back through the portal, and the Regent Lord stepped aside. From behind, a humming sound filled the air, resonant, deep, and sounding like nothing so much as heavy stones being dragged across the ground; a vibration in the soles of his boots reinforced that perception to the Conjurer. He knew his brethren on the other side of the portal were employing their arts to widen it so those waiting on this side might pass through.

Pointing down the game trail that marked the edge of this clearing in the hills, the Conjurer said, "My Lord, in the vale below stands a vacant stockade, of familiar design. I judge the Forgotten once lived within, and with little effort it can be made to serve. Throughout this area are campsites, for the stockade will serve temporarily as your court, but no more than a thousand can occupy the vale until more housing is built. I have marked trails so the trackers can lead bands to those campsites. They will serve as a defensive perimeter until the city walls can be erected."

To the Warleader, Undalyn said, "Let them begin. I want lookouts in the hills above us, sentries in the passes below. Let the workers build signal towers so the outer villages can be summoned when needed. Send out hunting parties and let it be known: should any member of the Clans be spied by human, elf, or dwarf, I will have his head on a pike before my throne. Any who espy us must die before word can reach others that we have returned. We shall decide when our cousins to the north and the rest who live here discover the true masters of this world have returned.

"The day will come when we will rid this land of our enemies," he said, looking back at the portal as it ceased its expansion. The first soldiers came through, each wearing the Clans armor: a heavy metal breastplate, pale yellow in hue, with peaked shoulders. The pale golden color came from the metals used to forge them, a mystery of the smiths closely held, giving the Taredhel stronger, lighter shielding than steel. Each was trimmed in the Clan colors, one for each of the Seven Stars, one for each color in the rainbow. Upon the heads of the standard-bearers rested the crested helms, more ornate than functional; each topped with a plume dyed the color of their Clan. The infantry carried their more functional helms tied to their belts.

The first hundred soldiers hurried away from the portal, splitting into squads, each led by a tracker who would lead them to various positions around the valley. Within hours, camps and watch stations would be in position and a secure perimeter would be thrown up around the valley. The Taredhel bridgehead would be established.

Laromendis watched patiently as heavy-bodied horses pulled massive wagons atop which rode females and the young. These were refugees from the outer villages and strongholds that had fallen before the demon horde.

The children were silent, but their eyes were wide with wonder. There was something in the very air of this world that called to each elf as they returned to their ancestral soil; the Conjurer could only liken it to a reawakening of something deep within that had been dormant for generations.

The Regent Lord knelt, removed his gauntlets, and picked up a handful of the soil of this world. He lifted it to his nose and sniffed, and said, "This land is rich with life. We shall reclaim this home, no matter what." He fell silent in reflection for a moment, his eyes distant as he drank in the sense of this place. Then he turned to Laromendis. "This is our world," whispered the Regent Lord. "Our world." He looked at the ragged elves who were the first to come to this land, and shook his head. Those in the city would be the last, with the defenders who held the demons at bay giving their lives to save their kin. A play of emotions crossed over the ruler's face, then he again showed only a mask. He said, "We must rest, recover, and grow, for we have lost too much in recent years."

Removing his fur mantle, as the day's heat grew, he took a deep breath. "The air here is sweet, despite the dwarves and others using it." He chuckled at his own joke.

Coming to his ruler's side, the Conjurer lowered his voice so that those coming through the portal would not hear him over the wagons' rumble, "Sire, there is but one other troubling thing."

"Tell me," said the Regent Lord.

"As I said before, there have been rumors of demons . . ."

The Regent Lord's eyes closed as if he was in pain. Softly, almost as if he could hardly bear to say the words, he uttered, "I put that out of my mind." He regarded Laromendis and asked, "Here, as well?"

"Rumors only, and I have seen no demon sign personally. And as you know, I have diligently searched for any hint they

are here. Still, I lack certain arts others have, which would ensure the demons' absence."

The Regent Lord looked at the wagons as they continued
to rumble through the portal, more warriors now appearing as
well, flanking the caravan of Taredhel females and young. There
was hardly one fighter without a wound or damage to his armor.
At one time the Taredhel ruled across the stars, traveling by
magic gates from world to world. But for almost a hundred years
the People had been battling the Demon Legion, from world to
world, as millions of the People perished.

The demons had reduced millions to thousands, and now
the last of their kind sought refuge on a world known only
through ancient lore, a world where the People had abided in
hallowed antiquity, before the time the gods warred and all was
in chaos.

The Conjurer smiled. "Yes, my lord. It is rich with life. Much
of it familiar. There are deer and bear, lions and wyverns; game
is plentiful. The corn tastes odd, but not unpleasant—sweeter
than what we know—and the dwarves, for all their despicable
flaws, sell their brewing to any and all. The humans and dwarves
have herds of cattle and sheep, and the seas are abundant as well.
There are riches beyond what we've known in a century." Then
he fell silent.

The Regent Lord stood and said, "You have something to
say. Say it."

"My lord," said the Conjurer, "should I offend you, take my
head, but as I am sworn to serve, I must speak only truth. If the
rumors of demons reaching here are true, and they do follow us,
we are left with two choices: to flee while the humans, dwarves,
and our primitive cousins battle the Demon Legion, yet again
seeking another world . . ."

"Where?" injected the Regent Lord. "I read every report. You
have found no alternative, only harsh places where life scarcely
survives, or barren rock . . . no, there is nowhere else to go."

"We stay and fight."

The Regent Lord said, "When my father was a boy, the Seven
Clans numbered two million swords, Conjurer." He looked on

as more wagons and beasts of burden emerged from the portal. Livestock was now coming through, a herd of razor-spine hogs, being herded by a wolflike dire dog. An especially large dog loped through the portal and came to the Regent Lord's side, licking the monarch's hand while wagging a bushy tail.

Roughly patting the beast's massive neck, the Regent Lord almost crooned as he said, "Sanshem, my good companion." He looked fondly upon the animal, perhaps the only being in all Creation for whom the Regent Lord felt genuine affection.

Looking back at the Conjurer, the Regent Lord said, "When my father took the throne, but four hundred twenty thousand swords could answer the call of the Taredhel battle horn.

"When I took the crown from my father's brow, *after demons had ripped his still beating heart from his chest*"—he almost shouted—"I had less than a third that number of warriors!" He stood up, patting the dog on its massive head. "Since our last battle, we have less than half that serving, with some youth training." He shook his head in open regret. "We have children learning to fight, barely more than babes, who have only smelled our own blood and the stench of demons since their birth!"

He gazed down into the lush forest below and said, "I am torn, Conjurer. The Demon Legion seems endless. No matter how many we kill, more appear soon after. How could we stand here in this valley, behind wooden walls caulked with mud, when we could not hold from behind the massive walls of Starwell, or keep them at bay with the death towers along the Gap of Doom? The Pamalan Dome collapsed and their fliers descended on the city like an evil hailstorm. Every magic known to the Taredhel defends Tarendamar, and the defenses are unmatched in our history. Yet the demons keep coming.

"So, I thought perhaps we might linger awhile here, while we seek another refuge, and then I came." He looked around at the valley as tree leaves rustled in the breeze, birds darted across the sky, and the only sound was the rumbling of wagons and the tread of boots on the soil. He took a deep breath. "No, this is where we shall stand; we have no other choice. And here we shall live or die as the Goddess will it, should the demons come."

The Conjurer nodded. It was not the time to say what he must say. Soon, but not today. Not after fleeing the Demon Legion across the tundra of Mistalik, hounded for months by creatures so foul and powerful that only the mightiest warriors could delay them, and only the most powerful magic could destroy them.

As the line of refugees continued to issue from the portal, the Conjurer knew one thing above all else: for the People to survive in this new land, no matter how abundant and hospitable, they would need allies. Which meant generations of making war on all who were not of the People would need be forgotten and aggression as a way of life need be set aside.

The Regent Lord nodded once to one of his heralds, standing near the portal, and the servant bowed slightly and darted through the magic opening. A moment later he returned, followed by a dozen older elves, dressed in the guild cloth of the geomancers.

Laromendis knew that they were much needed to repair the damage to the city defenses on Andcardia. He knew what this sight meant: these few remaining masters of earth magic would begin building a new city in the heart of this valley, and the repairs of the last bastion of defense for those behind would be left to lesser masters and apprentices to repair. It was an admission of a choice the Regent Lord had yet to voice.

A group of elders made their way through and came to stand before their Regent Lord, bowing as one. To the oldest of them the Regent Lord said, "Oversee the creation of our new home, my lords. Begin at once. Defend the valley and start down there." He pointed to a rise that overlooked the distant small lake that was the center of this valley. "Around that lake we shall plant the Seven Stars. On that rise build a new palace." He looked around, as if fixing the sights of Home in his mind. "Within the month, all who can be brought here shall come, and we shall seal this portal behind us.

"I return to Andcardia to oversee the fighting. We shall hold the demons at bay as long as possible." To the Conjurer he said, "What do you need, to find out the truth about demons here?"

Taking a breath, he simply answered, "My brother. No one among the People knows more of demon lore than he, my lord—" As the Regent Lord was about to object, Laromendis hurried to cut off the objection, "I know there are many who see him as the cause of the demon invasion—"

"If that were true," said the Regent Lord, "he already would be dead. I am not so gullible as to believe that he personally summoned the Demon Horde, Conjurer. But I do believe it was the meddling of those like him—and yourself—into realms prohibited by the Spellcrafters that somehow caused the magic barriers to be breached." The Conjurer almost winced at that, for he knew there was no breach of any "magic barrier," but rather somewhere a gate had been opened, a portal between the realms, and if that could be found . . . He turned his mind back to the Regent Lord, who said, "I simply hold him against your good behavior."

"You have my pledge, my lord."

The Regent Lord looked around once more, breathing deeply, as if to fix the sights, smells, and sounds of the place in his memory as he returned to the struggle.

"Very well. Return with me and change places, Laromendis. You shall be his guarantee."

"Ah—" began the Conjurer.

Smiling, the Regent Lord said, "When the last of the People are through the translocation portal, then shall I free you to be with your brother. For then no one on Andcardia will be alive. Until then, you are going to use your talents to defend against the Demon Legion."

"Ah," said Laromendis, nodding. No dungeon or cage in the courtyard for him; he would be at the battlements, sending demons back to whatever hell they came from. "Very well, my lord. It is as I would wish it, to serve in whatever way you judge right."

The Regent Lord stepped around a wagon rumbling through the portal, and through the magic curtain. Keeping his features set, the magic-user followed, satisfied that his plan was now under way. He had to make sure he had one minute, no more, with his brother, then he would gladly go and give his life if needed to save the People, but he prayed to an ancient goddess that that wouldn't be necessary. For to save the People, his arts and his brother's, and those of many more, who were considered less than elven by the Regent Lord, those would need to band together to save Midkemia.

And to do that, changes needed to be instituted, and quickly.

And that required a little treason.

He stepped through the portal and vanished.

# CHAPTER 6

## PREMONITION

Pug cast his spell.

The assembled students watched in rapt attention as a column of energy rose above the master sorcerer, a column of power speeding upward, unseen. They could sense the energy, though, and some, more attuned to the magic arts than others, almost felt it radiating on their skin. It was a basic skill he was teaching, usually left to those whose time was less valuable than that of ones in the Conclave of Shadows, but Pug felt the need to be with students from time to time. The lesson was simple: how to feel the presence of magic, to detect it when it was employed nearby. He had been astonished to discover over the years how many magicians and magical clerics couldn't tell a fireball had been cast until the flames singed their hair.

The young men and women, from many nations and a few alien worlds, were gathered to study under the tutelage of the greatest practitioner of the arcane arts on Midkemia. The lesson today was on perception and reaction to change in magic, and the first step in that was to recognize magic was being deployed. The lesson might seem fundamental to most of the students, but the three people who observed from a short distance away knew better: it was the first step in learning how to react to hostile magic directed at a magic-user by another, and it was that first instant of recognition of changing magic that kept a magician alive.

Magnus turned to his brother and mother, and said, "He seems to be fine."

Miranda shook her head. " 'Seems' is the word. It's another bout of melancholia."

"Nakor?" asked Caleb.

Miranda said, "I don't know. Maybe. It's been nearly ten years, and he hides it well when he thinks someone is watching, but those black moods come upon him still."

Caleb, Pug and Miranda's younger son, said, "Marie notices it, too." His wife was a woman of keen perception, and in the ten years since she had come to Sorcerer's Isle, she had become something of the mistress of the household, a position Miranda was more than happy to cede to her, as she had her own magical studies to conduct.

Magnus said, "I was there, and no one could have done more than Father did. Nakor chose his fate." Letting his voice drop a little, as if speaking to himself, he added, "As much as any of us can choose."

Miranda's dark eyes showed a mixture of hurt for her husband's pain, and impatience, an expression both sons knew well. A tenderhearted woman at times, at other times she could be as unwilling to wait as any child.

"Nakor?" asked Caleb again.

"He misses him," agreed Miranda. "More than he'd like anyone to know. That bandy-legged little vagabond had a unique mind, and even when I was furious with him he could make me laugh." She paused and turned away, motioning for her sons to follow her down the hill from where her husband conducted his instruction, leading them back toward the main villa. "But in the ten years since his death, Nakor's name usually comes up once or twice a month. Your father has mentioned him a half-dozen times in the last week. Something is on his mind, something new and troubling."

Villa Beata, "the beautiful home," had grown over the years. The single large square main house still commanded the heart of the vale in which it was nestled, but along the ridge line other buildings had been constructed, providing housing and study space for the students that Pug recruited to Sorcerer's Isle. They made their way down a long winding path toward what had once been the rearmost garden on the original property; now it was flanked on the north and south with low, barracks-like student housing.

Magnus said, "If Father is anticipating some new trouble, he's not mentioned it to me or anyone else, as far as I can tell."

Caleb said, "I've seen or heard nothing to suggest the present tranquility we enjoy is in peril."

Miranda said, "There's always peril. Just sometimes we don't see it coming."

Caleb smiled and said nothing. He had been given the responsibility, along with his brother and a pair of younger magicians, for coordinating all the intelligence gathered by the Conclave of Shadows' numerous agents, many placed in high office in the major nations on Midkemia. There was political rumbling in the Kingdom of the Isles, but then there always had been, so it wasn't seen as a major concern. Kesh was unusually tranquil, and Roldem's nobility continued their history of sitting comfortably on their island, secure in their own sense of superiority.

Once inside the house, they walked to the family's quarters, occupied only by Pug and Miranda since their sons had grown to manhood. Caleb lived with his wife in a small house close by, which Miranda had built for them when Marie had first come to Sorcerer's Isle with her son. Magnus still lived in the heart of the students' wing of the large estate, to be on hand should the need arise when his father was absent.

Sitting in her favorite chair, a large wooden one with upholstered seat and·back, Miranda said, "Something more than Nakor's death has been haunting your father for years." She glanced at both "boys," as she thought of her sons; only Caleb looked his age, well into his middle years, while Magnus still looked much as he had in his twenties, despite his snow-white hair and being the elder. Neither son betrayed any hint they knew of what she spoke.

"No one knows your father like I do," said Miranda. "He's a man of deep feelings and convictions, as you both know." She pointed first at Magnus then at Caleb. "But what you don't know is something happened to him before you were born, during the war with the Emerald Queen's army. He nearly died from the demon's magic that took him by surprise." She looked off to the left, into space, for a moment as she remembered. "I can't get him to admit anything about that time, as he lay near death and every healer we could find worked frantically to save him, but something in him changed after that.

"Nakor's death . . ." She stopped and said, "He was saddened by it, to be expected, but not . . ." Again she paused, as if thinking of exactly how she wanted to say what was on her mind. "It's more than just a wistful regret. Your father is as complex a man as I've known. He sees things, considers options, and makes choices before most men even understand what it is they are seeing.

"His mind works in ways that I can't begin to fathom. Oh, some of the magic—" she glanced at Magnus, "—discipline I recognize, but beyond that . . ."

She caught her own breath, realizing she was no closer to sharing her concerns than she had been minutes before. It was Caleb who said, "He's waiting for the other boot."

Magnus said, "What?"

"The old expression, waiting for the other boot to drop."
Still the older brother didn't seem to understand. "Comes from
wearing sandals, I guess," said Caleb with a smile. "You're in an
inn and someone on the floor above removes a boot before going
to bed. You hear the first hit the floor. So you wait until you hear
the second before your mind returns to what it was on before."

Magnus nodded. "He does appear distracted from time to
time."

"Preoccupied," said his mother. "He just hides it well, from
everyone but me."

"Father is anticipating something?" Magnus said rhetorically. He glanced out the window at the warm afternoon sun and
said, "Well, as you said, he masks it well." .

Caleb shrugged. "Why don't you ask him what he expects?"

"You think I haven't?" She stood up and crossed to stand
before her younger son. Looking into his eyes, she said, "He is
adroit at not telling me what he doesn't want me to know." She
smiled ruefully. "I just tell him to mind his own affairs and leave
me alone. He's more diplomatic than that." With an aggrieved
sound, she added, "I hate it when he does that!"

Both sons laughed. Their parents loved one another deeply,
as they did their sons, but both Magnus and Caleb knew their
parents' marriage was occasionally tense. Their mother was a
woman of strong will and older than her husband—though both
conceded that when both partners were over a century in age,
the difference was mostly academic. Still, they both knew something was bothering their father.

Pug had assumed a huge amount of responsibility over the
years since he returned to Midkemia from his life on the now
destroyed world of Kelewan. First he had ended the war between
the Tsurani and the Kingdom of the Isles, then he had founded
the colony of magicians called Stardock.

Magnus said, "And he has been visiting Stardock more often
than usual." . .

When Stardock had become rife with politics and intrigue,
he had quietly started his school here on Sorcerer's Island. The
outside world considered the island a place to avoid, and ships

from all nations gave it a wide berth; it was an attitude Pug encouraged with deftly planted rumors and occasionally a display of frightening images should a ship venture too closely.

The truth was that Pug was close to achieving his dream, creating the place Stardock was originally intended to be, an academy where magicians could come study and practice their arts, exchange information, and leave a wealth of knowledge to be passed on to future generations of magic-users. The mandate he hoped to leave as his personal legacy, Pug was building a haven for those who wished to be free from petty politics, the bigotry of superstition, and where those who learned were inculcated with the desire to serve and benefit their people rather than use their great arts for personal aggrandizement, gain, or dominion over others.

Miranda said, "I count that as another sign he's worried. He rarely bothers to check up over there, unless he's summoned. He's rarely pleased with the current political situation there."

"He had some good reasons," said Caleb. "There was that envoy from the Kingdom who had some nonsense to offer—what was it?"

"As soon as Father learned it involved once again pledging fealty to the Kingdom, he rejected it out of hand," reminded Magnus.

Miranda nodded. "He wouldn't hear the man out. He never told me, but last time I was at Stardock, one of the students took evil delight in telling me the envoy from the Kingdom suddenly found himself in the lake, about a hundred yards off the docks at Landreth."

Caleb laughed. "I assume the poor man could swim, else we'd be at war with the Kingdom. Drowning envoys doesn't sit well with kings."

Magnus said, "They would never openly start a war with Stardock. They still fear magic too much, and with that many spellcasters . . ." He left the thought unfinished. While a single magic-user could be quickly overcome by intent soldiers, a company of such, determined to ignore casualties, could eventually overwhelm the magician. But hundreds of magicians?

Miranda said, "The King's men are often stupid, but they are rarely suicidal."

Pug had learned bitter lessons from the Academy. He had bequeathed daily control of Stardock to those who lived there, at first angering the Kingdom of the Isles, which had considered the island in the middle of the Great Star Lake as one of their minor holdings, though they elevated it to the status of duchy to serve their own political ends.

To the south, the Empire of Great Kesh had sought to ensure their own interests were served by quickly persuading many young practitioners of magic to seek refuge at Stardock, while retaining their loyalty to the Empire. Two brothers, Watoom and Korsh—who, Pug was now certain, long after their deaths, had been Imperial agents—had almost succeeded in convincing the majority of students to the rightness of Kesh's claims. Only Nakor's time at the Academy, where he established a third faction, mirthfully called the Blue Riders—to honor a gift of a beautiful horse and blue cloak from the Empress herself—kept a precarious balance and prevented the brothers from success.

Pug had occasionally made a visit to the Academy, with two aims in mind: first, he wished everyone there to remember he still held title to the island, even though he had renounced his claim to Kingdom nobility. Second, he wished to maintain contact with a handful of agents of the Conclave, to keep an eye on whatever nonsense the current ruling triumvirate—the leaders of the three factions—were up to.

The "Hands of Korsh" were the most conservative, but they were as opposed to becoming a province of the Empire as they were of the Kingdom. But they perceived all who were not magic-users, and those who were but not within their faction, as possible enemies. "The Wand of Watoom" was more moderate in their policies toward outsiders, but decidedly pro-Keshian in their worldview.

The Blue Riders continued to delight Pug, for their leadership always seemed to somehow reflect Nakor's slightly mad and always manic views on magic. Many of them had adopted his notion that there really wasn't magic, but some mystical "stuff," as the little gambler had called it, that could be manipulated by anyone once they managed to achieve a certain level of familiarity with it.

They were almost entirely responsible for seeking out new students, while the more conservative factions waited until someone arrived at Stardock who met their more rigid standards of acceptance. Pug was grateful for that closed-mindedness, for it allowed the Blue Riders more opportunity to keep the island's population in balance.

Caleb said, "If Father's spending more time there, something is up, no doubt. Either he's alerting our agents to be on the watch for something, or they've already told him something's afoot."

Magnus said, "No, if it was that, by now he would have said something to one or all of us." He glanced out the window, as the breeze rustled the leaves of the old trees sheltering that side of the building from the afternoon heat during the summer. "No, it's something else."

The mother and two sons were silent as they pondered what could be disturbing Pug so deeply that despite his attempts to disguise his distress, they all could see it. Miranda finally stood and said, "Well, one thing about your father: when he judges it time to share his worries, you can be certain he will be totally forthright, and what he's worried about will be a very big problem."

She left the room and the brothers exchanged nods, for they knew she was understating the case. Whatever worried their father was likely to be more approaching disaster than a problem.

Pug dismissed his class and gathered up a few items he had employed to demonstrate the lessons of the day. He knew his family had been observing for a while, and was nearly certain as to the reason. He had attempted to conceal some grave concerns from them, but obviously failed. Still, he was reluctant to assume things worse than he knew them to be, and today was the day he would finally come to grips with the cause of his worries: a summons from the Oracle of Aal.

More than that, it had been the way in which it had arrived:

one moment Pug had been alone in his study, writing notes late into the night, and the next a man in a white robe had been at his elbow. As soon as he saw the man, he recognized him for what he was: one of the consorts or companions to the Oracle. Conventional human concepts were only an approximation. Gender with the Aal was a function of legacy; the bodies those spirits inhabited were human, so their physical makeup was unchanged, yet the driving mind within was alien. Pug had been apprehensive at first, for the Oracle herself had taken the dying body of a great dragon, her golden scales fused with a riot of gemstones by furious magic unleashed in the heat of battle, as the most dangerous of creatures, a Dreadlord, had been confronted by the dragon and Tomas, the legatee of the power of the Valheru.

That battle had been over a century prior, yet for Pug it might as well have been the day before; he could still conjure up vivid memories of the chaos that surrounded him, Macros the Black, and two Tsurani magicians who had joined him in trying to stem the return of the assembled host of the Valheru, the Dragon Lords, to Midkemia.

That battle under the now deserted city of Sethanon had been but the first of many encounters Pug had with agents of the Nameless, Nalar, God of Evil and the agency behind the Chaos Wars and the subsequent battles being waged by Pug and his allies against the forces of evil.

Pug paused to gather his thoughts. The strangest thing about the summons wasn't its being delivered personally by a minion of the Oracle; it was that he wasn't asked to come at once but at a future date, nearly a month away. And now that date was upon him.

Pug considered letting Miranda know what was occurring, but for some reason felt it best to hear out the Oracle first, then deal with his wife's moods. She would almost certainly wish to come with him, yet her name, nor that of Magnus, had been mentioned.

Besides, his encounters with the Oracle tended to be short, the longest lasting barely a half-hour. He would be back before the evening meal.

For ten years he had been practicing the art of transporting himself without the use of the Tsurani orbs. Those were becoming rarer as the years passed since the destruction of Kelewan. A few artificers from Kelewan had immigrated to LaMut, but most who survived the destruction of their home planet were now living on New Kelewan, as they had come to name their refuge.

Besides, though he would never admit it, Pug's vanity hated the fact his wife was effortlessly able to transport herself at will to places she barely knew, while he had to muster all his concentration.

Still, the chamber of the Oracle was unique and he had been there many times over the years. It should prove little difficulty to move there now. And now was the time.

He closed his eyes, willed himself to the chamber, and, as he appeared, heard the voice of the Oracle within his mind.

*Welcome, Sorcerer. Your timing is perfect.*

As Pug turned to regard the majesty that was the gem-encrusted form of the great golden dragon, a screech loud enough to cause her companions to cover their ears tore through the room.

Halfway between Pug and the Oracle something appeared, first a shadowy form, then it rapidly resolved itself into a figure. A demon rearing up at least twenty feet in height stood motionless for an instant, disoriented by the magic that had brought it to this place. Yet that muddle lasted but a moment. It quickly surveyed the room, judging the little figures around it scant risk, then turned its attention to the figure of the Oracle.

With a bellow that echoed in the vast chamber, the demon launched itself at the Oracle.

# CHAPTER 7

## PROPHESY

Pug unleashed a spell.

As the demon took a step toward the dragon form of the Oracle, a searing hot band of energy lashed out, wrapping itself around the demon's form like a lasso. Where it touched skin, evil-smelling black smoke erupted.

The creature towered over everyone in the cavern, save the Oracle herself. He had scales like those of a lizard or serpent, red and violet mottle in color. Massive shoulders and arms ended in huge black talons, and the apelike face was a mask of hatred and rage. He let forth with a roar that caused the walls of the cavern to shake, loosening soil, which rained down on everyone.

Huge fangs protruded down from the exaggerated

upper lip, and the demon's head was adorned with two long black horns that tapered backward to points, more like those of an antelope than a goat or ram. He shook his head in frustration and howled in outrage at being confined and injured.

Pug had limited experience with demons, and all of it bad. He did not hesitate to follow up his confinement spell with as powerful an assault as he could muster.

Tendrils of flaming white and purple energy shot forward, waving like the tentacles of a squid as they latched onto the creature's body. As each touched the demon's hide, more acrid black smoke was released and a tiny flame of dull orange shot upward.

The demon trembled as he fought against his confinement, then howled again in outrage and burst the binding spell. The shock that reverberated back through the tether and struck Pug's mind was like a physical blow.

The Oracle's mystic powers were nothing like the battle magic the greater dragons of Midkemia possessed, but physically she was still a force to fear. She lashed out with claws and teeth, sinking them deep into the demon's shoulder at the neck. Fountains of steaming black blood erupted and flowed down his back and chest as he lashed over his shoulder with the opposite claw, raking her muzzle, seeking to rip her eyes to blind her.

Pug shook off the shock of the magical backlash and sent out a spear of energy. This was one he had never employed before save in practice in an isolated part of his island.

Invisible, the energy still filled the cavern with a hissing noise, a counterpoint to the shouts and screams from the Oracle's companions as they hurled themselves at the demon.

The Oracle's companions were not without their own magic and strength, and while the first to reach the demon was eviscerated with one strike of the creature's claw, the next two were able to inflict injury. The dragon's maw held fast on the creature's shoulder, while Pug and the companions caused him as much damage as possible.

The invisible energy spear struck the demon full on in the chest and he stiffened, as if run through by cold iron. The creature's mouth moved, as if trying to speak or roar, and Pug suspected he was attempting some type of incantation. But the injury done by the spell was too much for him, and his eyes rolled up into its skull and it fell limp.

For a moment the Oracle held fast to the demon, now as listless as a child's doll, then she released his hold. Pug saw gashes in the dragon's snout, blood flowing freely down to drip on the still carcass of the demon, but knew them to be relatively trivial.

"Stand back!" instructed Pug as the Oracle's companions were still attacking the now fallen demon. "Back!" he commanded as calm returned to the room.

As he anticipated, the demon's body began to smoke, as if smoldering, and then abruptly came a flash of crimson flame, gone almost as soon as it was perceived. A stench of brimstone and putrefaction filled their nostrils, and several of the remaining companions fell back as if physically repelled by the odor.

Pug turned toward the towering figure of the Oracle of Aal and asked, "You wanted to see me?"

Over the years Pug and the Oracle of Aal had forged a trusting relationship, though Pug had never been convinced their aims were entirely the same. The Oracle, despite having the appearance of a mighty dragon, was as alien to the world of Midkemia as any creature he had ever encountered.

The Aal were rumored to be the oldest life in the universe; at least no other race could trace their lineage back as far. Even the Dragon Lords at the height of their power gave the Aal a wide berth and left them in peace.

When Pug had first encountered them, they were a dying race, as the world upon which they resided was ending its long life. Pug had offered those remaining passage to Midkemia, and through a series of circumstances—fate or coincidence, Pug still didn't know—the Oracle had found a host in the mindless body of Midkemia's single greatest creature, a golden dragon.

Her companions have found willing hosts among men and women of diverse backgrounds, many from among the lowest of the low. They were sought out over the years by practitioners of arcane arts even Pug didn't pretend to understand, and offered a unique place in this world, as servants and companions to the Oracle.

Pug allowed himself to believe no coercion was involved and those who were here were so willingly; it let him sleep better at night. But for whatever reasons, those in this cave were willing to give up their lives to protect this unique creature.

As many times as Pug had visited this cavern, he had still only a vague idea of this race's history and place in the order of things. His direct questions were always answered with vague responses and generalities, and he came to accept that he would only know what it was the Oracle wished him to know. He was content with that, for she had proven a valuable asset to his world's defense on more than one occasion. He could concede it to be self-interest, for if this world perished, she would along with it, but he judged her motives loftier than that; she seemed genuinely concerned with helping Pug and his Conclave reestablish a semblance of order in this part of a very big universe.

All this ran through Pug's mind as he waited for the Oracle to reply. She laid her head down on the floor so her companions could tend to her wounds, messy if not mortal. Two of her minions lay dead and would be disposed of as soon as she was healed.

Pug watched in fascination as magic he could barely recognize, let alone understand, was employed. He had seen enough clerical magic to discern those healing arts, but this was unlike anything he had witnessed before.

As best he could tell, it was as if each companion who tended a wound somehow caused the dragon body to repair itself, but at an accelerated rate. Yet the price seemed dear: each of those ministering to the dragon were aging before Pug's eyes, their faces becoming sallow and haggard, weight melting from their bodies. Somehow they were giving her their life essence. Before his eyes, her wounds healed, until, five minutes after they started, the companions left their mistress looking as she had before. They, however, had aged years in minutes.

"Impressive," said Pug.

"We are an old race, with many gifts." Indicating the bodies of her fallen attendants, who were being carried off, she added, "But we have limits, too."

"Can I assume this encounter was the reason you requested my appearance at a specific moment today?"

"What is, is as it should be, as it was, and as it will be again." Slowly she rose up, until her head was once again high above, her eyes staring distantly off into space as she saw visions no other could witness.

"Even for you that's unusually cryptic, my old friend," said Pug.

The Oracle stood silently for a long time.

Finally, Pug said, "Ah, I see. I must ask. What else have you seen, that troubles your mind?"

"Much, Sorcerer. I see a nexus coming, a blending of time and probability, a place of many outcomes. Beyond that I see nothing, so many possibilities flow from that moment. Or an end, should the worst outcome occur."

"Worst for you or for all of us?"

"They are one and the same, for should I fall, this world has fallen with me.

"I see havoc and destruction and the death of many, on a scale to dwarf all you've endured before combined, and I see a tipping of a precious balance, one which will cause the gods themselves to tremble in fear."

"I listen," said Pug quietly. Already his skin was crawling in anticipation of what he suspected. Summoned demons as powerful as the one he just faced required prodigious magic. Confining one and taking control was difficult enough, but to be able to subdue one, then send it by magic means into this cavern, that required a demon master of unmatched skill and power.

"A legion comes this way, Pug of Sorcerer's Isle. It rides hard and brings chaos and death in its wake. Others battle to withstand it, and they yield grudgingly, but they will soon be overwhelmed.

"The Dark One, he whose name cannot be uttered, is restless in his sleep, and in his fever dreaming he reaches out with the power of a Greater God. A passage between the realms he has envisioned, and as he dreams, it is so. He dreams of home, and wishes to return.

"The other Greater Gods soothe his restlessness, and stem his dreams, but they are overmatched. Only she who balances him can stop the madness."

Pug felt a cold tightening in his chest. "And she is dead," he said.

"She is," said the Oracle, "yet even in death she provides, for her legacy lives on, in the hearts of those who serve good.

"Find allies, Pug. Find those who in the past you have not sought out. Seek strength where you are weak, and find those who have knowledge where you are ignorant. Understand what comes soon."

The Oracle's head lowered again to the floor and Pug knew from experience her vision had drained her, especially after the battle with the demon. He had time for one, perhaps two more questions, and then she would enter a slumber that might last for days, even weeks. And once she was awakened again, those visions she just had would be lost.

Pug's mind raced and he thought of a dozen things he wished to ask. He finally said, "Tell me of the legion that comes?"

"Demons from the Fifth Circle, Pug. The demons come."

The hair on Pug's neck rose, and after the things he had seen in a very long life he was surprised to find himself shocked and alarmed. That demon wasn't the minion of some powerful human agency but an advance scout, an assassin from the demon realm, come to rid this world of its most powerful asset: forewarning.

Pug had fought demons before, and one had almost killed him, and he had witnessed the final struggle between Macros the Black and the Demon King Maag. The thought of a legion of such creatures numbed his mind, visiting him with a sense of despair he had rarely encountered. Even at the darkest moments in his life he had retained hope, and had sought to survive, so that when opportunity came, he could seize it. But this was an onslaught beyond imagining.

Even the danger posed by the Dasati during the Darkwar paled in comparison to the denizens of the Fifth Circle. The grass wilted under their heels, and their mere touch would burn flesh. Only those demons with powerful magic could contrive to exist in this realm without disastrous results, and the scope of that magic was majestic. Pug knew that for a legion of demons to enter this realm meant a repeat of what happened on the Saaur home world: utter and complete destruction.

"Who are those I need to seek out—" Pug began, but saw the dragon head's eyes were closed.

Pug glanced around the room and saw the silent companions watching him. They could provide no further aid to him, so he merely nodded a farewell and transported himself back to his study.

His wife was waiting and said, "Oh, there you are. I felt you depart and was about to get very angry with you."

He could tell Miranda was making light, but she did exhibit genuine concern. "I went to see the Oracle," said Pug flatly.

The tightening around her eyes communicated she understood he had heard nothing good.

"We need to find someone who knows a great deal about demons," said Pug.

Magnus and Miranda stood, while Caleb sat opposite his father. Pug had just finished recounting the Oracle's warning and Miranda said, "You're right. We need a demon master."

Magnus shook his head. "They are . . . difficult to find."

All understood that mastery of demons was one of the three forbidden arts; the other two were necromancy and arcane life. All were seen as being outside the bounds of respectable magic, dark arts that required misery and pain at the least, death and the rending of the very soul at the best.

Leso Varen, also known as Sidi, Pug's longtime adversary, had been a necromancer, as had a magician named Dahakan, whom Nakor had angered. And so had the false dark elf prophet, Murmandamus. In Pug's lifetime, he had encountered three magic-users who used the precious life force of others for their own dark purposes. Animating the dead to do their bidding had been the least of their offenses. Stealing fleeing spirits as bodies died created disharmony of staggering proportions in the universe.

Arcane life was the evil distortion of living creatures, modified to the magician's whim. Humans given animal powers, or animals blended into improbable creatures. Only necromancy was more evil.

Demon masters were more of a mystery, for often the advantages they realized from their control of demons came at a high price. Controlling demons in and of itself was not seen as inherently evil, but it was still considered a dark art, as there was little good one could achieve with a demon minion.

Pug sighed. "We need to send word through our agents to start reporting back any rumors of demons or summoners."

Caleb rose and said, "I'll send word out at once." As he started to leave the room, he paused, and said, "I think I remember some mention of something . . ." He returned to his father's desk, which he occupied when Pug was not at the school. Rifling through papers, he said, "Yes, a report from Muboy. A magic-user's banishing demons for a fee." He smiled ruefully. "They appear fortuitously and then the magician arrives."

Magnus said, "A confidence scheme, no doubt."

"We should still investigate," said Pug. To Caleb, he said, "You are in charge. I'm going to see to this myself." To Miranda, he said, "If you don't mind, Miranda, see if there's anything at Stardock on demon lore." To Magnus, he said, "And you should talk to the monks at That Which Was Sarth."

Both nodded agreement, and Miranda vanished.

Pug turned to his sons and said, "I was about to add, 'after lunch.'"

The sons chuckled, but in the wake of what their father had just told them, it was false mirth.

# CHAPTER 8

## DEMON MASTER

Gulamendis froze.

The sight that greeted him as he stepped through the portal to Midkemia was unexpected. He stood silently with his travel bag thrown over his left shoulder, and his brother's staff in his right hand. He drank in the vista, in wonder. He knew the Regent Lord had ordered geomancers away from repairing the bastions of Andcardia to constructing a new city on the ancient world they thought of as "Home," the planet of their origin.

When his brother had told him of finding this world, Gulamendis was halfway convinced Laromendis was either feigning the discovery or perhaps deluding himself, but one breath here and he knew: this was Home.

There was a resonance in the air, a feeling of solid-

ity underfoot, of being in touch with something fundamental, a
faint but almost palpable energy that seeped into the core of his
being. That made him know this was the world upon which his
race evolved; the very core of their existence began here. Emotions he thought he no longer possessed rose up and threatened
to sweep him away. It took him a moment to take another breath
and step away.

"It strikes everyone that way," said a voice to his right. Gulamendis saw a magician named Astranour standing beside the
gate. He was an aremancer, one who specialized in creating and
controlling the translocation portals and transporting devices
employed by the Taredhel. "My wife wept a moment after we
arrived." Looking out over the valley, he said, "It is . . . remarkable."

Gulamendis nodded, saying nothing, as he looked down the
trail—rather now a road—to the walls of the city. For that was
the other remarkable thing; he only had his brother's brief description of this valley in mind but what he saw now was something entirely unexpected. With a cursory farewell to Astranour,
Gulamendis moved purposely down the hillside.

Massive walls had already been erected, a third of the way to
encompassing the vast floor of the valley. The geomancers must
have exhausted themselves and their apprentices to have accomplished so much in so little time. Not too far away, at the current
end of the wall, he witnessed a half-dozen geomancers enchant-
ing massive piles of rocks, moving them into place by force of
their minds, while others readied the spells that would cause the
fundamental essence to flow into liquid, to be coaxed into new
shapes, then to be re-hardened as the magicians desired. The
magic was complex, requiring decades of study, and Gulamendis
was always impressed, not only with the sheer force of it, but the
artistry. Not only was simple rock turned into building material,
it was lent a beauty and elegance that was the hallmark of the
Taredhel. The wall was off-white in color, with a parapet, but the
merlons between the crenels were a deep yellow, almost golden-
rod color. From the distance, everything looked white and gold.
Barely a tenth completed, the city already spoke to the world of

its splendor. It would be the new capital for all elvenkind on this world.

In less than a week the outlines of the new city could be seen. Not named yet, he could hear people say, *"e'bar,"* in the ancient language, "Home," and he suspected that might come to be its name, no matter what the Regent's Meet might decide. Even while he walked, Gulamendis had a sense of the magic everywhere, a faint vibration in the fundamental fabric of this space—what the mancers called "the loops of being"—where elven will was being imposed on rock and mud. Vast boulevards were being cleared with flashes of blinding white light; he could imagine the heat as the incindiari, the magicians specializing in fire magic, burned away acres of undergrowth and detritus. Arboris had already worked their arts on the trees, literally commanding them to uproot and walk to where those magicians wanted them.

Gulamendis understood the scope of his race's power, and had seen evidence of it all his life, but never before had he witnessed so many practitioners of the arcane arts expending their skills so vigorously at the same time. It was positively intoxicating to contemplate.

As he watched, Gulamendis saw a team of drovers direct carts down a pathway toward a leveled patch of land. He knew that only hours before geomancers had fashioned the building pad with magic, completing in minutes what would have taken hours for workmen using picks, shovels, and drags to accomplish.

The massive horses were urged slowly forward, while the cleverly contrived carts gently tipped backward, depositing large rocks, some qualified as small boulders, in a roughly straight line. Lingering to observe magic with which he was barely familiar, Gulamendis was fascinated. These masters of the arcane controlled the very stuff of the world: the rock, soil, crystal, and sand.

Three younger magicians walked purposely to a position along the line of rocks, and as one they incanted a spell. Before the Demon Master's eyes the rock grew soft and began to flow. Two Master Geomancers, supervised by a Grand Master, moved to positions between the three younger spellcasters, and they began to control the rocks. A wall of stone rose up, liquid—like runny clay. When it was at the appropriate height, the Grand Master began his arts. First the surface smoothed, until it became an unbroken, almost eggshell-white flat, and along the top decorative designs appeared, carvings that would have taken an artisan with chisel and hammer months to achieve. Gulamendis understood the theory behind this craft, and knew that like his own spells that had been created to contain other spells, patterns such as this were combined and then unleashed in a series by simply incanting the master spell. Still, it was a wonder to behold.

Then came the crowning touch, as those patterns atop the wall were turned a reddish-gold color that the Demon Master knew was a blend of copper and gold. And he knew it was not a paint or gilt, but that this Grand Master's art allowed him to transmute what was once rock into a patina of metal.

The Taredhel were unmatched when it came to the arcane arts, and their control over the very elements of the world was breathtaking. Centuries of craftsmanship, passed along to artists, resulted in this spectacular creation. It was more than just a wall to a dwelling—one destined for someone of rank, given the size and splendor of the first wall—it was the near effortlessness of it that stunned the Demon Master. It was a testament in action, the legacy of scholars, artists, and masters of craft combined and handed down through generations. Like all those of his race, these magic-users took quiet pride in their efforts, but sought no praise, for to them it was what was expected. To do less was to court shame.

Gulamendis turned away. To one who labored for the most part in solitude, whose area of expertise were the darker arts, there was something almost too bright here, as if one might stare into the sun until one was blind. Not for the first time, the Demon Master—among the most despised of beings to his own kind—wondered at his people's appetite for power. Unlike the Forgotten, who had lusted after their ancient masters' might in a vain attempt to raise themselves up to the stature of the Dragon Host, the Taredhel only sought knowledge for its own reward, for after all, they were descendants of the Eldar, the true keepers of lore. Yet, not for the first time, the Demon Master wondered if there was much difference between the Taredhel and the Moredhel.

Gulamendis was required to report to the senior magician at the site, Grand Master Colsarius, but after that he was mandated by the Regent Lord himself to discover if there was any demon presence on this world.

Gulamendis didn't need to do much investigating; there was demon scent in the very air, but muted, faint, so distant that only one as sensitive to its existence as himself would recognize it. Magic had flavors and signatures, and if you knew the spellcaster well enough, you'd recognize his handiwork as easily as seeing the master's mark on a sword blade or fine piece of jewelry.

Still, it was the very faint, nearly absent, scent of demon that piqued Gulamendis's curiosity. He would have to go some distance from this place, as there was so much magic in play it would make detecting the exact location of the demons more difficult. Once he was alone, far from here, he could deduce where to begin his search. Besides, it was a good excuse to get away from oversight.

He had his own agenda, one that he and his brother and a handful of others had sworn to see fulfilled, even should it mean their deaths, for no one better knew the destruction coming headlong toward the Taredhel than the Demon Master.

Andcardia was lost, no matter what anyone still defending it might wish—the fervor in which the Regent Lord threw his remaining resources into building this city at the expense of defending Andcardia was proof he knew it, as well. That the Demon Legion would overwhelm Andcardia was as inevitable as the surge of the ocean tide, and like the ocean tide, relentless. Still, much had been revealed and more could be learned, for Gulamendis knew one thing above all else. Somewhere out there was a portal, a gate between worlds, that provided easy access from the Fifth Circle to this one, and while it stood open, demons could be easily summoned, or worse, find their way into this realm unaided.

He reached the end of the first completed section of the wall, through which this road passed, a huge gap waiting for majestic gates to be fashioned. Gulamendis had no doubt the Regent Lord would spend some time with the fabricators of those gates, ensuring their design and execution were as precise and ornate as they had been back on Andcardia. The Regent Lord fancied himself a man of taste and had taken a hand in the design of everything constructed by the Taredhel for over the last two centuries. That's why every façade was framed with ornate moldings and cornices, and rooftops were peaked, every roof topped with a spire. Gulamendis was forced to concede his race had a taste for the ostentatious, and he was in the minority, preferring simpler, more elegant designs.

He considered the reality he knew to be the Demon Gate. He and others in his calling had faced scorn and ridicule over that assertion, being accused of seeking to avoid complicity in the demon assault. But no matter whom he tried to convince, only a handful of magicians, almost to a man practitioners of the darker callings, believed him. One additional ally had proven a surprise, one of the ancient priests, the *Elta-Eldar*, for Gulamendis had made one observation in passing that had sent the ancient Loremaster to the archives.

That ancient had sought out Gulamendis when he had been imprisoned. He had asked questions and offered insights, then left the prisoner alone to sweat out his days and shiver through the nights.

It had been his apprentice, the Lorekeeper Tanderae, who had returned at last to speak on his master's behalf. Now Gulamendis saw the priest approaching.

"Gulamendis," he said in greeting.

"Fare you well, Tanderae?" answered the Demon Master.

"As well as one might expect, given our current circumstances." He glanced around as if to see whether anyone else was listening. He turned to walk next to Gulamendis and put his left hand on the Demon Master's shoulder, as if two old friends were speaking of personal matters. Lowering his voice, he said, "I suspect you have much to do, and need to be quickly about your business; I'll walk with you only a little way, for I also am hard pressed by many duties.

"I just want you to understand that much of what you have brought to the attention of myself and others has not gone unnoticed. You have our thanks."

Not entirely sure where this was leading, Gulamendis said, "I only serve."

"Yes," said Tanderae with a slight smile, lowering his voice even more, "yet there are those among the Lorekeepers, Loremasters, and Priesthood who would happily see you burned alive as a heretic."

Gulamendis said nothing.

"Like yourself, I have witnessed the fall of the greatest race from glory to ruin."

Still, Gulamendis kept quiet, as they walked past a circle of priests who were incanting a Star Stone. Having been raised by his mother in a small town on the frontier of the Empire of the Stars, he had never seen one created. Their fabrication was rare, yet now seven were being fashioned in this, the People's new home. He paused to observe this wonder, then finally he said, "None living has not been a witness to tragedy."

Tanderae nodded and was silent for a moment.

The Priests finished their spell, and hovering in the air was a dull grey object, looking nothing so much as like a large piece of unfinished ore, lead or tin. It began to glow, slightly at first and with a pulse. Over the next minute the glow brightened and the pulse quickened. In less than an hour, the stone would glow with the brightness of a star, and to look at it for more than a moment could blind a living being. But the magic would prepare the ground for the most holy of the People's artifacts, the living, breathing heart of the People, one of the seven great trees known as the Stars.

Almost muttering, Tanderae said, "I could be burned at the stake for saying this, but all of this is unnecessary."

Gulamendis turned to study the Lorekeeper. He looked much as any younger male of the People: tall, regal, with broad shoulders and a haughty expression. His features were unremarkable, much like Gulamendis's: straight nose, deep-set eyes, a strong chin, and high cheekbones. His hair was dark, however, unlike most of the People, a deep red, almost brown in color. "Unnecessary?"

Tanderae knelt. He gently rubbed his hand over the dirt of the valley floor, as if stroking a pet, and then picked up a loose clot of dirt. "This is the soil of Home, Gulamendis." He raised it to his face, sniffed at it, and said, "The magic is already here."

Standing again, he looked at the Demon Master. "We needed the tarmancer's Star Stones in the past, to ready the soil of an alien world so the Seven Stars would flourish." He took a long, slow, deep breath, and said, "The magic is in the air. I know you felt it when you first came through the portal."

Gulamendis nodded. "It's impossible not to."

"We could excavate the Seven Stars, wrap the roots of those mighty trees, and magic them through the portal and plant them, and they would thrive here. This is their home, too.

"But we are a People who are wed to tradition."

Gulamendis nodded in agreement. Entrenched beliefs were difficult to dislodge. So certain were those in power that some nameless demon master caused the invasion of this realm by the Demon Legion, it was only by fortune's favor he still lived.

Looking around, to ensure no one was eavesdropping, Tanderae continued. "You and your brother have lived on the fringes, my friend. Masters of Illusion are treated with indifference, but have no place on the Council of Magic. All of the builders, the geomancers, aremancers, the formers of things"—he indicated with a nod of his head the seven priests and magicians who now left the site where they had created the Star Stone—"and especially the tarmancers, they have convinced the People over the centuries they alone are to be entrusted with advising the Regent. Overcoming their bias . . ." He left the thought unfinished.

Quietly, Gulamendis said, "Why are you saying these things?"

With a slightly wry, slightly sad smile, Tanderae said, "I have no magic, Gulamendis. My only gift is a prodigious memory. I speak without false modesty when I say no Lorekeeper before me was as able as I to recall, word for word, every passage in every tome he has read. I know the history of our People better than any elf living, or any who came before me.

"And I see a pattern."

"Pattern?"

"We have much to talk about, but first you must find us a demon."

"I don't understand."

Taking Gulamendis's arm in his hand, the Lorekeeper gently turned him toward a distant gate. "We both know that your obligation to report to the Grand Master for assignment is a formality. You are a free agent, under direct order from the Regent Lord. You have two tasks . . ." He squinted a little as he studied the Demon Master's face. "No, you have three tasks," he said softly. "One of your own, I see."

Gulamendis stiffened slightly, but didn't break stride. "I am to seek out demon signs," he said. "If I find none, I rejoice."

"Oh, I suspect you will find some." He again studied the Demon Master while they walked toward the distant gate. "Perhaps you already have." Gulamendis stopped, and Tanderae smiled. "My other great gift is reading expressions and manner." He waited for the Demon Master to speak, then, when he did not, the Lorekeeper said, "Too long we have glorified power, Gulamendis. It is worthy of note, and when it serves, it is a grand thing, but to seek out power for its own sake makes us little different from those we call the Forgotten."

Gulamendis wondered for a brief instant if the Lorekeeper could read his thoughts, for this echoed what he had been thinking only moments before he had encountered Tanderae. Weighing his words carefully, he asked, "What do you advise?"

Again a quick look around to see they were not being overheard, and Tanderae started moving toward the distant gate. "I will speak to Grand Master Colsarius, which will discharge your obligation to report. He will consider it a burden I saved him from: a meeting with a demon lover." There was a wry smile and Gulamendis understood he meant the insult as humor. "He might take it upon himself to augment or extend the Regent

Lord's instructions to you, and I'd rather you weren't distracted from your tasks."

Gulamendis saw they were approaching the gate opposite the one through which he had entered the burgeoning city and said, "What do you know of my tasks, Tanderae?"

"I know the Regent Lord wants you to ensure we are not troubled by demons. And I'm also guessing he wishes someone with a great deal of experience skulking through dark places to investigate a few other things, such as how our distant kin on this world fare."

Gulamendis was impressed. His meeting with the Regent Lord had been in private, over the first good meal the Demon Master had been given in months. The Regent Lord was adamant: Laromendis would be kept hostage against his brother's good behavior while the Demon Master did the Regent Lord's bidding. And he had set two tasks, to see if they were free of demon taint in Midkemia and to travel the land to the north, discovering what he could about the elves, especially the so-called Elf Queen. Gulamendis wasn't certain, but he was clearly of the mind that the Regent Lord was in no hurry to surrender authority over the Taredhel to another, no matter what her lineage. She might claim descent from the true kings of Edhel, but it would take more than a garland for a crown and some leather-clad rustics bowing before her to convince him to bend his knee.

Tanderae said, "And there's another thing, but I don't know what it is . . ."

Gulamendis preferred it that way. This young Lorekeeper was too adept at discerning whole pictures from fragments and glimpses. He might prove a powerful ally, but he would be a deeply dangerous enemy. Still, Gulamendis wasn't without his own talents in seeing a larger picture when enough information was there. He studied Tanderae and said, "You have ambition, my friend. Is Master of Lore not enough?"

The young elf smiled, but it was a pained expression. "I am loyal, my friend. But the needs of my people come before any single elf's needs."

Gulamendis nodded and turned to walk out the gate. He understood completely. The young Lorekeeper, gifted only with a keen mind and facile wit, meant to be the next Regent Lord. Now he knew why he had sought out the Demon Master, and why this conversation. He wished the Elf Queen to know there were those within the ranks of the Taredhel who were ready to acknowledge her as rightful ruler of all the Edhel. In exchange for certain considerations, such as being named her Regent Lord in Elenbar, being first among them.

Gulamendis turned just as Tanderae was about to return to his other tasks and said, "Why are we having this conversation? You already knew my mission from the Regent Lord. But you expose yourself, even if only slightly, by talking as you have to me. Why?"

The Lorekeeper paused, turned back toward Gulamendis, and said, "Do you know the Tome of Akar-Ree?"

"I grew up in a tiny village on the frontier. As you can imagine, my education was not formal. I am self-taught."

"Impressive," said the Lorekeeper. "There are ancient volumes that have crumbled with time. Lacunae—holes in pages—often make already metaphorical and poetic lore even harder to understand.

"Your studies are among those forbidden for centuries, Gulamendis—if we can call them 'studies'—and what little we know of demons is either ancient lore or bitter recent experience.

"The Tome of Akar-Ree is a recounting of a great battle during the Chaos Wars, when gods and mortals struggled to seize the very heavens, and much of it is obscure reference to things the reader is supposed to already know, and some of it is imagery open to a myriad of interpretations.

"But there is one passage, clear as a clarion ringing in the cold air of dawn, without a hint of obscurity, and it is this: demons were summoned to fight in the battle, beings of the deeper realms, and other beings, of light, from the higher realms, answered. They came unbidden, for it was the nature of things that when a creature from the lower depths appeared here, his counterpart appeared somewhere else, and sought him out, and when they struggled, both were destroyed, or returned to their home realm—we don't know which."

"I didn't know that," whispered Gulamendis. He knew he was on the verge of hearing something very important.

"These higher beings, those in opposition to demons, have many names, most commonly they are called angels. Their glory is blinding and their power is equal to those of the demons summoned."

Gulamendis's mind raced, for he had summoned demons for years, yet this was the first he had heard of these other beings, these angels.

Tanderae smiled. "You see the question, don't you?"

Gulamendis nodded. "Where are the angels?"

Tanderae shrugged. "Unless this ancient tome is a work of the storyteller's art and has no valid history within, then the balance of our universe has been skewed since the time of the Chaos Wars. The host of demons who destroyed our worlds should have been met by an equal number of angels, and the Taredhel should have continued in peace and health across the worlds we inhabited."

"Why do you tell me this?"

Tanderae shrugged. "There may be no answer, or it may be that work is apocryphal at best. But what if it is true?" He placed his hand on Gulamendis's shoulder and gently turned him back toward the gate, indicating the conversation was at an end. "It is just that you are about to travel widely, while the rest of us labor to build this new city of glory and plan our conquest of this world, claiming it as ours alone. In those travels you may meet all manner of being, some who may be wise, or powerful, or have access to ancient knowledge, and it would be a shame if you didn't know the right question to ask. Journey safely." Without another word, he walked quickly away from the stunned Demon Master.

Gulamendis walked away from the nascent city, unsettled by what he had just heard, and more, by what he knew was coming. Gulamendis sighed to himself as he trudged up the hill. He didn't know if his tasks just got easier or more difficult.

# CHAPTER 9

## WARNING

Brandos paced.

Amirantha sat patiently in the anteroom, waiting for a summons that never seemed to come. This was his fourth day waiting for an audience with General Kaspar, Chancellor to the Maharaja of Muboya. The new palace in Maharta was an exercise in ostentation, something Amirantha had come to expect from royalty, but he was forced to admit that along with the ostentation came a fair dose of beauty. Some of the décor was actually tasteful, a rarity among those to whom fashion was a function of how much gold it cost to build something.

The two of them had arrived at the capital of the young and vibrant Kingdom of Muboya. The Maharaja had ended over twenty years of campaign and annexation when he reached the sea, uniting all the city states along the River Veedra, from the grasslands to the west to the City of the Serpent River to the east. It was the largest political entity on the continent of Novindus in history, and, like all young and sprawling nations comprised of diverse cultures, nearly impossible to govern.

While waiting, Amirantha had gained some sense of the tasks set before this Lord Kaspar. Nobles from many parts of the nation, envoys from other states in the Westlands and even from across the sea, paraded through this antechamber into his reception hall or private chambers or whatever it was Amirantha imagined behind massive wooden doors.

He and Brandos had presented themselves four days earlier, both wearing their finest clothing, so there was nothing of the vagabond or poor petitioner in their appearance. They simply told the secretary, a fussy and self-important little man, they wished to speak to Lord Kaspar on a matter of some urgency and importance to the Kingdom.

And for three days they had been soundly ignored.

Brandos sat down next to his friend, about the fifth or sixth time—Amirantha had lost count—and said, "Do we need to bribe the secretary?"

"Tried yesterday, and almost got us arrested." He turned to look at his companion and in low tones said, "Seems what we've heard about this Kaspar of Olasko is true; he's running a very principled state." He leaned back against the wall, carefully—he was conscious of his white robes with black and gold trim and the need to keep them free of dirty surfaces—and said, "Given the rogues and mountebanks who pass as government agents in most places, it's a surprise, but I'm not sure if it's pleasant or unsettling."

"Well, if you can't bribe to get in to see this General, and we seem to be growing moss waiting, do you have any other ideas? Not that I don't enjoy sitting and doing nothing for days on end . . ."

Amirantha said, "Very well. I guess I could send him a more compelling message."

The Warlock sat up, closed his eyes, and barely raised his right hand, but Brandos instantly recognized a summoning. This was hardly the time or place, in the old fighter's judgment, to call forth a demon, but he trusted Amirantha's instincts, even if they had come close to getting him killed on a number of occasions. More times though, they had saved his life.

A faint "pop" sound heralded the appearance of a tiny figure, about knee-high to the fighter. It was the imp Nalnar, oldest of the Warlock's summoned creatures. In their flimflamming of the gullible, Brandos and Amirantha had relied on a half-dozen summoned beings, all having different abilities to amaze and terrorize the onlookers out of their gold, but few posed any real danger.

The dark-skinned imp, his hue shifting from deep blue to purple, depending on the light, was the most intelligent. His bright yellow eyes with black irises regarded Amirantha from under flame-red brows. He grinned, revealing an array of razor-sharp teeth, and pointed one talon-tipped finger at the Warlock. "You have summoned me, Master. I await your bidding, Master."

The secretary looked up from his desk at the unusual sound of the imp's voice, and suddenly his eyes widened. Amirantha pointed to the entrance to Kaspar's office and said, "Beyond those doors is another room, in which resides a man of importance. He is General Kaspar, Chancellor to the Maharaja of Muboya. Bear to him a message that I, Amirantha of the Satumbria, seek audience, for I have a dire warning and need to speak with him now." Lowering his voice, he said, "Can you remember that, Nalnar?"

"I remember, Master," said the imp, as it leaped away, reaching a window in two bounds.

The secretary at the desk stood and shouted, "Guards!"

Instantly, guards from the corners of the large antechamber and by the doors raced to see what the problem was, as Amirantha calmly sat back down on the bench. Brandos looked on with some amusement as the secretary tried explaining that the two men quietly sitting on the bench had just conspired to make a tiny blue man appear, who had leaped out the window.

Unsure of what to do, the secretary ordered the guards to subdue the two on the bench, which brought a confused reaction from the guard sergeant, as the two men hardly appeared in need of subduing. Then the secretary realized that outside the window there was access to another window into the General's offices, and said, "Quick! Inside! Protect His Excellency."

The guards hurried through the door, with the frantic secretary a step behind. Brandos and Amirantha exchanged glances, stood slowly, and followed the excited man into the General's meeting room.

Kaspar of Olasko, General of the Armies of Muboya and the Maharaja's Chancellor, sat behind his desk, while the imp Nalnar sat quietly eating baked corn wafers and cheese off a plate. The General had pushed his chair back, obviously startled at first, but now calmly observing the imp at his meal.

The guards stood around, uncertain of what to do next, while the secretary shouted, "Excellency, are you safe?"

"Safe enough, it appears," said Kaspar. He was a round-faced man but otherwise slender and fit, his hair having turned steel-grey over the years. He once again affected the chin whiskers he had sported in his youth, but kept his upper lip and sideburns shaven. His mouth was set in a tight but slightly amused expression, as though he was annoyed at the interruption of his workday but found the novelty of it intriguing.

And it was clear he saw nothing remotely threatening in the situation. "It came in the window a moment ago and leaped upon my desk. Then it started eating my lunch."

Amirantha and Brandos exchanged knowing glances. Nalnar had a particular fondness for cheese.

As the imp ate with single-mindedness, Kaspar waved away the guards. "I think I'm safe," he observed.

The secretary, still looking frantic, shouted, "Arrest those men!" and pointed at Amirantha and Brandos.

With a single wave of his hand, Kaspar aborted the attempt. "Is this yours?" he said to Amirantha, pointing at Nalnar.

"In a manner of speaking," replied the Warlock.

Again with a wave of his hand, Kaspar dismissed the guards

and secretary. After the guards had left, Amirantha and Brandos noticed a man cowering in the corner, huddled down in abject terror. Kaspar half-rose out of his seat to address the man. "Lord Mora, perhaps it would be best if we continued our discussion on another day."

The man slowly rose, nodding vigorously but still unable or unwilling to speak. He quickly exited the room, leaving Kaspar alone with the imp and two strangers. "Now," said Kaspar, "what am I to make of all this?"

Amirantha's eyes half-closed and rolled upward in an expression of exasperation. "Nalnar!"

The imp jumped at his name. "Master?" he hissed.

"The message?"

Looking abashed, the imp lowered his head and said, "Amirantha of the Satumbria seeks audience, for he has a dire warning and needs to speak with you now."

"You forgot?"

"He had cheese," pleaded the imp.

Brandos shrugged. "It could have been worse. It could have been a plate of muffins."

"Muffins," agreed Amirantha.

"Muffins!" shrieked the imp as he started to look around the room.

Amirantha held out one hand and said, "Thou art dismissed, minion!"

The imp faded out of view and the Warlock said, "My lord Kaspar, I apologize, but I've been waiting without those doors for three days—"

"Four," corrected Brandos, "if you count this day."

Shooting his companion a dark look and a silent warning to not interrupt again, Amirantha said, "—days and judged it likely to be days more unless I resorted to something more dramatic."

Kaspar nodded, sat back down, and finally said, "I'm listening."

In efficient style, Amirantha told Kaspar of his encounter with the summoned demon, omitting the reason why they were summoning a demon in a cave in the first place. Still, he left out nothing critical, stressing how dangerous the creature was and that its appearance was a warning of far deeper dangers.

After he finished, Kaspar was silent for a while, then said, "Let me see if I have the right of this.

"You are the two mountebanks who have been fleecing the locals to the east and north of here by banishing demons you summon." When they didn't deny it, he continued. "But you thought enough of this danger to come see me, even though you knew I might decide to employ harsh judgment against you for your confidence tricks?"

Amirantha glanced at Brandos, who stood motionless, showing no emotion. "Yes," he said finally. "This is a dangerous enough issue that I felt the need to carry word.

"As I said, magic has a signature, each unique to whoever the caster is, and while only the most accomplished among us can discern that difference, it is there. And the man who distorted my magic to summon that demon is well known to me."

"Who is that?" asked Kaspar.

"My brother, Belasco."

"So, this is a family problem?" said Kaspar, his eyes narrowing, as if this was not the sort of answer he had expected.

Brandos shifted uneasily and said, "It's . . . an odd family, really."

"Apparently," said Kaspar, heaving himself out of his chair with a sigh. He moved to the window. "In my day I've traveled a lot, places even you would be surprised to hear of . . . Warlock?"

"It's a title of my people," said Amirantha, "the Satumbria."

"I've never heard of them," said Kaspar.

"They no longer exist," said Amirantha, and even Brandos looked surprised to hear that. "They were obliterated years ago by the armies of the Emerald Queen."

Kaspar nodded. "I've heard tales of that time," was all he said. He didn't think it necessary to explain he had served with men who had fought against those armies. He paused, then said, "Very well, Warlock. Let us say for a minute I believe what you say and that you are, indeed, very concerned.

"I am still not clear on why the concern."

"I thought I explained," said Amirantha, and a note of impatience seeped into his voice.

"Think of me as a slow student," said Kaspar dryly, as he sat on the edge of his desk, looking down at the two men. He motioned for them to bring their chairs closer and returned to sit behind his desk.

Amirantha sat, then for a moment stared at Kaspar of Olasko, second most powerful man in the Kingdom of Muboya. He recognized at once this was no ordinary courtier but a man who had seen much, and who could be very dangerous. Amirantha had no fondness for danger, preferring to give it a wide berth. Avoiding this man's displeasure was the safe course.

Slowly he said, "I was born in a village far to the north, one of a dozen inhabited by a people called the Satumbria. I suppose at one time or another we were nomadic, like some of the tribes to the east of us, but for many generations we had occupied a particularly nice valley, and the surrounding meadows.

"We paid tribute when we had to, to whichever city state or local robber baron claimed us, but for the most part we were left to our own devices and did as well as any poor farmers could expect in that time. We even had a town hall of sorts and a ruling council, which was more of an excuse for the men to sit around, argue, and drink.

"Our women were the caretakers of the children and the ancestors, and we worshipped our forebears as well as the gods." He paused. "In fact, we probably stinted in our devotion to the gods and paid more attention to our ancestors." He glanced at Brandos, who was paying close attention, as he hadn't heard parts of this story before.

"My mother had the vision, or second sight, as it was called. That made her both revered and feared. As was our custom, she was made to live apart, in a hut on a hill away from the village, but was provided food and other necessities. She was expected to live alone, yet be our eyes into the next world, providing guidance and wisdom.

"She was also to have lived a chaste existence, but as you

can see by my presence, that was never the case. She was, by any standard, a beautiful woman and men sought her out.

"She bore three sons. I was the youngest. None of us knew our father—or fathers, for we didn't know if we shared one. My mother was adamant about never mentioning who he or they might have been.

"In the end, it was the three of us, raised and taught by our mother." He shifted his weight in his chair, as if speaking of this made him uncomfortable.

If Kaspar was impatient to get to the point, he didn't show it, merely saying, "Go on."

"None of us could read—we came to that later. But we all were taught magic by our mother. All three of us inherited some of her gifts, though they manifested in different ways.

"We were all practitioners of what are called the 'dark arts,' for my mother was a woman of dark secrets. I suspect her gifts came at a price, perhaps through a compact with dark powers, but I only speculate.

"As a child, I sensed presences, the existence of things I could not see, and longed to call them to me. Nalnar was the first to answer, and while he is not overtly malicious, he has no natural sense of constraint. He injured me severely before I could subdue him. Once I bent him to my service, he became a lifelong companion. I can now summon him with a single word, and his obedience to me is absolute. Of all those I have summoned from the demon realm, he is my most reliable servant."

"You have others?" asked Kaspar.

"Yes," said Amirantha. "Several, most of whom are fully controllable."

"Most?"

"There are a few I have come to dominate lately, but upon whom I will not rely," said the Warlock, shifting his weight in his chair as if uneasy discussing his craft with another.

Brandos raised his eyebrows and in a semi-mocking tone said, "They tend to try to bite your head off until you get to know them better."

Kaspar was silent a moment, then said, "This is beyond me.

There are some people with whom I need to have you speak, but before then, I would hear the rest of your tale."

Amirantha let out his breath slowly, as if uncertain what to say next, then shrugged and said, "It's difficult to know how to explain. We were left to our own devices much of the time; Mother was a little mad, I'm certain, but she was also a woman of remarkable gifts.

"There were three of us, and I was the youngest, as I have said. It may be her madness was passed along to my eldest brother, for he was . . . different. He became obsessed at an early age with death, or more precisely, the actual moment of death, when life flees, and the meaning of that transition. He would often kill things just to watch them die.

"Our middle brother . . . he was less mad than our eldest brother, but that didn't make him sane. He had his own madness, but with him it was rage. He was born angry, and he stayed angry. We used to fight all the time, for he was frightened of our elder brother, and I was the youngest. So I became the target of all his ire. Only my mother prevented him from severely injuring me several times when we were children.

"It is how, ironically, I became a Warlock of Demons. My brother was administering a thrashing and I called to Nalnar to come help me, and he appeared. He's small, but he can be very nasty when he needs and has enough flame magic to burn down a good-size house if he's of a mind to. He drove off my brother and left him with a nasty set of scars. That's when my brother's hot anger turned to cold hatred.

"He's been trying to kill me ever since."

"And other people think they have family problems," Kaspar said dryly.

Amirantha studied the General for a long moment, then smiled. "It does appear absurd when narrated, doesn't it?"

"Somewhat, but I have seen many things in the last twenty years, things that before then I would have scoffed at and ridiculed.

"Still," added Kaspar, "you haven't gotten to why your family difficulties concern the Kingdom of Muboya."

"It's difficult to explain in a short time—"

"Oh, take all the time you need," said Kaspar, as he glanced through the doorway where his guards stood ready to answer his call. "As much trouble as you've caused to gain my attention, it would be foolish of me not to give it to you. After all, if you don't provide a compelling reason for unleashing that odd little friend of yours in my offices, you'll have ample time to contemplate your folly chained to the wall of the Maharaja's dungeon.

"So, please continue," said Kaspar agreeably.

Amirantha and Brandos exchanged glances, but said nothing to each other. The Warlock said, "After that fight, when Nalnar scared my brother, we three spent as much time apart from one another, and therefore from our mother, as we could manage once we reached a certain age.

"I spent a great deal of my time in caves near our hut, calling up Nalnar and learning as much as I could from him about the demon realm. It took a great deal of luck, frankly. I almost got killed a number of times until I began to puzzle out some sense of how these creatures are, how they respond to being in our realm, what drives them."

"This is all very interesting," said Kaspar. "Go on."

"My brothers meanwhile became immersed in their own areas of . . . interest. My eldest brother was probably the least talented among us, but the most driven. My other brother had flashes of brilliance, but no discipline. He's quick to learn, and has mastered many things. I fell somewhere in the middle, I suppose. I am very good at what I do, but what I do is within narrow limits." He looked at Kaspar. "I really don't understand much about other types of magic, if you must know."

"Your brother?" Kaspar prodded.

Amirantha sighed. "I suspect I'm having difficulty coming to the point because I want to acquaint you with just how difficult a task my brother achieved."

"Which brother?"

"The middle brother, Belasco."

"Continue."

Amirantha said, "I say with no false vanity that I know

perhaps as much as any man living what there is to know about demons. My knowledge is hardly exhaustive, as I discovered recently when encountering the battle demon my brother conjured into existence instead of the one I was summoning.

"That's the point of it, my lord Kaspar. Not only did my brother find me—and I have been successfully avoiding him for nearly fifty years—he found me in the middle of a conjuration that should be far beyond his ability to understand, let alone influence. Moreover, he introduced a component to my own magic of which I was unaware at the time, bending it to his will—no small feat alone—and almost got me killed, which I suspect was his goal.

"Here's the thing: if he has become that powerful he probably could have come up with a far simpler means of disposing of me, say conjuring up a massive ball of flames in the cave, which would certainly have incinerated me before I could have gotten magic wards up to protect me. But instead he chose to kill me in a fashion that was both ironic and insulting. He expected me to recognize at the last instant he was the author of my death, and wanted me to know that he's now better than I am at my craft."

Kaspar sighed. "So, your brother hates you and wishes you dead. Hardly an original tale. But we still haven't reached the point where I need fear for the safety of this Kingdom."

"The demon my brother conjured into being was of a type I've never encountered."

"So?" asked Kaspar, not seeing any significance.

"By our measure, demons tend to be stupid, or at the least are not very clever. Their existence is one I can scarcely imagine, and I have more knowledge of them than most men; it's a lifetime of combat and struggle, and guile serves better than intellect. One hallmark of intellect is reflection, and the idea of a reflective demon is . . . laughable, really.

"But they can be cunning. The demon I faced was not merely cunning, he was intelligent. Once he saw his usual rage and physical power were ineffective, he changed his approach and began to use magic."

"I know nothing of demons, but I have heard stories from those who have encountered one in the past," began Kaspar.

Amirantha looked intrigued. "I would like to speak to them if possible."

"More than possible," said Kaspar. "It's a near certainty, but I'm still not clear on why an intelligent magic-using demon is something I need worry over."

"There is a demon realm, General, a world apart from our own. I've read a few ancient records, but there is no certain knowledge of what that place is like. But we do know a few things. If demons could, they would happily invade our world, for here is an abundance of life that is intoxicating for them, and it is life that is mostly helpless against them. The stoutest warrior I know"—he indicated Brandos—"could keep that demon at bay only for a few moments, just long enough for me to effect its destruction.

"Imagine if you could, a dozen such coming into this palace at one time. I am the most powerful master of demons I have encountered—and there are not many of us in any event—and I could perhaps best two, even three such creatures given perfect circumstances."

"Life rarely provides perfect circumstances," offered Brandos.

"Yes," said Kaspar. "I think I see where this is going."

"Yes," said Amirantha. "Imagine now an army of such creatures."

Thinking of his past encounter with the Dasati Deathknights on the now destroyed world of Kelewan, Kaspar said, "I think I can imagine such." He sat lost in thought a moment, then asked, "How would you control such an army?"

Amirantha took a deep breath, the rise and fall of his shoulders communicating what he said next. "I have no idea. Perhaps they have rulers, or some sense of loyalty; my dealings with those I have mastered lead me to think everything in their realm is predicated either on power or usefulness; a demon will serve a greater demon rather than be destroyed; a demon will spare a lesser demon if he can be useful. Beyond that I have no notion of how such an army of creatures might be controlled."

Kaspar fell silent and said, "Yes, you most certainly need to speak with some friends of mine."

He moved toward the door and signaled for his secretary, who had been hovering outside the room with the guards, waiting for his master's command. "Secure quarters for these two and give them a good meal. Tomorrow I take them on a journey with me."

"Sir?" asked the secretary. "A journey?"

"Yes," said the General. "I'll inform the Maharaja personally, tonight."

"By sea or land?" asked the secretary.

"By land," said the General. "I'll need a half-dozen of my personal bodyguards."

"Only a half-dozen?"

"Six will do. Have two horses prepared for these two," said Kaspar, pointing at Amirantha and Brandos. "We'll need enough provisions for a week of traveling overland to the east. That will be all," he finished, waving the man away.

Returning to his desk, Kaspar sat down. Then he said, "Belasco, you say?"

"Yes," said the Warlock.

"He was the middle brother?"

"Yes," said Amirantha. "He's become something far greater than I imagined."

"Your eldest brother?" asked Kaspar. "What of him?"

"I don't know," said Amirantha. "He was, as I said, obsessed with death and dying. He was a powerful necromancer by the time I departed our home—somewhat in a hurry, I'm sorry to say, as my only reason for being there ended. My eldest brother had become fascinated by a necklace Mother had found—he'd remove it from her small cache of her most treasured things, bringing down her wrath.

"He claimed it spoke to him. Finally, one day, he murdered Mother." He spoke almost dispassionately, though there was a hint of feelings behind his words. "It was a particularly grue-

some and messy murder, but it provided him with a very powerful burst of magic.

"I caught a glimpse of him covered in her blood, invoking
some dark power as he stood wearing that necklace."

"Glimpse?" asked Kaspar.

"I was running for my life," said Amirantha. "Belasco had
already shown the presence of mind to flee, using some translocation spell or an invisibility spell or something of that sort. I
was forced to outrun my eldest brother, who was fatigued from
killing our mother, else I think he might have overtaken me.

"I was desperate and summoned a demon named
Wusbagh'rith, who carried me off. He's a foul creature, but he
has massive wings. Fortunately, I had enough control to get
miles away from Sidi before the demon tried to kill me."

Kaspar's eyes widened. "What did you say?"

"I said I had enough control to get miles away from my
brother before he tried to kill me."

"The name? What was your brother's name?"

"Sidi. Why?"

Kaspar took a deep breath, then let it out slowly. "Do you
know the name Leso Varen?"

"No," said Amirantha. "Should I?"

Kaspar regarded the Warlock. "You never saw your brother
Sidi again after he murdered your mother?"

"No, I saw him twice, once in the City of the Serpent River
and once across the sea in the town of Land's End, in the Kingdom of the Isles."

"I know the place," said Kaspar.

"Both times I avoided him before he saw me, but I never
spoke with him again, if that's what you're asking. If I could, I'd
happily cut his heart out and feed it to one of my demons. She
may have been a crazy witch, but she was our *mother*, and he
slaughtered her."

"Your brother is dead."

"You knew him?" asked Amirantha, showing the most emotion he had since entering Kaspar's palace.

"I had the unfortunate luck to have him guest with me for a

while. He used the name Leso Varen and caused me . . ." Kaspar stopped, as if weighing his words. Finally, he said, "He caused me great personal injury. But I do know that he was identified by someone I trust implicitly to have been a necromancer named Sidi before assuming that identity. And I know he is dead beyond reclaiming."

"General," said Amirantha. "Please, I must know how he died."

Kaspar nodded and quickly recounted the role Leso Varen played in the war with the Dasati. He glossed over the role played by the Conclave, choosing to allow Pug to decide how much to trust this Warlock and his companion. Kaspar was a good judge of men and thought the pair reliable enough if watched closely, but it wasn't his judgment to make.

Ten years after the fact, knowledge of what befell the Tsurani home world of Kelewan had spread throughout the land; many of the survivors had sought refuge in Muboya, a large cadre of Tsurani warriors personally serving as the Maharaja's core troops. But the details were shrouded in rumor and speculation, for even those who had lived through the horror of the Dasati invasion knew little of the truth about that war, that an army from another plane of reality had attempted to obliterate all life on Kelewan, in preparation for remaking it as their own.

Kaspar told the story as best he could, surprised at long-buried emotions that tried to rise up, for it had been one of the most difficult and horrific experiences of his life. "At the end, as best we can determine, your brother perished on the Dasati home world at the hands of some horror attempting to enter our realm, or he was obliterated with the utter destruction of Kelewan.

"More than one witness to his presence on Kelewan, in proximity to what we called the Black Sphere—the gateway to the Dasati home world—confirm this. I have friends who know more than I about such matters, and they are convinced that had he had one more soul vessel to which he might flee at his death, it would have had to be on Kelewan, and therefore it was also destroyed with the planet."

A mix of emotions played across Amirantha's face. "I . . . I guess I will accept what you say, General, and put aside . . . old hatred."

Brandos said, "That's a hell of a tale, General." He looked down, shook his head slowly, and said, "You hear stories . . . the entire world destroyed?" His expression told Kaspar the old fighter didn't want to believe this, but did.

Kaspar just nodded, remaining silent.

Amirantha looked away for a moment, then turned and looked Kaspar in the eye. Whatever pain and regret had flashed there for a moment was now replaced with a clear-eyed certainty. "That doesn't change anything, though. I must stress this: whatever troubles Sidi caused you are as nothing to what Belasco is capable of."

"Are you sure?" asked the General.

"Absolutely. For while Belasco was always the dabbler, he learned many things. He had a prodigious curiosity and he would undertake something single-mindedly until he mastered it.

"And while Sidi was insane, Belasco is insane and brilliant. Of the two, he's far more dangerous."

Kaspar was silent while he weighed the warning. He sighed. "Leso was as dangerous a man as any I've met, so to hear you say your other brother is more so . . ." He fell silent a moment. Finally, he said, "I'll have you escorted to your quarters. We leave at first light." He walked out of the room, leaving Amirantha and Brandos sitting in their chairs.

After a moment, a court page appeared, flanked by two soldiers-at-arms. Brandos rose and looked at his friend. "Well, I guess we're going on another journey."

"Apparently so," said Amirantha.

# CHAPTER 10

## THREAT

Sandreena swung her mace.

The massive weapon took the other rider in the stomach—he had been coming in high and she ducked under his blow and struck hard—lifting him out of his saddle. She knew her art well enough to know he was done for the time being. If he wasn't passing out because he couldn't catch his breath, he was likely to be lying on the ground stunned from the fall.

She had happened upon a wagon being attacked by bandits, four raggedly dressed thugs with surprisingly good weapons. The merchant and what appeared to be two sons furiously battled the more experienced brigands with a poor assortment of weapons: one battered shield and an old sword, two clubs, and a lot of determination. Still, they gave good account of themselves and had held the bandits at bay for a few minutes before Sandreena had ridden over the rise and seen the conflict.

The three remaining riders saw one of their own go down suddenly, and a fully armored knight riding toward them. Without a word they turned their horses and put heels to them, galloping off. Sandreena weighed giving chase, then decided the struggle was over; besides, they were heading straight up into the hills and her heavier mount would soon fall farther behind; also, they knew the terrain and she didn't. While she had no doubt she could easily best the three of them, given what she saw of their light armor and untrained fighting skills, she didn't relish fighting her way out of an ambush.

She paused a minute to ensure the bandits weren't doubling back to recommence the attack, then turned to see the two boys stripping the bandit on the ground. She judged that meant he was dead.

She rode over to the wagon, where the man sat regarding her suspiciously, holding his very old and battered sword at the ready, in case one brigand had merely driven off others. She raised her visor off her full helm and said, "Stay your weapon, sir. I am a Knight-Adamant of the Order of the Shield of the Weak."

His suspicious expression didn't leave. "So you say," he said in an oddly accented Keshian dialect. He turned to the boys and shouted something in a language she didn't understand, or think she had heard before, then turned back to her. "Well, if you expect thanks or reward, you're mistaken. My boys and I had things well in hand." The boys gathered up everything, including the robber's filthy smallclothes—leaving him lying nude in the road—and then ran off after the brigand's horse, which was cropping grass a short distance off the road.

"Looks like a good horse," said the man on the wagon, and Sandreena couldn't tell if he was addressing her or talking to himself. Then the driver seemed intent on inspecting the content of his wagon, against the remote possibility that one of the bandits had somehow managed to pilfer an item or two while the conflict was under way.

Finally content nothing was missing, he shouted something to the boys, who were having a little trouble corralling the horse, which seemed to like the idea of cropping grass better than having another rider on her back. At last, one of the boys reached down, grabbed up a long clump of grass, and held it out for the horse to sniff at while his brother gently reached out and snagged the reins. If the horse objected to such a turn of events, she hid her disappointment well and came along quietly.

The driver shouted more instructions to the boys in the strange language, seemingly convinced they couldn't tie the horse's reins to the back of the wagon without his oversight. When they were at last done, and back in the wagon, the driver turned and sat down, finding the patient Sandreena still looking directly at him.

"What?" he demanded. "I'm not going to pay you."

"I'm not asking for payment."

"Good, then get out of my way. I have business."

Sighing at the man's impossible rudeness, Sandreena said, "One question. Do you know the village of Akrakon?"

"Yes," he answered, then with a flick of the reins he started his team forward, deftly moving the horses just enough to skirt around where Sandreena waited.

As he rode past, she shouted, "Where is it?"

"You said 'one question,' and I answered," was his reply and the boys burst out laughing.

Suddenly out of patience, Sandreena turned and urged her horse forward, quickly overtaking the wagon. With one swift motion she reached over, grabbed the man by the collar, hauled him off the seat, and deposited him in the dirt.

"Try again," she said, her voice almost hissing with menace.

"All right," said the man, rolling away from her and to his feet in a deft move. With three strides he was back alongside his wagon and then back on the seat. "Akrakon is down the road, maybe five miles. You'll be there by supper."

"Thank you," she said, putting heels to her horse and moving down the road at a lazy canter. She wished to put as much distance as possible between herself and the obnoxious man.

Then she remembered what the Father-Bishop had said about the villagers being one of the more annoying tribes of the region. She had thought that meant they were fractious and rebellious. Perhaps he simply meant they were rude.

As the man had predicted, Sandreena rode into the village of Akrakon near supper time. Two boys were running through the center of the village, perhaps coming down the hill from overseeing a flock, or working in a field, intent on reaching home for the day's final meal. She pulled up her mount before them and said, "Has this place an inn?"

Neither boy answered, but one pointed over his shoulder as he darted around one side of Sandreena's mount, his companion dodging around the other. Shaking her head at the lack of civility demonstrated so far by these people, Sandreena wondered how much information she might extract about the goings-on in the mountains above the village. She might have to club it out of them.

She had never seen a region like this one. Since leaving Krondor and riding through the Roldem city of Pointer's Head, she had passed miles of coastal lands, but none like this.

Both the Kingdom of the Isles and Roldem held claims to the long strip of coastal land running between the southern shores of the Sea of Kingdoms and mountains called the Peaks of Tranquility.

She assumed the tranquility was reserved for those who lived south of that massive barrier of mountains and hills, for the region between the Kingdom city of Timons and Pointer's Head was anything but tranquil. Two other cities rested between them, Deep Taunton and Mallow's Haven, none of which properly acknowledged either Kingdom as sovereign. The local nobles and merchants had done a fair job for decades playing one kingdom off another, building their own alliances, and keeping free of close supervision.

Only the massive barrier of mountains kept Great Kesh from also claiming the region; they had in the past, but those attempts to annex the area had resulted in Roldem and the Kingdom putting aside their own interests to drive Kesh south.

Sandreena vaguely recalled from her history that the last battle had been over a century before, when a Kingdom Duke from Bas-Tyra had driven Kesh out of Deep Taunton. But at least that land was rich with forests and farms.

This side of the Peaks of the Quor left little to covet. Since riding north out of the port city of Ithra, she had seen nothing but rocky bluffs, stone-strewn beaches, a difficult road cut through in a dozen places by swiftly running streams hurling down from the peaks above. The woods above looked dark and uninviting, and those few villages she had encountered were small fishing enclaves, where the inhabitants scraped out a harsh existence.

Somewhere above her, she knew, had to be some farming communities, else those fishing villages would have vanished ages before. They had no gardens or fields nearby, so one must deduce that they traded their catch for vegetables, fruits, and other necessities. But if there were farming enclaves in the region, she didn't encounter them. Still, there were occasional trails and pathways leading up into the hills, some with recent wagon tracks.

But what was strangest to Sandreena was that there was no authority in the region. If Kesh claimed this part of the peninsula, they vested nothing in that ownership; gone were the usual outposts and patrols, governors or minor nobles. It was as if this rocky coastline was all but forgotten by the Empire.

She rode through the village and judged this the most prosperous place she had seen since leaving Ithar, and it was a poor one at best. There were nothing like shops that were recognizable as such. Only a smithy at the end of the street was obvious, for the huge chimney was belching smoke, and there was another shop she had just passed that appeared to be a woodworker, probably the local barrel-maker, cartwright, wheelwright, and woodcarver all in one. It was a very strange place, from her experience. And it was quiet, as if everyone went about their business without fuss, trying to stay inconspicuous. Even the few children she saw were sullen and stared at her with suspicious eyes.

Reaching the indicated building, she could scarcely believe this was the inn. A large, ramshackle house, perhaps. Still, there was a hitching rail in front, with two horses tied in place. She rode around the building, leisurely, looking for anything that might resemble a stable, finding only a large corral where a tumble-down, run-in shed stood, with one side completely collapsed. Her mount had endured worse.

She quickly dismounted and untacked the animal. She put her saddle and bridle on a rail obviously used for such—it still was slightly sheltered by what remained of the roof and the three still standing walls. She quickly brushed down her horse, and picked out the hooves. A well close by provided clean water, and she drew out grain from the sack she carried behind her saddle.

Ensuring everything was as secure as it was likely to be, she turned her attention to her own needs. She expected a bath would be out of the question—and vowed to bathe at the first stream, lake, or river she found—but hoped at least the bed was something more than a bag full of straw.

She didn't worry about her horse's tack, as her mount was a well-trained warhorse. Anyone foolish enough to come up without her standing there would be in for a very rude shock.

Sandreena made her way around the modest building to the entrance and entered. The interior of the inn was no more promising than the exterior. A low ceiling would cause a tall man to duck, and Sandreena felt cramped. The long bar and one table provided all the accommodation for eating and drinking, and Sandreena assumed large gatherings were not customary.

A single door to the back seemed the only other passage, and when no one appeared after a minute, she shouted, "Hello, the inn! Is anyone here?"

Quickly, a woman's voice answered: "Who's there?"

"Someone in need of a meal and a room," and muttering more to herself than the disembodied voice, she added, "and a hot bath if that's possible in this hovel."

A pinched-faced woman of middle years appeared from the lone door at the rear of the building. She wore plain grey home-spun, a stained apron faded to yellow, and a blue scarf over her grey-shot black hair. "What do you need?" she asked in curt tones.

Sandreena felt a sudden urge to turn around, ride back to Krondor, and strangle the Father-Bishop. Biting back a frustrated and angry retort, she simply said, "Something to drink. Ale?"

"No ale," said the woman. "Beer."

Sandreena nodded. Not a fan of the lighter brew, she still felt the need to wet her throat before anything else. The mug appeared before her, and she took a drink. It was weak and sour, but it was wet. "Food?" she asked after she drained a third of the mug.

"I have some *homush* cooking. Should be ready in a few minutes." Sandreena had no idea what *homush* was, but she had eaten a wide variety of things in her travels and discovered that if the locals were eating it, it wouldn't kill you. "I sometimes have mutton, but there was no one here to slaughter a sheep this week. I'm waiting for my husband and sons. They are due back from trading in Dunam."

Sandreena nodded. She had ridden through Dunam on her way from the port city of Ithra. It was a small trading town half-way between here and Ithra, with a small harbor. She assumed it was where the locals had their goods shipped, which seemed likely if that's where the innkeeper and his sons went for supplies. She had seen other towns like it, ancient communities left over from the days of coastal sailing, before the big deep-water ships started plying their trade, leaving the smaller stops along the once prosperous trade routes to wither away.

She looked at the older woman and said, "Two-horse rig, with a bay and a dapple grey pulling it?"

"That's my Enos," said the woman. "Did you see them?"

"They should be rolling in any time now," said Sandreena. "I chanced across them on the road a little while back. They were fighting off some bandits."

"Bandits! Black Caps?"

Sandreena said, "I don't know about any black caps, but they were a scruffy lot. One of them died, and the others rode off. Your man and the boys are fine."

The woman didn't lose her strained expression, but a hint of relief showed in her eyes. All she said was, "Food is almost ready. It is four coppers for the beer. The meal is two."

Sandreena reached into her belt purse and pulled out a silver real. Kingdom's silver spent as well as Kesh's in this part of the world. "I need a room."

The woman nodded as she scooped up the silver coin. "I have one through there."

"Bath?"

The woman shook her head. "You can bathe down in the creek. No one will bother you."

Sandreena rolled her eyes, but said nothing. The bed was probably filled with straw and bugs. Well, it was still better than sleeping on the ground next to her horse in the run-in. "You have any fresh hay or grain for my horse?"

"When my husband gets here," was the reply. "He went to buy supplies. We were running low on many things." There was a hint of concern in the woman's otherwise stern tone, and Sandreena wondered why she sounded that way discussing something as unremarkable as an innkeeper traveling to get a wagonload of supplies for his inn, especially now having been told he was close to arriving safely. Sandreena had been in dozens of villages like this one over the years, and had a good sense of when things were normal and when they were not. Something was very out of place here, and she wondered if it was related to her mission.

"Well," she said, "I'm for a quick rinse. Will you ask one of your boys to see to my horse when they get here?"

"That will cost extra," said the woman without hesitation.

"Why am I not surprised," muttered Sandreena. She took another silver coin out of her purse and put it on the counter. "I may be here for two or three days. If there are more costs, let me know."

She walked out of the building and past the shed. She re-
trieved a bundle from her saddle kit, and moved through the
small meadow south of the shed. No one had to tell her where
the creek was, as she had been north of stream for most of the
last five miles along the road into town, and the lands sloped
downward in, past the run-in shed. Logic made it unlikely the
stream was in the other direction.

She quickly found it and noticed with some satisfaction it
was isolated and free from casual observation. Not modest by
any stretch of imagination, she still enjoyed her moments of privacy.

She removed her cloak, and the Order's tabard, letting them
both fall to the ground. She removed her heavy leather gauntlets and tossed them onto the cloak. Doffing her helm, she set it
down on the ground next to the cloak. The coif and mail shirt
were annoying to remove without help, as always, and she knew
she must look a sight bending at the waist and shaking them off
once she had lifted them as high as she could. There was one advantage to being a temple knight rather than a Knight-Adamant,
and that was having a squire at hand to help. Some errant knights
had squires, just as some mendicant friars of her order had beg-
ging acolytes, but she preferred her solitude.

Stripping off her head covering, tunic, trousers, and smallclothes, she waded into the stream. Snowmelt from the high
mountains, the water lingered in a lake above, where it basked in
the hot sun before spilling down toward the ocean. She'd bathed
in far colder.

As she did each time she found herself bathing outside, she
revisited the conflicts and contradictions her body raised within
her. In the cloistered baths at the temple, or in the privacy of a
tub in an inn, she felt confined but protected, and in the temple
the meditative aspect of bathing and steaming also helped her
distance her thoughts from her body. Outside, it was the opposite; she felt somehow more exposed yet somehow more fundamental, almost primitive in nature.

She enjoyed being a woman, yet she always felt it a burden.
She despised the men who had used her when she was young,

but occasionally she longed for a gentle man's hand on her body. She knew men found her beautiful, so she hid it under armor and arms, rejecting the allures of her former trade. Gone were the unguents and colors, the soft silks and jewelry. Her face was hidden behind a helm's faceplate as often as not, and her body under armor and tabard.

She sighed in perplexity as she scrubbed at her hair with the very costly Keshian soap she had purchased the year before. The bar was almost gone, and she used it only on her hair and body, letting a pummeling on hard rocks serve for her clothing. She paused and luxuriated as much as possible outside in the cool breeze, in the faint scent of lilacs that the soap-maker had instilled in his product. She knew that on her way back to Krondor she must secure another bar of soap; it was her only indulgence in an otherwise austere existence.

Feeling an unexpected twinge of sadness, she wondered if her life would end in bloodshed and pain, or if she might find another life after this one, perhaps with a good man, being a mother. She shook her head, as much in frustration as to shed water, and pushed aside that often visiting feeling of futility. The Goddess often tested her faithful and doubt was not unexpected, and the priests and priestesses had prepared her for these moments, yet it was difficult.

She put aside her doubts and set about vigorously pounding out her trail-dirty clothing on a flat rock, using the method Brother Mathias had taught her: thoroughly soak the article, twist it as much as she could into a rope, and slam that twisted cloth as hard as she could against the rock; keep soaking, twisting, and pounding until clean. She had no idea why her clothes ended up cleaner, but they did. Then she conceded she had no idea how soap worked in cleaning anything, but was content to just accept that it did. She spent a few minutes pounding clean her tunic, pants, cloak, and smallclothes, then hung them to drip on a nearby tree branch.

Sandreena ignored the breeze off the mountain, which raised gooseflesh on her body, waiting patiently to dry enough to don her fresh clothing. This was the part she hated most, for now she could do nothing but let the air dry her. Now she wished for a towel and realized she really would have preferred being sent somewhere with at least a tub and hot water.

Finally judging herself dry enough, she put on her clean smallclothes. She pulled on a fresh tunic and trousers, leggings, and clean head-covering she wore under her mail coif to keep her hair from becoming tangled in the metal links.

Once she had clothes on, she audibly sighed and pulled on her boots. Again she wondered about taking a squire as she struggled to get the stubborn things back on.

By the time she was dressed, the clothes hanging on the tree were no longer dripping, though they were still thoroughly soaked. She gathered them up and carried them up the hill to the inn, her helm under her arm and her mace in her left hand.

Reaching the inn, she saw another horse in the run-in next to hers and recognized it as the bandit's mount the boys on the wagon had seized. She then found the wagon at the back door, being unloaded by the two boys she had encountered earlier in the day. She shouted, "One of you see my horse gets a bag of grain and I'll give you a copper."

Both boys looked at one another, as if weighing the offer against what their father might do if they left off the unloading. Silently, they nodded and two fists were raised, pumping up and down twice and on the third pump, one shouted "odd," and the other shouted "even." Both boys had two fingers extended, and the one who had shouted "even" smiled and leaped down from the wagon, lifting a bag of grain off the ground and carrying it to the run-in shed. The other boy glowered at Sandreena but said nothing as he continued his work.

Inside the inn, Sandreena spread her cloak out over the back of a chair closest to the fire and put her wet tunic, trousers, leggings, and smallclothes down next to it on the floor.

"Supper is ready," said the woman as she came out from the kitchen. If she had any objections to the guest drying her clothing before the fire, she did not voice them.

Sandreena put her bag and weapons under the table, but close at hand. Years on the road had taught her that the unexpected was far worse a source of pain and misery than trouble you saw coming.

Glancing around the room, she reaffirmed there were only two entrances: the one from outside, and the one from the back of the building, where she assumed both her room and the kitchen lay, as well as the family's quarters. As inns went, this wasn't the worst—that honor went to a hovel in Kesh, which had four walls and a roof. There were no tables or chairs, no bar, and no rooms. Everyone ate on the floor from cooking done before an open fireplace and slept where they ate. But this inn was only marginally better.

When the woman appeared, she was followed by the man from the wagon and the two boys. As food was placed before her, the man said, "You. From the road."

Sandreena nodded, not entirely sure if that was an accusation or a question.

"You said you'd pay my boy a copper to feed your horse."

"Yes."

"Give it to me."

Sandreena didn't argue, but pulled out a coin and put it on the table. The man snapped it up. "That is for his work. The oats are two more."

She put a silver coin on the table and said, "For today and tomorrow. If I stay longer, I'll pay in advance."

The man only nodded. "I'm Enos, this is Ivet, and my boys are Nicolo and Pitor. Your room is at the end of the hall."

Sandreena nodded. "My temple got reports of bandits. I see they were true."

The man paused as he started to turn away, and then turned back toward her. "Why does your temple know this? Who told them?"

Sandreena was a little surprised at the question rather than a simple admission. The man seemed more concerned with how the information reached the Temple of Dala than with someone arriving to help.

"Does that matter?"

The man shrugged.

"I don't know. I was simply ordered here by my Father-Bishop. It seems the Empire is too busy elsewhere to protect you."

"Protect?" said Enos with a bitter, barking laugh. "Those are worse than bandits. The tax men. They come, they take, they leave. They do nothing for us.

"Pirates and bandits. Smugglers and . . ." He stopped himself. "We don't need help. We manage."

Sandreena weighed her words carefully. She said, "I'm sure, and I'm not here to help you."

The man's eyes narrowed, as if he didn't understand, but he said nothing.

"I'm here to get information to take back to my temple."

"What sort of information?" asked Enos suspiciously.

Sandreena said, "Just why this out-of-the-way village is being ravaged."

The look of alarm that was barely hidden by Enos and Ivet was noticeable, but the boys positively went white with fear. There was something here that was far from ordinary, and she felt as if she had just stuck a stick into a hornet's nest.

She didn't need the sudden look of panic that descended on the family before her to warn her something bad was about to happen. She had too many unpleasant encounters in the last few years to be taken completely unawares, but she had let her attacker get too close.

She stood and, in a single fluid motion, kicked her chair straight back as she lifted the table and turned it over, then kneeling and having her mace in her hand before she was fully turned. The chair had struck a man in the legs, slowing him just long enough that she was ready as he swung his sword at her, trying to remove her head from her shoulders.

He, however, didn't expect her to move so quickly, and was shocked for a brief instant as he tried to regain his balance, just before her mace slammed into the side of his head. The blow propelled the man sideways and down, landing him in a heap on the floor. It also knocked off a black leather hat he had worn.

Sandreena had seen enough bodies hitting the ground to

know this man wasn't going to answer any questions. She hadn't intended to kill him, but battle-honed reflexes had taken over.

For a moment she inspected the body. Her would-be assassin wore a dark maroon tunic, black trousers, and black leather boots. He had a black cape, tied with a golden clasp, which looked more a gentleman's garb for an evening out in Roldem than any sort of serviceable travel wear, so she assumed he had stolen it.

The side of his head was caved in, with blood running from nose and ears, and his eyes were set wide in an expression of surprise. They had been a vivid blue, but there was something about the eyes of the dead that always made them look greyish to Sandreena, no matter what the original color.

She knelt down and inspected him. There was no belt purse, only an ordinary dagger, and no other signs of who he might have been. The only personal item she discovered was a chain around his neck, from which hung a token, a black balled fist made out of iron or some other base metal.

She picked up the leather hat and turned to Enos and his family. "A Black Cap, I presume?"

Enos's eyes were wide with terror and he seemed unable to speak. He merely nodded.

Sandreena stood, righted the table and chair, and, ignoring the body on the floor, sat down. "I think you need to tell me some things," she said.

Softly, in a whisper, Enos said, "We are all going to die."

# CHAPTER 11

## UPHEAVAL

Gulamendis howled.

A primal sound erupted from his throat as he threw back his head and unleashed his frustration in the only way he could. The sound was quickly engulfed in the endless pounding of waves on the rocks, as the Demon Master of the Taredhel stood on the bluffs above. He knew this moment was coming, but against hope he labored on, seeking the source of the demon signs he had encountered.

An emotional people, the Taredhel still knew how to keep within themselves when required. On the rocky bluffs of this wilderness, miles from any sign of habitation, human, dwarf, or anything remotely intelligent, he felt no such constraint. He raised his hand and conjured up a seething mass of mal energy, a writhing ball of mystic black tendrils within a dark purple sphere of light, and hurled it down toward the rocks below.

The ball struck a massive boulder and, in a satisfying display of pyrotechnics, exploded in a purple flame of blinding brilliance. It released dark clouds of smoke and sent a scintillating show of silver and white sparks in all directions, and when the ocean breeze blew away the smoke, all was as it had been before. The only sign of Gulamendis's outburst was a patch of bare rock, devoid of moss and lichen. Otherwise, the ocean and the rocks below were indifferent.

Gulamendis chuckled at his own childish outburst, and sat down to ponder his next move in this terrible and dangerous game. His original plan was simple: follow the demon sign long enough to establish exactly what it was. He had almost complete certainty that what he detected was a conjuration, for there was a difference, almost as if the lingering residue had a different quality, or flavor, between summoned demons and those that entered this realm unbidden. He had noticed that the first time he had encountered demons along the frontier on Diaziala, when the first conflict erupted in what would be this long and bitter war his people were losing.

He had become intrigued. Who was this summoner of demons, this being who could order them into this realm, as he did? For in his travels, Gulamendis had met few who could, and none who could match his abilities. He would be first to admit he had been lucky over the years, yet he also would take credit for learning what there was luck brought to him. He was an apt student of his craft, as his brother had been with magic of the mind.

He sighed and stood up. The demon was across that sea, and while he had no certainty, he suspected it was a very long way off, perhaps on the other side of this world. He had demons he could conjure that could fly, could carry him, but none could cross such a vast distance.

Besides, there were more important matters closer at hand than satisfying his academic and professional curiosities. Finding the other demon master would have to wait.

He was now faced with the task set before him by the Regent Lord: to investigate the elves to the north, in a place called Elvandar. He felt a strange tugging at the thought, for while the Taredhel had established their own order of things, their own view of the universe, still at heart they were Edhel, the People, and ancient ties still abided.

He considered what he knew of this region. He stood on the bluffs overlooking the sea, in a land the humans called the Far Coast. He believed himself to be near a city called Carse, south of another human population center, Crydee. North of that was the Elven Forest, if his brother's intelligence was accurate, and Laromendis was nothing if not thorough. He weighed what he had in his travel bag and judged it a difficult journey on foot.

He took one very long look around his position, knowing deep down he was unobserved, but still being cautious. He closed his eyes and began a summoning, and within a moment a huge steed appeared before him. Hell spawn, it might be, a demon of a lower cast, but it was very much like a horse, and he could ride it. Moreover, if it stayed uninjured, it could run as fast as the swiftest horse. In any case, it was a sight to behold.

The creature blinked its huge black eyes against the light of day. It looked around and snorted. It had been summoned by this elf before and knew better than to attack or try to escape, for this was its master. It lowered its head and waited.

It looked as much like a huge dog as it did a horse, though the legs were long and the body slender. It had a pointed snout, almost lizard-like, and the ears flattened back against the creature's skull, like a cat's when angry. A stub of a tail didn't wag in greeting, but rather trembled slightly, a warning among its own kind that it was ready to attack.

Gulamendis closed his eyes again, using a spell taught him by his brother, a glamour that would have any onlooker, save those with exceptional magic ability, see only a horse. It was akin to the spell Laro had used to disguise himself as a human while he traveled this land, and it had served him well.

Gripping the creature's scaly hide at the withers, the elf

leaped onto the creature's back and, using his legs, turned it northeast. There was a good-sized road a few miles in that direction, and it would take him to the human town of Crydee. There he might investigate a little, before traveling north to see his long-lost kin.

Gulamendis moved his demonic mount through the fields. He had taken to riding off the road, just in sight of it, and found a game trail through the barrier land between the fields of a scattering of farms south of Crydee. He had abandoned what the locals called the King's Highway when he found humans staring at him. At first he worried about his mount somehow not being disguised effectively by his illusion spell—he knew he was nowhere close to being the master his brother was—but he realized the second time some human children had risen up in the back of their parents' wagon, shouting and pointing, it was the mere fact of being an elf that had caused the excitement. Despite this region's proximity to the Elven Forest, it was apparent that elves rarely ventured south of what was called the River Boundary, and that he was the object of much scrutiny and comment.

At least, from what he could overhear, these humans gave no hint they perceived him to be any different, in attire, manner, or mount, from the local elves. Still, he decided stealth served him better than trying to play the part of a local elf, and at first opportunity turned eastward, away from the road.

He could ride along between the boundaries of these farms, most of the time being within sight of the road, without attracting too much notice. The crops were ripening, but not ready for harvest, so the fields tended to be unoccupied, and on those few occasions when he spied humans in the fields, he avoided them. His perceptions were clearly superior to theirs, so he felt no risk of detection.

When he came to a relatively close cluster of farmhouses, he rode farther eastward, into the woodlands that led into the deeper forest, called the Green Heart by the locals, and moved north. In these woods he felt a strange disquiet, the echoes of presences that were both somehow familiar and yet alien. It was times like these he wished he had had more time to speak with his brother on what Laromendis had discovered about this place.

As he returned to the strip of boundary land between farms, the sun set in the west, providing an unusually brilliant display of red, orange, pink, and gold light against grey clouds on the horizon. Gulamendis found himself holding back emotions, for it was hardly the first spectacular sunset he had seen over an ocean, but it was the first he had seen over an ocean on Mid-kemia. When last he had looked out over the seascape, it had been a grey and forlorn day, with haze masking the boundary between sea and sky.

Every day he spent on this world reinforced one thing over all others: this was their Home. And something was wrong.

He couldn't put his finger on the exact nature of this sense of wrongness, merely that he felt out of phase with this place. And he knew deep down that the wrongness was within himself, not with this place. Perhaps the generations on other worlds, away from the nurturing magic that was Midkemia, had changed the People. He didn't know, but he also knew concerns such as this one were academic compared to the immediate need to find his distant kin and discover what sort of allies they might be.

For as certain as he sat on this masked demon, riding along in the evening's twilight, he knew he alone from those laboring in the valley to the southeast understood the threat that was poised to strike this world. Deep inside him, another certainty was rising: this would be the last battle. If the Demon Legion found its way to Midkemia, if they discovered a path from And-cardia to this world, their Home, then all of the Edhel, every last elf born of this soil, every last elf returned from distant worlds, all would perish.

Crydee had proven an interesting and entertaining diversion for a short while. Gulamendis had easily avoided a noisy and ill-orga-nized town watch that had marched the perimeter of the town with little attention to details. It was clear this was a place untroubled by conflict for some years now. He had ridden quietly through an otherwise dark street past one or two buildings with lights on, but attracted no attention to himself.

The harbor had a tidy waterfront, with a long neck of land to the north boundary running out to a stone tower that appeared to be more of a watchtower than a lighthouse. There was a light, but it was hardly a beacon, being more of a single brazier that gave a faint illumination. Gulamendis assumed no ships were scheduled to arrive after dark, and any arriving unannounced would do well to lie off the coast and wait for dawn to enter the harbor.

He turned his mount northeast from the mouth of the harbor and skirted the town along its northern boundary. He was curious about the castle high above the town, on a steep rise, but knew it would be guarded by men more able than the town watch he had avoided. He still knew little about these humans, but he was an elf of keen observation and sharp wits.

Their social organization showed them to be in command of the region. Whatever neighbors might have troubled them in the past—elves, dwarves, goblins, or trolls—they had been driven out or disposed of. That made the humans dangerous.

His race had not encountered humans in centuries, and those encounters had always ended in bloody war. While some human tribes had been relatively peaceful, a large number had proven warlike and aggressive, and after several failed treaties with various tribes, the stance of the Taredhel had shifted from peaceful contact and negotiation to preemptive obliteration.

The dwarves had proven more troublesome in some ways, less in others. They were much tougher and difficult to root out of their underground communities, but they also were far less aggressive, willing to stay within their own territories without problems. Only twice had warfare erupted with dwarven clans, but both had been protracted, bloody wars.

Gulamendis realized with a sigh that those histories were now academic, for every world in which the Taredhel had encountered humans or dwarves had been overrun by the Demon Legion. With a sinking sensation in his stomach, the Demon Master wondered if he was on a fool's errand. Even if he could find potential allies among these humans and the other races on Midkemia, would his own people welcome their aid?

Turning his mount around, he rode past the local inn, which seemed lively enough by his standards. A steady sound of voices, some laughter, and music, if that's what it could be called. Taredhel musicians played a very soft and lyrical type of music that was supposed to mimic the lofty emotions of the magician's experience, as a means to share that bliss with those who had no magic. As Gulamendis's experiences with magic hardly contained any that could be called lyrical, he felt as the soldiers, farmers, and laborers must have felt listening to the great singers and musicians of his people on festival days—not that there had been many of those since the coming of the Demon Legion.

The Priests also kept traditional songs of prayer and welcoming, as well as other, more primitive music and instruments, as a way to keep in touch with the original culture of the Edhel. It was seen as more devout—or academic, depending on one's view of faith—and rarely heard outside the temple.

The music coming out of the inn was boisterous, loud, dissonant, and as best as the elf could tell, fun. Those singing seemed to be enjoying themselves greatly. He could not understand a word, as he spoke no human tongue, let alone one of this world. His brother had several spells that allowed him to understand and be understood, but there was neither time nor circumstance for him to teach Gulamendis. Had he not learned the spell of disguising his demons years before from his brother, Gulamendis would have had to ride through the forest the entire way north.

Leaving Crydee town behind, Gulamendis wondered how fared his brother, and then bleakly wondered if he still lived.

Laromendis pointed his wand at a demon climbing the wall and unleashed a bolt of energy that struck the creature in the face. Clawing at its eyes, the demon fell over backward, having lost its purchase on the stone wall. The wand had been given to him by a magician named Sufalendel, for which Laromendis was eternally grateful, for at the moment his more subtle illusion magic was next to useless.

He stood on the northernmost wall of Tarendamar, shoulder to shoulder with soldiers, priests, and magicians, attempting to repulse the fourth attack this day, as the demons sought to swarm the defenses, gaining access into the last bastion of the Taredhel on Andcardia.

The great barrier had been erected in a massive circle around the city of Tarendamar, over a hundred miles in radius. Other defenses had been placed around the planet, huge traps designed to obliterate demons by the hundreds, death towers that spewed evil mystic fire at any moving body within a hundred yards, a network of tunnels under the mountains to the north of the city, and all had proven useless.

The demons had scourged the planet, leaving nothing living in their wake. Within a year of finding the portal to Andcardia, they had driven the widely scattered population of the world to Tarendamar, forcing the total abandonment of over four hundred other cities around the planet, and countless towns and farming villages. Entire forests had been defoliated, and lakes and seas now churned on silent shores, devoid of life. The demons left nothing alive behind them, feasting on any creature they found, no matter how small. Scouts had reported not even insects abided after the demons departed.

The only advantage the Taredhel possessed over the demons, besides their superior arts, was the demons' single-mindedness. They had elected to attack the barrier in one location, a canyon that funneled them into the defenders' strongest position— merely, it was assumed, because it was the shortest route from the portal to the city. Certainly, early in the war, they had attacked on many fronts. Now they came in a straight line from the gate to the city.

Laromendis glanced upward, out of habit. Had any fliers been overhead, warning would have been passed. He once again marveled at this powerful magic, a huge, invisible wall of energy, only hinted at when struck by a demon's magic or falling body. The spellcasters had originally erected a dome, but at huge cost, until it was discovered there was a height above which the demons apparently could not fly. The spell was adjusted and the dome lowered, gaining the defenders weeks, even months, before the magic that fueled the barrier was exhausted. Laromendis caught his breath and kept his thoughts to himself. Around him, grim-faced soldiers, magicians, and priests awaited the next assault, despite, to a man, sharing the same thought: this was pointless; eventually the city would fall. But the Conjurer wouldn't be the first to speak aloud those words, lest someone turn his ire upon Laromendis. Besides, while the city might fall, each hour here on the wall gave more of the Taredhel the opportunity to flee through the portal to Midkemia. Thinking of Home, Laromendis wished fervently he was now there, with his brother.

Then a voice shouted, "Here they come!"

Three times since before sunrise the demons had been beaten back, leaving thousands of rotting corpses littering the planes outside the wall. So high were the dead piled that the last assault ran up the bodies of their fallen brethren as if they were an earthen ramp, gaining them an additional twenty feet on the wall from which to launch their assault.

Laromendis held a dagger in his left hand, against magic not proving effective, and watched for a moment, catching his breath, as another wave of fliers approached, coming low and fast. These were the most dangerous and unpredictable of the Demon Legion, for it was unclear where they would strike next. Something had changed in the last two days, as the fliers—some of them, at least—were now able to pierce the barrier.

The hand-to-hand fighting was now the order of the day, and again the Taredhel had the upper hand. Despite each demon being physically the match of any two elven warriors, the elves employed magic arts unparalleled. Not only were magic-users able to cast spells that would wither demons in their tracks, or stun and confuse them, many of the weapons used had been enchanted to cause far more damage than would be expected. Swords would cause flaming wounds or festering agony, arrows would stun with mystic shock, and high above, green flames of death rained down on the attackers from death towers constructed over the last month. The demons would eventually take this position, but they paid an unimaginable price in doing so.

The fliers dove. In the previous onslaughts they had hit the top of the wall, trying to create a breach in the defenses, so the crawlers—as Laromendis thought of them, those demons that could scamper up a wall of stone like spiders—could gain access to the top of the defenses, make their way to the gates, and open them. One time before, they had purposefully overshot the wall to land in the open bailey between the defenses and the outer city, and mount an assault on the gate's defenders. The few who had survived the transit through the barrier had been quickly dispatched by "flying" companies, squads of the best soldiers ready to rush to any position needed.

The death towers began to spit their evil green energy at the approaching fliers, and Laromendis watched in fascination. Necromancy was an art so dark no magic-user admitted to an interest, yet here was something so anti-life it must have been the art of necromancy that had conjured it into existence. Even if no necromancer lived, the forbidden volumes and tomes must have been taken from the vaults of the Regent's library. No sane being could imagine these hideous engines of death, let alone design one. Could those who designed the towers do so and remain untouched by madness?

The huge black towers had been erected along the wall, each topped with a crystal of some material so black it seemed to drink in the light. Nothing reflected off the surface of those crystals. Each pulsed with wicked energies that unleashed a bolt of green light, which flew forward, toward the fliers. The green pulse didn't even need to strike those creatures, merely coming close to them, and their lives were sucked out of them. Silver-white lights, like tiny bolts of lightning, flew from their bodies into those passing green bolts, and the fliers stiffened in midair, falling in rigor to their death below. Those farthest from the death bolts kept coming, to be received with death by any elf on the walls of the city.

The fighting was the bloodiest of the war so far. Every effort was being made to hold the monsters outside the city walls as long as possible. The translocation portal in the center of the city was being employed to transport the Seven Stars, and every magician who could be spared from that task was on the walls, lending their skills and arts to the city's defense.

A scampering demon came up the wall so quickly Laromendis was almost taken unaware. He flicked his right hand and the bolt of energy from his wand missed the creature entirely. But it was enough to distract the creature and he sliced at its neck with his dagger. The creature's neck was like a tree trunk, and he barely cut into it, but it was enough pain to distract it from its task of climbing the walls and it lost its purchase, falling backward onto another climbing demon. Laromendis wondered if others noticed what he did; the fliers were now breaching the energy barrier at an alarming rate.

"We can't keep this up much longer," he said to no one in particular.

A veteran soldier next to him grunted, which he took to be agreement. The warrior was too busy cutting off the head of a flier who had gotten past the death tower defenses to speak. He was ignoring a serious gash in his left shoulder, which Laromendis was certain would cause him to faint from blood loss if he didn't get the wound tended to quickly.

"Get that shoulder dressed!" he shouted. "I'll hold them!"

He conjured up an illusion, one of those he had prepared against this sort of contingency. A creature appeared in the air above him, a regal wrathbird, seventeen feet of wingspread and all anger and muscle. Talons that could cut a man in half and a beak that could snap through armor were suddenly confronting the remaining demons on the wall. The illusion was so real that they hesitated, which was all Laromendis wished for. He aimed his wand at the closest and sent a death bolt to strike it full in the face. It fell clawing its own eyes out in agony before it died.

The conjuration was so lifelike, defenders nearby fell away, uncertain of where the danger came from. The creature was one of the most feared predators on the planets ruled by the Clan of the Seven Stars, and the illusion was so vivid, they could smell the carrion stench from its breath, feel the wind off its wings, and see the vivid ruby highlights on its black feathers. The beak of the creature was dripping in blood and the eyes were alight with rage and hatred. The illusion would remain for at least another minute before it would begin to waver and start dissipating.

Laromendis cast his wand down again and another demon fell. Archers were now targeting those on the wall, while the heavy engines poured rocks and hot oil, boiling water, and flaming refuse upon those at the base of the wall. The corpses already piled high ignited and the foul smoke that spiraled upward choked defenders and attackers as well.

The attack faltered, and then the retreat began. Coughing from the rising smoke, the Conjurer moved to where a bucket of water waited, picked it up, and drank from it. He had no idea his throat could be this parched. He ignored the bitter metallic flavor of the water, thinking it wise to not contemplate what made it taste so. Catching his breath, Laromendis looked out over the battlefield and saw something new: a half-dozen larger demons stood equally spaced out along the battle line, directing other demons. He was no expert, but he had read every report he could contrive to sneak a peek at, and this was the first time he could recall anything that looked like organization from the Legion. Usually they just came unexpectedly, a flood of creatures that flew, crawled, ran, and hopped at defenders in waves. Most of them had no weapons, just teeth and claws, but a few carried swords of some alien metal or wore rudimentary armor.

But these looked like field commanders, wearing armor of a finer make, and they had other demons at their side, each holding a banner of some fashion. The battlefield was too smoky, the light failing, and the standards too distant for him to make out any devices or patterns on them.

He looked around and wondered if he was the only one to notice. Nowhere did he see any sign of any soldier, officer, or footman, Regent's Guard or City Watch, moving to carry word to the Regent Lord's command. Nor were there any magicians or priests making their way down the long stone steps to the bailey below. Most were catching their breath, drinking water, or tending to the wounded. A few sat, back against the wall, legs outstretched, in exhaustion. All were waiting for the next onslaught.

Laromendis looked around again, and finally decided to take matters into his own hands. The officer detailed to get him to the wall and find him his place in the defenses was nowhere to be seen. Either his duties had caused him to move or he was dead. Either way, Laromendis had no one to tell him not to go. He decided his time on the wall was over.

Making his way down the long stone steps to the outer bailey, he saw a cluster of officers gathered around a figure Laromendis knew well: Lord General Mantranos, second in command only to the Regent Lord in the army, and a critical force in the Regent's Meet. He was white-haired and battle-scarred, but still as keen a military mind as the People had ever known. Years of fighting the Demon Legion had brought his skills in the field to near perfection. He had never been able to defeat them; no commander of the Taredhel had ever won a victory, but he had repulsed them, slowed them down, and cost them more blood than any elven commander before him.

Knowing better than to try to speak directly to the Lord General, the Conjurer studied the group around him. A half-dozen senior commanders were looking down at a hastily drawn map of the northern defenses, now covered with marks in chalk.

Behind them, ready to carry commands to any position along the defensive front were a half-dozen junior officers. Seeing he was being ignored, Laromendis used his arts to shift his appearance to that of a messenger, covered in blood spatter and nursing an injured arm. He made his way up to stand next to a junior officer and said, "Sir!"

The young commander turned and saw what the Conjurer wished him to see, and said, "Report!"

"From the wall, sir. I'm to tell you the Legion has officers!"

The Lord General couldn't avoid overhearing the report. He turned his attention to Laromendis and said, "What? Repeat that!"

"Sir," said Laromendis, trying his best to sound near fainting from his wounds. "There are a half-dozen demon officers taking the field, with standard-bearers beside them. They're rallying the demons for another assault."

"Who told you to report this?" demanded the Lord General.

Feigning weakness and disorientation, Laromendis said, "Why . . . it was an officer . . . my lord . . ." He waved vaguely toward the outer wall. "Up there."

To one of his younger officers, the general said, "Go see what the truth is." To Laromendis he said, "Go have your wounds seen to; you're of no use to us as you are. If you're not fit for duty, go to the portal and leave with the others."

Laromendis bowed as best he could, then moved away. As soon as he was out of sight, he dropped his illusion and hurried toward the translocation portal. As far as the Conjurer was concerned, he had the permission of the military commander of all Andcardia to leave for Home, and he wasn't going to debate the finer points of this with anyone.

He reached the translocation portal and saw something truly awe-inspiring. A massive tree, oak-like in form but bearing much larger leaves of a shimmering golden color, was being carried by magic, floating yards above the earth as it was guided by ropes tied to *godos*, the massive oxen-like creatures native to this world. Slowly, it was being pulled through the translocation portal while a stream of refugees moved alongside. The Conjurer got in line with those waiting to go through and watched as the last two of the Seven Stars were conjured into the air and tied to the teams of *godos*. Within an hour the trees would be safely back on their native soil, after millennia away, and at that moment, Andcardia would be a memory.

For at that moment, the Regent Lord would order those remaining on the wall to flee to the portal. Those who reached it before the demons would find refuge, and those who arrived too late would die on this world. Two priests watched as the Conjurer and others around him stepped forward to pass through the portal. Laromendis knew they would give their lives, for it would be their responsibility to destroy the translocation device, the clever machine that housed the magic that let this portal exist. Without it, the demons would have to find their own way to Midkemia.

Until this battle, the demons had been clever enough to find and hold gates to each world they attacked, but this was different. Or at least the Regent Lord and every Taredhel hoped so, especially Laromendis. For there was only one gate to Midkemia, and despite its massive size, it was just as easy to destroy as the others. Break the machine, and the gate collapsed. Without the machine, the destination would be unknowable. Or that was the theory.

Stepping through the portal, Laromendis found himself confronted with a sight to make him falter. When last he had stood on this hill, a pastoral valley was all that lay before him. Now, a city was rising up, and from the look of things, in rapid fashion.

At least the outer walls, thought the magic-user, as he moved down the road to the newly erected walls. The walls would encircle the entirety of the city within a week or so, he judged. Few buildings were erected; mostly wood huts and canvas tents were providing shelter, but as night fell here, he saw a veritable tapestry of campfires. He had no idea how many of his people had come through this gate, but it must be in the tens of thousands. Watch fires along the upper ridges showed other encampments, and he was certain the commanders here would have already sent out groups, families even, to secure and then occupy the villages he had discovered on his last journey through this region. There was easily room for fifty thousand Taredhel in this valley and in the meadows above.

Without a twinge of guilt for having deserted his post, the Conjurer counted himself lucky to be alive. Moreover, he was without oversight, for while someone here might recognize him, he was fairly certain no one in authority would take a minute to question his presence. They were otherwise occupied and apparently very busy.

He looked around. "Now," he whispered to himself. "Which way did Gulamendis go?"

Gulamendis rode quietly along the banks of the river. He had reached the River Boundary earlier in the day and went looking for a ford to cross over. But when he found one, he discovered a discomfort, an inability to cross over into the Elven Forest, and decided to look for another way across.

Now, hours later, he was at the third likely crossing point and still he couldn't bring himself to cross. He stopped and dismounted. Perhaps there was a geas or some other conjuration that prevented him from riding his demon steed into this ancient and sacred forest. He dismissed the mount with a wave of his hand and waited.

He listened. The breeze in the branches sang to him as no other place he had visited, yet there was something odd in the sound, something he didn't quite understand. This land was native to his race, yet he felt alien here, as if he was out of rhythm with this place.

He sighed and sat down on the bank, to ponder his next act. He looked at the bank of the river, less than one hundred yards away, and the water running swiftly over the shallow rocks. It would be effortless to simply stand and walk into the water, making his way to the other side. In his mind he could see himself doing this without any difficulty.

Yet when he tried to step into the water, he could not.

He closed his eyes and used his skills to see if there were wards or a geas in place. There was something, but it wasn't magic as he understood it. This was something more akin to a feeling, as if he had heard an old, familiar melody, but couldn't quite remember it days later. There was a haunting quality to it that disturbed him as much as it called to him.

From behind he heard a voice ask, "Having trouble crossing?"

The accent was odd, but he understood the words as he quickly came to his feet, his hand going to the hilt of his belt. Gulamendis stood looking down at an elf who was a few inches shorter than he was. "Yes," he said slowly. "I am having trouble crossing."

The elf tilted his head to one side, as if trying to judge something by the manner of Gulamendis's speech. Like all of his race, he was patient, so he said nothing for a long minute, then said, "Nothing of you is familiar, yet you are kin; that I can plainly see. Who are you and from where do you hail?"

"I am Gulamendis, of a modest but ancient line, recently a citizen in the city of Tarendamar."

"Star Home," said the elf. "I have never heard of such a place. Tell me, where is it?"

"On another world, if you can imagine such."

The elf shrugged. "I have met those from other worlds, so I can imagine such. But I have never met any of our kin from another world, save those Eldar who returned to us from Kelewan—"

"Eldar?" asked Gulamendis. "Others of the Eldar are here?"

The elf nodded. He was dressed in green leather, from tunic to boots, and across his back carried a finely crafted longbow. "Yes. Are you of the Eldar?"

"Once," said Gulamendis, "my people were, though we now call ourselves the Taredhel."

"The People of the Stars," said the elf. He smiled. "I like that. Come, you may enter Elvandar and we bid you welcome. I presume you wish to speak with the Queen?"

"Yes," said Gulamendis as he walked into the water, now completely able to do so. "I thought a geas or wards prevented my entrance."

"More," said the elf. "The very woods of Elvandar do not permit anyone to enter without welcome, unless powerful magic is used. Only once in memory have invaders reached the heart of our lands, and they were magicians of great power."

Suddenly two other elves appeared from out of the trees, and Gulamendis halted. The first to speak to him said, "I am Cristasia, and these are my companions Lorathan and Gorandis. We've been watching you for a while, wondering what the problem was."

The one called Gorandis said, "Are all your people as tall as you?"

Gulamendis noticed he was a good six inches taller than the

tallest of the three, Cristasia, and he nodded. "I am of average height. Some are taller, but not many."

The elves exchanged glances, and then Gorandis said, "Well, we are three days from the Queen's court, so we should be off." To Cristasia and Lorathan he said, "Continue the patrol and I will guide him."

They nodded and seemed to melt back into the trees as Gorandis started to run up a trail. Gulamendis hesitated then started to run after the elf. He quickly caught up and said, "Do you not have mounts?"

"We do, sometimes," answered the forest elf. "We seldom use them unless the journey is long. Three days is hardly worth the bother."

"I'm not used to running," said Gulamendis, realizing that he was going to be pressed to keep up with this woodland elf.

They wended their way through the woods, moving rapidly along what appeared to be narrow game trails. Twice Gulamendis faltered and once he fell, and Gorandis said, "You have no woodcraft, do you?"

"No," admitted the elf. "I am city-born and my time in the wild has been unpleasant."

The wood elf laughed. "A city elf! I have never heard of such. Even those who came from across the sea lived on farms or small villages.

"Well, there is something new every day, as they say." He turned and started running again. "We were wondering if you were trying to be noticed, the way you trudged along the riverbank."

"You saw me?"

"We've been watching you for nearly the entire day," he replied.

Gulamendis felt nothing so much as annoyance that this rustic was mocking him. Even more irritating was that he was certainly correct; he had no wood skills and had no desire to gain any.

Sandreena awoke instantly; she had her mace in her right hand and gripping her helmet in her left as she started to rise. She was already on her feet with her helmet in place before she was completely aware of what had awakened her. She had crawled out the tiny window of the room she had been given by Enos and made her way as quietly as possible to bed down next to her horse. From her perspective, there was little to choose between the run-in shed and the room. Both had dirt floors, evidence of recent use as a privy, straw to sleep on, and a plethora of bugs with whom to share the straw.

Besides, her horse was well trained and would alert her to any approaching danger, which is what had just occurred. The slight snorting sounds and pawing of the ground would probably not alert anyone nearby, but to Sandreena it was as vivid a warning as any alarm bell in a watchtower. Someone was approaching the little inn in stealthy fashion, and it was almost certain they planned nothing good for the one guest in residence.

As was her habit when outside, she slept in her armor. It was hardly the most restful way to sleep, but she had grown accustomed to it over the years. Moving as lightly as she could, shield high on her left arm, mace in her right, she kept her faceplate up, giving herself the most area of visibility before encountering the enemy.

As she suspected, two figures garbed in black were skulking through the open garden behind the house, heading toward the window that would have been her room. She didn't hesitate, assuming it would only be instants after she saw them that they would see her. She flipped down her visor and charged.

Three steps from her first target, they saw her looming up out of the gloom and before he could turn to meet her, the first assassin was down from a savage blow to his head. Sandreena doubted he would rise to trouble her again. The other assailant had wheeled around, following her movement, so as she turned, he was already lunging at her with a long sword. She caught the sword's point on her shield, expertly turning it so that the blade slid along, letting the motion carry the man in black toward her. She punched him as hard in the face as she could with her right hand, still clutching her mace, and the force drove the man backward. Blood flowed down his face from his shattered nose, and he was blinded for a moment. Sandreena swept downward with her mace, catching his heel, causing him to trip backward. He slammed his head against the ground and for a moment was stunned.

She calmly kicked him hard in the side of the head, and he went limp. She really didn't care if the kick killed him—though she thought he was tougher than that—but she would like to question one of these Black Caps.

Enos and his family had been reticent to the point where she had threatened to leave them there, to answer for the death of the man she had killed. That had terrified them even more than the possibility of being accused of helping her had.

She really didn't feel sorry for putting them through all that—they had no way of knowing she couldn't leave them abandoned because of both temple practice and personal ethics—they were rude and annoying people. She suspected that even under the best of circumstances they'd be cold and rude to strangers.

She quickly checked, and the first man was dead. The second was unconscious and likely to stay that way for a while. She dragged off the body and hid it under old straw on the other side of the run-in shed. These two might have friends.

She knelt to examine the unconscious man and saw his breathing was shallow and fast. She had done more damage than intended. She might not have meant to kill him with the kick to the head, but those things were difficult to control in the heat of the moment; she might have two bodies to bury come first light.

As she began to rise, she sensed someone behind her, and as she spun to defend herself, a blow struck her on the side of the head, glancing down to crack hard into her shoulder. The force of the blow drove her to her knees and only her armor prevented her from suffering a broken shoulder or worse. But the glancing strike to her helmet had caused her just enough disorientation that she was open to another blow from behind. Her last thoughts were, *There are two of them!* before she collapsed into a dazed semiconsciousness.

There was a hot flash of pain, and then her side went numb, and another pain somewhere else, but she wasn't sure where, then came darkness.

After three days of running, Gulamendis was now certain that
if he never had to set foot in woodlands again, he would be content. He would return to the new city, to Home, gladly and never
set foot beyond its walls should he be permitted. Whatever sense
of wonder and magic he had first encountered was now gone, replaced by fatigued legs and sore feet. He kept up with his rustic
cousin by pure act of will, and a tiny bit of magic he used when
training demons—it dulled the pain.

His companion had been less than talkative. At night when
they camped, the young elf—he had given his age as less than
fifty years—had been content to sit by a fire, chewing on dried
fruit and meat, and replied to Gulamendis's questions with
short, vague answers. The Demon Master didn't know if Gorandis was especially adept at avoiding conversation or stupid. The
second night, there was almost no conversation, and Gulamendis
quickly fell into an exhausted sleep.

Throughout the following day they moved quickly and
Gulamendis grew used to the grueling pace. He grudgingly
conceded his distant kin possessed skills he had disdained until
he attempted to duplicate them. Rustic they might be, but they
were superb woodsmen, and, no doubt, hunters. Toward twilight
he could feel the change around him.

It was something in the very air of this forest, he felt. That
tug of emotions so alien yet so proper he first felt upon reaching
this world, Home, that feeling grew stronger with every passing minute, as if they were nearing the source of that wonderful
sense of place.

Then he entered the clearing and saw Elvandar.

Across the open meadow he could see a huge city of trees rising upward. Gigantic boles, dwarfing any oaks imagined, stood
together. They were linked by gracefully arching bridges of
branches, flat across the tops, on which elves could be seen crossing from bole to bole.

Gulamendis looked up and saw the trunks rise until they
were lost in a sea of leaves and branches, foliage of deep green,
made almost blue-black in the evening gloom, but still somehow

alight with a soft glow of their own. Here and there Gulamendis could glimpse a tree with golden, silver, or even white foliage, sparkling with pale glimmers. A soft glow permeated the entire area, and Gulamendis dropped to his knees, wetness flowing down his cheeks as tears came unbidden. "I had no idea," he whispered.

Gorandis stopped and turned to look at his companion. Whatever emotions played across the Taredhel's face, it kept the Eledhel runner from chiding him. This was a moment of deep, personal feeling.

"The stars," whispered Gulamendis. "You have so many."

"Stars?" asked Gorandis.

He pointed. "The trees. We call those . . . we have seven of them, brought with us from this world ages ago. They are the Seven Stars. We are the Clan of the Seven Stars."

Gorandis cocked his head to one side, as if trying to remember something. Then he said, "This is how Elvandar has always been."

What greeted the Demon Master was a thicket of massive trees, so many he couldn't tell how far back into the deep forest they ran. He counted and there were a score within sight, and another behind. Moreover, he saw colors of leaves he had never seen before. The Seven Stars numbered four trees of copper bronze leaves, two of a vivid yellow, and one of silver. But here he saw blue leaves, deep green, red, orange, silver, and gold. And all were brilliant with lights that made the shimmering glow of the Seven Stars pale in comparison.

Pulling himself to his feet, the Demon Master said, "There are so many."

Gorandis shrugged. "I don't know how many, but there are a lot of them. We've had babies and needed room, so the Spell-weavers have planted saplings, and the Master of the Green has urged them to grow quickly." He motioned for Gulamendis to follow. "Come, see for yourself."

Gulamendis towered over most of the elves he passed, being nearly seven feet in height. His clothes marked him as alien even if his look hadn't. Nowhere did he see the vivid red color of hair to match his own or his brother's. He saw dark red-brown, and many blond elves, but most had brown or dark brown hair, and their brows were less arched, and their features less finely drawn. To his eye, these were a plain people of unappealing aspect.

The rustic elf took him up a stairway carved out of the living wood of a massive tree, and along branches so wide their backs had been flattened to make boulevards. Upward they climbed, and deeper into the forest they traveled, until at last they reached a massive platform.

Then the Demon Master got an even bigger shock than when first seeing the heart of Elvandar.

Sitting around the edge of the platform were the assembled council of elves, the Spellweavers, the Eldar, and others, but the center was dominated by two thrones. The woman who sat in the highest of the two was regal in her bearing, though by Gulamendis's standards her clothing was simple, lacking any of the delicate needlework and gems he took for granted among the Taredhel's ladies. She wore a circlet of gold upon her brow, and her features were lovely, if soft by his people's standards.

But it was the being sitting next to her that shocked the Demon Master. He sat on a slightly lower throne, but that he was her consort was undoubted. They held hands without thought, as couples long-together do. But he was so much more. For even wearing a simple russet-color tunic and leggings, without armor and arms, he was a warrior born, projecting power like no other being the Demon Master had encountered. In his bones and to the heart of his being he knew this creature: a Valheru.

"Welcome," said the Queen. "We would know your name and from whence you come."

Softly, without taking his eyes off of the man next to the queen, he said, "I am Gulamendis, My Lady. I am a Demon Master of the Clan of the Seven Stars. I come seeking the . . ." He stopped and looked around, feeling both drawn by these people and repulsed by them. There was something profoundly familiar about them, yet there was so much that he didn't understand. Finally, he said, "I seek help."

"How may we aid you?" asked the Elf Queen, but she glanced at her companion.

Taking a breath, Gulamendis said, "Our lore tells us we came from this place, in the days of madness, when the gods fought in the heavens above." His eyes locked with those of the Queen's companion. "We fled from this place, across a bridge to the stars, and we abided."

A robed elf stood and said, "As did my people, Gulamendis. We were Lorekeepers, Eldar, and abided for centuries on another world before returning here."

"Cousin," said Gulamendis. "We were once Eldar, according to our lore. We took the name Clan of the Seven Stars and call ourselves Taredhel."

The man sitting next to the Queen spoke. "You departed before the war's end."

Gulamendis nodded, fearful of speaking to the Valheru. Creatures of legend, they were the ultimate masters of the People, and to find one here was terrifying.

"I am Tomas, Warleader of Elvandar," said the man, standing, and when he approached, Gulamendis could see there was something different in his manner. "I wear the mantle of one lost ages past, and I bear his memories, but I am more. I will tell you that tale at length, some other time, but for now this you must hear from me: you are a free people. That was said in the time of the Chaos Wars, and as it was true then, so it is true now. Abide and rest, and share with us your story, Gulamendis of the Taredhel, for you have found friends if you would have us so."

Despite being nearly half a head taller than Tomas, Gulamendis felt small in his presence. He didn't fully understand the meaning of his words, but found them reassuring. If this was, indeed, a Valheru, he claimed no dominion over these people, or the Taredhel.

Then a strange odor registered on the Demon Master's senses. He had smelled its like while passing through the human town. It was a weed they burned and inhaled. He glanced at the throne and realized that standing in the shadow behind it was a small figure. An old dwarf with nearly white hair stepped out of the shadows, fixing Gulamendis with a skeptical look and drew a long puff off his pipe.

The dwarf said, "About time you showed up, lad. We carried word of you here nearly a month back, and I was growing tired of waiting for you to get here."

Tomas smiled and the Queen laughed, her green eyes merry, but the Demon Master was unsettled. They knew he was coming? How? Three weeks ago he was in a cage, as his brother bargained for his life.

Gulamendis hid his confusion and nodded. He couldn't bring himself to smile at a dwarf. He turned to the Elf Queen and said, "My lady, I am bereft of wits and in need of rest and food. If we could speak tomorrow, I will give a better account of myself."

"That is fine," said Queen Aglaranna. She motioned for Gorandis and said, "Take him to rest and eat and we shall meet again tomorrow." To Gulamendis she said, "Rest and be well, for we have ample time to discuss so many things."

The Demon Master nodded, bowed, and allowed himself to be led away by his woodland guide. He wished what the Queen had said was true, for that would mean a clean escape from Andcardia and the way between the worlds closed off for good and all. But in the pit of his stomach he feared it would not be true, and that in quickly diminishing days, a danger of horrific proportion was coming to this idyllic place.

# CHAPTER 12

## SURVIVAL

All she knew was pain.

Something vague urged Sandreena to do something, but she couldn't grasp what that might be. She could barely breathe, and muted pain would suddenly rise up to cut through her like a hot blade. In the distance, someone groaned.

A pain behind her eyes roused her, and she thought she felt hands behind her head, lifting it. They were strong but gentle. Water touched her lips.

Thirsty. Her throat was parched and her eyes felt as if sand had been packed behind the lids. She tried to open them, but found the effort more than she could manage. A voice softly said, "Ah, I think you'll live."

Again a firm but gentle hand lifted her head as water touched her lips. She drank deeply, and then the pain returned.

A groan escaped her lips as she again tried to open her eyes, and at last managed. Her vision swam and images went in and out of focus as she tried to see what the light and dark shapes before her were.

"Slowly," said a soft, male voice.

Sandreena sipped as more water was put to her lips. It tasted metallic and she realized it was the flavor of dried blood, and from the sourness of her expression, most likely her own. She tried to move, and then the pain hit her.

She almost wept from it. There was no part of her that didn't hurt, and worse than anything she could remember—and she had endured her fair share of wounds. She blinked, and felt a wet cloth across her face, gently wiping around her eyes.

Shapes and images began to resolve themselves and she saw she was in a dimly lit cave. The single flame, a floating wick of some fashion in a bowl of oil, gave yellowish highlights to an otherwise grey and black environment. She still could not make out the features of the figure hovering over her, for he had the single flame behind him.

Almost whispering, he said, "Maybe you'll live."

"What happened?" she tried to say, but the words were little more than a sigh.

"I'll pretend I understand you," he said, moving to where he had a cloth on the floor of the cave, next to the flame. She could see him, though the vision in her left eye was blurry. Closing it made it easier to see.

He looked ancient, yet there was an old ironwood quality to his touch that told her despite his age this man was still strong. His features were craggy, a sharp nose and deep-set eyes, under a heavy brow, a jutting jaw covered in a grey beard. There was nothing appealing about this old man, yet she could imagine when he was young he might have had a certain presence. Some women found that more appealing than a handsome face.

His hands worked quickly as he spoke. "Someone wanted you very dead." He paused as he considered what to add to the bowl of water he had on the cloth before him. "You were stabbed several times, stripped naked, then thrown off the cliffs. They tossed some clothing after you."

Sandreena could barely move. Her body was heavily bandaged, with what felt like lumpy cloth rags. She reeked of something alien, and she barely had the strength to speak. "Who . . . are you?"

"Me?" asked the old man, smiling. "I keep to myself. The people around here don't like strangers."

"So I . . . discovered," she said, letting her head fall back and her eyes close. "I . . ."

"You need to rest," he said. "I fished you out three days ago. Didn't know if you'd make it." With a chuckle, he said, "You are a mess, girl."

As she felt herself drift off, she whispered, "You're not the first to say that."

Time passed as an alternating series of dreamless sleep and short periods of consciousness. Sandreena knew she had spoken to the man at least once, perhaps more often, but couldn't remember anything said. She finally awoke with a clear head, though it still throbbed as she tried to sit up. She was under a pile of skins, seal or otter, or some other creatures' pelts, on a pile of what could best be called filthy rags. For a pillow, her blood-stained tabard had been rolled up and put under her head. She realized she was nude, save for a mass of rags that served as bandages. She was hardly worried about modesty; besides, most of her was covered by the bandages. She ached terribly and did a quick inventory. She had at least a dozen cuts, several of them deep. She lifted one bandage on her leg, tied around and knotted, and saw a puckered purplish wound roughly sewn together. From the pain in her back she knew she had a deep cut there, and when she coughed, the pain almost caused her to pass out again.

She took a deep breath and it hurt. But rather than the raw, stabbing pain of a fresh wound, the pains she endured were the dull, constant ache of wounds healing. Not for the first time she wished she had had the gift for the majestic healing spells some of her and other orders could offer from truly blessed priests and monks. She could hurry healing along, if the wounds weren't too bad, but she needed focus and strength, two commodities she lacked at the moment.

She was alone. She struggled to sit up even more, and putting a fur behind her back, to cushion her against the cave wall, was an exhausting task, but she managed. She was tired of lying on her back. And she wanted questions answered.

She dozed off, and when she opened her eyes again, the old man was sitting beside the fire, boiling water. He glanced over and grinned. "Crab!" he said with enthusiasm. "I thought you might be ready for something beside broth."

She saw he had fashioned an interesting cook pot, using hard, tanned hides stretched over a wooden frame, making a large, shallow bowl. She had seen its like before, and had been surprised it didn't go up in flames when put over the fire, but she had seen that as long as there was enough water in the container, and if the fire didn't reach the wood itself, the water would steam and eventually boil, but the hides would only scorch, not burn.

Weakly, she asked, "Where did you get crab?"

He pointed out the cave mouth. "There's a pool, at the base of the rocks, and when the tide is high, they swim in. Some good fish, too, when the tide is out, but I have to catch them by hand—it's harder. With the crabs"—he made a dipping motion with his hand—"you just scoop them up from behind, and. they can't pinch." He reached into a sack and plucked out a large one, dropping it in the steaming water. With a shrug, he said, "No butter," then he started laughing as if this were a very funny joke. As thankful as Sandreena was to this man for her life, it was obvious he was a little mad.

"How did you find me?" she asked, her voice raspy.

Hearing her tone, he stopped overseeing the boiling water and scuttled to her side, and took up a water skin. "I left this here for you, but you didn't find it." He held up the water skin and she drank eagerly. The water was bitter with minerals and badly tanned leather flavors, but it quenched her thirst eventually.

He sat back, looking at the makeshift boiling pot for a moment, then said, "I was looking for crabs and found you on the rocks. Almost dead. I carried you back here."

She narrowed her eyes slightly. He didn't look strong enough to carry her, but she had learned early in life that appearances could be misleading. "The last thing I remember was killing an assassin, maybe two, and then someone coming up behind me." She fell silent a moment, then said, "I got overconfident."

The old man laughed, a harsh, barking sound. "That's why I have no confidence at all! I'm a mouse! I hide in cracks and crevices, behind the walls, under the floor!"

"You've survived," observed Sandreena as the old man used two sticks to pull the crabs out of the boiling water. He put one on another poorly tanned skin, perhaps a rabbit or hare, and picked up a rock. He smashed the crab's shell repeatedly, until she could easily get at the steaming meat inside. He carried the makeshift platter to her, and put it on her lap.

"Yes, I've survived," he said, with a note of bitterness in his voice. "I've survived," he repeated.

"Who are you?" she asked.

"Who am I?" he responded. He sat back as if considering a difficult question. "Those in the village call me the hermit, when they even admit I'm around." He looked around, as if somehow he could see through the cave's walls and was considering the larger surroundings outside. "I came from over the mountains, a long time ago."

"How long?"

"A long time," he said as if that were ample explanation.

"Do you have a name?"

Again he looked as if he had to think about this. Finally he said, "I did, I'm certain, but it's been so long since anyone's used it, I can't rightly remember what it might be."

She shifted her weight and felt the pain in her side. "Ribs?"

"I think they kicked you for a while," he said. "Ruthia"—

he invoked the name of the Goddess of Luck—"must have been watching over you."

She laughed and instantly regretted it. It hurt everywhere.

"No, you should be dead," insisted the old man, nodding vigorously. "Six deep wounds, any of which should have killed you, and none did. Lots of other cuts, but none so bad, but together they could have bled you to death. I think they knocked you out, stripped you naked, then cut you up a bit—I guess they were upset with you."

"Well, I killed one of them, probably another as well."

"Yes," he said, nodding as if in agreement. "That would make them upset. After they took your armor and your weapons, they threw you over the cliff—they must have thought you already dead.

"You should have died on the rocks, but the tide was in and you landed in the only deep pool near the village." Again he nodded vigorously. "Ruthia!"

"I'll make an offering in her shrine, first opportunity." She wasn't jesting, as she took devotion very seriously, though her order and Ruthia's saw the world in very different lights; hers always trying to balance things, theirs accepting chaos and imbalance as inevitable.

"That would be good," agreed the hermit. "The water was very cold, and that seemed to staunch the bleeding, and you were only there a short while, else you would have drowned before you washed up on the rocks. I found you and carried you here." He reached over and held up what appeared to be another bunch of skins and furs. "Look, I made you this."

Not entirely sure what it was he was offering, she said, "Thank you."

"You can wear this when you feel better."

This struck her: she was more than two weeks' travel by horse from the nearest Temple and even if there was a Keshian authority nearby, which there wasn't, they would have no interest in a girl wrapped in skins claiming to be a Knight-Adamant of the Order of the Shield of the Weak. On foot she was a month away from help, if she got strong enough to walk, and without weapons or coin, her chances of reaching the Temple down in Ithra were close to none.

She lay back and sighed, then started to nibble at the crab. It was surprisingly good, if a little salty.

"What?" he asked, hearing her sigh.

"I guess I'm going to have to find those who did this to me."

He looked at her as if she were the mad one. "Why?"

"They have my weapons, and armor, and a very good horse. I want them back."

He laughed, a short, barking sound, then stopped, then laughed again, full-throated and deep. After a minute of laughter, she heard him say, "Ah, don't say I never warned you: you're asking a lot of Ruthia after all she's already done for you."

"Perhaps," answered Sandreena. "But when I'm done with that bunch, they'll be the ones praying for mercy." She ate more crab and the hermit fell silent.

Days passed, and finally Sandreena returned to an awareness of time. She had no idea how long she had lingered in the cave, but knew it was at least three weeks, perhaps a month. She would sport a nasty assortment of scars, for the hermit had sewn her up with some sort of fiber, perhaps stripped from seaweed or a plant close by. She'd been tended by all manner of healers, from the finest magic-using priests in the temples to village medicine women with their poultices and teas. She found it oddly amusing that she was recovering from the worst collection of injuries in her life, perhaps more than all her previous fights and mishaps combined, with the help of the most primitive ministrations ever. The only thing worse would have been to crawl off into a cave and lick her wounds like a dog.

As she began picking out her stitches with a fish bone—the ones she could reach—she reminded herself she needed to thank this hermit, as well as her Goddess—and perhaps the hermit was correct, she needed to include Ruthia as well—for her life. That she was still alive was proof that some benevolent force was looking out for her.

By the time the hermit returned, she had removed all the

stitches she could reach and, without words, she held out the fish bone and motioned to her naked back. He nodded and sat down and quickly had those stitches out. She could feel a little blood and tenderness, but at last she could move without the constant tugging.

She pulled on the rough hide dress he had made for her and said, "There, that's better."

"I was going to wait a little longer; some of those wounds were deep," said the hermit.

"One thing I know is wounds, and another is my own body," Sandreena said. "I've healed enough so those stitches would only start being a problem if we waited much longer to cut them out." She indicated the cave with her hand. "You don't have a lot of chirurgeon's tools here."

He found that very funny and laughed deeply. "I did once." Then he stopped. He tilted his head as if listening for something. "Did I?"

Whatever had happened to this man, long enough ago, it was lost in even his own memory. A tragedy, illness, or a vengeful god, whatever the cause, most of his memory and mind were gone. Still, he had visited kindness on a stranger with no hope of recompense; she was without even the most fundamental possessions. He had found her as naked as the day she was born, and as helpless.

Still, she felt a debt. "Once I settle matters with those killers, is there anything I can do for you?"

He was silent a long time, then he said, "I would like a real pot." Then his eyes widened and he sat up. "No, a kettle!" He nodded vigorously. "Yes, a fine iron kettle!" His eyes grew even wider. "And a knife! A knife so I can clean my catch! Yes, that would be wonderful."

Sandreena felt her heart break. His desires were so modest and his gratitude for even the possibly empty promise of those minor treasures moved her. "That and more," she whispered.

There was silence in the cave while he built up the little fire he kept banked during the day; the sun was setting and soon it would be very dark. She lay back and closed her eyes. She needed rest. In a day, two at the most, she had to leave this cave, and then some men wearing black caps had to die.

Sandreena hefted the small tree branch. The makeshift club was her only weapon, and she felt even more underdressed in the otter skins she wore than she had when she was naked. Her bloody, shredded clothing and tabard were unwearable. Being undressed under a pile of rags was one thing, wearing them in place of armor was another.

She was as steady on her feet as she was going to be on her current diet of crabmeat, shellfish, and the occasional wild tuber the hermit cooked up. She could use a good meal, but knew she wouldn't have one until she put paid to these injuries and got whatever of her armor and clothing back. She hoped her horse was all right; it was one of the best mounts she had ever ridden. The mare was dependable, even-tempered, and meaner than a tavern rat when needed.

Sandreena approached the back of the tavern, the last place she had any memory of, and the logical starting point for finding her attackers. She hoped Enos and his family were all right, despite their being particularly unpleasant people.

There were no lights on and there should be. It was twilight and even if there were no guests, Ivet should be in the kitchen preparing a meal for her husband and sons. By the time she reached the window, she knew in her bones they were not all right.

She quickly made her way to the one door in the rear of the building, where she had seen the boys unloading the wagon. The door was open, and in the kitchen she found the first body. Ivet lay sprawled across the floor, her head at an awkward angle. Sandreena quickly judged someone had merely grabbed the woman from behind and broken her neck. Her clothing was intact, so she was spared being raped before she was killed. Sandreena knew that dead was dead, but at least it had been quick and relatively painless.

The Knight-Adamant had no idea why Ivet was killed, whether for offering a room and food to a traveler, or to ensure no one knew who had killed the wandering knight, or just for the pleasure of killing. She knew without looking that the father and boys would be dead in another part of the inn. She did wonder if some of those pathetic weapons she had seen them use might still be around.

She found the three swords and a badly scarred buckler shield stored in a food locker. The weapons were so inferior the murderers left them behind, even though they pillaged about every piece of food in the inn. She found a bag of millet. For one desperate moment the thought of even that simple grain caused her mouth to water in anticipation. She inspected the bag in the gloom and found the millet unroasted. She'd have to find a pan, start a fire, then boil water . . . She threw the bag aside and kept searching.

In another corner of the kitchen she found a platter with an apple on it. It was hardly fresh, but still edible and Sandreena devoured it in moments. She sighed. She would probably end up dead in the next few hours, but if she survived, she vowed she'd never get this hungry again.

She returned outside with the buckler and the best of the three swords—still duller than any sword not used on a practice pell should be—and went to the window where she found the men she killed. Given where she was standing in the run-in shed when she was struck from behind, she assumed that whoever saw her kill his companions must have been standing . . . There! She fixed the point in her mind and hurried over. Given the time between her short fight and being attacked herself, this was the most logical place for her assailants to be watching. She studied the landscape in the fading light. Soon the moons would be up and she'd be able to travel, but now she had to deduce where to go next.

She patiently waited until the larger moon rose, quickly followed by the middle moon. The small moon wouldn't rise for another few hours, so while it wasn't what was known as Three Moons Bright, there would be enough illumination for her to find her way. She studied the foothills behind the inn, sweeping up into the mountains to the east, looking for obvious trails or paths. As the moons rose over the mountains, the landscape below them remained shrouded in shadows. Then, after nearly an hour standing there, she saw it. A cleft between two small hills and a gentle rise into what appeared to be a notch in the mountains. Had there been fog, or rain, or even heavy mist, she would not have seen it, even in the daylight.

She began a steady trot toward that notch, hoping she'd reach it before sunrise. At this moment, she could not gauge the distance, and her memory was suspect. Things she should easily remember were difficult for her to recall. She'd had the problem before, when she had taken a blow to the head, and she had no doubt that if one of those Black Caps hadn't kicked her in the head, she most certainly must have struck it on the rocks in her fall. Either way, she vowed, those murderous bastards had much to answer for. She hefted her poor sword and knew that she'd still have gone after them, even if that tree-branch club had been her only weapon.

The sun had been up for nearly two hours when she found the trail. Six or seven horses, one most certainly her own. She lacked any expertise in the wilds, though she had spent enough time traveling the countryside she could read basic trail signs, and she knew she was on the right path. She continued on, having to stop to rest far more often than she liked. Her injuries and lack of good food had weakened her more than she cared to admit to herself, and she knew any dreams of walking into a camp of five or six thugs and quickly dispatching them were just that, dreams. She still had her temple magic, though she had never tried to invoke any when her concentration was this poor. Still, those spells and mantras had been drilled into her countless times by the teaching priests, monks, and sisters of her Order. And they were spells not to be ignored if her wrath was behind them, and it was. She might fail, but if she died, she'd take a lot of them . . . The soul crystal! She didn't have it. It was among the other items in her belt pouch. She cursed herself for a fool. She couldn't die fighting, at least not yet; her mission was incomplete and she had no means to get the information back to the Father-Bishop in Krondor.

Not for the first time in her life, Sandreena chided herself for being rash. As many times as she had dealt with thugs and robbers, she should have scouted around for someone holding the horses or standing lookout before she hit the two at the window. But she was certain they'd discover her missing and raise alarm . . . she realized that she had had no right choice in the matter. Either one would have brought a very difficult struggle. Still, she continued in her self-condemning mood, had she found and taken out those who eventually ambushed her, at least she would have known there were two more coming from the house and been ready.

With a sigh, she let go of this second-guessing. Regret was a trap and it crippled, she reminded herself.

She was another hour up the trail when she heard the voices. Before she understood why, the hair on her arms and neck stood up and a chill puckered her skin in gooseflesh. Rather than the common camp noises she expected, the muffled speech, the sound of horses tied to a picket, perhaps laughing or the sound of weapons being cleaned, there was a rhythmic chanting. She didn't recognize the language, but there was something in the sound that set her teeth on edge. This was no natural language of Kesh or the Kingdom. She spoke a fair number of them and recognized a lot more, and this had nothing of those tongues. She wasn't sure it was even human speech.

She saw the path she was following led into a cleft between two low rocks, and assumed a small valley or plateau was on the other side. She quickly picked the left side to climb and scampered up. She judged that if there were sentries just beyond the gap, she didn't want to run into another ambush. Still, she found it odd there were no lookouts atop the rocks, for it was the logical place to put them.

She reached the top and looked down on a scene of horror. There were no sentries or lookouts, for no sane man or woman would knowingly approach this place.

A man in a dark orange robe trimmed in black, a magician of some fashion, by the look of him, stood erect, holding a huge black wooden staff over his head. The staff was topped by some kind of crystal globe, which pulsed with an evil purple light. Just looking at it made Sandreena's eyes sting.

She swallowed her own bile back down, fighting hard not to retch at what greeted her. Over toward another pathway leading up into the mountains stood what looked to be a band of fighters. They were dressed in a variety of clothing, but all had the look of hard-bitten, experienced warriors. Sandreena judged them likely to be well-paid mercenaries and ex-soldiers, from many different lands, not fanatics. Many of them looked away from the carnage before them, and some who looked were pale and obviously shaken by what was taking place.

Around a large flat stone altar, a half-dozen priests and priestesses were kneeling, their robes thrown back so their chests and backs were bare. Behind them stood others likewise dressed, their backs stripped raw from flails. These were lying heavily on the backs of those kneeling before some ritual offering of blood and pain, but to whom?

In the middle of the stone was a pile of bodies. At least a dozen men and women, and one small arm that Sandreena was certain belonged to one of Enos's two boys. Now she realized that had she searched the inn, she would have found them missing, not dead in their sleeping room, as she assumed. The raiders must have startled Ivet, whom they killed to keep from raising an alarm. They then must have seized the husband and sons, tying and gagging them. Another half-dozen villagers were obviously dragged away as well, from the body count.

Atop the pile the last victim lay struggling, his arms and legs held in place by a set of ropes, each held fast by more monks or priests or whatever those murderous dogs were. Sandreena quietly spat to keep her stomach from turning. She had seen many things to make a soldier weep, but nothing like this.

The magician finished his incantation and a thing appeared in the air above the victim. The man cried out in abject terror as a black form materialized out of nowhere, a thing of long, spiderlike limbs, a hawk's razor-sharp beak, and huge bat wings. It hovered above the shrieking man for a moment, then dove to land with a heavy thud on his stomach.

Throwing back its head, the demon howled, a sound that set Sandreena's teeth on edge, and she saw several of the mercenaries draw a step farther away, while others winced at the cry. The demon cocked its head as it looked at the screaming man upon whom it sat, looking for an instant like some bird of prey from a nightmare, pulled back one of the very long, spindly arms, and, with stunning speed, drove it into the man's chest. The sound was one Sandreena was all too familiar with: the ripping of flesh and cracking of bones, and the man's screams were cut off as his body convulsed in pain and his lungs were ripped asunder. Before the man's life fled, he was forced to endure a moment when the creature ripped out his heart and began devouring it.

Sandreena had seen many horrific things in her life, from the degradation and abuses she suffered as a child in a brothel to the blood of battle. She had witnessed men dying in their own excrement, put out of their misery by their friends and thanking them for it; children murdered and entire villages slaughtered for the meager goods they harbored; but nothing in her life hit her as being so basically evil as what she was watching now.

Now the suppliants all bowed before the conjured creature and the chanting renewed its urgency. The creature flew to land upon the upraised staff of the magician who staggered slightly under its weight. *It must be heavier than it looks,* thought Sandreena. *But it can fly . . . ?*

Magic, she thought, counting herself a fool. And this thing hailed from some nether region where the natural laws were different. Still, it looked as if the magician was struggling.

Then he fell. And with a shriek of rage, the conjured creature vanished, leaving behind a foul, oily smoke, the stench of which reached Sandreena in her perch. The wail that went up from the assembled suppliants was that of a mother who lost her child.

The magician began to rise, but the worshippers leaped at him with bare hands outstretched like claws, or wheeling their flails, and he went down beneath the onslaught. Before Sandreena's eyes they literally tore the man apart. Sandreena took a long, slow breath, and wished she understood what it was she saw.

From their expressions, the fighting men who stood apart

also were shocked. Many of them had weapons half-drawn, as if expecting to be attacked in turn. Sandreena then noticed a fact that had eluded her during the chaos of the last few minutes. These men wore an assortment of head coverings—tied bandannas, scarves, flop hats, foragers' caps, kepis, cocked hats, and berets—but all of them were black. These were the Black Caps the villagers had spoken of, the men Father-Bishop Creegan had alerted her might be in the air. Whatever else they might be, they certainly were more than simple pirates and smugglers.

She sat back, scooting down below the top of the rock, so as not to be seen. Why would a band of cutthroats come to this isolated mountain valley? Why would they be in league with a bunch of demonic cultists? And what was that bloody ritual she had just witnessed?

She knew she had to find her way back to Krondor, but she also knew that there would be questions. The Father-Bishop would ask her questions for hours, and at this moment, she would answer most of them, "I don't know." But someone in the Temple would be able to give some insight into what this was she had observed, which meant she needed to push aside her revulsion and continue watching. Taking a breath, she rose up again.

A quick count put the total at thirty fighting men and two dozen cultists. The mangled corpses, including the dead magician, were left on the ground. From the way everyone was moving, this was not their camp. She slid along the top of the rock and tried to stay deep in shadows. The moons overhead were making it easy enough for anyone to see her, if they were vigilant. Then again, she considered, they thought her dead and anyone else a terrified villager. And they had been gathered around several fires, so their vision would be weaker.

The cultists all hitched up their robes, ignoring the bloody shreds of flesh on their backs and shoulders. Sandreena wondered if they had some magic to prevent festering. Else many of them would be ill within two days. Maybe they just didn't care.

Cults were anathema to the organized temples. On the level of faith, they almost always were predicated on bad doctrine or some half-baked heretical theory. On the level of getting along with the neighbors, they created distrust and fear. Sandreena, as a Knight-Adamant, wasn't always recognized as a temple functionary, and even when she was identified as a member of a religious martial order, it wasn't always the first thing on other people's minds that she could use magic.

Priests and priestesses in the temples in big cities were one thing. Town priests and monks and priors also were viewed as part of the fabric of the society. But in the smaller villages in out-of-the-way places, anyone practicing any kind of magic was to be feared.

She vowed that if the Father-Bishop didn't forbid her, she'd personally inform the Temple of Lims-Kragma in Krondor of what was taking place here. No one had less patience with evil death magic than the followers of the Goddess of Death; they were content that everyone eventually would come to their Mistress. They didn't see any need to hurry anyone along. And most death magic, or necromancy, perverted and twisted the soul energy, leaving the dying body a further insult to the Goddess, as that soul couldn't find the Goddess's Hall, to be judged and reborn. Sandreena had no doubt a full company of the Drawers of the Web, that Temple's martial order, would be quickly dispatched to come down here and clean up this mess.

Still, she considered, she had her own duty to her own temple first. As she anticipated, the fighters began trudging up the hill, speaking softly among themselves, and they kept a discreet distance between themselves and the cultists. They were heading up the draw to the east of the temple where the carnage had occurred. She waited until she was looking at the back of the last cultists, then slipped down to follow.

Gripping her poor sword and shield much tighter than necessary, she started trailing more than fifty killers.

Sandreena was getting cramps in her legs. Abuse, fatigue, lack of food and water, all were taking their toll, as was a considerable amount of tension. She found what she sought, the Black Caps camp. There were another dozen people there, ten who seemed prisoners, two guards. The prisoners did the menial work, from what she could see—tending the fires; cooking meals; cleaning clothing, weapons, and tack. Everyone at the camp was subdued, and if news of the fate of the magician had reached the prisoners, they apparently had no joy in it.

Sandreena found her horse tied to a picket at the rear of the camp. The camp had the look of one that had been established for a while: wooden lean-tos built up to shacks and even one good-size cabin. The four fighters who entered there looked to be the leaders of the mercenaries, as Sandreena thought of them. That might be a good thing, as mercenaries often knew when to quit; fanatic cultists never did.

She considered the possibility of getting to her horse and riding out of here. Unless every single person in the camp was a sound sleeper, she had almost no chance at all. She wished she knew where her belt pouch had ended up. If any of the cut-throats who had ambushed and tried to kill her had found the Soul Gem, they might have kept it under the mistaken impression it was a precious stone. It had the look of a moonstone or milk opal, depending on the light, but if any magic-user examined it, they would quickly come to understand it was holy magic, and probably destroy it.

What to do? She was torn between the need to report back the location of this camp and the desire to learn as much as possible. Moreover, she was hardly equipped to travel, and needed to replace her missing arms and armor. She might be able to pick off a sentry and take what she needed.

She waited as the camp quieted down. It was, however, a restless quiet. Those she thought of as the cultists were outright sullen, sitting in small clumps as far away from the others as they could. Those prisoners who carried food and drink to them positively cringed when spoken to, and the fighters kept a respectful distance. Sandreena had no idea what lay at the heart of this difference, but it was clear neither side considered this a happy circumstance.

Sandreena weighed her options. She decided to wait for the camp to settle in for the night. Whatever else, the smell of cooking food was causing her stomach to knot.

If nothing else, she'd try to steal something to eat before she turned and fled. Getting information back was paramount, but she could hardly achieve that goal if she died from exhaustion and hunger. Letting out a long sigh of resignation, she put her chin on her forearm and tried to get comfortable atop the rocks.

Hours passed, but as the large moon was setting and the small moon was rising, the last of the captive servants bedded down for the night. There was light coming from the door of what she thought of as the leader's hut. She had identified one fighter, a black-bearded thug who sported lots of rings and gold chains around his neck, as the likely leader of the mercenaries. He and two others had retired to that hut after eating.

Sandreena carefully made her way down the rocks and through the camp. The cultists all were bedded down in rude leather-and-wood shelters; the evening's slaughter seemed to have exhausted them. The fighters were scattered through a dozen small huts and lean-tos. Reaching the side of the big hut, Sandreena listened.

"Remember that inn in Roldem?" said a voice.

"Which inn? There's a lot of them in Roldem," came the answer.

"You know the one. Where we were playing *lin-lan* and you got into that fight with that Royal Navy sailor over him trying to take back part of his bet when no one was looking?" said the first voice.

"Ya, that one. What about it?" said the second voice.

"They had this lamb pie, with peas and carrots and those little onions, you know those?"

"Ya, I know those onions."

"Well, they had this pie, you see, and it had something else in it, some kind of spice or herb, I'm thinking. But it was really special."

"What about the pie?" asked the second voice, impatience rising in his voice.

"I love that pie, that's all."

A third voice said, "You can sit and talk all night about the greatest meal you've ever had, but it won't change anything." This voice was deep and raspy, and its tone left no doubt who was in charge. Sandreena would bet her life this was the leader. Ironically, she considered that she probably was betting her life being here. Still, a lack of boldness had never been her problem. And she knew she would never survive a journey back to the nearest outpost of her Order, in Ithra, without weapons and armor and a horse.

"Ya," said the first voice.

The man she now thought of as the leader said, "I don't see any other way. We need to just kill them all as fast as we can, before they can start using their magic, then grab what we can and get out of here."

The first voice said, "Ya."

But the second voice said, "Even with Purdon dead, the rest of them can still do some nasty things and, besides, there's Belasco. He doesn't seem the type to forget betrayal. And we did take his gold."

"We took his gold," said the leader, "to keep things around here under control. But what we didn't do was drink the demon's piss. We're not like them. We may be dogs, but we're our own dogs, not his."

The room fell quiet and then the leader said, "There's something else. One of the old boys in Pointer's Head told me a story, 'bout a bunch like us got sent here ten years or so ago. The reason the subject came up . . ."—there was a pause—"somebody was wearing a black headscarf in the tavern."

"Sorry," said the first voice.

"Anyway, he said that a bunch of fellows had sailed all the way around from the Sunsets, and that they provisioned here and someone said they were heading to the peaks."

"Peaks?" asked the first voice.

"This is the Peaks of the Quor, you idiot."

"Oh, I didn't know," came the plaintive response.

"How can you be camped in a place for four bloody months and not know what it's called?"

"Nobody told me!"

The leader said, "This thing with that girl, in the armor. She had temple knight written all over her."

"So?" asked the second voice.

"So, if one of the temples is sending one of their knights to investigate, things here are getting too twitchy." A moment of silence, and he continued. "I signed on to terrorize some locals, maybe deal with a constable or two from Ithra if they showed up. But I've seen those temple knights in a fight. A murder cult sprang up down in Kesh ten years ago, and they were hiding out at the docks in Hansulé. A bunch of those knights from Lims-Kragma showed up and it wasn't a pretty sight. Magic every-where, and they didn't take prisoners. Slaughtered every one of those cult fighters like they was lambs."

"Magic!" said the first voice, like it was a curse.

"The gold is good," said the second.

"But not if you're dead. Can't spend it here, and Lims-Kragma don't give you a better turn at the Wheel if you brought a little gold with you."

Silence followed for almost a full minute, then the second voice asked, "What do we do?"

"This morning, before they wake, I want you to quietly wake up Blakeny, Wallace, Garton, and that murderous little rat Allistair. The seven of us are just going to quickly and quietly go over and start killing. We hit them hard, fast, and they're all dead before they know it. Then we kill those villagers, grab what we can, and ride south. Then I don't know about you, but I'm on the first ship outbound, I don't care where. Maybe I'll head down to that other land, Novindus. Or the Sunsets.

"But something's coming here, something I want no part of, and the faster we get away from here, the better."

"What about our gold?" asked the second voice.

"Purdon was supposed to have it," replied the leader.

"The magician?" asked the first voice.

"Yes," said the leader. "So if no one's disturbed his kit since they murdered him for failing to bring in the right demon, it should all be there."

"How much?" asked the second voice.

"Does it matter?" asked the leader. "It's gold, it's whatever there is, and we take it. If any of the boys don't like it, they're free to stay and see who Belasco sends to replace Purdon. They can explain to the next bunch of those blood-drinking whores and pimps why the first batch is all lying around dead."

"Okay," said the second voice. "It's time."

"No," said the leader. "An hour before sunrise. That'll put us in the saddle as soon as the sun comes up, and we head south."

"How much longer is that?" asked the second voice.

Sandreena glanced at the rising small moon and knew the answer. She had an hour to figure out what to do next.

# CHAPTER 13

## CONCLAVE

Sandreena took a deep breath.

Sandreena had no love for anyone in this camp, but she had sympathy for the villagers being used as slaves. She struggled for a long time, deciding what her best course of action would be, but finally rejected all the choices that didn't involve trying to save the slaves. She slowly worked her way over to where they were sleeping, and gently nudged a young woman. The woman awoke suddenly and was about to shout, as Sandreena's hand clamped down over her mouth. "Shh," she whispered. "If you want to live, make no sound. Do you understand me?"

The young woman nodded her head up and down. "In a few minutes the guards are going to kill the cultists. Then they'll kill you and your friends. Help me wake them up quietly and flee silently. Do you understand?"

Again the woman nodded, and Sandreena let go of her. There were eleven other sleeping villagers, all of whom looked exhausted and underfed. They were normally listless, but their fear energized them. The young woman who was the first one Sandreena awoke said, "What do we do?"

"Go north," she said. "Find a safe place to hide for a day. Those cutthroats will ride east to Akrakon. Then south to Ithra. After they've gone, it should be safe for you to go home."

"Who are you?" asked a man standing behind the young woman.

"I'm a Knight-Adamant from the Temple of Dala in Krondor. If I can get out of here alive, I'm going to try to find help to come up here in case others like those Black Cap bastards return."

"Thank you," said one old woman, obviously frightened.

"Don't thank me yet. I haven't made it out of here alive, either." Looking at the young woman, she said, "Remember this: if I don't get out, someone has to go to Ithra. There's a Keshian garrison there and a shrine to Dala. Go to the shrine first and tell whoever's there that Sandreena of the Shield of the Weak spoke to you. Tell them what you've seen and heard, and then tell them there's someone behind all this named Belasco." She looked the young woman in the eye. "Can you remember that?"

The young woman nodded. "Sandreena," she said softly, looking at the Knight-Adamant, as if trying to burn her face in her memory. "Belasco is behind all this."

"Good. The monk at the shrine will talk to the garrison commander and maybe the Empire will send someone up here. If they don't, my Temple certainly will. Now go!" she hissed.

The prisoners needed no further prodding; they turned as one and began scrambling over the rocks to the north. Sandreena knew that if they could get a half-hour start, the fighters wouldn't bother to hunt them down. Glancing at the moon, she realized a half-hour was about all she had, too.

She hurried to where the horses were picketed. In their certainty that they had no threats up here in the hills, the Black Caps had gotten complacent to the point of sloppiness. She approached the horses slowly, for she didn't want nickering and stomping to alert those three murderers in the big hut or any light sleepers close by.

She reached the side of her own mount and saw the mare was unharmed. She patted it on the neck as she looked for any sign of her tack. It was in a heap nearby and Sandreena quickly tacked up her horse. She saw nothing that resembled her armor or arms, let alone the little pouch with the Soul Gem in it. Most likely her armor had been apportioned to some of the smaller men, one of the leaders had her mace and shield.

Regretting her inability to get more information than she had, she put all that behind her. She considered for a brief instant trying to muffle her horse's hooves, but there was nothing at hand that would easily lend itself to doing so, and she didn't have the time. Sandreena quietly led her horse away from the others a short distance and paused, waiting to see if the sound of hooves on the ground attracted notice. When no alarm was raised, she slowly moved through the heart of the sleeping camp, and a short way down the trail. Tying her horse to a bush, she hurried back up to the rock from which she first observed the camp.

The balance of the hour passed quickly and as she anticipated, the three murderers from the hut were quietly awakening their companions. No one appeared to notice the absence of the dozen prisoners—their attention seemed focused on the sleeping cultists.

Sandreena felt torn; her Order's very mandate would be to ride in and attempt to balance this conflict, which would almost certainly get her instantly killed. Yet it galled her to see cold-blooded murder, even if those being slaughtered were monsters such as these cultists. And she didn't relish the notion of the mercenaries riding off without penalty. Some of those men, perhaps even those in the hut she had overheard, those were the men who sliced her up and threw her into the sea as food for the crabs.

Without thinking about it too long, she picked up a rock and threw it hard at the foot of a sleeping cultist, where it jutted out of his lean-to, just as the fighters started to cross the clearing to where the cultists slept. It struck as she hoped, and in the dark, none of the fighters took note.

But the man whose foot she struck came away with an outcry, and before anyone could ascertain what happened, chaos erupted. The waking cultists saw a band of armed men moving toward them and reacted with the only weapons they possessed—their magic.

Green energies shot out and several of those with weapons screamed in pain, while the other fighters shouted in outrage and charged. Sandreena scampered down the rock face, not wishing or needing to see further carnage. She knew the thirty-odd swords would eventually dispose of the two dozen cultists, but a lot fewer of the fighters were going to ride safely away from this hellish place.

Sandreena rode down the trail at a nice canter, knowing those fighting for their lives behind her wouldn't hear a thing.

Sandreena worked her way up the rocks to the cave where the hermit had tended to her. She called out, "Hello! Are you here?" as she entered. It took some moments for her sight to adjust to the gloom after riding through the sunrise, and when she was inside, her eyes widened.

She carried a small kettle and an assortment of cooking items: a knife, ladle, several spoons, and two earthen bowls. She had raided the inn passing through town, knowing the previous owners had no use for any of the items. When there was no answer, she moved deeper into the cave.

The hermit sat back against the wall, his eyes closed. "Wake up, old man!" Sandreena said, for she had no time to tarry, but wanted to make good on her promise. The hermit didn't move.

She put down her burden and knelt next to him. She knew before she touched him the old man was dead. She quickly examined him and found no wounds. He simply had died during the night while he slept. There were no expressions of pain, no contortions of the body, so he must have never awakened.

Sighing, she reminded herself that sometimes people just

died. He was old and this was a harsh way to live and it was his time.

She said a quick silent prayer to her Goddess to see him on his way to Lims-Kragma's Hall, and then left the cave. She mounted her horse and turned it toward the south. With one last look around the forlorn seascape and rocky coasts, all greys and browns, black and white, she wondered if there was anyone in the world besides herself that would note the passing of that strange old man. She put aside that question, for her only goal now was to somehow get to Ithra alive and send her warning to the Temple in Krondor.

Pug of Sorcerer's Isle, perhaps the greatest practitioner of magic in the entirety of the world of Midkemia, waved his hand and created a barrier to protect himself and his companion from the blinding, choking smoke. He looked at an elf Spellweaver named Temar, and said, "This is the worst I've seen in a hundred years."

Temar nodded. "I've seen a few that match, but not many. It's a bad combination, Pug, drought and lightning."

Temar was from the elven community at Baranor. For ten years Pug and Miranda had visited the elven enclave in the remote mountain area of Kesh known as the Peaks of the Quor, attempting to understand those strange aliens and those they protected, the Sven'ga-ri, and the equally odd race known as the Quor, who protected them.

"It hasn't been especially dry until a week ago," said Temar. "But the undergrowth here is so thick that it was almost a certainty lightning would start something like this." He glanced around and pointed with his hand to the north. "We're getting an especially bad dry wind that's doing us double disservice; it's pushing the flames and drying out everything before them."

"Rain?" asked Pug.

The elf gave Pug a wry smile. "I'm good at weather magic, Pug, but not that good. There's not enough moisture in the air, nor is there any rain close enough for me to summon. I could attempt it, but I know the effort would be a waste."

A loud pop in the air alerted them to the arrival of Magnus.

The elf was unfazed by the sudden appearance of the human magician, but Pug was startled to see he was not alone. "Father," greeted the tall, white-haired magician.

"Who is this?" asked Pug.

"This is Amirantha, someone you need to speak with."

"This couldn't wait until I return?"

"I think not," answered Magnus.

Pug nodded. "We're concerned about this fire," he said, pointing to the raging flames on the next ridge. "It's not entirely likely that it will reach Baranor, but it might. Conditions here are not good." Turning to Amirantha, he said, "Sorry to be short on social pleasantries, but time is fleeting."

Temar also nodded a brief greeting. "It's going to be getting very hot here in the next hour, Pug."

Magnus asked, "Can you not turn the wind, blow it back on itself?"

"I can command the wind," answered the elf, "but not over so wide a front. And, like all things with fundamental elements, there is a price to pay."

"So rain is out of the question?" asked Amirantha, looking at the rapidly approaching inferno.

"There is no hope of rain," said Temar.

"Perhaps I can help," said Amirantha. "Please stand away from me."

Pug, Magnus, and Temar moved away, then farther as Amirantha motioned them to move a little more. When he judged them safely away, he held up his hand, closed his eyes, and incanted a spell. From his hand a brilliant white light, blinding even in this daylight, shot down to burn a line in the ground. In seconds it inscribed a circle around the Warlock. He looked at the circle on the ground, nodded in satisfaction, then stepped out of it, being careful not to step on the burned line as he took up position between himself and the others.

He began another spell, this one longer and more involved, and then something huge appeared in the circle. For lack of a better description, Pug saw it as a thing of water, a huge being in roughly man shape but clearly a fluid being. Surging waves within the form were masked by ripples across the surface of it, and bubbles and foam seemed to deck its shoulders like a mantle. It cried out in a language that sounded like the roar of rapids or the pounding of waves and rushed Amirantha. The Warlock stood motionless, and when the creature reached the boundary of the circle, it recoiled.

Amirantha said, "Summoned you I have, and my bidding you will do." The creature in the circle seemed disinclined to agree. Amirantha began another spell, and then the thing in the circle grew quiet. Amirantha pointed to the advancing flames and said one word, then the circle vanished.

The water creature grew. Pug and the others stepped back in amazement as it doubled in size in a few seconds. Amirantha turned his back and walked slowly to where they stood and said, "This should take care of the problem."

The water being continued to grow and soon was over twenty feet in height, then it sprang into the air. Like a bowshot, it was gone, arching high into the sky, and then suddenly it vanished. Rain fell.

There was not a cloud in the sky, yet rain poured down over the flames.

Amirantha said, "It's not enough to completely extinguish the fire, but it should cool things off enough so the flames won't reach this far." He glanced at Temar. "And perhaps it will give our friend here the time he needs for a more permanent solution?"

Temar nodded. "I can feel the weather change. In a half-day, there will be enough moisture in the air for me to call down rain. Thank you."

Amirantha nodded and smiled. Pug said, "What was that creature? I've never seen one like it before."

"It was a simple water elemental. A very minor demon. Nasty if you don't contain it, as it can quickly fill your lungs with water—my first encounter with one was painful." He glanced at the water still falling and said, "Water and fire are natural enemies among elementals. Once I got it to listen, pointing out the fire made it eager to go kill." He chuckled. "Elementals are not among the brightest of creatures."

"Will you have any problem controlling it?" asked Magnus, obviously curious.

"No," said Amirantha. "Actually, the elemental will give itself up to the fire; they sort of cancel one another in the demon realm, and once that creature runs out of water to rain down on the fire . . . Well, it saves me the trouble of banishing it back to the demon realm."

"It's a demon?" asked Pug.

"Not entirely, but close enough in some respects." He glanced around. "Interesting place. I don't believe I've ever been here before."

"You travel a lot?" asked Pug, finding something about this newcomer's manner wryly amusing.

"Quite a bit, many years ago. I have settled down a bit, recently." He looked around and said, "Given the time of day when we arrived at your very interesting island, and when we departed—after a fascinating discussion with your son—and the position of the sun now, I assume we are again many miles to the east of where I was a few minutes ago." He glanced at Pug and said, "Somewhere in Kesh." Then he glanced around and added, "Perhaps the Peaks of the Quor."

"I'm impressed," said Pug. "Seeing as you claim to have never been here before."

"I haven't," said Amirantha with a friendly smile. "But given the angle of the sun and the time of day, the fact we're standing on mountains, looking down at what can only be sea coast, there weren't a lot of other likely candidates. I may not have been here, but I have studied a map or two."

Pug glanced at his son. "My demon expert?" His son nodded. "Where did you find him?"

Magnus said, "Actually, Kaspar brought him to the island last night."

Amirantha smiled. "It was morning when we left Maharta."

"Maharta?" asked Pug.

"Currently close to my home." He glanced at the other two men and the elf and said, "If we're going to talk, may I suggest we retire someplace a bit less smoky?"

Pug glanced at Temar, who said, "Go. I can easily return to Baranor." Originally from Elvandar, Temar had elected to come to Baranor with others of his kind to revitalize the dying Sun Elves, a pocket of elven guardians who had been placed in the mountains ages ago by the Dragon Lords.

Duty-bound, they had remained even though the toll had been terrible. When discovered by Kaspar of Olasko and his men ten years before, the Sun Elves were barely able to defend themselves from a band of void creatures that had somehow reached Midkemia and taken up residency a few miles away from the elven enclave.

Now many of those, known as the Glamredhel, those rustic elves who had once lived north of the Teeth of the World mountains, had migrated to Baranor, swelling the population and revitalizing the community. Temar was originally from the Tsurani world of Kelewan, an Eldar Spellweaver who had come out of simple curiosity, liked what he found, and remained. He, as much as Pug and the other magicians, was fascinated by the mysterious Sven'ga-ri and their Quor protectors.

Speaking to the Quor was as frustrating an undertaking as Pug could imagine, for they appeared primitive, even simple at times, while at other times they made observations that hinted at a deep, perhaps even profound understanding of things beyond Pug's own considerable intellect. Over one hundred times Pug had come to speak with the Quor and the Sven'ga-ri, and each time he felt as if he had gained a tiny bit of insight, yet no whole picture emerged. He was convinced the Quor were not native to this world, but nothing they said indicated that. They spoke without regard for time, being content to live in the moment, and their only concerns for past and future revolved around protecting the Sven'ga-ri.

Those alien beings were most certainly not originally of this world, yet somehow they were connected to Midkemia in a vital, perhaps essential way. They didn't communicate in any fashion Pug understood, but rather filled the air around them—or the minds of those with whom they spoke—with music. Their music was unlike anything Pug had heard from the dozens of races he had encountered over the years; it was pure feelings distilled.

Pug wished to remain and study the Quor and Sven'ga-ri as originally planned, but it was clear his son thought the arrival of this stranger a more pressing matter. Besides, he had asked them to find him an expert on demons.

Pug said to Temar, "Farewell. I will return again, soon."

"You are always welcome," said the elf, who bowed slightly to the others, then turned and began descending toward the pathway that would lead him home.

Both Pug and Magnus reached out and took a grip on Amirantha's arms, and suddenly they were standing in Pug's study. Amirantha said, "I am now convinced that is the most wonderful thing a magician can achieve. To go where one wants by thought!"

Magnus and Pug exchanged glances. In their experience, no practiced magician was unaware of the ability to transport either via a Tsurani orb or through spells that take years to master. Even if he had never utilized the talent, he must have been exposed to it.

Pug moved behind his desk and motioned for Amirantha to take a seat opposite, while Magnus remained standing near the door. Pug said, "You are welcome here, Amirantha."

The man smiled, though it was clearly not a genuine sign of pleasure but a social concession. "I came with a friend, who I believe is being held hostage somewhere against my good behavior?"

Pug glanced at Magnus, who said, "Your friend is hardly being held hostage, but I didn't feel the need to drag both of you along to find my father. I brought you with me in case he was unable to return here. If you'd like, I'll send for Brandos."

"I'd like that very much, thank you."

Magnus left the room, leaving Pug and Amirantha alone. "Why don't you tell me why Kaspar thought it important to bring you here?"

Amirantha smiled and this time it was a genuinely amused smile. "And thereby betray his relationship to another authority besides the Maharaja to whom he's sworn fealty?"

"Hardly a betrayal," said Pug. "Kaspar's relationship to the Conclave of Shadows predates his taking service with the Maharaja. His service to his lord and to us is not in conflict. Our interest and the interests of the Kingdom of Muboya are never in conflict and occasionally overlap.

"Now, again, why did you come here?"

Amirantha paused, framing his response, then began recounting his experiences since the surprise summoning of a battle demon in a cave. Pug listened silently, asking no questions nor offering any comment. When Amirantha reached the part of the narrative where he met Kaspar and recounted his relationship with his two brothers, Pug stiffened in his seat and his eyes narrowed, but again he said nothing.

"So, we rode out at sunrise in a display of overland travel, but once we were out of the city, in a small woodland thicket, the General and his soldiers dismounted, we were told to dismount, and for a brief moment I was almost convinced that Brandos and I had been brought to this out-of-the-way place to be murdered.

"Of course," he quickly added, "that was merely my . . . suspicious nature. The General could have just as easily had us tossed into the dungeon in Maharta and been done with it.

"Your son appeared as if out of nowhere and we vanished. I assume the soldiers merely camp out until Kaspar returns, then they all ride back into the city in a few days and it looks like he went for a quick visit somewhere."

"Something like that," said Pug, his eyes fixed on Amirantha.

"Where is Kaspar, by the way?"

"If I know Kaspar, he's probably fishing off the north beach. He takes these little holidays when he can. If he returns to Maharta too quickly, people start asking questions. He'll guest with us for another three days, then head back."

Amirantha seemed amused by that, just as Magnus returned with Brandos, with Caleb trailing behind. Introductions were made, and the old fighter sat down in a chair in the corner, content to let his friend do the talking. Pug said, "I need to ask you about your brother."

"Which one?" asked Amirantha.

"Sidi," replied Pug.

"Ah, I take it then you've encountered him."

"Several times, never with a good outcome."

"Kaspar informs me he is dead. Is that true?"

"To an absolute certainty," replied Pug. He alone pieced together reports from Jommy Killaroo that he had seen a Tsurani great one singing a Kingdom tavern song as he walked toward the Dasati Black Mound, their magic beachhead on the world of Kelewan. That description matched up with Miranda's identifying the body inhabited by Varen, or Sidi, who could jump from body to body. Either he had been on Kelewan when the planet was destroyed, or stranded on the Dasati home world where Pug had no doubt he would eventually perish. Despite his not-inconsiderable power, Sidi would not have the time to adapt to that environment before death overtook him.

Amirantha sighed. "Good. He, like Belasco and myself, was a bastard, but he was a murderous one, and he slaughtered our mother for the sheer fun of it."

Brandos had heard the story before, but shook his head as he always did. Seeing the gesture, Pug gave the old fighter a quizzical look.

"Just, well, it's an interesting family."

Magnus was forced to chuckle and decided he liked the old fighter.

Amirantha looked slightly annoyed, but remained calm as he said, "I am not my brothers."

"Apparently," said Pug. "Had you been like Sidi, I doubt you'd have come looking for someone in authority to speak with.

"Now, as we know very little about the demon realm, what exactly do you wish us to know?"

Amirantha looked uncomfortable for the first time. "I've heard of your Academy at Stardock, Pug. No user of magic hasn't. I first became aware of it fifty years ago, or so.

"I even visited there when traveling in Great Kesh, some years after, and realized that my sort wouldn't be welcome. So

I noted with some amusement the self-congratulating smugness of a few magicians I spoke with in an inn in Shamata, then went about my business."

Pug nodded. He would have had a different reaction to the Warlock, but he knew the students and instructors around at that time were a conservative group of Keshians who would have made it clear that any summoner of demons was not a "proper" magician.

Amirantha continued. "I was hardly surprised, you understand, even if I was slightly disappointed. I do not know who trained you, if you were an apprentice or how such things were done on the Tsurani world—I did hear that is where you came into this Greater Path of Magic, as some call it. But I and my brothers, we were raised by a mad witch, and we learned our craft the hard way. I hear you have many volumes of lore in Stardock, tomes, books, scrolls, epistles, and even a fine collection of stone and clay tablets, all to the end of allowing magicians to learn from others who came before them.

"My brothers and I had none of that. And we were . . . influenced by a mother who had made a compact with dark powers, I am certain. The madness, if you will, seemed to dilute with each child. If you encountered Sidi, you must know he was insane before he was out of boyhood.

"Belasco is different, but his rages are uncontrollable, and he hates easily.

"I have had my . . . difficulties, and it would be reasonable to say have made a fair number of mistakes. I have learned, however, that to constantly be battling for no good cause, to be angry without reason, is harming no one but myself. In the end, I have endeavored to find my own little place in the world and live there contentedly."

"By tricking the gullible out of their gold?" asked Pug.

"Ah, that," said Amirantha. "My reputation precedes me."

"To be truthful, there are not a lot of demon masters alive. It's one of the problems we face."

"Problems?" asked the Warlock.

"More on that later. Continue telling us about this event that caused you to seek us out."

"Allow me to presume that while you are a master of many arcane arts, you know little of demons."

"A fair assumption for the moment," said Pug, "though I have encountered more than my share and have had to destroy them." He thought it best for the moment to forgo mentioning one almost killed him.

"I don't know what sort of child you were, Pug, but I liked to poke around in things. I'd sit over an anthill and prod it with a twig to see how the ants would react. My eldest brother liked to see things die, and my middle brother liked to hurt things. In my defense, I think my curiosities were the most harmless, except perhaps to the ants." He smiled, and seeing no reaction, continued. "We spent a great deal of time alone. Our mother had little use for us after we could be set aside, as she had her own interests.

"Looking back on my childhood, it's surprising any of us survived. My mother provided charms and potions, wards and minor enchantments for local villagers, who endured her proximity because they occasionally found her useful. We three boys were shown at a very early age our presence in that village wouldn't be tolerated. Each of us in turn was allowed to wander into the village, without our mother stopping Sidi, or either of them stopping Belasco, or any of them stopping me. Each of us in turn was beaten and chased from the village. I had the dogs set on me." He rolled up the sleeve on his left arm, showing old bite marks. "I've had this all my life. I was seven."

Magnus said, "Harsh."

"In a way, yes," said Amirantha. "But in another way I like to think I was tempered to endure a great many hardships. It's why I'm still able to sit here and speak with you, rather than having had my entrails spread around some cave by a demon years ago.

"My curiosity about poking in things led me to a cave a few miles from my mother's hut, and there I found ancient runes cut into the wall. Some primitive shaman, I think, because even at the age of ten I could feel the power in it. I had some lessons from my mother by then, minor cantrips and spells, things that would hardly amuse you, let alone impress, I'm certain; still I was something of a prodigy, or at least my mother said so. My brothers, as could be expected, hated me even more for having shown talent at an earlier age than they did.

"I was alone in this cave I mentioned, and suddenly something on the wall seemed to make sense to me. I don't know if there were ancient powers still abiding in the runes, or if some native ability I had seized on them, but I remember thinking there was something out there I could play with.

"I conjured Nalnar, and we had a very rough-and-tumble introduction. He's not malicious, at least not compared to his brethren, but like all manner of demons he can be unpredictable and combative. Fortunately, as demons go, he was also very young, and while he managed to singe my hair a little, I beat him into submission.

"We then spent a good month learning to speak with one another—the demon language has sounds almost impossible for a human to make, without magic, and at that time I had no magic to speak of. I would bring him here once or twice a week over two years, and learn what I could from him."

Pug and Magnus now looked thoroughly fascinated.

"When Sidi slaughtered our mother, Belasco and I went our separate ways. Our final parting was him accusing me of being complicit in our mother's death though I'm certain he knew that false; he just liked having other people to blame.

"I've encountered him a number of times over the years, and despite two civil conversations, most of the time he tries to kill me. I've been avoiding both my brothers for over a century now."

Both Magnus and Pug were unfazed by this revelation. Given how long Sidi had been a thorn in Pug's side, that his younger brother was also long-lived came as no surprise.

"After fleeing my brothers, I wandered and Nalnar, my little demon friend, was instrumental in keeping me alive. He's nimble and clever, and for nearly two years I had him stealing things for me, a pie from a window, a new pair of trousers from a wash-line, a coin from a beggar's bowl. And while I was alone a lot, I had him to talk to.

"I learned of the demon realm."

Pug said, "Stop now. I think from this point forward, there are things here I wish for others to hear." To Magnus he said, "See our guests are comfortable and let me know when—"

Amirantha sat bolt upright in his chair and said, "Demons!"

"What?" asked Magnus.

"Where?" asked Pug.

"Here, close." He stood, and his head turned as if he was listening for or trying to see something. Then he pointed to the north. "There. Not far. More than one."

"How do you know?" asked Caleb.

Flashing an angry expression, Amirantha said, "Trust me." To Pug he said, "They are powerful. We must go meet them, now."

"North?" asked Pug.

Then Magnus said, "Kaspar. He's fishing on the north beach."

"Take us there," said Pug.

Brandos said, "I should go. I'm the only sword you've got that knows how to fight demons."

Pug glanced around the room and said, "We all go."

Magnus reached out and Pug took one hand; Amirantha and Brandos understood and reached out, Caleb standing between them. When the circle was complete, Magnus incanted his spell and suddenly they were on the cliffs above the beach on the north shore of the island.

Kaspar of Olasko was giving a good account of himself as he confronted two red horrors. They had bat-like wings, which they were using to keep away from Kaspar's sword. It was clear the struggle had only been taking place for a few moments, as the two winged monsters were being effectively kept at bay.

Pug shouted to Amirantha, "Can you do anything?"

"I've never seen their like," answered the Warlock. "But I

have something that might help." He reached into his belt pouch and withdrew a stone, which he tossed at Kaspar's feet. "Run toward us!" he commanded.

Kaspar was no stranger to military obedience and recognized a command when it was issued. He swung hard, and as the two creatures withdrew, he turned and sprinted toward Pug and his companions.

The demons hesitated a moment, and then a pulse of energy erupted from the stone in a barely visible sphere, like a concussion from an explosion. The two creatures were hurled back, over the edge of the cliffs, and fell from view.

Kaspar reached them, and, almost out of breath, said, "That was timely."

Amirantha shouted, "They are not done!"

Pug nodded and waved the others back and took three purposeful steps toward the cliffs. The two red-winged horrors, looking nothing so much as smaller versions of the monster that attacked the Oracle, save these had curving horns, like those of bighorn rams, rose up from the edge of the cliff. Pug shot out his left hand and a wave of force slammed into the leftmost one, driving it back again, while from his right hand a withering lash of pale-silver energy sprang out and wrapped itself around the other demon. The creature howled in agony as the energy leeched life from its body.

Magnus came up behind his father and cast a bolt of blackness, which engulfed the demon on the left. It convulsed within the sphere and tried to howl, but seemed unable to utter a sound. Amirantha hurried up to stand behind them and said, "These are something like elementals. Air or fire creatures. They do not like the touch of land."

"How do they feel about water?" asked Magnus, and with a cast of his hand he launched the one he faced into a high arc over the beach below to slam into the water. With an eruption of green flame and hissing steam, the creature vanished.

Pug did the same with his, and in a moment all was quiet. "I should have recognized them," said Pug. "I faced such outside of Stardock, many years ago."

Kaspar said, "I was coming back up from the beach and just had cleared the top of the rocks when they appeared, out of the air." He said, "I almost left my sword in the room you set aside for me." He laughed. "I don't know how well I could have stood them off with a fishing pole." He carried a long surf pole, but it hardly looked equal to the task of being a cudgel.

Pug looked at Amirantha. The Warlock said, "This was no coincidence."

"I didn't think it was," said Pug. "Your brother?"

"I don't know," said the Warlock. "I used a stone I've prepared to repulse a demon, giving me time to run if I need it. I didn't engage them with magic, so I have no feel for it . . ." He closed his eyes as if trying to sense something and said, "No, I only feel the lingering presence of those two demons."

"How did you know they were there?" asked Magnus.

"The more I deal with demons," said the Warlock, "the easier it is to sense them and the farther away I can sense them. Time was I wouldn't know if there was a demon in the next room. Now I can feel them miles away. Comes from having dealt with them for over a hundred and twenty years."

Kaspar said, "Well, I'm glad you did. They were giving me hell to pay and, truth to tell, I'm not as quick on my feet as I once was."

Pug looked out over the water, growing dark as dusk approached. "So, who is sending these?"

Amirantha said, "I don't know, but whoever it was isn't very adept at the mastery of demons."

"Why do you say that?" asked Magnus.

"Those two are minor demons, little more than elementals of the air, really. Not intelligent, not powerful. Sending these to an island that's home to magicians as powerful as you two is like turning two attack dogs loose on an army." He looked around. "This is more to get your attention, I think, or to let you know someone knows you're here."

"Let's go back to the house," said Pug. "There's a bottle of wine we can share before supper and," he looked at Magnus, "before your mother gets home. Where is she?"

"Still at the Academy."

Pug shrugged. "She's there longer than I would have guessed." To the others he said, "If you don't mind, let's walk. The way is short, fresh air clears the head, and I've been jumping from place to place so much over the last few days I could use a small dose of the familiar."

No one objected, and they started to walk back to the house in the middle of the island.

# CHAPTER 14

## BARGAINS

Tomas looked over the forest.

Spreading out below him was the home he had known most of his life. From the royal couple's private balcony, the view was stunning. The great trees of Elvandar were laid out in a fashion that at first glance appeared chaotic but there was a pattern, and once the eye became accustomed to it, much was revealed. From here Tomas could see the great meadow, where children played as parents watched over them while they repaired bows, made arrows, loomed cloth, or prepared food for feasts. In the distance he could see the top of a hill where an ancient watch fire waited to be lit should trouble breach the outer forest. No such warning was needed for the inner forest, on this side of the river the humans called Boundary, for only powerful magic could allow the uninvited to enter the heart of Elvandar, and such an intrusion would be felt by all who lived within the glades.

As a boy in Crydee, he had imagined heroics and great feats as a warrior in service to the king, but fate decreed something far more than his boyish flights of fancy could conjure. He was the heir to the white-and-gold armor of the Valheru, and with that came the knowledge of a being dead long ages before he was born. He had seen a thousand things in memory he had not witnessed in life, yet they were as vivid to him as if he had lived them firsthand.

His companion at the time he found the armor stood at his side, regarding the vista silently with his friend. The dwarves and elves had long had a cool but civil relationship until Tomas had gained the armor of the long-dead Valheru, Ashen-Shugar. As a battle companion, Tomas had saved many dwarves during the war with the Tsurani, and as the avatar of a long-dead Dragon Lord, he had commanded nearly blind obedience in the elves. During the Riftwar, a bond between the elves of Elvandar and the dwarves of the Grey Towers and Stone Mountain had been forged that had led to a far more cordial relationship than before the war.

Dolgan had remained Tomas's friend for over a century, always a calm source of counsel with a very practical view of the world around him. Tomas welcomed the old dwarf's presence, though not the reason it had brought him. After delivering his warning to the Elf Queen, Alystan of Natal had departed, for he had many duties now delayed by carrying that warning, but Dolgan had decided to linger. It had been almost six years since he had visited with his friends in the north, and he felt the need.

He also knew Tomas nearly as well as the Queen did, or Tomas's boyhood friend Pug, and the King of the dwarves in the west knew his friend was as disturbed by the arrival of this alien elf as the Dwarf King had been. "It's something to ponder, isn't it, lad?" he finally said.

Tomas always smiled at being called "lad," by Dolgan. "That it is, Dolgan."

"I knew there was something afoot that day in the mines of Mac Mordain Cadal, when I found you eating fish with a dragon." The old dwarf laughed, and said, "That alone was a tale worth a hundred nights by the fire of boys and girls fetching me another ale so I'd finish it. But what came after, Tomas. The Tsurani and what changed in you and who you became." He gave an emphatic nod, and then said, "But it has all turned out for the best."

"Has it?" The tall, blond-haired, once-human warrior regarded his old friend with blue eyes filled with concern.

"You've done a fair bit beyond your pledge to protect your adopted home, my friend. You've raised a fine son in Calis, and you've given a wonderful woman all the love a man can give. That alone merits praise. But more, you've been a redoubt to your people. It's been pretty peaceful up here in Elvandar while the rest of the world has endured some pretty nasty times."

Tomas nodded. Elvandar was untouched when the Emerald Queen's army had ravaged the Kingdom.

"Well, I've given you plenty to ponder, and not near so much as our new friend," Dolgan said with a nod toward where Gulamendis was being housed. "He's a queer one, that's for certain, and if it weren't for the ears and all those elvish ways, I'd think he was a tall human, that's a fact."

Tomas smiled. He enjoyed his visits with Dolgan, as infrequent as they were becoming. The dwarf would probably live another hundred years, with luck and good care, but nothing was forever, and even the most robust of the long-lived race was mortal.

Lately, Tomas had been filled with a sense of foreboding, a feeling he could not shake that something was coming, something very powerful, and the world as he knew it would change as a result, and not for the better. That feeling had deepened with the arrival of the alien elf.

Looking at Dolgan, Tomas said, "So you're leaving then?"

"Aye, lad. I think I'll wander up to Stone Mountain and visit old Hathorn. He's a bit elderly now and doesn't get out much. Need to chat a bit with his son, Locklan, about this and that. Dwarves' business, you know."

Tomas nodded. "I understand. Would you like some company along the way?" Tomas didn't want to insult his friend by suggesting he needed bodyguards. After all, the dwarf had run all the way from the Grey Towers with only Alystan of Natal.

"No. It's a short run and I could use some time to think. Besides, it's been very peaceful these days, since you chased the Dark Brothers north. The goblins around these parts may be stupid, but they're not stupid enough to trouble me." He patted the legendary hammer at his side.

Tomas grinned. Dolgan had found the Hammer of Tholin, the sign of his kingship, in the same cavern the then-boy from Crydee had found the armor of white and gold.

The armor that gave him his power, that provided him with the link through time to a life not his own was safely stored in his quarters, next to the ceremonial gowns and jewelry worn by his wife. Yet he needed no armor for anyone to see the power in him. He was arguably the most dangerous being on this world, perhaps only rivaled by his boyhood friend Pug, whose magic made him almost a force of nature. But Tomas's great strength and Valheru magic didn't give him the ability to see the future.

"Then fare you well, my old friend," said Tomas.

"Fare you well, lad."

Just then Aglaranna appeared and Dolgan said, "Ah, lovely. Saves me the trouble of tracking you down to say good-bye, my lady."

"You are leaving, Dolgan?"

"Aye, off to visit kin in Stone Mountain, then home before my boy makes too big a mess of things."

"Then travel well and visit again soon, my friend," she said.

He bowed and departed.

Tomas stared out again over the forest below, and his wife regarded him for a moment. She knew his moods better than any being living, and she loved him with a depth of her heart she barely believed possible. She had loved her first husband, the last King of the Elves, but it had been a love of slow building, a comfortable affection that came from necessity, for it had been her fate since birth to rule at his side. But with Tomas, passions she had never imagined had sprung into her heart as soon as she had seen him as a man, no longer the boy she had first beheld, and he had looked at her with a man's eyes. Since then they had been as one, and she knew his heart and mind. She knew he was thoughtfully considering this new elf who had come among them.

And she knew he was troubled.

Aglaranna, Queen of the Elves and his wife for a century, came to stand behind him and put her arms around him, a gesture that never failed to give him comfort. "What troubles you, husband?" she asked softly.

He turned with a smile, gazing into the face he counted the most marvelous sight he had ever beheld. "Have I told you how beautiful you are?" he asked with a sheen of moisture in his eyes.

She couldn't help but smile. "Only every day, my lord."

He grimaced and said, "If it grows old . . ."

"No," she interrupted. "I'll endure you saying so if you must."

The banter was just what he needed and it caused him to relax. "I'm concerned," he said.

"I know. You are concerned over our guest."

Tomas nodded. "My memories of Ashen-Shugar are not complete. Many have come to me over the years, but still there are holes. Of all my memories of the Edhel, I have no recollection of any like this Gulamendis."

"He is very strange," agreed the Queen. "Even the Moredhel resemble us in so many ways. But this . . . elf, he is different."

"Dolgan said but for the ears, he is as different from us as a human would be."

Aglaranna laughed, a musical sound that always delighted Tomas. "My love, have you been with us so long you've forgotten you are human?"

He smiled and folded her into his arms, her head resting snugly under his chin. "I am what I am. Yes, I was born human, but that was lifetimes ago. Only Calis"—he mentioned their son—"understands what it is to live half in one world and half in another."

"I thank our ancestors he found Ellia and her sons."

Tomas said, "Yes. A family can save a soul." He was thinking of his own, and how he nearly succumbed to the madness of the Dragon Lords when he first wore the battle armor of white and gold. His wife and son had given him an anchor to hold him firm in the teeth of rages that came in battle or desires to dominate that were never entirely gone. His son likewise had a reason to live beyond mere survival: a foster family he had grown to love deeply.

Tomas was silent and, in the way of her people, Aglaranna was content to accept silence. After a few minutes of just enjoying one another's quiet touch, Tomas said, "You rule in Elvandar, my love, so all decisions are yours. Still, as Warleader, my duty is to be wary."

"I understand, and always welcome your counsel."

He smiled. "Not always."

She returned the smile. "Most of the time."

Acaila appeared at the edge of the royal couple's private chamber, seeking admission, and Tomas waved him over. The ancient elf was the leader of those who had returned to Elvandar from an enclave under the ice on the world of Kelewan. With the death of Tathar, the Queen's closest advisor and senior Spellweaver since the time of her father, Acaila had become the leader of the Queen's Council. He bowed and said, "Majesty, Lord Tomas."

The Queen asked, "This Gulamendis, what do you make of him?"

Acaila moved to a waiting chair as indicated by the Queen. Sitting on the wooden seat, two large U-shaped pieces of wood cleverly joined and padded with a down-stuffed cushion, the ancient elf indicated his gratitude at the privilege. "It is most difficult, my Queen," he began. "That he is of the Eldar, there can be no doubt. What he knows of our ancient lore is not much, but it is what I would expect from one who was not raised as a Lorekeeper or Spellweaver. To find him a master of demons, however . . ." He leaned to the right and put his right hand to his face, his index finger tapping on his bony cheek. His age was incalculable, and he was doubtless the oldest elf living. His hair was now as white as snow, but his blue eyes were still alight with curiosity. "What troubles me is less the matter of his . . . dark studies, for he would not be the first among the Eldar to find such practices fascinating. Rather it is his other . . . attitudes."

"What attitudes?" asked Tomas.

"He hides it well, but he feels superior to all here. He counts his 'star people' a superior expression of the Eldar tradition." The old man sat back a little and sighed. "He considers us primitives, rustics at best. Wood lore is as alien to him as it was to many of the Ocedhel, who came to us from across the sea."

"What else troubles you?"

"There are many secrets in this elf," said Acaila. "He is here for more than he says. I sense he desperately wishes aid for his people, and despises himself for feeling the need to ask for help."

Tomas was no stranger to feeling conflicted over difficult decisions, so he asked, "Is he torn because he feels we are inferior?"

"No, it is more than that. In talking of our lore and how it differs, he is an academic in many ways, like all the Eldar; he loves knowledge for its own sake. But it's how that knowledge is to be used that goes to the heart of his troubles." Sighing, the old elf said, "I do not know, but I suspect he has his own, personal agenda, and that is what we must uncover before we take all he says on trust."

Tomas and the Queen said nothing and waited.

Acaila said, "These elves, these Taredhel . . . they are unexpected."

Tomas merely nodded.

"You know our origins more intimately than anyone alive; can you have imagined the Eldar taking the path these Taredhel took?"

Tomas was quiet a long moment as he considered those memories he had inherited from the Dragon Lord, Ashen-Shugar. Finally, he said, with a slight sigh, "No, but remember the Valheru were arrogant beyond any other race's imagining. They hardly understood the obvious differences between those of you who served close at hand and those who labored in the field."

The old Eldar nodded agreement. "We were Lorekeepers and among the most trusted, those who were the Eldar. When my ancestors fled to the north of Kelewan, abandoned there by the Dragon Host, we assumed others would do as we did, abide and hope that someday we would be found, as we were.

"When we returned here, finding the division between Eledhel, Moredhel, and Glamredhel . . . even discovering the Ocedhel, all seemed logical, as if our basic nature was fashioned by circumstance, but these Taredhel . . ." The old elf shrugged. "They are strange." He fell silent.

A patient race, elves thought in terms of years where humans worried about days. "We have time to uncover these things," suggested Tomas.

"That is where I must disagree, Lord Tomas," said the leader of the Eldar. "There is an urgency in this Gulamendis, a sense of time being limited, that leads me to believe we shall see the heart of this matter sooner rather than later." He sighed. "What I don't know is if we will like what we see. I don't think we will."

"Are these Taredhel to be like the Moredhel, rather than like ourselves?" asked the Queen.

Acaila shook his head. "No, different from both, Your Majesty, different from we who were the Eldar." He looked out and waved his hand. "This is the place of seeds, where we sprang at the dawn of time, before the war in heaven and the freeing of the People." He used the original word, Edhel, that encompassed all the tribes of elves. "But like seeds, if you move them to different soil, the tree that grows will take on a different character. Some will grow strong and straight, others will be stunted and bent, while still others become something far different than what they were before." It was clear to Aglaranna and Tomas he was speaking of the Eledhel, Moredhel, and Taredhel. "Those who lived to the north, they have come to abide with us and some have moved on to Baranor. Others from across the sea have returned to us. Is it not reasonable to think that those who have lived centuries on other worlds would be any less strange to us than those who merely lived on another part of this world?"

Tomas nodded. To those who always lived in Elvandar, the

Glamredhel—those who lived to the north of the Teeth of the World—were barbaric, almost primitive, while the Ocedhel—those who lived across the ocean—were almost too human in their ways. "To live on other worlds for generations, yes, I can see how they would become alien to us."

"Yet at their hearts, they are us," said the old Eldar. "They have lore that is lost to us, as we have lore lost to them. For us to join with them in some fashion would benefit us both."

Tomas looked dubious. He knew much of what that lore contained, from his memories of the ancient Dragon Lord, Ashen-Shugar, and some of it deserved to remain lost. This caused him to consider something, and he asked, "Is he concerned over my presence?"

"Perhaps," said Acaila. "Gulamendis asked questions about you, but no more than I think any newcomer might. His fear and curiosity are balanced. No, there is something else he fears, more immediate than any concern about your Valheru nature accreting itself and trying to establish dominion over his people.

"In fact," said the old elf with a wry smile, "though he tries to hide it, he believes to a near certainty that you would fail. These people, I think, are arrogant to the point of thinking themselves supreme of all the races."

Aglaranna said, "That has never been our way."

"Not your way, Majesty, but it is the way of the Moredhel."

Tomas nodded and the Queen said, "I must admit that is so."

"But the Moredhel were menials, house slaves, those forced to build the abomination that was Sar-Sargoth"—he spoke of the monstrous city north of the Teeth of the World—"for their masters, and its twin, Sar-Isbandia, for their own glory, ages ago," said Acaila.

Tomas shook his head. "You lead me to think we have encountered a race of Eldar with the ambitions of the Moredhel."

"Not quite," said Acaila. "That would be simple, but these elves, these Star Elves, they've become something even more dangerous. From what he has said, Gulamendis is representative of these people. They are physically bigger, and I think have strength far in excess of our own." He smiled and nodded at Tomas. "Your own being the exception, my lord."

Tomas nodded, his expression indicating it was of no importance. Despite his majestic abilities, he was without vanity. He had endured too much and caused too much pain to others, coming into his power, to consider himself other than the luckiest of beings, having avoided succumbing to the ancient Valheru madness. Finding forgiveness from those he wronged had made him profoundly humble.

"More," said Acaila, "his magic is . . . dark."

"How so?" asked the Queen.

"I have not seen him employ any spellcraft, yet there is power in him. It's hidden well, but it is there. He asks questions. He is insightful, perceptive, and has a keen mind, perhaps as intelligent as any I've encountered, yet there is something about him that troubles me."

"Me, as well," said Tomas. "He brings danger."

Both the Queen and Acaila looked at the Warleader. Tomas said, "So far I don't see him as being a danger, but there's something he's hiding, something that will be a danger."

The Queen said, "He is strange." She paused, then added, "There is no sense of kinship when he is before me."

Acaila nodded. "These Taredhel have changed far more than any of our kin during their time out among the stars." He looked thoughtful. "Though he does seem almost enthralled by our great trees; he calls them 'the stars,' at times. When he is not with the Spellweavers he wanders the forest floor, touching the boles, almost as if he disbelieves they are real."

Aglaranna said, "We may be as strange and unexpected to him as he is to us. We think of ourselves as unchanged since the time of the Chaos Wars, but that is probably not true." She looked at her husband, knowing Tomas had memories of those days.

"You are a stronger people, more noble, more at one with the world around you. You have risen." He looked back out over the forest below. "These Taredhel have risen, too, but in a very different fashion."

"He talks of cities," said Acaila. "Great cities of stone and glass, with massive walls and sky-vaulting towers, elven cities."

Aglaranna said, "That sounds strange to my ear, elven cities."

"He hides things," said Acaila, "but makes a common error speaking of things he assumes we already know. Like geomancers—Spellweavers who work with rock, stone, and mud as our Spellweavers work with the living magic of our forest.

"Others who command fire, water, and air."

"Elementalists," said Tomas. "I remember." He looked out over the forests again. "When the Valheru were gripped by the madness of Drakin-Korin, and built their first city at Sar-Sargoth, they gave that magic to their chosen builders." He turned to see the Queen and Acaila looking at him intently. He smiled. "You don't think the Valheru dirtied their hands building that city, do you?" he asked wryly.

Acaila said, "Then what happened to those who built Sar-Isbandia?"

Tomas shrugged. "Those who remained here, who became the Moredhel, they lost those arts, apparently. Their magic-users have never been a strong presence, or a threat to us." Tomas paused, then said, "What this says to me is these Taredhel may be more of the Moredhel than Eledhel."

Aglaranna said, "We are all Edhel."

Acaila inclined his head in a gesture they both read to mean "I wish it were so."

Tomas spoke, "Yes, it would be a noble thing if all the tribes of the Edhel were as one." He looked at his wife. "For every Moredhel who finds his way here, who returns to us and forsakes the Dark Path, we have slain a dozen. It is in their nature to seek out power." He looked at Acaila. "And it appears the Taredhel have found that power."

Aglaranna said, "What do you propose, husband?"

"I think it is time for me to have a private discussion with our guest." He turned to Acaila and said, "Ask Gulamendis to meet with me at the entrance to the Holy Grove."

The old Eldar bowed slightly, then bowed deeper to the

Queen, and departed. After he was gone, Aglaranna said, "Why the Holy Grove, Tomas?"

"This Gulamendis seems to be struggling with something, that thing I see as bringing danger. I don't presume to know what it is, but I do know that there is no place on this world that can give any elf more strength to make difficult choices than the Holy Grove. Acaila says Gulamendis is almost consumed by wonder over these ancient trees."

She nodded. "I understand."

Tomas sighed deeply. "And I think I need to provide one more, additional prod."

She watched silently as her husband went into their quarters to don his white-and-gold armor.

Gulamendis followed the elf detailed to escort him to his meeting with Lord Tomas. He found her a fair example of the females of the Eledhel, though their women were too dainty for his taste. Most of the Taredhel women stood as tall as the Eledhel men and were more striking—then he considered it was mostly a matter of taste and that this female was attractive in a rough-hewn fashion.

They passed down a path in the woods that took them some distance from the heart of Elvandar, away from the majestic trees the Demon Master could not help but think of as "stars." When they reached a clearing, she halted and said, "Lord Tomas will meet with you shortly."

He said, "Thank you," and she left him alone.

At first glance, there was nothing remarkable about this clearing, but he did feel a faint, gentle flow of energy. It was nothing he could identify, yet it did feel familiar, as if he heard the echo of a song he couldn't quite remember. Since arriving at Elvandar, Gulamendis found himself feeling an unexpected conflict; his agenda was anything but simple, but it was straightforward: establish a relationship with these primitive elves and use them as a means to recruit allies against the Demon Legion. He had no doubt the demons eventually would follow the Taredhel to this world.

The blame heaped upon him and others who explored demon

lore was unfounded; it was by no arts of his or any other Tared-hel magic-user the demons reached the first outpost of the Clan of the Seven Stars, the colony on the world of Estandarin. And it certainly was no fault of any demon master the colonists had not destroyed the translocation portal before the demons reached the translocation hub in Shadin City on Dastin-Barin. From there they spread like a cancer, infecting four other Taredhel worlds.

At first the Taredhel were supremely confident they could crush the attackers, for they had never known defeat in any conflict. But the demons appeared endless. Despite taking un-counted casualties, the demons were unrelenting.

The Demon Masters knew the truth, but no one in the Re-gent's Meet would listen to them; there was a gate, somewhere, on Estandarin perhaps, through which the demons were pouring into this realm. Gulamendis tried to find other Demon Masters with whom to consult, but their years of isolation and distrust, as well as several having been killed outright as being respon-sible for the war, made it impossible for any coherent picture of the demon realm to be drawn.

He only knew what he knew from his years of study and consulting with his handful of trained demons. But whatever the truth behind the demons reach into this realm, he was certain somehow they would follow from Andcardia to Midkemia. If he was wrong, no harm done in gulling these elves into allying with the Taredhel; they would be allowed to serve . . . yet . . . There was something about this Queen, this Aglaranna. She may truly be of the ancient line, for when he beheld her for the first time, Gulamendis felt something deep, basic, and . . . something right. This woodland was not familiar to him, yet there was something profoundly familiar to him.

As if reading his mind, a voice from behind said, "It is the ancient home."

Gulamendis turned and felt a shock close to a physical blow. Tomas, the Warleader of Elvandar, stood behind him wearing a suit of armor, white and gold, but in a style alien and arcane. The golden dragon on his tabard captured the Demon Master's eyes, and when he finally looked Tomas in the face, he saw something behind his eyes he had not seen before, when in the Queen's Council. Within this being resided an ancient power, and now he let it show through.

The Demon Master felt himself tremble, albeit slightly, for instincts long-stilled in his people awoke, and he found himself in awe and terror of another being for the first time in his life. Generations of arrogance and a self-aggrandizing certainty of superiority fell away. If his experience with the Demon Legion had given him doubts about his people's supremacy, one look at this being, this avatar of an ancient power, and he was humbled.

Almost whispering, Gulamendis said, "Ancient One . . ."

Tomas held up his hand and the Demon Master fell silent. "This demonstration is to cut to the heart of this matter, Gulamendis."

"Master," whispered the Taredhel magic-user. Even though he stood nearly six inches taller than Tomas, the Demon Master felt dwarfed in the presence of this icon of the ancient race that ruled over all elves.

Tomas said, "This is the Holy Grove. This is the heart of Elvandar, and the fundamental essence of your race springs from here."

Gulamendis turned to regard the young trees and then he recognized it. This grove was where the saplings of the great trees the Taredhel called "the Stars," were tended and nurtured. He had seen the majestic boles of the mature "stars," but this was the first time he saw them being cultivated. He knew with certainty than when his ancestors fled from this world, this is where they uprooted the Seven Stars to carry them to Andcardia.

"Yes," said the Demon Master.

"This is where the Edhel began," said Tomas.

"Yes," repeated Gulamendis.

"It is a time for plain speaking. Why are you here?"

The Taredhel looked away from Tomas and back to the grove. He said, "I have reasons for what I do, Lord Tomas." As he spoke, his feeling of being overwhelmed by the presence of the man in ancient armor diminished, though it never fully left. He took a deep breath. "We are fleeing a horde of demons, beings who have swept across every world the Taredhel have taken as their own." He looked at Tomas. "How many live here?"

Tomas thought a moment and said, "Within the heart of Elvandar, ten thousand and a few more."

"Throughout the world?"

Tomas said, "We only guess, but the Moredhel to the north likely number more, perhaps as many as twice our numbers, but they are widely scattered and fight among themselves more than they trouble us."

"Others?"

"Across the sea, perhaps four, five thousand of those we call Ocedhel. Down in Baranor, another thousand and some, most of whom migrated from here."

"Perhaps thirty thousand among the scattered tribes of the Edhel," said Gulamendis. He reached out and gripped Tomas's tabard front as if needing to hang on to something. Hoarse with emotion, he said, "We were millions! We were the Eldar! *We* were. Acaila's band were what we were when we left Home, but we made ourselves so much more than you can imagine, Dragon Lord."

He let go of Tomas's tabard and turned away, moisture in his eyes as he look around. At last he said, "This is like looking into the past, for me." He turned, hands outstretched. "We can never be this." He made a sweeping gesture. "We can never return to living in trees." His eyes welled up and tears ran down his face. "No matter how beautiful or venerated those trees are. We have become something else."

Looking directly into Tomas's eyes, he said, "We will never wander into these woods to ask to be taken in, to have 'returned,' as I have heard tell. The Moredhel were the least of us—we call them the Forgotten, for they were those base servants who were permitted to serve *us*, the Eldar! They envied us, their betters. *You* remember!"

Tomas nodded. Since he donned the white-and-gold armor of a long-dead Valheru, memories came unbidden over the years, sometimes triggered by circumstances or a word, other times seemingly at random. His memories of the long-dead Ashen-

Shugar were not complete, but many of the things said by Gulamendis he knew to be true.

Gulamendis made a sweeping gesture with his hand. "You permitted this, Lord. You and your brethren. This was where the elves arose, to serve the Valheru! Without this, we are nothing." He turned and again looked directly into Tomas's eyes, his expression almost defiant. "We took this with us! We uprooted seven saplings from this grove, bound their roots as a mother wraps a child, and we carried them across a bridge to another world.

"The foundation of our history was that journey. Before that"—he again waved at the grove—"may as well be myth, for we arrived on Andcardia with what we carried, seven saplings, a few tools, and our knowledge.

"We planted those seven trees, our Seven Stars, and we built our home around them. First, hovels of wood and animal hide, but we mastered that world, and now our cities make those of any other world look like rude mud huts. We are a prideful race, we of the Seven Stars, Lord, but we have *earned* that pride."

Tomas nodded. "I take no issue with who you are, Gulamendis. I need only know your purpose in coming here. If it is not to take refuge from the Demon Horde, what is it?"

"To find a way to save what is left of the Clans of the Seven Stars."

"Explain," said Tomas, crossing his arms before him.

"We cannot survive if the Demon Legion follows us to Midkemia. None of us."

Tomas said nothing, regarding Gulamendis coolly.

"We need you, and the humans and the dwarves. We need anyone who will resist the Demon Legion."

Tomas said nothing for a long moment, then asked, "Why not simply tell us this when you first came to us?"

"I needed to . . ." Gulamendis paused, looked completely around the grove, then said, "This calls to me. It's . . . powerful. I see you, Valheru, and fear, hate, and a dread all echo through my being. I thought . . ." He paused, gathered his thoughts, and said, "When my brother and I, and a few others, conceived of our plan, we knew we must quickly find those already on this world, our Home, who would unite with us should the Demon Legion come.

"So you understand clearly, when you remember the days before the time of chaos, when the gods raged across the sky, and the Dragon Lords rose to challenge them, in that time *we*, the Taredhel . . . we stood first among your servants."

Tomas closed his eyes a moment, and then opened them to look at Gulamendis. "The Eldar were our most trusted servants."

The use of the word "our" was not lost on the Demon Master. He said, "Acaila and his brethren are descendants of librarians. They were stranded on the world . . ."

"Kelewan," supplied Tomas.

"Kelewan," echoed Gulamendis. "One of the Dragon Host abandoned them there. What they achieved was remarkable given their limited resources.

"But we are the true Eldar. We were your housecarls, your ministers, your emissaries when you needed to negotiate with one another, and we were your lovers."

Tomas again closed his eyes and memories of elven females of astonishing beauty kept near his throne—Ashen-Shugar's throne—returned to him. He nodded. "Yes, you were first among our slaves." There was a hard edge to his voice, and he didn't fully understand why he felt the need to emphasize the elves' position relative to the Valheru.

Gulamendis's eyes narrowed and his expression was almost defiant. "We are more than what we were, Tomas," he whispered and his tone was full of menace. "I have no doubt you could cut me down with your golden sword before I could take a step. I will not contest that, but should you face a dozen of us in the field, you would be challenged. And we number in the thousands."

"A threat?"

"No, a warning, perhaps not even that; let's call it a courtesy. We do not come to you as lesser beings. We come to you as equals." He looked back at the grove and said, "We venerated those who had the responsibility for these groves. They were the most fundamental of us, those closest to the soil of this world, and the very life-giving things nature offered.

"But they were gardeners. Your Queen's ancestors were gardeners, nothing more."

Tomas said nothing for a moment, now fully understanding. "You view them as your inferiors."

"They are rustics. They are farmers and hunters and fishers of the sea, nothing more. Those are honorable crafts, but they are not who we were or have become.

"We are the scholars, the academics, the explorers, the crafters of devices and weapons." He pointed to Tomas's chest. "That armor, that sword, my ancestors crafted it for you. The devices that let you fly to other worlds, they were our invention.

"How do you think we were able to flee during the time of madness and find safe haven on Andcardia? We were the builders of the translocation portals and we were the ones who took the tools and tomes, scrolls and books. We were forced to contrive the means to do by arts what you did through hereditary magic. It was the dragons who could carry you across the void to other worlds not your own. We bowed to your might, because we could not command dragons to carry us, but we found ways to achieve what you achieved, and we did it without you!" He looked back again at the grove. His voice softened. "And we took from here that which reminded us of our beginning.

"But we are not who we once were, and we have returned here out of need. But we will take what is ours, without asking your leave."

"You present a troubling attitude, Gulamendis, if it is shared by all of your people."

With a wry smile, the Demon Master said, "I am moderate in my view. The Regent Lord will look upon your wife as a threat."

Tomas's eyes narrowed as anger rose up, and he said, "You do your cause little good. Let any threaten my Queen and they will know the extent of my power, Gulamendis."

"I am not a threat. But you should know there are others among my people who will see *you* as one.

"We thought it would be fairly simple. We assumed the elves remaining on this world would be in ascendance, as we have been for thousands of years, and that any other races we might choose to deal with would be an afterthought. Then my brother spent months exploring this land."

Tomas said, "It was your brother then who was seen in the valley north of Dolgan's holdings?"

"He was seen?"

"Humans number some gifted trackers and your brother was not adept at hiding his passage. A Ranger of Natal came across his spoor and was curious as to why there were tracks and yet he could not recall who made them moments after seeing your brother. So he followed and when your brother established a rift—"

"Rift?" said Gulamendis.

"His way home."

"We call it a portal," said the Demon Master.

"Ah," said Tomas. "That is when your brother revealed himself. He was closest to King Dolgan's village, and from there came to see my Queen. You can imagine the concern at the appearance of an elf unlike any encountered in the memory of any elf or dwarf."

At the mention of Dolgan, Gulamendis's features darkened. "We've had issues with the dwarves in the past, and they have never come to an easy conclusion."

Tomas's eyes narrowed. "Dolgan is among my oldest friends, a dwarf of gentle heart and iron resolve. I have placed my life in his trust on more than one occasion and he has proven stalwart. I trust him as I trust few others."

Gulamendis inclined his head slightly as if to say it was of no serious concern.

Tomas said, "So then, to the heart of it. Why have you come here?"

"To seek an alliance should the demons come, and to help you understand that while you and your lady command respect, that is all; obedience will not be offered. We are no other race's thrall."

It was Tomas's turn to indicate by a small gesture that this was not important. "Your ancestors fled this world before the one whose armor I wore took to the skies to tell all below that they were now a free people.

"We seek dominion over no one. The Moredhel to the north have declared us enemy, from time before remembering, and for reasons lost in antiquity, so we defend ourselves when they venture south, but those among them who choose to return to their ancestral home are welcome. Many among us spent their youth in the north. We welcomed the Ocedhel from across the sea, yet many remain in that land, unwilling to join us. We have no issue with them. And when we discovered the Anoredhel endured to the south, we also claimed no sovereignty over them."

"The Sun People?" asked Gulamendis. "I have not heard of these."

"The protectors of the Quor and Sven'ga-ri."

Again, a questioning look. "I should know these names, but I do not."

"A matter for another time," said Tomas. "Very well, your position is clear. You seek our help but do not wish to serve. As we have no wish for your service, we are in accord." His expression was reinforced in his next utterance: "But any attempt by your Clan of the Seven Stars to assume dominion over others of our people will be thwarted.

"Not only will I draw a sword, I have allies who will answer my call."

"Dwarves? Humans?"

"Stout warriors and powerful sorcerers, Gulamendis. Do not let your past history blind you to this fact; they are your equal in many ways,"—he thought of Pug—"and some will prove your better.

"Consider this a caution. Midkemia may be your ancestral home, but it is home to many others, descendants of those who came here during the Chaos Wars, and their claim is perhaps even more enduring than yours. Your ancestors left, while theirs stayed."

"We understand one another. Any differences between our

people must be put aside until after the Demon Legion has been dealt with."

"And keep in mind we will not trouble you so long as you do not trouble us, but should the day come when we are opposed, I will be without pity." His expression left no doubt in Gulamendis's mind it wasn't an idle threat. "Is there anything else?"

The Demon Master said, "I and some others understand this world will be different than what we might wish it to be. But the Regent Lord, and those priests, magicians, and soldiers who make up the Regent's Meet, they will not so easily come to understand that accommodations must be reached. Were you to bring them here, as you had me come, they would see this as a challenge, a threat, one to be answered and swiftly.

"The Clans of the Seven Stars cannot endure here unless we make changes and come to different accommodations with the other races on this world. We need a change in leadership to achieve that goal."

"Treason," said Tomas.

"Reason," said Gulamendis. "The strength of our race is also a weakness, for we have never been vanquished until we met the demons. It is inconceivable to us that another mortal race might be our equal, let alone our superior.

"It would be better for all of us if we had a different perspective when the time came for us to aid one another." He looked one more time at the grove. "We must return here and take what lessons we have forgotten, Tomas." He then looked at Tomas and said, "Just as some of your people must come and learn from us. Only that way can conflict be avoided."

"That sounds promising," said Tomas. "Little else of what you said does."

"I understand."

"Come," said Tomas, "we must travel."

"Where?"

"There are others you must meet, humans, who are my friends, and, more important, who hold the safety of this world paramount. Perhaps after you've met Pug and his associates you'll rethink your feelings of superiority."

Gulamendis looked dubious but said nothing.

Tomas closed his eyes and spoke softly, but the words were powerful and Gulamendis felt magic forming. For nearly five minutes they stood motionless, then the sound of gigantic wings came and a shadow passed over them. Gulamendis looked up and if his first sight of Tomas had visited a shock upon him, what he beheld now nearly forced him to his knees in awe and terror.

A great golden dragon hovered above, lazy beats of its wings keeping it aloft. In some speech only Tomas could understand it seemed to question the human-turned-Dragon-Lord, and Tomas spoke aloud in the same language.

"He's agreed to carry us."

"Carry us?" said the Demon Master.

As gently as a falling feather, the dragon touched down before them, lowering his head until it rested on the ground. "Come," said Tomas, walking over to a portion of the neck where he could climb aboard. "Sit behind me and behold more of this world you call Home."

Gulamendis was mute. He could barely nod and it took all his resolve to meekly follow Tomas and climb aboard the dragon behind him.

# CHAPTER 15

## PLOTTING

Sandreena awoke.

Before she was fully conscious she had her hand reaching for the haft of her mace and was about to attack whoever was standing above her. A strong hand grabbed her wrist and prevented her from finding her weapon, and she found herself too weak to break that grasp. A voice spoke softly: "Now, none of that. You're safe."

She blinked and realized there was no mace next to her. It had been taken by the . . . whoever those Black Caps were. She had a sword, but now it was gone. She blinked again, trying to focus her eyes and remember where she was.

She lay in a simple bed of wood, a straw-stuffed mattress suspended on a rope lattice, in a small monk's cell. Memory returned. She was in the Temple in Ithra. She had arrived nearly dead on her feet, her horse in little better condition ... she didn't know, when. She tried to speak, the face above her indistinct in the dim light of the room. "How long?" she managed to barely croak.

"Almost a day," said the voice; now she could tell it was a man. The hand released her wrist and a moment later slipped in behind her head, helping her sit up a little as a cup of cold, clean water touched her lips. She sipped and as moisture awoke her thirst, started to drink. After she drained the cup, she could speak clearly. "More."

The man stood up. He had been kneeling by her bedside, and she now got a good look at him. He was a dark-haired man, somewhere in his mid-thirties, she thought. Heavyset, but not fat. He wore a deep plum–colored tunic and black trousers, simple but of fine weave, and his boots were of fine craftsmanship. He appeared unarmed. His features were plain, even unremarkable, but there was something about his dark eyes that said he was not someone to be underestimated.

"Who are you?" she asked weakly.

"I'm Zane."

After another drink of water, she said, "Just Zane?"

He shrugged and smiled. It was a simple expression, but without guile. That made him either straightforward or dangerous. She'd assume the latter until the former proved out. "Well, if you care, I've a couple of titles that I never use, one from Roldem, another from the Kingdom of the Isles, and I may be entitled to some honorific from Kesh, but I'm not entirely sure. Zane will do."

He turned to indicate those outside the door. "The monks tell me you're called Sandreena and you are a Knight-Adamant of the Order of the Shield of the Weak. Is that correct?"

"Yes," said Sandreena. "I'm assuming you're harmless, else the Brothers would never have allowed you into my quarters while I was unconscious."

He feigned a look of injury. "Harmless?" He shook his head

slightly. "I'm no menace to you, certainly, but harmless?" He sighed as he sat back down next to her. "You need your rest, but before you fall asleep again, there are a couple of things I need to know."

Feeling herself slipping back into unconsciousness, she said, "That may have to wait . . ."

When she awoke again, Zane was still there, but he was dressed in different fashion. She could see that the light from the high window above was different as well—grey. "Ah, there you are again," said Zane. He had been standing near the door, apparently watching her, and came to sit on the edge of the bed again.

"Water?"

"Yes, thank you," she said and allowed him to help her drink. Gathering her thoughts, she asked, "Who are you, again?"

"Zane," he replied.

"I mean, who sent you?"

"Ah, to that," he said, standing up as she appeared more lucid this time and able to drink without aid. "I am presently a friend of the Father-Bishop Creegan. Well, associate is perhaps a better choice of words."

"But you are not of the Temple?" she asked.

"No," he said with what passed for a regretful smile. "I tend to discover myself praying to Ban-ath or Ruthia more often than not." He looked at her. "I try not to find myself on the side needing Dala's intervention."

"And as an associate of the good Father-Bishop," said Sandreena, elbowing herself upright, "I assume you're here to ask me about what I've uncovered."

He reached under the bed and pulled out a folded blanket. He put it behind her as a makeshift pillow and said, "Yes, to the heart of it." He added, "If you feel up to talking."

"I'm a little hungry, but I could talk before I eat."

He nodded and stood, moved to the door, and spoke to someone outside. While sitting up, Sandreena took stock of herself. Someone had bathed her, for she was clean, and redressed her wounds, which now itched as they were almost fully healed. She was wearing a simple white shift of bleached linen, and her hair smelled clean to her.

She had been nearly dead when she rode into town. She had endured a week on the road with no food and only what water she could find in creeks and one farmer's well. She vaguely recalled finding a stand of berries along the way, but they had made her sick to her stomach.

Her exact recollection of things was hazy after she had started on her journey south. She remembered reaching a hillside overlooking the town of Ithra, and then nothing until she was spoken to by someone at the town gate, perhaps a warden or town watchman. Then she was at the entrance to the temple and trying to speak to someone, a monk perhaps, then awaking today.

The last week on the road had been a blur of hazy memories. Her wounds had stiffened, as she suspected they would, since she hardly had the best time recuperating in that damp cave, and she was woefully malnourished. Somewhere along the way time became meaningless. Training had evidently taken hold, for she had somehow managed to keep her horse watered and find grazing along the way. Perhaps she had slept while the animal had cropped grass. In any event, it was clear to Sandreena the Goddess had been watching over her.

She vaguely recalled finding her way past the city watch, who regarded the ragged woman with some suspicion, but she had said something about finding the temple, and slightly crazy pilgrims and mystics were hardly unusual, even in as out-of-the-way a place as Ithra—and even if they rode a fine horse.

"So, you work for Creegan," she said as she pushed herself upright. Every part of her ached and she felt shockingly weak. It was a feeling she didn't like.

"Work with him is more the case," said Zane. He looked over his shoulder at her as they waited for food to arrive. "Or rather, I work for people who work with him." He saw a monk approaching and said nothing while a tray was brought into the room, placed on Sandreena's lap, and the monk departed. While she ate, Zane said, "Your Order's resources are spread out right now, and you were the only high-level temple knight around, apparently. So the Father-Bishop asked us to keep an eye out for you."

"You just happened to be in Ithra?"

"This was where they sent me. We have other people in Dosra, Min, and Pointer's Head just in case you showed up there. If none of us heard from you in another week, someone else would have been sent north. There's a strong suspicion something important is taking place in that very isolated village you went to . . ."

"Akrakon," she supplied. She said nothing more, concentrating on eating the vegetable soup and coarse bread, which comprised her meal. She didn't think this man would be standing around in the middle of the monastery if he were any sort of risk, but his claim to affiliation with the temple in Krondor didn't make it a fact. As he observed, there were no other highly placed members of the Order nearby; the monks and lay Brothers of the Order in this little temple were far removed from Temple politics and intrigue.

When she said nothing for a while, Zane smiled and said, "Fair enough. You can report directly to the Father-Bishop if you wish. I was given no instructions about learning what you know, just to see you got safely home, or, failing that, that whoever followed you had a better chance of getting the intelligence . . . we need."

She wondered which "we" he spoke of—the Temple, the Father-Bishop and himself, or whoever his masters were. "Good," she said. "You going to ride with me to Krondor?" she asked between mouthfuls of soup and chewy bread.

"Something like that," he said with a smile. "I'll wait until you're done."

She said nothing while she finished, then watched him take away her tray. When he returned, she was standing on wobbly legs and needed a moment. "I'm weak as a kitten," she supplied.

A monk arrived with some clothing, and Sandreena was annoyed to see it was a dress. Seeing her expression, Zane shrugged. "It was the best we could do on short notice. I had to buy it off one of the shopkeeper's wives." Lowering his voice as the monk departed, he said, "And I think the Brothers never considered you might prefer tunic and trousers. I think you may have been the first Knight-Adamant they've seen in recent memory." Lowering his voice even more, he added, "or ever." Looking over his shoulder as he handed her the dress, he said, "Certainly the first woman."

She pulled off the shift and donned the dress, ignoring Zane's presence. "There aren't many of us," she acknowledged, and her tone was grudging. "It's thankless work and not for those of weak constitution. It doesn't appeal to many, man or woman." She held out the sides of the dress, which was obviously a size or two too large for her, and said, "Am I supposed to ride in this?"

"Ah, no," said Zane. He drew an object from his belt pouch and said, "Stand next to me."

She moved a step closer and he said, "This is a bit faster."

Suddenly they were in a room somewhere else. It was earlier in the day, from the brightness of the light, and noticeably warmer. There was a trio of men in the room as they appeared.

Sandreena looked around, then her eyes widened. She took one step toward one of the men and drew back her fist. Before anyone could react, she unloaded a punishing blow to the jaw of a man wearing a white robe with purple trim. He went backward, skidding across the floor, slamming into the wall.

Shaking his head and blinking his eyes for a moment, Amirantha looked up and said, "Why, Sandreena. Good to see you again, too."

Pug stood dumbfounded. Few things could surprise him at his age and with his experience, but the sudden appearance of Zane and the woman, who immediately knocked Amirantha across the room, succeeded.

Brandos grinned. "You're looking a little off, girl. Normally, you would have broken his jaw."

Seeing the old fighter, she returned his smile and came to hug him. "You old fraud. How are you?"

He hugged her back and said, "Well enough. I had wondered how you were, from time to time."

Pug said, "Obviously, I don't need to make any introductions."

Sandreena said, "Only who you are."

"My name is Pug and this is my island."

She frowned. "The Black Sorcerer?"

He smiled slightly. "It's a long story. Let's say for the moment we all represent interests that have a common goal."

"Which is?"

Getting off the floor, rubbing his sore jaw, Amirantha said, "Discovering where some unwelcome demons are coming from."

She fixed him with a baleful look. "This another of your confidences?"

He held up his hands, palms outward. "No. In fact, an unexpected demon nearly gutted me a few weeks ago."

"Too bad," she said.

Brandos grinned. He knew she meant too bad the demon hadn't succeeded. "I've missed you, girl."

She gave him a dubious expression. "You're a good enough man, Brandos, but I can't say much for the company you keep."

"If we can put aside the personal animosity for a while, we have others coming to meet with us," Pug said.

"Who are you?" asked Sandreena again. "I mean, who are you to bring me here?"

Pug knew an exasperated tone when he heard one. "Father-Bishop Creegan will be here shortly. I think I'll leave it to him to explain your role in this. However, before he arrives, perhaps you'd care to give us a brief idea of what it was you encountered up in the Peaks of the Quor."

"No," she said. "I wouldn't care to."

Pug shook his head slightly and said, "Zane, if you would show Sandreena to her quarters, we'll wait for the rest of our guests."

"Yes, Grandfather," he said. He motioned for Sandreena to follow him. She cast another baleful glance at Amirantha as she followed Zane out of the room.

As they walked down the hallway, she took notice of her

surroundings. The building was low and had doors that opened on gardens. She said, "Grandfather? He doesn't look more than ten years older than you."

"Appearances can be deceiving," said Zane. "Pug is my stepfather's father and he's old enough to be . . ." He shrugged. "You'll see." He led her to a room and said, "You can rest here and if you get hungry, just pick up that bell and ring it. Someone will escort you to the dining hall." He pointed to a small, tulip-shaped bell that rested on a table next to a bed. "Is there anything I can do for you in the meantime?"

Reaching down, she tugged at the ill-fitting dress and said, "Yes, if you could find me clothes that fit, I'd be grateful. Trousers and a tunic, please?"

He said, "I'll see what I can do. I'll be back shortly."

She sat on the bed after he left, and put her elbows on her knees, burying her face in her hands. "Oh, Goddess," she said softly. "What have I done to deserve this? Amirantha, again?"

By the time Zane returned with clean clothing, she was asleep again, curled up on the bed like a child, and he could tell from the dried tracks on her face she had been weeping.

Pug sat near the door to the kitchen, dining with his wife, two sons, and Amirantha and Brandos at a table large enough to accommodate twice the number. A large kettle of stew sat steaming in the middle, with platters of hot bread, cheeses, meats, fruits, and vegetables placed around it.

The Warlock observed, "This is a . . . fascinating place. I always assumed your students were, and work was done, at Stardock."

Pug inclined his head slightly as he said, "That's what we want people to think. My predecessor here on this island, Macros, created the legend of the Black Sorcerer to maintain privacy. We have continued the illusion to keep that privacy. Moreover, the Academy at Stardock is a busy place, and much is accomplished there, but this is where the real work, research, and education of the exceptional students take place."

Brandos said, around a mouthful of bread and cheese, "I assume that either you've decided to trust us, or you're going to kill us." He pointed to his bowl of stew. "This is very good, by the way."

Miranda smiled. There was something very fundamental and unself-conscious about this veteran fighting man that appealed to her. "If we wished you dead, Brandos," she said, "you wouldn't be eating up the cook's good stew."

"That's a relief," he said. "Though, as last meals go, this wouldn't be bad."

Magnus and Caleb both laughed, and Amirantha said, "Well, then, if we're not to be killed, are we to be trusted?"

Pug regarded the Warlock and said, "I'm not sure 'trusted' is the word I'd employ; rather, consider yourself 'accepted for the time being.' Demons are an issue for us, at the moment, and it appears we have little knowledge of them here and at Stardock."

Magnus said, "The monks at That Which Was Sarth weren't especially helpful either; most of their records are pretty straightforward, 'on this date a demon appeared, Brother Iganthal or Father Boreus banished it,' or was eaten by it and someone else did the banishing. But as to the nature and ways of demons, they were surprisingly vague."

"Not really," said Amirantha. He looked at Pug as he spoke, as if addressing him specifically. "It's difficult to negotiate with demons, and the power they bring is intoxicating, addictive even. But there's a price, and if I have managed to endure these encounters, it's because I was never willing to pay the price."

"Your life?" asked Caleb.

The Warlock shook his head. "My soul, for lack of a better term. I may not be a particularly good man, but I'm willing to stand before Lims-Kragma when my time comes, for an accounting of all I've done, good or ill. I'll take whatever passes for justice among the gods, but what I won't do is give up my place on the Wheel of Life for eternity to gain whatever it is I think is worth gaining in this life."

"It would have to be a great deal," agreed Magnus.

"It's not so simple, is it?" asked Pug.

Amirantha shook his head as he put down his large spoon,

apparently finished eating. "If some agency of evil came to you and offered you a bargain, it would be a matter of strength of character, perhaps, or even fear of losing one's place on the Wheel, but the agencies of darkness are far more subtle than that.

"There's a force out there," he continued, picking up his cup of wine and sipping, then setting it down, "that is hardly that overt.

"I'm convinced my brother, the man you knew as Leso Varen, was more than half-mad when he killed our mother. Something had already reached out and touched his heart, finding a willing minion. I knew my brother well; his vanity would never let him bend his knee to another, but that vanity could easily lead him to be manipulated."

Remembering a conversation with the God of Thieves, where Ban-ath had revealed that Macros's vanity had been his biggest ally in manipulating the otherwise crafty sorcerer, Pug could only nod agreement.

"While my brothers and I were disinclined to speak, we did have mutual acquaintances. As you may already understand, those of us who practice what are called the 'dark arts' often find our needs drive us to deal with a more unsavory stripe of fellow— thieves, bandits, renegades, and the like. People who can secure goods that otherwise would be impossible for us to obtain.

"This is less true in my own calling, for most of what I need I make, for wards, stones of power, and other items that over the years have proven useful in following my interest, to discover as much as possible of demon lore and the realm from which they come, without—"

"Having your head ripped off," inserted Brandos.

"—I was about to say something else, but he makes my point." Idly picking up his spoon and poking at what remained of the food before him, the Warlock said, "Those who need living human subjects must deal with slavers, and those who need the death of others—such as my brother did—also must deal with slavers or warlords or others guaranteed to engender mayhem. Cults become particularly useful."

At the mention of cults, Pug asked Caleb, "Did Zane . . . ?"

"No," said Caleb to his father. "He said Sandreena preferred to wait until Father-Bishop Creegan arrives."

"Creegan here?" asked Amirantha, his eyebrows rising as his only sign of surprise.

"We have many friends."

"Indeed," said the Warlock.

"You know him?"

"We've met," said Amirantha.

Brandos said, "Not to worry. Creegan might have Amirantha burned as a heretic, but he won't punch him in the jaw. He's far too well-mannered for that."

Amirantha smiled ruefully. "He's a practical man. He disapproves of my interests, but he's never tried to interfere with them."

"It helps that we live on different sides of the world," observed Brandos. "Big ocean between us, and all that." He winked at Pug and his family. "Keeps things civil."

Magnus smiled and shook his head, and Caleb laughed.

Miranda asked, "So, why the punch to the jaw—sorry I wasn't there to see it. Sounds like it was entertaining."

Brandos said, "Well, it's a long story—"

Amirantha interrupted. "It has to do with the Father-Bishop, as well. I was traveling through the Principality about four, five?" He looked at Brandos, who nodded. "Five years ago. There was a story making the rounds about a demon sighted up the coast from the city of Krondor, near a village with the unlikely name of Yellow Mule."

"Good tavern," observed Brandos.

"Good tavern," agreed Amirantha. "We were in residence there, attempting to discern the validity of the rumor when we encountered Sandreena, who also had come looking to rid the region of this demon.

"Our interests seemed to overlap—"

"And Sandreena is a very good-looking young woman; my friend here is particularly fond of that."

Amirantha frowned at his companion, who tried hard not to look smug as he continued to eat. "We joined forces."

Pug looked thoughtful, then said, "I'm usually apprised of something as unusual as a demon sighting, especially that close to Krondor." He glanced at Magnus and Caleb, who both shrugged, then at Miranda.

"I read the report; it came from our friend at the Prince's palace."

Pug's eyebrows raised and he said, "Oh?"

"It seemed nothing worth bothering you about. A demon was sighted, some locals disposed of it, nothing further."

Brandos and Amirantha exchanged a look of surprise and Brandos said, "Locals?"

Amirantha said, "Father-Bishop Creegan probably left our names out of any report."

Pug smiled. "Not unlike him. He's ambitious. But, please, continue."

"Not much more to tell," said Amirantha. "A . . . very strange man, a little mad I think, had wandered into the village and claimed he was a prophet of some sort or another and did some fairly impressive things; at least they were according to the villagers.

"He healed some wounds, somehow rid a small orchard of a blight, and he did a fair job of predicting the weather. He gathered together a little group of followers and after a year or so had them convinced he was an avatar of a god.

"Then it got nasty, according to what we heard."

"Yes," agreed Brandos. "People who didn't fall in with this bunch were suddenly stricken by illness, or had their cows' milk sour, crops got blight."

"Curses," said Pug. "Witch work."

"Maybe," said Amirantha. "My mother was called a witch more times than I can remember. My title, Warlock, literally means 'caller of spirits,' in the ancient Satumbria language, but it's used to mean 'male witch.'"

Brandos said, "Never could quite understand all these names; you use magic or you don't, right?" He addressed that question to Pug.

Pug couldn't help but laugh. "You have no idea how many conversations I've endured on that very question over the years, my friend."

Amirantha returned to his narrative. "Over the course of a week we discovered there were others involved with this cult, men who would mysteriously arrive in the middle of the night then vanish."

"Magicians?" asked Magnus.

Amirantha shrugged. "Or renegade priests of some order or another, but they were a conduit for information or instructions between this false prophet and whoever was ultimately behind all the goings-on in Yellow Mule."

"The locals were a pretty happy lot until they started dying off," said Brandos. "This prophet, called himself Jaymen, he blamed us! Can you believe that?"

Pug nodded. "Go on."

Amirantha said, "So, as I said, by then Sandreena and I had concluded we had similar interests and we joined forces. She was trying to save the villagers—apparently whatever reports were getting down to the Prince of Krondor's Coastal Wardens Office were being ignored—and I was very interested in the demon scent."

"Scent?" asked Pug.

"Yes," said Amirantha. "You've encountered demons, right?"

"Yes," said Pug, with an emphatic nod. "Not with the best results, I might add."

"Did you notice how they smell?"

Pug recalled vividly his encounter with the demon who had disguised himself as the Emerald Queen, and yet the memory was a blur. He had been full of vanity and his own sense of power, and had come flying in—literally—from overhead, only to be blasted from the sky in a scorching ball of flames that had almost ended his life.

"I can't say as I had the time to notice any smell," said Pug. He looked at Miranda and Magnus. "I've run into several demons over the years, and except for one who smelled of burning brimstone, the rest were . . . sweaty? Some pungent . . . musky odor."

Amirantha laughed. "I'm sorry, I didn't literally mean their odor. I mean, how their magic smells."

Pug's eyes narrowed and he said, "This sounds a lot like a conversation I had once with a tribal shaman down in Kesh, many years ago. He claimed he could tell which magician fashioned a ward or cast a spell."

Amirantha's eyes grew wide. "You can't?" He glanced at the others, then at Brandos, and said, "But I thought every magician could . . . sense whose spell it was, I mean, if they knew the other magician, had encountered their spellcraft before."

Magnus exchanged glances with his mother and father, and then said, "An assumption based on limited contact with other practitioners of magic." He thought on this a moment, then said, "I believe I can, as well."

"Really?" said Pug.

"You've never said anything," added his mother.

"I never really gave it much thought," said Magnus. "It's not something I do consciously. If you or Mother translocate into or out of the next room, I just know which of you it is."

Pug's eyes widened slightly.

"If I'm in my quarters, I know who's teaching the students, most of the time, just from the way the magic 'feels' in the background."

Miranda shook her head slightly. "I had no idea."

Pug said to Amirantha, "After the current problems are concluded, perhaps I could persuade you to linger a bit, for I would like to see more of this ability you and my son speak of."

"I don't know if it's an ability, in the sense of something that can be taught."

"Maybe it's a quality that can be recognized," said Pug. "Something we do and give no thought to, like blinking or breathing."

"Actually," said Brandos, "I give a fair amount of thought to breathing, usually when something is trying to keep me from doing it."

Amirantha's gaze narrowed at the quip but he withheld comment. To Pug he said, "Brandos must return home soon, else his wife, Samantha, will have my head on a stick, but I will stay for a while if I can help." He smiled. "Besides, there's a great deal here that piques my curiosity, for you've codified magic I've barely heard of. As I said, for those of us who practice the so-called dark arts, there's little social opportunity to meet with other magic-users."

Pug said, "Agreed."

Sandreena appeared, guided by one of Pug's students. The Knight-Adamant of the Order of the Shield of the Weak wore a man's tunic and trousers, both of which fit well enough, and sandals. Pug indicated she should join them at the table, and she took a chair next to Miranda, on the opposite side of the table from Amirantha.

"Did you sleep well?" Miranda asked in neutral tones.

"Yes," said the still exhausted girl.

"You should have one of our healers look at those wounds."

Sandreena took a bowl and helped herself to the stew. "They are fine. I've sewn up enough of them to know if they're festering. I'm just going to have some new scars."

Miranda said, "There's a priest of Killian who can make those scars fade, if you care to visit his temple."

"Why?" said Sandreena. She looked directly at Amirantha as she said, "Scars are useful to remind me that being careless is a way to end up hurt."

Amirantha inclined his head slightly, as if in agreement, but said nothing.

Brandos said, "Well, that was fine, but if you have no more use for me, I think I'd like to get out and stretch my legs; otherwise I'll be napping and I find it a bothersome habit—makes me feel like I'm getting old."

Miranda smiled and said, "I'll have one of the students show you around; there are a few places that wouldn't be safe to blunder into." She signaled and a young man in a dark robe approached. Miranda instructed him to show Brandos around the rest of the community he hadn't seen so far, and they left.

Pug asked Amirantha, "You care to look around?"

The Warlock said, "If it's all the same to you, I'd just as

soon wait here for Creegan to arrive and get that out of the way."

Pug and Miranda exchanged brief looks, but said nothing. Magnus said, "We sent word to all our agents that Sandreena had turned up safe and was here, so he should be along any time now."

Amirantha said, "Well, then, if you have no objection, might I inquire into your stock of wine?"

Pug laughed and motioned another student over and said, "Do you prefer red or white?"

The Warlock said, "Yes."

Miranda laughed with her husband and Pug said, "Fetch a bottle of wine from the cellar—see if we still have some of that old Ravensburg red—I think there are a few bottles left. Bring it up and fetch some goblets." He looked around the table. Magnus, Caleb, and Miranda indicated they were fine, so Pug said, "Two goblets."

Sandreena held up a hand with one finger extended, and Pug said, "Make that three."

The student hurried off and Miranda said, "I've been organizing some old documents that have been languishing in the cellar over at Stardock, so-called demon lore, Amirantha. If you'd like to look at it later I'd appreciate your appraisal of its worth. There isn't much, so it shouldn't take very long."

The Warlock inclined his head, indicating he was willing.

Magnus said, "Well, I have a lesson to conduct after lunch, which it now is, so I'd better be getting along. I will see you all later."

Caleb also stood up as his brother departed, and said, "And there are household accounts and other matters which also need attending." He took his leave of the guests as well.

The wine appeared and Amirantha was impressed at the quality of the vintage. As they sipped in silence, Pug's expression caused Amirantha to turn.

From a door across the room he saw a tall, red-headed man enter, with Father-Bishop Creegan behind him. Amirantha muttered, "There goes a pleasant moment."

Sandreena began to rise, but the Father-Bishop waved her back into her chair. "Finish eating, girl," he said. Looking at Amirantha, he said, "I thought you were dead."

"Hoped, you mean," said the Warlock. "Creegan," he said in greeting.

Pug rose and said, "Wine?"

Glancing around the table, the Father-Bishop nodded and pulled out his own chair.

Pug looked at the red-headed man and said, "Jommy, wine?"

Grinning, and suddenly looking much younger than he did a moment before, the man said, "Of course."

Pug motioned for two more goblets and Father-Bishop Creegan said to Sandreena, "What did you find?"

Sandreena began slowly, starting with the assault of the innkeeper's wagon on the road to Akrakon. She omitted nothing she could remember, concerned that a detail that she didn't realize was important might provide critical information to the Father-Bishop and his companions. Occasionally she let her eyes drift to Amirantha, who sat motionless, listening as closely as anyone else at the table. Finally she recounted visiting the cave to find the old hermit dead.

When she was finished, she added, "Most of the journey from Akrakon to Ithra is a blur to me, still. I was fevered and passed out a few times. My horse was stalwart and saw to my protection when I lay at her feet. I recall something of entering Ithra and speaking to a guard and finding the monks at the temple. After that, well, it is nothing of this mission."

Father-Bishop Creegan looked at Amirantha. "What of the summoning and the murder of the magician?"

Amirantha shrugged. "It is obvious the cultists weren't happy with the results." He fell silent for a minute, then said, "I can only surmise, but the sacrifices were designed to call forth . . . something, but instead they invoked a series of minor demons . . . from Sandreena's description, I think I know their ilk: a particularly nasty little thing I call a 'ripper,' bat wings, huge talon on the forefinger of the hand-like extension on the leading edge of the wings." Sandreena nodded. "Whoever that unlucky magician was, he was attempting craft far beyond his ability and paid the ultimate price. He was fishing in unknown waters, using bait that could have landed him a shark as easily as a mackerel." He was silent a moment longer, then asked Sandreena, "All the demons, they were identical?"

She nodded.

"Then he had a summoning ritual that was bringing forth what it was he called for. They vanished after they killed the sacrifice?"

Again she nodded.

He sighed. "Murderous fools. Somehow they managed to get their hands on a ritual of summoning and probably thought they could amend it to call forth something other than what appeared. Those who don't know demon magic . . ." He looked at Pug. "If I understand some of your craft, it would be as if you were trying to call down rain, and decided to substitute the word 'snow' and get snow."

Pug said, "I'm not a master of weather magic; that would be Temar, but your example holds. The entire structure of the spell would have to be crafted differently."

Amirantha nodded in agreement. "So it is with a summoning. If I could contrive one spell of summoning and just change the name of the demon, my life would have been a lot simpler."

"Or shorter," said Sandreena wryly. Pug and Father-Bishop Creegan looked at her and she said, "I've seen him work. He can . . . take liberties and put himself and *others*," she added with emphasis, "at risk." Letting her voice return to normal, she looked at the Warlock and added, "You're an arrogant bastard, Amirantha."

Amirantha inclined his head slightly, as if conceding the point. "But I know more of demon lore than any man I've met." He looked at Pug. "Someone is attempting to master in short order what takes years to master. I suspect that means someone feels there is an issue of time involved."

Pug was silent for a moment, then said, "Jommy, tell Amirantha and the others"—and he indicated Father-Bishop

Creegan and Sandreena—"about that encounter you had when we first discovered the Sun Elves and the Quor."

Jommy was unknown to Sandreena and Amirantha. He looked at them, and said, "Ten years ago I was still a lad in training and had been given over to the less than tender care of one Kaspar of Olasko."

Amirantha laughed. He said, "He's here, you know."

Glancing at Pug, he said, "Fishing?"

Pug nodded. "Even the demons couldn't stop him."

Jommy looked uncertain as to what that meant, but continued on. "In any event, the General had myself and some other lads training at the same time; we were undertaking a mission for . . ." not knowing if the newcomers knew there was a secret organization behind this seemingly straightforward school for magic, he said, "Pug, and, well, we were spending some miserable times sitting in the rain waiting for pirates."

"Pirates?" said Amirantha.

"Well, that was the report." He gave Pug a narrow look. "Sometimes we lads in the front only get to hear what we get to hear. Anyway, this ship lay off the west coast of the peninsula where the Peaks of the Quor are, and three boats came ashore. This bunch looked like pirates, save they all wore these black headscarves."

Sandreena glanced at the others around the table. "Black Caps?"

"Could be," said Father-Bishop Creegan. "If so, they've been keeping to themselves for quite a while."

"Even the level of magic Sandreena observed doesn't come easily. If magicians are trying to learn demon summoning, ten years is not unreasonable a time to hide and study."

Jommy said, "They had this magician, and he had this . . . thing he summoned."

Now interested, Amirantha said, "Describe it."

"Big, and mean, looking like nothing so much as the hazy outline of a man, only bigger, maybe seven, eight feet tall. It had smoke all around it, like a cloak or mantle draped over its shoulders. It spoke some language the magician understood, and its voice was hollow, distant. It took shape and it was . . . hard to describe. The skin rippled, like thick cream when you tip the pitcher, or a banner waving in a breeze. If that makes sense."

Amirantha nodded. "Yes, it does."

"It had eyes like burning embers, bright and red, and then the skin got hard, like dark smoking rock. I can't tell you much more after that, because General Kaspar ordered a charge, and all hell broke loose around me.

"I do know the thing got bigger as it fought, and when it hit something, it burned them. After a minute, it was covered in fire, flames of yellow and white covering it from head to foot. Saw a shield get scorched and a man's tunic catch on fire. Smoke came off it like a campfire. I don't know if we had a prayer until the elves showed up and . . . banished it, I guess you'd say."

"How did they do that?" asked Amirantha, keenly interested.

"I don't really know," said Jommy. "Didn't think to ask. One minute we were scrambling to stay alive, the next there was this bright shaft of light and the thing just froze a minute, then the fire went out. It was raining, did I mention? Anyway, as soon as it froze, and the fire went out, the rain started steaming off its skin, and then all of a sudden it just fell apart."

Amirantha said, "That was not a true demon. That was a bound elemental servant."

Pug said, "What is the difference?"

Amirantha said, "I can only speak from experience, and mine is limited. I knew a magician by name of Celik, who was fascinated with the properties of the elements, earth, air, water, and fire.

"He contended there was this essence of each element, an aspect that was akin to life, but not true life. But with the right spells, that . . . I'm searching for words here, for like myself, Celik was a man who had learned through trial and error and had the scars to prove it. He called these creatures elemental servants. They came from someplace . . . not the demon realm, I am certain, but some other place, some plane of existence unknown to us."

"Fascinating," said Pug. His experience with his son and

Nakor, the little gambler who had been a friend for many years, on the next plane of existence, when they confronted the Dasati invasion of Kelewan, had fueled Pug's curiosity about the various planes of existence. To his continuing frustration, there was as little information on those realms as there was on demons.

"Well, whatever it was, it was one very scary thing to have bearing down at you," said Jommy. "But I'm not sure what it has to do with whatever it is you all were investigating back in the Peaks of the Quor."

"Neither do I," said Pug. "These Black Caps serve someone, or something, and for over ten years they've been interested in the Peaks of the Quor."

Father-Bishop Creegan said, "The Sven'ga-ri. While we still know nothing of their nature beyond the sheer beauty of their being, we know they are beings of power, and that they drew those wraiths—"

"Wraiths?" interrupted Amirantha. "You've encountered wraiths?"

"I did," said Jommy. "Or something enough like a wraith to not be much of a difference."

Amirantha said, "Tell me."

Jommy spoke of being harried up the trail by strangely humanoid creatures who rode on the backs of wolflike mounts, and who were almost impossible to see as anything other than dark places in his field of vision.

Miranda had been silent for the entire narrative, but she said, "I helped obliterate them." She described their camp and turned to her husband.

"As best we can tell, they are creatures of the void, something akin to the Dread, like wraiths or specters," said Pug. "I've encountered the Dread on two occasions and their lesser kin a few more times."

"My respect for you is now without limit," said Amirantha with no humor or irony intended. "No man living, to the best of my knowledge, has encountered the Dread.

"Wraiths and specters are also not of the demon realm. They are . . . something else."

"What?" asked Jommy.

"We don't know," said Pug. "We only know that they come from someplace beyond the Seven Hells or Heavens." He looked at Amirantha and said, "They are creatures of the void."

Amirantha said, "I have a feeling there's more here than I'm being told, which is certainly your prerogative." He narrowed his gaze as he studied Pug. "And you already know a great deal about the demon realm, I warrant."

Pug was silent as those around the table studied him. Miranda's expression asked a question, but everyone else had an expectant look. Sandreena put down her spoon, as Father-Bishop Creegan did with his goblet. Pug saw two students standing ready to serve, and a pair conducting some independent study on the other side of the dining hall while they snacked on fruit and cheese. Pug pointed to them and said, "You may leave us, and ask them to find another place for their studies, as well. Thank you."

The two students hurried across the room, and soon the dining hall was empty save for those at Pug's table.

Miranda finally said, "Tell them. Tell them all. They deserve to know."

Quietly, Pug began. "You all know of the invasion of the Kingdom of the Isles by the armies of the Emerald Queen. To most of you, it's history; to Miranda and me, we lived through it."

Amirantha remained quiet, but he had witnessed the devastation wrought by the Emerald Queen's armies in his homeland, when he had been a young man.

"There are things about those times of which I will not speak. There are questions I will not answer. But what I will tell you is only the truth." No one spoke, but there was a general acceptance of those statements in their expressions.

Miranda knew of what he was speaking, for she had been there. She remembered everything Nakor had said about the Fifth Circle and what transpired there, as they stood on the devastated world of Shila, had seen her father, Macros, battle the Demon King Maarg, and had spoken with the possessed demon, controlled by the Saaur Lorekeeper Hanam. Only Miranda, Pug, and Magnus knew that throughout all the years Nakor had been one of their closest confidants, he had also been a tool of Ban-ath, also called Kalkin, the God of Thieves and Liars.

Pug said, "One of the reasons your High Priest in Rillanon made our introduction, many years ago, Father-Bishop, was that much of what occurs here is in service to a much higher order, a fact not known by the majority of those who labor here." He looked from face to face, seeing his wife, the Warlock, the Prelate, his foster grandson, and the Knight-Adamant. "You have all come into this for different reasons, or so you assume." He looked for a long moment at Amirantha and said, "Your role is not clear to me yet, but I suspect it is vital we found you.

"Demons have begun appearing in unexpected locations, without the benefit of being summoned." At that, Amirantha's eyes widened slightly, but he said nothing.

Pug fell silent another moment, then said, "Father-Bishop Creegan, Jommy, and of course Miranda know this, but you two do not." He pointed to Amirantha and Sandreena. "Within the community of this island some of us serve a higher calling, through an organization called the Conclave of Shadows.

"We are by necessity a highly secret organization that has a very special relationship with the rulers of the three mightiest nations here on the continent of Triagia."

Creegan added, "Which also means they have influences in all the lesser kingdoms as well."

"And given Kaspar's role in conducting me here," said the Warlock, "with the Kingdom of Muboya on the other side of the world." He sounded impressed.

"We are also well established with other groups, including several of the major temples. Our purpose is not to subvert or even influence these entities, political and secular, but rather to keep open our lines of communications, to serve a greater good."

"And that greater good would be—?" asked the Warlock.

Jommy barked a laugh, then said, "The survival of the world." He leaned forward and all mirth vanished from his expression. In that instant, Amirantha could see that under the affable, smiling, open expression of this young man, there was a hard-bitten veteran of some terrible struggles. "I've seen things. I've lived through things no man should have survived, and I've watched people I cared about die." He paused and then said, "There is no one in the Conclave for whom I wouldn't lay down my life, and I'm certain each of them would lay down their life for me.

"It's not blind loyalty either. These people make a difference."

Pug said, "Enough, Jommy. We're not here to convince Amirantha we're an agency of good and those we oppose are servants of evil."

The Warlock nodded. "No need. As such things go, I already know that. At least I know you believe you're serving good."

"Adroit comment," said Miranda.

The Warlock smiled. "Many of the people who've tried to kill me over the years thought they were serving a greater good."

Jommy laughed. "I've had a similar experience over the years."

Sandreena looked impatient and sounded the same as she said, "The demons?"

"Yes," said Amirantha. "What is it you know about the demon realm?"

"There are graduated levels of reality," began Pug. "This is what would be considered by some to be the first level of Hell."

Jommy laughed. "At times I think that's too generous." He saw Miranda's expression darken and said, "I'll be quiet now."

"We fought demons on the world of Shila, home to the Saaur, and found our way to the passage from where they were coming. We destroyed the rift between Shila and here and escaped." He neglected to mention that Macros, Miranda's father, died holding the most powerful demon of the Fifth Circle at bay long enough for them to succeed.

"We know the demons are ruled by a creature named Maarg, and he has captains. Of these we know little, save his first captain a hundred years ago was named Tugor.

"They have intelligence, after a fashion, but it is very unlike our own."

"Agreed," said Amirantha. "So far my experience confirms they can be cunning, even clever, but there is a limit to their creative nature."

Pug nodded. "They seem drawn to the higher planes as a moth is to a flame."

Amirantha said, "Such is the case. That is why any summoning must have a containment spell or ward accompanying it, else the creature will devour everything in sight.

"Even the tiny imps, like my Nalnar, would run rampant to the best of his ability if unhampered." With a smile he said, "He has a particular fondness for baked goods."

Miranda didn't seem amused by the image. "Most of those we encountered were meat-eaters," she said coldly.

"Again, such is the case," said Amirantha. "Even more, those of the highest level I believe can draw life energy directly out of living beings using their own particular brand of magic."

"We know they have magic," said Pug, "for there was a demon utilizing an illusion to convince all who saw him he was the Emerald Queen."

Amirantha said, "I would know nothing about that, as I have never encountered a demon with the power to create such an illusion. That the demon could do such a feat surprises me. They tend to be a fairly direct lot in their use of magic.

"From what the few demons I can trust have told me—"

"Trust?" interrupted Miranda. "You have demons you can trust?"

" 'Trust,' perhaps, is the wrong word. They are predictable, and reliable in that they will do what I wish and tell me what I want to know because they see me as powerful; they know I can destroy them as well as banish them back to the demon realm."

"What have they told you?" asked Pug, shifting the topic back.

"They have cities, or something like social organization," said Amirantha. "Not cities such as we would recognize, but warrens in the caves of mountains, or hives perhaps might be a better analogy.

"They feed on one another, constantly, but I have the sense there is something here I'm not fully understanding." He paused, and looked at Pug, Miranda, and the others, and said, "I have no certain knowledge, but I have an intuition that they never really die. I think their essence is consumed either by another demon or it somehow returns to some fundamental state in their realm."

"Otherwise," said Jommy, "why haven't they run out of food already?"

"Yes," said Amirantha. "They do not farm or fish, and to the best of my ability to judge from what I've been told, their realm is devoid of any life except for demon life, as we understand life."

Pug considered how alien the Dasati realm of the second plane of existence had been, and how much farther removed the demon realm was, and said, "Perhaps it is something we shall never understand.

"To our present concerns; the Saaur are a race of warriors and magic-users that are the equal of any I've encountered, and the demons crushed them after seventeen years of struggle. The Saaur's empire encompassed an entire world and millions died fighting the demons.

"Our concern of course is, why are demons now appearing with increased frequency here in Midkemia?"

Amirantha said, "There are several possible theories."

"I'd like to hear them all," said Pug, "but for the moment, your most likely."

"Someone is bringing them here."

"Your brother?" asked Pug.

Amirantha nodded. "At least the one that tried to kill me, the event that had me off looking for Kaspar to tell someone something bad was occurring. And if he's able to subvert my spells and . . ." He sighed. "He's either grown far more powerful than I thought possible, or he's allied with others. Either way, it's to no good end."

Father-Bishop Creegan asked, "Whom does he serve?"

"Himself," said Amirantha.

"Runs in the family, I see," said Sandreena.

Ignoring the barb, Amirantha said, "Belasco is not mad the way Sidi was, but he is not entirely rational, either. He easily flies into rages that cause him to do things . . ." He shrugged. "Sidi was completely demented, and, as a result, unpredictable. I'm not sure he even knew why he did half the things he did all his life. Since childhood he was driven by impulses, needs, desires that I can only begin to imagine.

"Belasco, however, he is driven by hatred. He hates whatever he cannot have, whatever he cannot control, or whatever he cannot understand."

Jommy sighed. "That is a lot of hate."

"Indeed," said Amirantha. "If someone or something, an agency we have encountered before or identified, perhaps this organization of Black Caps as you called them"—he indicated Sandreena—"has offered him greater power, greater wealth, greater understanding, in other words spoken to his vanities and desires, then he would serve another.

"I am certain if he is in service, eventually his plan will be to surpass and supplant whomever or whatever he currently serves, but that's another topic. For the moment, he is either working on another's behalf, or for himself, but either way he seems determined to facilitate bringing some very nasty creatures into our world.

"The demon I encountered, the one that began this adventure for me, he was unlike anything I've run afoul of before; he was a battle demon *and* a spellcaster. I can't emphasize how unprecedented that is. In no lore have I encountered or through my own personal experience seen or heard of such a creature.

"Demons tend to fall into two groups, with the magic-users being the far smaller. Their race is dominated by raw power, and often magic is more subtle. Those that use magic tend to be cleverer, more manipulative, even seductive with their arts."

Sandreena said, "Which reminds me, how is Darthea these days?"

Amirantha hesitated a moment, then ignored the comment.

"I've often wondered how the little creatures like Nalnar survive."

Pug said, "We think it's a system of fealty, being useful, buying protection from more powerful demons further up the hierarchy. Maarg rules through his captains, and they in turn have minions. We assume those like your imp serve a useful purpose, perhaps as intelligence-gatherers, but perhaps through nothing more important than carrying out the trash.

"Whatever the truth of it may be, we do know that we are confounded by ignorance and need more intelligence." Looking at Amirantha, he said, "What can you do to help us?"

The Warlock said, "Whatever I might. Even were my brother not involved somehow, I would find this entire prospect fascinating. There is nowhere else I'd rather be at the moment."

A student stuck his head through the door and said, "Sir!"

"What is it?" Pug asked.

"Distant sentry reports a dragon heading this way."

Pug rose quickly and said, "Dragons do not trouble us. It can only be Tomas."

"Tomas?" asked Amirantha.

As Miranda, Pug, and Jommy made toward the door where the student had appeared, Father-Bishop Creegan said, "Why don't you two come along? This is something you may never see again in your life."

They hurried outside, where Pug and his family had quickly gathered. Amirantha saw Brandos had joined them, as well as the young man named Zane. In the distance they could see a speck in the sky grow larger, becoming something birdlike, and then resolving itself into something akin to a wyvern or drake on the wing.

It kept growing in size, and each time Amirantha thought it was now close enough to begin landing, it just kept coming. Finally it loomed up out of the sky, massive, with wings impossible to measure cracking like thunder as it halted its descent.

"Amazing!" said Sandreena, and Amirantha could only nod. He felt pain and looked down and saw she was clutching his arm, squeezing it tight enough to leave a bruise.

Kaspar walked up from a dell to the north of the landing site, and joined them. To Jommy he said, "I never thought I'd see this again."

"Me neither, General," replied the red-headed young man.

The dragon descended itself gently to the ground and lowered its massive head. Pug was surprised to note two figures climbed down. Tomas he was expecting, but the second visitor to this island was a figure completely new to him.

It looked like an elf, but seven feet tall, with hair the color of a red-rooster's comb. It wore robes that appeared to be woven from light satin, with embroidered edges of purple and gold, and across its back carried a staff that reeked of arcane energy.

Tomas embraced Pug, who said, "Welcome, old friend."

Tomas made his greetings to Miranda and the others known to him, then turned and said, "Pug, Miranda, may I present my companion, Gulamendis, Demon Master of the Clans of the Seven Stars—the Taredhel, or Star Elves in our tongue."

Amirantha turned to Father-Bishop Creegan and Sandreena and said, "Now I am certain there is nowhere else on this world I'd rather be this moment."

# CHAPTER 16

## ALLIES

The dragon leaped into the sky.

Tomas bid it farewell and said he would call it again if needed, though as often as not, when he visited Pug, one of the magicians transported him home in much swifter, if less dramatic, fashion. Everyone watched in silent awe the spectacle of a great golden dragon winging its way into the blue vault above.

Pug glanced at those standing near him and felt a pang. Here were some of the people he loved most in the world, his wife, his surviving children, his oldest friend. Again, as he had in the past, he felt a burden of fore-boding threaten to overwhelm him. Only Nakor, now dead, had known what Pug knew. Miranda had learned most of it, though he held back one painful and terrifying thing: he was doomed to watch everyone he loved die before him.

He had told Tomas some of the truth behind the manipulations of the god Ban-ath over the years, and even less to Father-Bishop Creegan, but not the entire truth: that most of his life had been spent as a tool for the Trickster to ensure the survival of this very world. He had no doubt that if the God of Thieves and Liars wasn't the primary agency behind what was occurring now, he was involved somehow. Pug pushed aside his rising sense of sadness, realizing that part of what triggered this was his need to communicate some of the truth—again, only a part—to others. There was no one alive who fully knew the burden Pug carried every day of his life.

Pug motioned to Tomas and his companion and said, "Come, we have much to discuss." He turned to Father-Bishop Creegan and said, "Join us, please," and then with a nod indicated Amirantha was to attend as well. To Sandreena he said, "I believe you could use new clothing and some arms?"

She nodded, still agape at what she just witnessed. Pug motioned for one of the students who had observed Tomas's arrival, and instructed him to take Sandreena in tow and find her what she needed.

Pug said, "Excuse me a moment," then went to speak privately with Miranda. They conferred quietly and briefly, then she nodded and departed, hurrying off to another part of the house.

Pug motioned for his guests to join him and led them to the private quarters set aside for him and his family. An open garden with several benches served as a casual meeting place, and while this gathering lacked any aspect of the social about it, the privacy afforded here was needed. There was no one on the island Pug didn't trust, but many of his students were young, excitable, and prone to gossip.

"If anyone wishes any refreshments," said Pug, "I'll send for them."

As Amirantha and Father-Bishop Creegan had just finished a repast in the dining hall, it fell to Tomas and Gulamendis to decline.

"Very well," said Pug. He glanced from face to face, then said, "Too many times in my life I assumed coincidence, only to find later that some higher agency was at work. I may say things that either surprise or alarm you, but what I say will be not conjecture but truth. There is something here bringing us all to council, something of the gods, or perhaps fate." He looked at the strange elf from another world and said, "Let us begin with our newest guest. Tell us your tale, Gulamendis."

The elf studied the three human faces before him, his own an unreadable mask, but he did glance at Tomas, who subtly nodded he should cooperate, and the elf began to tell his tale. He started slowly and began with the history of his people as it pertained to this current crisis.

Time seemed to halt for Amirantha, Father-Bishop Creegan, and Pug as the elf painted images with his words. He spoke of a struggling band of refugees, fleeing this world for another, and a few thousand survivors mastering the land around them. He evoked images of the reverent elves planting the saplings of the great trees they called the Seven Stars and building their first city around those trees, then expanding their control over the world.

His tale became a people's epic as the elves who had fled to the stars became masters of all they beheld. Arts flourished, music, healing, and scholarship. They encountered other races, and Gulamendis was unapologetic in recounting how those encounters became conflict and how relentless and unforgiving the Taredhel were. Those who would not yield were destroyed. And few yielded.

The client races withered and died out, so that after five centuries, on all the worlds of the Clan of the Seven Stars, only elves endured.

Pug remained stoic during the narrative, but Tomas, his oldest living friend, could see the subtle signs of concern as the tall elf spoke. These were a harsh and unforgiving people, as relentless in their own fashion as the Moredhel but so much more powerful.

"For nearly a millennium, we had peace and we flourished," said Gulamendis. "Then we came to a new world. It was devoid of life, but life had once abided. We saw the rubble of structures and the remnants of civilization. We investigated and discovered another portal, one not of our fashioning. Our aremancers studied it while others scoured the world, seeking clues as to what happened. Those who worked with the portal unraveled its secrets and we opened it to yet another world. And there we met the demons."

He looked from face to face and asked, "Have any of you faced a demon?"

Pug said, "Of one stripe or another, all of us at different times."

Looking at Amirantha, Gulamendis said, "You are a summoner, yes?"

Amirantha nodded. "I am."

"You understand then, better than these others, what is required to bring a demon across the realms to our own dimension."

"Yes," said Amirantha. "The magic is complex and difficult to master."

With a smile that could only be called ironic, the elf said, "That is why there are so few of us. Those who lack talent do not survive the learning process."

He paused, and said, "We are explorers, and for centuries we used our translocation portals, what you call 'rifts,' to reach other worlds.

"Explorers died and most worlds we found were uninhabitable, but over the centuries we moved through the stars.

"Of late, for two hundred years or so, some have spoken of finding this world, our Home, the world from which we sprang. Some were against this, thinking it likely this world was destroyed by the war between the Valheru"—he glanced at Tomas—"and the new gods.

"Others dreamed of finding this world free of strife, as it was in our oldest myths." Again he glanced at Tomas. "Though it was judged likely we might again face our former masters." He took a deep breath. "Until I met Tomas I, like most of my people, thought we had risen high enough in our ability that we could vanquish the Valheru should they endure." He lowered his eyes. "I fear that proud certainty of our own power is why we fall before the demons."

"Tell us of the demons," urged Pug.

"One of our explorers found a world, desolate beyond measure. Barren rock and empty oceans, but once lush."

"How could you judge that?" asked Father-Bishop Creegan.

"The world had been inhabited; there were ruins of great cities. In those cities we found artifacts belonging to the people who had lived on that world. Within were sprawling gardens with irrigation systems of clever design. Given the volume of water employed, we assume that hot, dusty world was once tropical, or at least verdant on every hand. Vast plains of farming land, again with miles of irrigation systems still in evidence, lay exposed to relentless hot winds, stripping them down to rock and sand. From the age of the artifacts and buildings, we judged the world depopulated less than a century.

"Yet there was not a hint of life. Of the great race that once inhabited this world, we found nothing, not even bones, and there was little remaining to give us any hint of who they might be. They were physically small, we think, because their doorways were short and their rooms tiny by our measure, yet they built majestic monuments to their own glory, great pyramids of stone. We found art, paintings and tapestries, though few showed any hint of their maker; they tended to abstract designs of rich color. We found a few likenesses, and we think they may have been a race akin to the dwarves.

"They may have had libraries or great schools, but of books, tomes, or scrolls we found nothing but ash. Fires raged throughout their cities, across every vista, and we wondered who or what had caused this planetwide catastrophe.

"In the deepest vault of one of those great stone buildings we found words, hastily scrawled over murals on a wall. Words painted with the most indelible paint they knew, so that this tiny legacy of this race might endure.

"It took our Lorekeepers years to unravel their meaning, but they simply said, 'Why have our gods deserted us? Why are we to perish?' And a word that we could not translate followed by ' . . . are without this hall. So we will end. Should any read this, cry for the . . .' and another word we could not translate."

"Demons?" asked Amirantha.

"Later experience led us to believe so."

Pug said, "If demons somehow came to that world, and ran free, eventually all life as we know it would end. Once they ran out of prey, they would turn on one another, and eventually one would survive. He would finally starve to death."

Amirantha and Gulamendis exchanged questioning looks, and the Warlock said, "I've never conjured a demon to this realm that remained long enough to starve to death."

The elf smiled as he nodded agreement. "I have fed a few, along the way, but as with you, when they have done my bidding I banish them back to their own realm. Until we encountered the Demon Legion, I had never even considered how an unfettered demon would behave in our realm."

Amirantha said, "I have encountered a few." He glanced at Father-Bishop Creegan and said, "Not everything I do is a confidence trick. I have rid this world of several serious evils over the years."

"No doubt," said the cleric dryly.

Amirantha turned his attention back to Gulamendis. "One weak-willed would-be demon master, overstepping his limitations, to his very short regret, and a demon would be running loose. I have hunted down and dispatched a dozen over the years."

Jommy appeared at the doorway and entered the garden. Pug motioned him over and the red-headed noble said, "Miranda is gone, she asked me to tell you. She'll be back soon." He glanced around, and said, "Should I leave?"

Pug shook his head no, and said, "Stay. You'll be neck-deep in whatever we run into as much as any of the rest of us."

Jommy moved off to one side and took a seat on the bench beside where Tomas stood.

Gulamendis said, "Among my people, I am considered something of an outcast." He noted Amirantha's slight smile in acknowledgment. "Many of my people mistakenly blame me and others who are students of demon lore for the assaults."

"Even though you found proof of demon incursion into other worlds decades before you encountered the Demon Legion?"

Gulamendis nodded sadly. "It is the nature of things that many people are more interested in affixing blame than fixing the problem."

Amirantha said, "We hadn't encountered any of the problems you've mentioned on any significant scale until recently." He sat back. "I'm not sure we are, even now. It is almost certain that much of what I've recently seen with unexpected demon encounters is the work of one agency, a summoner who has the ability to wreak havoc for . . . his own reasons." He shrugged.

"How certain are you of this?" asked Gulamendis.

"Absolutely, for he interfered with one of my summonings and almost got me killed. I tried calling forth a familiar demon and instead got the most aggressive battle demon I've ever encountered."

"Fascinating," said the elf. "I've never heard of a summons being distorted that way. I've had them interrupted, abruptly at times, but never . . . perverted in such a fashion." His eyes narrowed. "It would involve magic of extreme power . . ."

"And subtlety," added the Warlock. "At key instances changes in the summoning would need to be introduced."

The two demon experts seemed on the verge of discussing the specifics when Pug interrupted. "I'm as fascinated by this as either of you, but we need to consider the larger picture. Why?"

"Why?" repeated Amirantha. "Well, as I've said, my brother has been trying to kill me for years."

"Your brother?" asked Gulamendis.

"I'll explain," said Amirantha. To Pug he said, "As I said, I'm surprised he has developed the skills needed, but not that he's trying to kill me."

"Why now?" asked Pug. "Why after all these years, and

in a way that would be the most likely to create echoing chaos around you? If he's as powerful as you say, and he has knowledge of your whereabouts, why not just drop a ball of fire into the room with you?"

"Fire wards are part of the proactive spells," said Amirantha while Gulamendis nodded in agreement. "But I see your point. He could easily have dropped a very large rock on my head while I walked to the cave."

"Unless he couldn't see you," added Jommy. When all eyes turned to him, he said, "Sorry."

"No need to be sorry," said Pug. "That is a good point."

Amirantha said, "It means he sees me with magic, not sight."

"So he could be anywhere," added Gulamendis, "but he needs you to be working your arts to know exactly where you are at the moment."

Pug said, "My feelings, entirely. But to be able to spy upon you, somehow, so as to know when you're actively conjuring a demon . . . ?" Pug shrugged, as if asking how.

Gulamendis slowly shook his head. "That is very subtle and very powerful magic craft, even for my people."

Pug said, "I have been a student of magic for most of my life, and am well into my second century of study, yet there is so much more we do not know than what we do.

"I also have difficulty imagining how your brother is able to do this."

"My magic signature, for lack of a better term, would be as familiar to Belasco as his is to me," said Amirantha. "As yours and your wife's are, apparently, to your son Magnus."

"But how is he able to know where you will be, until you actually begin to conjure?"

"That," said Amirantha, "is, indeed, the question."

"Spies?" offered Jommy.

Amirantha said, "Only Brandos, and perhaps his wife, Samantha, might know where I'm going to be when next I conjure. I trust them as family."

"What about demon spies?" asked Jommy. "I mean, I don't

really know how this conjuring of demons works, do I? But maybe he's got a demon somewhere whose job is to alert him when you're calling up some other demon."

Amirantha and Gulamendis both looked thunderstruck. The human demon master spoke first. "I don't know . . . ?"

"Is that possible?" asked the elf.

Jommy shrugged. "You two are the demon lore experts. You don't know?"

Gulamendis seemed insulted by the remark, but said nothing. Amirantha said, "There is far more that we don't know, as Pug observed, than we do."

Jommy shrugged. "So, why don't you ask?"

"Ask whom?" Gulamendis's tone was cold.

Jommy grinned. "Ask the demons?"

Amirantha looked stunned. Then he laughed aloud. "Oh, gods and fishes," he exclaimed. The Star Elf also looked astonished at the suggestion, then he started to chuckle.

Amirantha said, "I suspect my new friend here has fallen prey to the same failing as I have, to wit, being so focused on mastering our particular arts—which is part of staying alive— that we neglected a broader curiosity about those very creatures we employ to do our bidding."

"What do you do now?" asked Creegan.

Amirantha stood and said, "Why, we summon a demon and start asking questions!"

With a single gesture and a word, he executed a spell. Pug and Jommy both felt the familiar sensation, like hair rising on the arms, when standing near a powerful spell. Tomas remained standing, but his hand fell to the hilt of his sword.

Creegan stood reflexively and stepped back as a puff of black smoke revealed a small, blue-skinned imp. "Nalnar!" shouted Amirantha. "You are summoned."

"Master," said the creature, looking around the group.

Gulamendis laughed in obvious delight. "It's Chokin!"

"Chokin?" asked Pug.

"I have an imp that serves me—two, actually, Choyal and Chokin. This one looks like Chokin."

Hearing that name, the imp regarded Gulamendis. "Chokin?" he asked in a high-pitched voice.

"Do you know Chokin?" asked Amirantha.

Nodding vigorously, Nalnar said, "We be of blood, and he is my elder. Choyal is my younger."

"Brothers?" asked Gulamendis.

"What is brothers?" asked the imp.

"You are of the same mother or father," said the Warlock.

"Mother? Father? Not understand, master."

"Apparently they don't have parents," said Jommy, fascinated by his first look at a creature from the demonic realm that wasn't trying to kill him.

"What do you mean he's of your blood?" asked Amirantha.

"We spawn together. Choyal, Chokin, Lanlar, Jodo, Takesh, Tadal, Nimno, Jadru, and Nalnar! We nine. Jodo and Lanlar no more. Seven only now." He lowered his head, an expression of sadness totally unexpected on a face that alien.

"What happened to your . . . brothers?" asked Amirantha.

"Eaten," he replied. Looking from face to face, the imp asked, "Master needs Nalnar?"

Amirantha looked at Pug. "Could we have something for Nalnar to nibble on? He's more cooperative if we feed him."

"Certainly. What do you require?"

Looking at the imp, who now had an eager expression on his blue face, Amirantha said, "I think a plate of cheese and bread, perhaps a small slice of sausage, and any fruit would keep him occupied."

The imp looked positively thrilled at the prospect of food. Pug used his arts to summon a student waiting close by, and the young woman was sent to the kitchen to fetch the food.

While the food was being fetched, Sandreena appeared, now wearing a clean and new suit of clothing and fine, highly polished armor. She even sported a new tabard with the symbol of her Order on it. Father-Bishop Creegan looked at Pug and said, "Impressive. How did you happen to have the tabard?"

Sandreena said, "More, how did you happen to have an entire suit of armor that fits me perfectly?"

Pug smiled. "We have resources."

The imp began jumping up and down excitedly, "Sandreena! Nalnar love Sandreena."

The female Knight-Adamant of the Order of the Shield of the Weak looked upon the imp with widened eyes. "Nalnar?" Looking at Amirantha with hooded eyes, she said, "Putting on a show, are we?"

Amirantha chose to say nothing.

Pug said, "We have discovered that despite Amirantha and Gulamendis's experience with demons, we are still ignorant of their realm. We thought we might begin by interrogating one of its more tractable inhabitants."

Sandreena sat, saying, "Well, my experience with this little monstrosity is it's a little more intelligent than a dog, less reliable, and prone to very rude and inappropriate behavior at inopportune times." She looked at Amirantha. "Why not Darthea? I'm certain you and she have had many quiet conversations."

Amirantha looked uncomfortable, but said nothing.

"Darthea?" asked Jommy.

Sandreena's expression as she glanced at Amirantha was poisonous, and the Warlock seemed genuinely embarrassed. She said, "Not all the residents of the demon realm are hideous. Some are . . . beautiful."

Jommy closed his eyes in sympathetic pain for the Warlock, while Father-Bishop Creegan looked appalled. "A succubus?"

"Succubus?" asked Jommy, his eyes wide with fascination.

Father-Bishop Creegan said, "We scarcely believe the lore, but the succubi are female demons of incredible beauty who seduce the righteous into acts of depravity and worse."

Amirantha took a deep breath and said, "Those legends are vastly overstated." He looked at the faces now regarding him and said, "Each demon survives as he or she must, with whatever gifts they have. The succubi are . . . gifted with the ability to resemble a female of great beauty of many races. It's an illusion."

Gulamendis smiled and said, "My brother would be fascinated by such illusion. That is his area of expertise."

Amirantha said, "Enough. I'm past one hundred years old and

have put embarrassment over my personal proclivities behind me; I've outlived a dozen lovers, so if I seek comfort with someone who will be here in another hundred years, that is my affair."

Sandreena flushed and her anger was visible, though she was silent.

He turned to her and said, "Again, as I have said on three other occasions, if I have hurt you, I am deeply sorry." Then his expression turned hard, and his voice firm, as he added, "But I made you no oath that I broke, nor did I promise you anything. If you cannot forgive me, that is *your* burden, not mine." Looking at Pug, he said, "May we please return to the matter at hand?"

Pug had lived too many years to find this sort of discourse anything but banal. He nodded and said, "Please, speak to your minion." Seeing the refreshments for the imp were at the door, he waved in the student carrying the tray and indicated she should put it before Nalnar.

Without leave, the imp began devouring the cheese, bread, and fruit. Amirantha sighed and, with a slight inclination of his head, indicated he understood Pug's impatience with Sandreena's ire and the sordid aspects of it. He said, "Nalnar, tell me of those with whom you were spawned."

"Yes, master?" said the imp.

"Perhaps if you were more specific?" suggested Gulamendis.

Nodding, Amirantha said, "Tell me of Choda, Nimno . . ." he struggled to recall the other names " . . . and the others with whom you were spawned."

"Tell?" asked the imp. He said, "Tell what, master?"

"Tell us of your life, what you do when you are not summoned here."

"We live, we die, we fight . . ." A light seemed to enter the creature's eyes, and he said, "We began. We were not, then we were. Hundreds of us swimming in the beginning place. We fought. We ate, we grew. Of the hundreds, fifty endured. Fifty crawled out of the beginning place, and we fought for those bigger and hungry. We were the clever ones, we nine. We banded together and killed those who waited, and devoured them. We became strong, and we were nine together. Those who waited ran from us and sought out those weak ones who didn't band together." He shrugged. "We left the beginning place and hid."

"Hid?" asked Amirantha. "From whom did you hide?"

"All who were bigger, stronger, and hungry," answered the imp as he impaled a piece of cheese on a talon and devoured it. "Nalnar thirsty!" With a narrowing gaze, he looked at Amirantha and asked, "Wine?"

"No!" said Amirantha. He looked at Pug and added, "You do not want to see him drunk." To the imp he said, "Water."

"Water," the imp repeated.

Pug motioned for the student, who stood watching with fascination, and had to wave vigorously to get her attention. The young woman nodded vigorously and hurried off, returning moments later with a goblet of water.

The imp drank greedily, then dropped the cup. He looked around the gathered onlookers, then howled in glee. Amirantha sighed and, with a wave of his hand, banished the creature.

"Why?" asked Pug quietly.

It was Gulamendis who answered. "They grow intoxicated with our food, even water, and become bold. We only feed them as a reward after we're done with their service. It's why he banished him." He nodded approval to Amirantha.

Amirantha said, "He was of no further use as he would become fractious and wish to lie—he needs to regain his sobriety in his own realm."

"I have had similar difficulty with imps," said the elf.

"We need more information," said Tomas quietly.

Gulamendis inclined his head respectfully and said, "Yes, Ancient One, and I have seen the error of my lack of curiosity."

"As have I," added Amirantha. "But in your case, I wonder," he said to Gulamendis. "When your people ran afoul of demons, did it not occur to you to seek information?"

Gulamendis said, "How reliable are your sources among the demons?"

Amirantha shrugged. "I have not had the need to establish that."

"Precisely," said Gulamendis.

Pug observed the Star Elf and thought he detected a slight bridling at the implied insult that he should have done more. "I'm certain Gulamendis had his own concerns that were pressing."

Showing the elven self-constraint Pug had observed with Aglaranna's people, Gulamendis merely nodded slightly. "Indeed. My standing with my people has never been high, and once the nature of the Demon Legion was established, let's say of those few of us who are concerned with the nature of demons, we were not given opportunity to help.

"Some were executed outright—"

"Executed?" interrupted Tomas. "How is that possible?"

Gulamendis seemed thrown off balance by the question. "By order of the Regent Lord. Some of us were imprisoned and questioned, tortured, while others were summarily executed. It was believed by the Regent's Meet, or at least the majority voting, that we were responsible for this invasion."

Tomas's expression was a mix of disbelief and outrage. "Executed," he whispered. "Elf killing elf." He lowered his eyes as if overcome by sadness for a moment. Then he looked at the Taredhel Demon Master. "I think in days to come I may have to speak to your rulers, to this Regent Lord."

Gulamendis did not like the direction that remark was heading, so he said, "I did try to ascertain what I could of the Demon Legion from my summoned demons, but time was not my ally. I was imprisoned and confined under guard. The best I could do was summon Choyal, one of my imps, for a brief time at night, and send him to the kitchen to steal food and drink so I wouldn't perish in my cage."

Pug asked, "Why were you spared?"

"To guarantee my brother's good behavior."

"Explain, please," asked Pug.

"As the Demon Legion pressed us, the search for a safe haven became more pressing. Our capital world, Andcardia, would eventually fall; the Regent Lord and the Regent's Meet knew this long before it was apparent to the rest of the population.

"Great meetings were held in the squares of our cities, and glorious banners were unfurled and flowers rained down on warriors marching off to fight the demons. Every type of elven magic was unleashed—we have spell-shattering weapons that cause demon magicians to falter so our armored fighters can close in and kill them; we have death towers that unleash massive bolts of foul energy that destroys demon flesh on contact; war machines of terrible aspect were erected and unleashed on them.

"And still the demons came."

Pug said, "Let us go back to that world your people discovered, the one devoid of life. If that wasn't where you encountered the demons, where?"

"Our translocation portals work with a certain degree of imprecision. I do not understand the issues, as it is magic that is alien to me." He inclined his head toward Pug. "You would most certainly know what the portal masters speak of; I do not.

"I only know that in years past, it was decided a hub would be constructed, one that all worlds would connect to, a centralized hall of magic where anyone wishing to travel between the worlds of the Clans of the Seven Stars could easily find passage.

"So, from any world one need only step through one gate to the hub world, called Komilis, and from there to the final destination."

Pug nodded slightly as he mused, "It would forestall the need for dozens of rifts, for each world would only need one rift-way, and only the magicians on Komilis would need to tend to many gates."

"Precisely," said Gulamendis. "But when our exploration team found the world of the demons . . ."

"They overran the gate and gained access to your hub world," said Sandreena. Her tone left no doubt she thought this was a military blunder of unforgivable proportion.

Gulamendis said nothing, but his expression said he agreed with her tone. "The struggle over the central city of Komilis lasted years.

"The demons took control of the hub long enough to find their way to all our worlds."

"Didn't you try to destroy the gates?" asked Pug.

"Yes," said Gulamendis, "but it was too late. They had found their way to all our worlds."

"And if they overrun the gate from Andcardia to Midkemia before you can close it," said Pug, "they'll be here."

"Or they are here already," said Amirantha.

"I think you'd know if they were here," said Gulamendis dryly.

"Not necessarily," said Amirantha. "That demon I told you of, the one conjured in by my brother, have you ever seen its like?"

Gulamendis said, "I can't be sure, but I think not."

"A battle demon who is also a magic-user?"

"No," said the elf. "I have not seen its like."

Amirantha said, "I have a theory. It is only surmise, but it fits what we know so far."

"I would welcome it," said Pug.

"There is another agency at work," said the Warlock.

"Your brother?" suggested Pug.

Amirantha shook his head. "Perhaps, but unlikely. Belasco is many things, but he is no fanatic. However, he would willingly serve those who are.

"What Sandreena described as a failed summoning means someone is desperately trying to gate demons into this realm, and is willing to risk mistakes—even catastrophic ones—to achieve this goal.

"What I should have pointed out when Sandreena told us of the failed summoning is that had the summoner been slightly more gifted, those demons he conjured would have remained in our realm a great deal longer."

"And grown more powerful," added Gulamendis.

"Which is beside the point, really," said the Warlock. "The point is some agency knows this world exists and is trying to bring demons here, and is willing to unleash madness to achieve that goal.

"Moreover, it may be completely unrelated to the danger our elf friend here has come to warn us of."

"Why do you say that?" asked Father-Bishop Creegan, his doubts about Amirantha's presence being set aside for a moment.

"Because if I have my timeline correct, these occurrences have preceded his arrival by a decade?" He looked at Jommy.

"Yes," said the red-headed noble. "It was about ten years ago when we ran into that bunch of Black Caps off the shore of the peninsula."

"And your brother arrived here, what, less than a year ago?" said Amirantha to Gulamendis. The elf nodded. Looking around the room, the Warlock said, "The demons were trying to come here before they reached Gulamendis's home world."

"I'm not convinced these are unrelated problems," said Pug, "but even if they are, they both must be confronted.

"We can't have lunatics running around trying to bring demons into our realm in wholesale fashion." Amirantha's expression revealed he was unsure if Pug was putting him in that category. "And if the Demon Legion follows the Star Elves to this world . . ." He left the thought unfinished.

"Two problems, then," said Jommy.

Tomas said, "What do we do?" His question was directed at Pug.

Pug hesitated a moment. As leader of the Conclave of Shadows he had been expected to give instructions for decades, but he still found it difficult sometimes to simply order men of vast power and experience, rather than let them suggest their best course of action. Finally, he said, "I think Father-Bishop Creegan, Amirantha, Sandreena, and whoever they wish to recruit from here should return to Akrakon and start looking for any signs of who is trying to bring demons here."

Jommy said, "I'll go, too, if you have no objection. I saw that first monster come ashore ten years back and think it might be time to finally get to the bottom of who these Black Caps are."

Pug nodded. Looking at Tomas, he said, "I think you and I

should travel with Gulamendis to greet the newcomers to our world and assess the risk of the Demon Legion following them here."

Gulamendis said, "There could be difficulties."

Tomas said, "You've made me aware of those possible difficulties. Still, we have no choice. We cannot ignore an incursion of the size your arrival heralds. Moreover, it will not be ignored by the Kingdom of the Isles once Alystan of Natal's report wends its way to the Prince's court in Krondor. A detachment of riders will certainly be dispatched to ride from Carse or Tulan Garrison to investigate. Dolgan's dwarves will also certainly send someone up to keep an eye on your people."

"That would be unwise," said Gulamendis.

"Why?" asked Pug.

"Because the Regent Lord has given orders that any who blunder across our valley are to be killed on sight."

"What!" said Tomas. "Your valley!"

Gulamendis said, "We are a people facing extinction! We will dig in and we will fight if we are threatened, by humans, dwarves, or even our distant kin. It would be better if you let me approach the Regent's Meet first, to let them know I've made contact and that you are interested in helping prevent the demons' arrival here."

Tomas glanced at Pug, who nodded slightly.

"Very well," said the Warleader of Elvandar. "I can summon a dragon and land you within a short distance of your outposts."

"No need," said the Demon Master. "I can summon a flier." He saw Pug's expression and quickly added, "It will be completely under my control and dismissed when I arrive."

Tomas said, "Leave as you will, but tell your leaders that I will be along within three days—I will return to my Queen and then I will come to your new home, and I will bring members of my lady's council, and we shall sit with your Regent and discuss what we shall do should the Demon Legion come.

"But your leaders would be well advised to reconsider their

attitude toward those who may approach the boundaries of your encampment in the mountains, Gulamendis. Despite your leaders' beliefs in their superiority, you are a people who are few in numbers, hard punished by a war seemingly without end, and you will need help. Those who come to you may do so inadvertently or out of curiosity, so treat them with respect." He left unsaid that should that message not be received well by the Regent Lord, Tomas would not be pleased, and even a Valheru of such a strange origin was still a being to be respected, if not outright feared.

The elven Demon Master nodded, and bowed to those in the garden. To Amirantha he said, "We must sit down and soon; we have much to discuss. There is much to learn."

"Agreed," said the Warlock, standing to bow slightly in respect.

As he made ready to depart, Gulamendis said, "There are so many things I would learn from you and your companions, Pug. But I am not typical of my people." He glanced at Tomas and said, "Your old friend may speak of words we had, and realize that I am frank when I say we will not welcome your people's overtures until we know we are safe."

He looked up at the sky above and said, "Home. It is a myth, yet here I stand, under the same sky looked upon by my ancestors."

Looking again at Tomas, he said, "And I am not the best interlocutor you could have chosen, Lord Tomas, for most of my people blame me and those like me for the demon invasion. No matter what we say, they will not believe there is a demon gate out there somewhere through which these creatures travel."

"Demon gate?" asked Pug. "You said nothing of this."

"It's almost a myth as well. A rumor, as much as anything else. It is said that one Demon Master, prior to his execution, pleaded to tell the Regent's Meet that he knew how the demons came into our realm: through a demon gate. He never said how he knew, though it may be he gleaned the information from one of his summoned creatures. But it also may be that is but a hope we who practice my craft hold on to, to give us hope that some day we shall be forgiven for this horror visited on our people."

Calmly, Pug said, "I know there's a demon gate."

For the first time, Gulamendis's composure cracked and something akin to hope played across his face. "How do you know?"

"Because I have been there."

# CHAPTER 17

## DETERMINATION

Gulamendis looked stunned.

Slowly, he asked, "You've been there?"

"Shila."

"Shila?"

"The world from which the Saaur—a race living on this world now—were driven by the demons. It must be the gate where I saw Macros battle Maarg, the Demon King."

Gulamendis sat down, now completely stunned. "Maarg?"

Amirantha said, "We've heard legends . . ."

Gulamendis stood, held his hand aloft, and conjured a spell. In a moment, a twin to Amirantha's imp stood before him, wrapped in dissipating smoke. The creature looked surprised to be surrounded by so many onlookers, and spun in place before acknowledging Gulamendis. "Master?" he asked, looking meek and pathetic.

Gulamendis said, "Tell us of Maarg."

Instantly, the imp shrieked in terror and spun in place, as if seeking a way out. "No!" he cried in a shrill voice. "No! No! No!"

The creature was obviously terrified, but Gulamendis held out his hand. "Tell us of the Demon King!" he commanded.

The imp looked around, a crazed feral cast to his features, his eyes hooded as if he sought escape or a route for attack. He crouched with clawed hands extended as if he would rend anything that he could reach. "No!" he shrieked, a sound of rage and terror. "No! No! No!" he kept repeating.

Gulamendis's eyes narrowed and he said, "He has never disobeyed me before." He stuck out his left hand, palm up, and incanted something in a language Pug and the others did not understand, but it caused a reaction from Amirantha, who seemed as shaken by the imp's behavior as the others. "Tell me!" said the Taredhel, and with a closing of his hand some magic was enacted, for the imp doubled over holding his stomach, suddenly in terrible pain.

"Master, no!" cried the imp, the rage and fear in his eyes now gone, his expression one of pleading.

"By ward and word, spell and will, *tell me of the Demon King!*" Again he opened and closed his hand and the imp shrieked in agony. Then, with a wave, he released his magic and the imp drew a deep gasp of air.

The creature cringed and whispered as if terrified of being overheard outside the room. "The Demon King is greatest of all! He hears what is said; he sees what is done. He rends and eats, and no one escapes him. He rails at the gate, waiting for the final opening." Suddenly the creature's eyes widened and it stiffened as if struck from behind, then its eyes rolled up and he fell forward.

Amirantha stood and with a sweeping arc of both hands in opposite directions, inscribed a dome of energy above the garden. "Brace yourself!" he shouted.

From above, the sky exploded, the calm blue of the afternoon instantly changed to a raging blast of yellow and white, blinding anyone who glanced upward. Even through the mystic shield the heat swept down over them like waves of torment. Pug was but an instant behind the Warlock with his own counter-spell, and the heat vanished as he neutralized the inferno.

Gulamendis, Father-Bishop Creegan, and Sandreena were all just reacting, as Jommy dove for the ground, seeking to be as close to the cool soil as humanly possible.

The flames above vanished, and Pug swept his hand around him in a circular motion, incanting another spell of protection.

Then from another part of the building a massive silver bolt of energy sped into the sky, arching quickly out of view.

Amirantha said, "What was that?"

Pug glanced around to make sure everyone was all right, then knelt to examine the fallen form of the imp. "That would be my wife. Whoever sent that mystic comet down on our heads is about to be suddenly repaid. It's a nasty trick she's known since before I met her. If our attacker has no protective wards in place, he's about to get back worse than he gave. That energy bolt requires far more protection than mystic fire does. It could melt a house." Dropping the arm of the imp, he said, "It's dead." Looking at Gulamendis, he added, "I think."

"As dead as it can be here in this realm. It will slowly re-form back in the . . ." He pointed. "Look."

The figure of the imp faded into transparency, then mist, then was gone within a moment.

"It will re-form, as I said, and I will be able to summon it once more."

"With demons, there's dead, and then there's dead," said Amirantha. "I was going to ask you later how your warriors have been killing them."

"With every weapon and spell we can muster," said Gulamendis.

"There's one of your problems, then," said Jommy.

Both demon masters looked at him and Amirantha said, "Yes, he's right."

Gulamendis nodded. "No one believed me when I would tell them that short of complete destruction through very powerful magic, the demons were only banished to their own realm."

"And if they rested up a bit, they could come back through any open gate into this realm," said Jommy.

"An army that cannot be destroyed, only delayed?" asked Tomas.

"Oh, demons can be destroyed," said Sandreena. "I've destroyed more than one myself. Completely and utterly."

Father-Bishop Creegan indicated agreement. "It's the magic of the gods that obliterates them. If you even can stun one long enough to utter a specific oath or spell, the creature is utterly destroyed." Yet he sounded worried. "But those are rare cases, Pug. Most of our magic is banishment. We do not belabor the difference when we teach that magic, but the majority of demons we deal with are merely sent back to the demon realm."

"How difficult will it be to deal with a host of them?" asked Tomas pointedly.

The old cleric visibly sagged as he admitted, "Impossible. Even if I should muster ever priest, priestess, monk, and nun of every god, as well as all the martial orders, each would only be able to destroy one or two each day. The magic is difficult and exhausting."

Pug let out a sigh as Miranda came storming into the garden. "What was that?" she asked accusingly. "We've got half the outer buildings on fire and a lot of very frightened students, not to mention a few who were badly burned. It's a miracle no one was killed."

Magnus also appeared and looked ready to do battle. When he saw his mother's mood, he said nothing.

Pug glanced at his elder son and said, "Caleb? The others?"

"Everyone is fine, as far as I can tell," he answered. "Whoever erected that barrier saved this building and this is where most of the heat struck. Some fires in the outer buildings, but they are being quickly dealt with."

"Good," said Pug. Looking at his wife, he said, "That retaliatory bolt you threw back along the path of the incoming spell, do you have any sense of where it went?"

She nodded. "To the southeast, to somewhere near the Peaks of the Quor, I think."

"Well, someone has just gotten a rude awakening if they've survived that," said Pug. To Magnus he said, "I want you to pass the word: we're now on a war footing. Send the younger students away, either back to their home worlds or to Stardock. Send messages to everyone to return here as quickly as possible—I want every master magician in council in the next few days."

Gulamendis moved over to stand next to Amirantha. "These human magicians are . . . impressive."

"You would do well not to underestimate them," cautioned the Warlock.

"I don't understand" said Gulamendis.

Amirantha gifted the Taredhel Demon Master with a slight smile. "I think you do."

The elf lowered his voice and said, "I will not, but others of my kind . . . even the harsh lessons of the Demon Legion are lost on them. Arrogance is a relative term among my race."

Amirantha saw Pug, Tomas, Miranda, and Magnus were in a deep conversation, while Father-Bishop Creegan was speaking intently with Sandreena, and Jommy seemed more intent on watching the pair of them than the two demon experts. The Warlock gently took Gulamendis by the elbow, led him a few more feet away, and said in a low voice, "Let me speak candidly, my new friend. You and I understand things about what is coming that few others on this world can only imagine in a nightmare. And we've had but glimpses into that realm from which those nightmares come.

"Perhaps those you left behind have faced them, but until the Demon Legion arrives, we have much work to do."

"What are you proposing?" asked Gulamendis.

"From chaos comes opportunity," said the Warlock. "You and I will never fully be accepted by our people, but here"—he waved his hand in a small circle—"this place is unique. I know you haven't had the time to visit, but there are creatures from other worlds here, intelligent beings who are studying with Pug and his magicians." He looked back at the sorcerer, who he saw was now watching him speak with the elf. "These people have something special here, and it could be ours as well."

The elf said, "I sense what you mean." He also looked back to see Pug watching over his wife's shoulder, as she spoke to their son and Tomas. He nodded once, then said, "In a very short time I have come to understand that my view of things, radical and even treasonous to my people's thinking, is perhaps not radical enough."

"Think of it, people who wish only to seek knowledge. Isn't that why you began poking around in dark caves when you were a child?"

Gulamendis broke out in a laugh, which caused others to turn and look. He held up a hand. "It is an unseemly jest," he said to the others. Then to Amirantha, he said, "Yes, that is exactly why I began as you say. Turning over rocks to see what was under them. Pushing sticks into hollow trees to see what was inside. Never-ending curiosity that took me places no one else even imagined. You as well?"

Amirantha nodded. "Over a century ago. I will tell you sometime of my mother, who was a mad witch, and my brothers, two evil bastards if there ever were, but let me say for the first time in my life I sense something here that might welcome us, and I think we'd be fools to not take advantage. Think of being able to study without fear, and having others nearby to support your work, to aid you if need be. The knowledge we could discover."

Gulamendis inclined his head a moment, as if thinking, then said, "Perhaps if time permits, I'll find my brother alive and bring him here as well. He would also enjoy this atmosphere."

"Good," said Amirantha. "I know trust is hard earned, especially to those like us, but I'll avow this moment, on my blood, that if you serve to forestall the Demon Legion, I will serve along with you, and should we prevail, I'll call you brother."

The elf studied the human before him, seeing a steel resolve in his features. He said, "Why do I think this is an unusual position you find yourself in?"

"Because trust comes hard to me, and I've spent my life watching people I have come to care for die. I find it easier to be aloof and to keep within myself, and when I spend time with people, it is usually to rid them of their gold."

"A frank admission."

"I am not a man with pride, Gulamendis. I have vanity, but that is not the same. I have done little in my life for which I feel a sense of achievement." He nodded toward Sandreena. "That young woman was someone who came to feel something for me, and I repaid her affections with callous abandonment."

"Ah, that would explain her attitude when she looks at you," said the elf.

"In many ways she's as strong a woman as one can imagine—certainly the better of most men when it comes to skill at arms—but strong of mind and will, as well. What is not apparent is that she's also easily hurt." His voice fell off at the end of the remark and the elf remained silent. Amirantha went on. "The strength hides the vulnerable nature of her heart. She was ill used by men as a child and I assumed that made her callous; quite the opposite, in fact. I do not know how it is with your race, Gulamendis, but with us such matters are often confounding, and from the highest goal of my race, finding love, can come the most harm."

"It is not that different, though we have much more time than humans to discover what is truly of value. My brother and I are both counted young by our people, barely halfway through our first century of life. And like you we live on the fringe of our society, so finding a woman who will bear that social stigma makes it even harder." He glanced over to where Sandreena stood and said, "Perhaps in all this you can reach across the breach between you?"

"I will never repair that breach," Amirantha said quietly, "but I choose, if I might, to live a better life."

"Upon that we can agree," said the elf. "All wish a better life."

"Come, let us return and make plans to help where we might."

They returned to the discussion taking place, and found Pug

giving detailed instructions as to what must be done and how quickly. He turned to Gulamendis and said, "Return to your people and let them know of Tomas's arrival, for he will come within three days and speak to your council. We will not wait upon your leaders to act, but we will welcome them as allies should they choose to join with us." To Amirantha he said, "I have a difficult task for you, should you be willing."

"I'm not prone to taking needless risk, but under the circumstances, I am willing to serve." He glanced around. "I like what I see, Pug, and would gladly linger here to study, and share what I know."

"After," said Pug, and Amirantha did not need to be told what that meant. To his wife, the sorcerer said, "It would be valuable if you took the Warlock with you, as well as Sandreena"—Amirantha tried hard not to wince—"and discover what you can of where that bolt of fire came from. Whoever sent it knew we were questioning the imp, and that worries me in several ways."

Miranda said, "Who can overhear what is said here?"

"Someone who has links to that imp," said Amirantha. "You may not understand fully, but those like Gulamendis and myself, who master demons, we think we are utterly in control, but for another entity to be able to eavesdrop on what is said by a demon under our sway . . . it is most disturbing." ·

"Very well," said Miranda, hugging her husband. "Do I dare ask where you and Magnus will be?"

"I must return to Shila," said Pug, and the color drained from Miranda's face. She had stood alongside her husband and watched her father battle the Demon King on that world. Macros had held Maarg at bay just long enough for Pug to destroy the rift that led to the demon realm—or so he had thought.

Strange alien creatures, the Shangri, had constructed the rift, in the ancient city of Ahsart, the Saaur holy city. Pug and she had entered the rift, collapsing it from within. But something Pug had said to her years ago on that world returned: if the rift somehow survived, it could be reopened. She said, "What if the rift to Midkemia had closed as we planned, but the one to Shila, to the demon realm, did not?"

Pug closed his eyes and said, "I have thought the same. When I first saw that rift I did not understand how unique it was. Since I've visited the Dasati world on the next plane of existence, now I realize what a feat it would be to create a rift to reach down to the Fifth Circle. I underestimated the nature of that creation, I fear."

"Still," said Magnus, who had listened to his parents' discussion, "even if the rift between the demon realm and Shila existed, how would the demons have gotten off that world to raid into the elves' worlds?"

"What if Shila was the world the elves found, the one where the demons swarmed into their rift, reaching their portal hub?" said Miranda.

"We'll know soon enough," said Pug. To Magnus he said, "You are coming with me. Pick two others who can keep their wits about them." He kissed his wife on the cheek and said, "I've got to see what damage has been done before I leave, and speak to a few others, but before night falls, we shall be gone. I suggest you do likewise."

Miranda watched him walk away and said to Magnus, "Now is when he will miss Nakor like he hasn't in ten years."

Her son could only nod silently.


Gulamendis approached the north end of the valley that contained his new home—E'bar, as he thought of it, Home. He knew the sight of a winged demon speeding toward the city walls would net him a harsh welcome, so he directed the creature to land in a small clearing enough distance from an outpost to keep from being filled with arrows or, worse, incinerated by a magic blast of flame.

He dismissed his winged horror, which, despite its appearance—mostly drooling jaws and massive claws under gigantic raven's pinions—was a reliable if bony steed. The Demon Master looked around to see if anyone noticed his approach, and decided if they did they were slow in coming to investigate. Given the level of alertness that became a way of life for the Taredhel, that was unlikely. He judged having come in low over the tree-tops for the last few miles was a wise choice.

He worked his way down the hillside until he approached the first outpost on the trail he was using, and he halted within sight of the walls. He waved his hand back and forth and waited to be hailed by the sentry. When a question was called out in his native tongue, he replied and was bid walk slowly forward.

At the gate he paused while they opened it, and when he stepped inside he was impressed. While the city below was growing at prodigious speed—by dint of magic and the focus of massive effort—here in this former Moredhel village, only the sinew and sweat of those detailed to live here were resurrecting the place. Yet it looked as if the work was almost done. Walls had been repaired, hut roofs re-thatched, streets cleared of brush, and a new well sunk in the village square.

A guardsman in the uniform of the Starblood Host said, "Your name?"

"Gulamendis, on the Regent Lord's business," he answered.

"Proceed, but halt at the last hut and see Lacomis."

He moved through a very busy village and noticed even the children were helping with the final cleanup and repair. Taking note, he judged fifty warriors and their families were now ensconced here and soon would be getting on with the business of hunting, fishing, and farming. He thought that should the Demon Legion not come, which he judged unlikely, or should they be defeated, again unlikely, this quiet little village might not be a bad place to settle.

He reached the last hut and knocked on the side of the door. A voice said, "A minute," then an elderly elf stuck his head out. "Who are you?"

"Gulamendis. On the Regent Lord's business. The guard told me to announce myself to you."

The elf stepped out of the hut and, from his robes, the Demon Master could see he was a magic-user, one unknown to him. Gulamendis had little to do with members of the Starblood Host over the years so that didn't surprise him. "Stand over there," said the old elf.

Gulamendis moved to the indicated spot, and the old elf

closed his eyes, waved his hand, and the Demon Master felt a mild magic gathering in the air around them. After a moment, the old elf opened his eyes and said, "Yes, you're who you say."

"Worried about infiltrators?" asked Gulamendis.

"Worried about everything," said the old magic-user. He smiled. "So far we've only encountered squirrels, mice, and a few foxes, but until we completely secure this valley, we have orders to be wary."

"Understood," said the Demon Master. "I must go."

"Walk with the Stars," said the old man, returning to his hut.

Moving down the hillside from the village, Gulamendis was impressed at the work done in his absence. The road a mile south of the village was now being paved with stone. A pair of young geomancers were directing workers, who would dump baskets of stone into piles across the road. The magicians would then use their craft to reform the loose pebbles and rocks into flat, form-fitting pavers that provided easy travel for wagon and mounted rider alike.

Gulamendis nodded in greeting as he passed the work crew. Another mile down the road and he encountered a lone galas-mancer, a master of plants, who was digging a small hole beside the road, using a simple wooden stick. He placed a seed in it, and closed his eyes. Waving his hand, he called forth a small plant that rose up before Gulamendis's eyes. It was a glow tree, native to the world of Selborna. Midkemia might be Home, but the Taredhel were returning with the best they had found on other worlds. The tree would grow to a height of ten or twelve feet above the roadway and illuminate all around it in a soft, bluish glow, making night travel safe and easy. Gulamendis considered it was discoveries such as this that had robbed his people of the legendary woodlore they had once possessed. He had no doubt those elves he had encountered in Elvandar had no need of light to move effortlessly through the woods at night.

The magic used by the galasmancer would cause the tree to grow at a furious rate, reaching maturity in months instead of years. At this time next year, there would be a line of trees along every highway out of E'bar, all making magical light in the night. He considered it would be quite the vision from the hills above the valley.

Now that he was on paved road, the journey went quickly. Cresting a rise, the city came into sight and he stopped. His people might prove to be many things in the days to come, but they were artists! The city was already breathtaking, one to rival Tarendamar when it was completed.

The outer wall was nearing completion, with massive gates being erected at the entrance that was his destination. Beasts of burden and magic would lift the huge wooden gates into place, securing them on balance so perfect a child could push one open with a single hand, yet, once secured, only rams of the most massive force could breach them. They were painted white, as were the walls, which had been faced with some limestone or other material that made the city almost sparkle in the afternoon sun.

Spires were already rising from the central palace, and outer buildings were being raised. Gulamendis considered that there was enough room here for every surviving elf from Andcardia, and quite a bit more. Cynically, he did not imagine the Regent Lord was considering an invitation to their lost kin to come reside here. He was anticipating a successful transition to Midkemia and the need for expansion in the future. He planned on seeing his descendants playing in the streets of this city.

As he reached the gate and moved past guards, who seemed unconcerned with another elf entering the city, he wondered how wise it was to put all this energy into such splendor, when defense was paramount. Then he took note of an outer tower rising above the gate, and saw recessed within the white façade, under the golden roof, a black presence, a crystalline form of baleful aspect. The Regent Lord was building death towers on the walls!

Sighing at how even under this beauty the ugly reality of their situation endured, Gulamendis moved purposely toward the city center. The city was manifesting itself as he had anticipated, with a great Pavilion of the Stars at the center of the valley, with the Seven Stars planted around it. The trees of ancient myth somehow seemed slightly less impressive to Gulamendis now that he had traveled to the Holy Grove in Elvandar and had seen countless trees growing in all directions from the Queen's balcony.

To the south rose the new palace of the Regent, still under construction, as most of the geomancers had been tasked with building the outer defenses. Still, even as others labored to erect massive walls and towers, some artisans were at work decorating the façades already complete. The palace—for there was no other word that would do justice to this building—was white, with royal purple stonework resembling rope knot-work twisting around each opening. The rooftops and the spires were golden in the sun, the materials chosen not apparent to Gulamendis, but some quartz or glass stone, he was certain. Yet from this distance, the top of the structure looked to be topped in gold.

He walked up the broad steps of the main entrance, noticing guards detailed along the way. Already the Regent Lord was exercising his appetite for pomp and ritual, for these soldiers were among the best remaining, and could have been struggling with the enemy on Andcardia, buying more time for more of the People to flee to Midkemia.

As he neared the portal, a vast open arching doorway, he saw several of the honor guards still showing signs of recent combat, a bandage under a tunic collar, or a slight lean to one side to remove pressure from an injured leg or foot. With a sinking feeling in the pit of his stomach, Gulamendis knew that meant the struggle on Andcardia was over, or nearly so. These warriors were being rewarded for service by being placed in the Regent's own personal guard.

As he crossed the vast marble floor, cleverly set off with borders of sparkling rose quartz between the massive slabs, he was hailed by a figure approaching him from the left. Tanderae motioned for the Demon Master to come closer. "Fare you well, Gulamendis?" he asked loudly enough to be overheard.

"Well enough," answered Gulamendis. Both knew exactly what was being discussed.

The Lorekeeper motioned for the Demon Master to walk with him, and in a low voice said, "Before you see the Regent Lord, have a refreshment with me, please?"

Gulamendis recognized it was not a request. He followed the Lorekeeper into a small apartment overlooking a huge central courtyard. Tanderae motioned for Gulamendis to look out.

Looking down, the Demon Master could see the construction of a device, a massive latticework of golden metal, with large spheres of polished stone and gears, topped by a magnificent crystal. "The Sun Tower," said Tanderae. "Our leader has decided to employ the sun to provide energy for the defenses of this new city."

"The death towers?"

"You noticed."

"Difficult not to if you just glance into the cupolas atop the towers. I've seen them up close before, in the battle of Antaria, and they are not something easily forgotten."

"I'll take your word on that. I have no desire to ever see one used."

"Have they named the city yet?"

"No, but everyone calls it E'bar, so I expect that will be what it becomes. So, tell me of what you've discovered."

Gulamendis sat as the Lorekeeper poured two goblets of wine. He sipped and found the vintage reminiscent of what he had tasted on Pug's island. "Very good."

"Local," said the Lorekeeper. "We sent raiders to the east and brought back everything not planted in the ground—and some things that were."

"Raiders!"

"A small town. We made it look as if the Moredhel had returned from the north. Our soldiers wore dark cloaks and left survivors to carry the word that the Forgotten had fled northward, as if moving once again out of the region. Two of our trailbreakers even left miles of false trails leading away from here."

Thinking of what he had heard and seen, and about his own brother's being detected by a Ranger of Natal, he said,

"We should not underestimate these humans, Tanderae. They count able men in their ranks, and those trails may not conceal our presence here for long. And their magic-users are not to be trifled with."

"I know," said Tanderae. "I counseled caution, and almost lost my place in the Regent's Meet."

Gulamendis sat in a cushioned chair and sighed. "It will be hard enough to convince these people to trust us, to ally with us against the Demon Legion, without pillaging their towns and villages."

"The Regent Lord has little use for the idea of allies. Subject people, perhaps," said Tanderae. He glanced toward the window as he added, "He grows consumed with creating a new home for our people, and he will hear of nothing else. I am convinced he plans to move against our neighbors once this place is complete."

Gulamendis said, "I must report to the Regent Lord soon, but let me tell you what I have found." Quickly, but in detail, Gulamendis recounted his experiences since reaching the Queen's court and then Sorcerer's Isle. He omitted one detail, that of Tomas's nature, as he did not want the conversation shunted off on a tangent. He wanted the full disclosure of facts to outweigh the certain emotion that would greet his news of the wearer of Dragon Armor living in Elvandar.

The Lorekeeper listened without comment, and when Gulamendis finished, he had questions. The give-and-take added another half-hour to the conversation, and at the end, the Lorekeeper said, "These sound like impressive beings."

"I saw little of the dwarven king, which was as I would wish it"—his people's distaste for dwarves was almost inbred; of all the competing races in the stars the dwarves had proven the most difficult to conquer—"but he was at ease with the elves in Elvandar, and has strong ties with the humans of the area.

"Our cousins are as you would expect them, rustic, at one with the forest, deeply imbued with a sense of nature we have long ago forgotten." He lowered his voice, more out of habit than necessity. "We would do well not to underestimate them, either, Tanderae. They may appear primitive, but their magic is strong if subtle. They have groves of trees that dwarf our Seven Stars, ancestors of our Seven Stars! And they are as one with the land under their feet. I saw no overt wards or other magical barriers, but I could not bring myself to cross the river into their land until I was bid enter. It might be we could mount an army on the opposite shore from Elvandar yet never step on that sacred land." He sighed. "It worries me, fascinates me, and, somehow, it pleases me. It's seeing ourselves in the mirror of time."

"I will go there, someday," said Tanderae. "If we survive."

"The war?"

"Badly. You may have noticed those who line the steps to this palace are recruited from the survivors of the last battle of Andcardia, those fit enough to stand watch. Many more still linger at death's door, tended by the few healers we have left." He sipped his wine and said, "These humans make fine wine, do they not?"

"Indeed," agreed Gulamendis. "My brother?"

"No one has seen him," said Tanderae, but then he laughed. "Of course, he could be standing next to them looking like anyone and they'd never know."

"A few would," said Gulamendis.

"There's a reason your brother was counted first-most among the Circle of Light."

Gulamendis frowned.

Tanderae held up his hand, palm outstretched to indicate no harm intended. "This is not a secret, Gulamendis, even if we are expected not to speak of such things any longer.

"The demise of the Circle of Light is regrettable, in my opinion." He sipped his wine. "It was foolish for the Regent's Meet to insist that all magic-users fall under their purview. And when they stumbled across those like you . . ."

"My brother objected."

"Indeed." Sipping his wine again, Tanderae seemed to be choosing his words carefully. "Had he not been so preeminent among those of the Circle, he might have suffered more harshly than . . . Well, let's say despite his vanities and eccentricities, the Regent Lord and the Meet recognize a valuable resource.

"They say Laromendis can create illusion so vivid that should his subject be shown a knife plunging into his chest his heart will stop as if the blade is real."

"So they say," replied the Demon Master noncommittally.

"Such ability is rare, and I suspect that once we get our new home built and turn our attention to dealing with our neighbors, we will give more credit to those of you who've been . . . let's say not properly recognized for the work you've done on our behalf." He put down his wine for a moment. "What do you think of these humans?"

"We are more like them than we are like our kin in Elvandar," Gulamendis replied flatly. "They wear their emotions on their faces like the shirts on their backs, but they have very keen minds among them, and talent to rival our own. I saw just enough from their magic-users to conclude that these are people we need to respect, for they are as endless as the sand on the beach and we . . ." He shrugged.

" . . . are but a shadow of our former might. Yes, I know all too well," said the Lorekeeper. It was implicit in his profession that he would know more of the history of the Taredhel than any other.

"There is one among them, by name Pug, he may be among the most puissant magic-users I have encountered." Gulamendis lowered his voice. "He claims to have been to the world housing the Demon Gate. He claims he can return."

Tanderae looked stunned. "If true . . ."

"I think it is. I think he can provide the proof that no one among the Taredhel brought the demon wrath down upon us. It was simply bad fortune that exposed us to the Demon Legion. And, moreover, he claims to have the ability to close the gate for all time."

"Astonishing," said the Lorekeeper.

Gulamendis said, "When we last spoke, I was uncertain of how to receive your comments, but now that I have been out and among the humans, our kin, and even met a dwarf, I think nothing in our past has prepared us for this world. It is very different, with many questions, and those questions may have answers we will not entirely care to hear.

"Yet, it is also a place of opportunity and, perhaps, even evolution so we may become even greater than before."

"What of this Queen?"

"I think she is of the blood. I think her claim valid. You would be better able to judge, but there is something about her that speaks . . . no, it sings to your heart and mind. To see the Stars in their majesty, as they were before we fled to other worlds, to imagine what it must have been like here, at Home, when the world was young." He sighed. "Our kin in Elvandar are truly one with the land beneath their feet, something we have lost."

"Those in Elvandar are more fundamentally who we were than any among our people," began the Lorekeeper. "We named the finest among them rulers, partially in secret defiance of the . . . ancient ones, but also to honor them as being more closely linked to the very magic of this world. They were the grove guardians, the protectors of the Stars. Even those of us among the fleeing Eldar venerated them." He finished his wine. "It's ironic that was the reason they chose to remain, so as not to relinquish their responsibility toward the sacred trees.

"I'm pleased to see they have endured." He stood up and said, "I intercepted the report that you had been seen coming down from the hills so we might have this chat before you report to the Regent Lord. But we have tarried long enough. I'll escort you so there's no further delay. Is there anything else you need to tell me before we see our lord and master?"

Gulamendis stood. He had been weighing the possibility that he had found an ally in Tanderae against the one that the Lorekeeper saw him only as a usable tool or weapon. He judged it time to test that. "One thing. The Queen's consort will be arriving in three days to speak with the Regent Lord."

Tanderae's expression revealed volumes. "Is he coming to establish a claim?"

"This Queen has no desire for sovereignty. She will avow we are a free people. No, it's something else."

"What?"

"Her consort wears the armor of . . . the Ancients."

Tanderae's concern deepened visibly. "That is both odd and disturbing. A likeness or an artifact?"

"More than an artifact," said the Demon Master, beginning to perversely enjoy the mounting discomfort in the Lorekeeper. He might trust the elf, but that didn't mean he had to like him.

"More?" Tanderae's eyes narrowed.

"Her consort is by name Tomas; he is Warleader of Elvandar. He is Valheru."

Tanderae was visibly shaken. "How can this be?" he whispered. "If the Ancients still ruled, we would have been greeted by fire and sword; the humans, dwarves, goblins, all would have been obliterated."

"There is much to explain," said Gulamendis. "He is Valheru, and he is human, and I only know part of his story, but when he arrives, you will see without a doubt that he is a Dragon Lord."

"And he comes to us as an envoy?"

"Yes," said Gulamendis. "Now, may I suggest you keep that part of the report to the Regent for later, because I do not know how our coming envoy would react to being greeted with magic and fire."

Tanderae took a deep breath, and then he began to chuckle. "Your levity tells me I need not worry, though I will need more reassurance. Still, it might be worth a quick death from the Regent's personal guards to see the expression on his face when the Queen's consort arrives."

"For you, perhaps, not me. If you don't tell him, I most certainly will. It is part of my charge to him, and my brother's life and my own hang in the balance."

"I wonder what has become of your brother."

"He is almost certainly here if he had the means," said Gulamendis. "And if he's here, he's out looking for me."

"What are the chances he'll find you?"

"Good," said the Demon Master. "We have the knack for tracking each other down. He thinks as I, and will trace my route, but once he decides it's time to return, he will come back."

They left the private room and the Lorekeeper said, "Let us get this over with. The Regent Lord will be . . . unhappy, with much of what you have to tell him."

With a hint of foreboding in his voice, Gulamendis said, "A fact of which I am painfully aware."

# CHAPTER 18

## EXPLORATION

Sandreena held up her hand.

She had not been comfortable with the selection being assumed by the sorcerer, with the Father-Bishop being relegated to what looked to be, at best, an advisor. Yet, these people had treated her well, seen to her care, and provided her with everything she needed, without question or obligation. She had been transported by the woman, Miranda, who seemed a magic-user of significant power and ability, along with Amirantha, who could easily be the last person in the world she would ever care to see again.

Now they worked their way up the trail toward the site of the muddled sacrifices she had observed less than two weeks before, though it felt like ages. Something ahead moved, which is why she had signaled for a halt. Brandos brought up the rear, for despite Amirantha's and Miranda's significant power, a second sword was welcome. And despite her distaste for Amirantha, Sandreena had a fondness for the old fighter, who was steadfast and honest, or as honest as any companion of Amirantha was likely to be. She gave him credit for at least attempting to warn her that Amirantha was not a man to grow close to. More than once in the last five years she had wished she had listened.

The sounds coming from ahead were furtive, either an animal in the evening brush or someone doing a bad job of hiding. She indicated she would scout ahead, and not for the first time in her life wished she had made a less cumbersome choice in armor and arms. Still, with practice she had learned to move in a relatively quiet fashion.

In almost a duck-walk, she moved in a low crouch, slowly, until she could raise her head enough to see what lay ahead. As she suspected, there was a sentry who was not being particularly attentive to her route, but who was showing no signs of being sleepy or otherwise easy to approach. She slowly retreated.

Reaching the other three, she whispered, "One lookout. He's too far away for me to reach without a loud rush."

Miranda said, "I'll deal with him."

She moved forward without much attempt at stealth, though in the deep evening shadows on the narrow canyon, her dark dress served effectively as camouflage. Still, she made enough noise and there was enough movement that the sentry looked up when she was about a dozen yards away.

"Huh?" was all he managed to get out.

With a single wave of her hand, Miranda sent out a bolt of energy that compressed the air before it, enough to deliver a punishing blow to the man's face. He somersaulted completely backward, to land on the rocks behind him, smacking his head hard enough to render him motionless.

They hurried forward and Amirantha asked, "Is he dead?"

Kneeling, Sandreena inspected the fallen guard and said,

"No, but with that blow to the back of his head he's not going anywhere for many hours."

"Scout ahead," said Miranda.

Sandreena did as asked and, in less than five minutes, she returned, her face drained of color. "We have to move, now!" She motioned for the others to follow and hurried forward without any attempt at concealment.

They reached a rise from which Sandreena had been able to climb a slight ridge to oversee the ritual the last time she had been here. She motioned for them to follow and when they neared the top of the rise, they understood why she had abandoned silence.

There were voices, chanting in unison, and when they cleared the rise, they saw there must have been a hundred of them. A huge fire was burning, flames leaping thirty feet into the air, and around it stood a dozen robed bedecked men and women. In a semicircle around them the others were gathered, men and a few women, dressed in a variety of garb, all fashion and manner, from all parts of the world, Keshian, the Kingdom, Novindus, and the Eastern Kingdoms. But all wore a black head cover. Tied scarves, flop hats, leather caps, it didn't matter; everyone covered their head in black.

Miranda said, "Well, there's your Black Caps and it looks like most of them have shown up for something important."

"I think I know," whispered Amirantha. "It's a summoning, but it's different."

"How's it different?" asked Miranda.

"I don't know. It's just . . . different." He whispered, yet there was an urgency in his voice. "Something very wrong is about to happen." He looked at Miranda. "Be ready."

"For what?" she asked.

"Anything, but whatever it is, it will be very bad." His skin crawled, and he felt powers gathering that were dark and terrible beyond anything he had ever encountered in a long life of dealing with infernal beings.

Three men appeared to come from the other end of the canyon, one wearing robes of bright red trimmed in black and silver piping. The other two, one on either side, wore black, like the others. The two black-clad figures were hooded, their features obscured by the deep shadows. The red-robed man had his head uncovered, and he smiled broadly as he came to face the semicircle of gathered adherents. He stepped up onto a large rock, and held up his hand for silence. Instantly, the chanting ceased.

"Servants of Dahun . . ." he began.

"Damn," swore Amirantha.

"What?" asked Miranda.

It was Sandreena who answered, "Dahun is a demon prince."

"One of Maarg's Captains," said Amirantha. "If I understand everything told to me in the last few days, which I almost certainly don't . . ." He pointed. "But I know that man, and I know that anything he's involved with is going to be something very bad."

"Who is he?"

"That," said Amirantha, "is my brother, Belasco."

"Evil-looking bastard," said Sandreena. "I can see the resemblance."

Miranda shot a dark look at Sandreena, then realized it was the young knight's manner of dealing with fear. Miranda had none of either Sandreena's or Amirantha's experience with demons, but she had faced enough dark magic in her life to sense this situation was verging on becoming something bad.

"In four nights," said Belasco, "we shall greet our master and begin the transformation of this world into our master's domain, and we, his blessed servants, will be his first chosen, ruling at his side."

"First to be eaten, most likely," said Brandos.

"Well, I'm hardly the one to condemn lying to those who are about to be gulled, but I only took their gold, not their lives," said Amirantha.

With a grudging tone, Sandreena said, "For that small difference, you might find Lims-Kragma lets you return to life as something a little higher-born than a cockroach."

Miranda said, "We have four more nights to decide what to do."

Amirantha said, "No, we have until that guard wakes up."

Sandreena said, "Will he know he was struck by a spell?"

Miranda said, "Normally he'd wake up feeling like he'd been on a three-day drunk, but the way he hit his head . . ."

"Well," whispered Brandos, "we could finish the job on the way out and make it look as if he simply fell off his perch and broke his skull on the rocks."

"Someone in that bunch is a tracker and would see we were here," said Sandreena.

"If there was some way we could convince that fellow he had just fallen asleep," said Miranda.

"I have an idea," said Amirantha. "Come on, we must hurry."

He led them back down the trail to where the still-recumbent guard sprawled across the rocks. He motioned for them to follow him past, a good thirty yards down the narrow trail. "Just be silent," he whispered. "Can you wake the guard when I tell you?"

Miranda said, "I believe so, though why would I want to?"

"Just wait and do it when I tell you, then all of you get down out of sight."

He closed his eyes and reached inside his belt pouch, pulling out a crystal. Holding it tightly, he muttered an incantation and suddenly a puff of dark, fetid smoke erupted from the ground.

Stepping out of the smoke was a woman, tall, stunning in appearance, and nude.

The newly summoned demon looked around with large, expressive brown eyes. Miranda was forced to admit she was certain to be most men's perfect female fantasy: long legs, round buttocks, a flat stomach, breasts that defied age, and perfect skin. Thick brown hair tumbled down to her lower back, and she had a face that was without flaw. Her full lips parted in a smile and she said, "Master! I love you!"

Sandreena said, "Darthea? Really, Amirantha, is this the

time for that?" Her expression was venomous and her color was rising, her cheeks flushed with anger.

"Shut up," said Amirantha impatiently to Sandreena. He held up his hand and said to the demon, "Not now. I have a task for you." He took the beautiful demon by the elbow and pointed to the unconscious man. He whispered a series of instructions, then said, "Can you remember that?"

"Yes, master," she replied and with dainty steps, unmindful of the sharp rocks beneath her bare feet, she hurried to the sentry.

"When she reaches his side, wake him," said the Warlock.

Miranda waited, then when the female demon knelt next to the unconscious man, Amirantha signaled it was time.

Miranda closed her eyes briefly, then pointed her hand, and they were rewarded with a groan from the sentry.

Amirantha waved the others out of sight and crouched down.

"Oh, you poor man," said Darthea to the recovering warrior. "I'm so sorry. I did not mean to startle you like that, having you fall off the rock and hit your head. Here, let me help you up."

The stunning nude woman helped the man to his feet and, as reason returned to him, his eyes widened in disbelief. Amirantha spoke a short, quiet phrase, and suddenly she was gone, vanishing with a tiny puff of smoke.

The blinking, confused sentry looked around, then, with knees wobbly, sat down and rubbed his tender head.

Amirantha crawled back to where the others waited and motioned for them to follow. When they were far enough away to transport without being detected, Miranda said, "That was interesting."

Brandos laughed quietly. "He's certain now he slipped and hit his skull on a rock, because who in their right mind would think he was startled by a naked beauty in this gloomy backside of the universe? And I pity the man if he tries to tell the story to any of those cutthroats he's in league with."

"He'll keep quiet," said Sandreena grudgingly.

"You've bought us four more nights," said Miranda. "What now?"

"We return in four nights and see how much magic it's going to take to ruin a very powerful summoning."

"We have as much as you'll need."

"I have no doubt," said the Warlock, "but I'd like to see it done without you or me or anyone else dying in the process."

"There's always a risk," said Miranda.

"Let's go somewhere to talk about it," said Amirantha.

"Grab his arm," Miranda said to Brandos, who complied. She reached out and gripped Sandreena and Amirantha and suddenly they were back in the garden on Sorcerer's Isle.

"I have got to learn to do that," said Amirantha.

"It takes years," said Miranda.

He smiled. "I'm willing."

"Well, if we survive this, maybe. Right now you need to decide who or what we need, and how we're best served to deal with this mess. I can manage perhaps one more person when I transport that way." She seemed distressed as she said, "If Magnus was here, together we could get as many as nine or ten people to that spot. If he and Pug were here . . . well, if Pug were here I wouldn't worry as much." She fell silent.

Brandos said, "Besides magic, there are a lot of swords and evil men willing to use them back there. I've been around magicians long enough to know you don't have time to cast more than that first spell if someone's busy trying to cut off your head."

"We need two plans," said Miranda. "One if we have to do this alone, and another if Pug and Magnus return."

"Are there others here who can fill in for your husband and son?" asked Amirantha.

"All the magicians I know who could help us in a fight like this are either dead or on the world of New Kelewan. Most of the students here have never been in a fight, let alone a battle." She thought for a minute, then said, "Sandreena, how many magic-using priests in your Order can handle demons?"

"Some. I know banishment spells as well as most of them. It's part of our training."

Amirantha agreed. "If she has a weakness, it's to use her mace first, but when she's able, she can banish a minor demon as well as I can. I've seen her do it."

Sandreena scowled, not sure if she was being complimented or insulted.

"You're coming with us, then," said Miranda.

"I wouldn't miss it," said the Knight-Adamant.

Miranda said, "Rest, and get something to eat if you're hungry. I have more plans to make."

She hurried out of the garden, and Brandos said, "Well, food sounds good. Coming?"

"In a moment," said Amirantha.

Brandos looked from the Warlock's face to the young woman's and nodded, turned, and left them alone.

Expectantly, Sandreena said, "What?"

Amirantha took a deep breath. "I have no idea what will happen in four days, and I know I can't talk you out of coming."

"Why would you try to?" she asked.

"I know things ended badly between us—"

"There was no 'between us,'" she interrupted. "We spent some time together and you lied to me to get me into your bed."

"It was your bed, actually," said Amirantha. "And I never lied. I just didn't tell you the entire truth."

"A fine distinction, I'm sure, but we have other things with which to concern ourselves, don't you agree?" He nodded. "Why would you try to talk me out of coming along?"

"You're the most resourceful woman I know," said Amirantha, "but you have a decided knack to rush in without hesitation."

"I'm a Knight-Adamant," she reminded him.

"A fact of which I am painfully aware, but you sometimes underestimate risks. Look, you never told me what happened before you got here, but I've seen you look better. You almost got yourself killed again, didn't you?"

"I appreciate your show of concern, but it's too late." She spun on him and poked him hard in the chest with an armored finger. He winced but stayed silent. "I was a whore, Amirantha, and no man showed me anything but contempt or lust until I met Brother Mathias. After that, it was bloodshed and mayhem, and I found a calling, but even then, men only looked at me with hate or with lust.

"Then you came along with your damned charm and funny sayings, and made me feel as if someone could actually see beneath the surface . . ." She took a breath as if to calm herself, and said, "I can face your demons, Amirantha. I can face a room full of armed cutthroats. I just can't face your falsehoods." She took a step and then turned to say, "One thing, though. Darthea: you've done well in changing her looks. Though the goat's hooves and horns did add a certain exotic quality to her."

Without saying anything more she turned and left the Warlock standing alone in the garden. For over a hundred years Amirantha had been willing to take advantage of the passing generosity of women when it suited him, for often they repaid his kindness with the only currency they possessed, their bodies. But when he was ninety years of age, he happened to chance upon one he had known in his youth. She was now an old and faded grandmother, content to sit in the shade and card wool while her daughters and their families worked hard on a farm. She didn't recognize him as he asked for and was given a cup of water.

For a long moment he stood watching her as she watched her granddaughters, and he realized that when the granddaughters were old and at the end of their lives, he most likely would still be as he was that minute, and he would watch them watching their granddaughters. At that moment, whatever spark of affection he felt for humanity was damped. The only woman he had truly cared for in any fashion after that encounter was Samantha, but only because she made Brandos happy.

His feelings for Brandos were still a mystery to the Warlock, perhaps he saw him as the son he would never have. But now, when they were together, people mistook the fighting man for the elder and Amirantha knew the day would come when his companion would either die in battle or have to quit the adventurous life to sit at home, next to Samantha as she carded wool, watching their grandchildren.

He took a deep breath. Sandreena was a confusion he had no answer for. There was something about her that tasked him, something that made him desperately want for her to forgive his cavalier behavior toward her years earlier, and that desire troubled him deeply. Shaking his head in irritation at himself, he turned to find Brandos and get something to eat.

Gulamendis knew his life was hanging by the barest thread as he spoke to the Regent Lord about Tomas's pending arrival. It had been clear from the first moment of reporting to the Regent Lord and the attending members of the Meet that Undalyn was ready to declare war on their cousins to the north should he feel the impulse. As the members of the Meet were for the most part handpicked by him over the years, to replace older members who had fallen to the demons over the last thirty years, Gulamendis knew he would get no support in arguing against any position the Regent Lord took.

Even Tanderae would only be able to offer subtle influence, to shade how things were presented, but he, too, risked being swept away by the Regent Lord's wrath. He was not yet the new Loremaster, first among the Lorekeepers, though it was rumored the position would be his soon. Gulamendis knew that should it come to a choice between his rise to power or supporting the Demon Master, Tanderae would happily light the fire around Gulamendis himself.

Slowly, step by step, Gulamendis recounted his journey, his frustration at not being able to locate the demon source, his ride up the Far Coast, and his eventual discussion with the Queen and her Consort. He thought it best to omit discussion of his journey to Sorcerer's Isle until after he saw if he was going to survive what he had to say next.

"The Queen is sending her Consort in two more days to greet you, my lord," said Gulamendis.

"Her Consort?" He glanced around. "There is no King?"

"Her King made his journey to the Blessed Isle many years ago, and to ensure the King's son inherits, her second husband rejected the crown. Prince Calen will rule in Elvandar after his mother."

The Regent Lord said, "Odd. One should think that any elf would aspire to rule in Elvandar."

Gulamendis could already see the Regent Lord's mind turning. If he could somehow rid the world of this consort, he would be—in his own mind—the logical suitor for the Elf Queen's hand, after a suitable period of mourning, of course. Long before departing on this journey, Gulamendis has begun to suspect that the strain of command for thirty years of war, of losing so many close companions, of watching his people being systematically obliterated had taken its toll on the Regent Lord. After having seen the Elf Queen, Tomas, Pug, and others, he was now certain: the Regent Lord was unfit to rule, perhaps he was even mad.

What had begun almost as a jest between himself and his brother—that they were going to have to practice a little subversion—now seemed closer to what was needed, an act of treason. Gulamendis lacked the nobility of spirit he had seen in Tomas, who he sensed would gladly give up his life to defend Elvandar, but at this moment, if he thought he had an opportunity to end his people's suffering by killing the Regent, he thought he would.

Still, there already were wards in place, against the coming of the Demon Legion or others, but they were just as effective against Gulamendis's powers. Perhaps one of the human magicians might turn this hall into a fire pit before the Regent's guards might react, but Gulamendis knew he would be dead before he might be halfway through a summoning.

Mustering up the courage to say what needed to be said, Gulamendis spoke softly: "He's not an elf, my lord."

The Regent Lord blinked, as if confounded by his own senses. "What?" he asked.

"I said the Queen's Consort is not an elf."

With a tone bordering on outright revulsion, the Regent Lord said, "What is he?"

Calmly, Gulamendis said, "He was born human."

Anger rose up in the Regent Lord and he said, "Whatever claim she may have held to the most noble line in our ancestry is fouled by such a mating. A human!"

Taking a deep breath, Gulamendis said, "I said he was born a human, my lord, but today he is far more than that. He wears an Ancient One's armor."

The Regent Lord looked as if Gulamendis had struck him a blow across the face. Almost whispering, he said, "He *dares*?"

"More," said Gulamendis, judging it time to give the full truth and hope the Regent Lord continued to be stunned enough not to feel the need to affix blame to the messenger. Glossing over the very complex story Tomas had told him, Gulamendis said, "He was gifted the armor by the greatest of the great golden dragons"—he knew it was false, but he needed to glorify Tomas as much as possible to prepare the Regent Lord for the shock of meeting him—"in reward for some great deed. The armor's magic transformed the human, and he does more than wear an Ancient One's armor, he carries his—" at the last moment he decided to omit the facts of Tomas having Ashen-Shugar's memories and instead said, "—his powers. In all but heart and spirit, he is Valheru."

Now the Regent Lord was reeling. He looked around the nearly finished meeting hall and moved to the large chair—not quite a throne—set on a small dais for him to rest on, and he slowly lowered himself into it.

Of all the possibilities since Laromendis returned from his discovery of this world, this was one never considered. It had been feared the Valheru might have survived the Chaos Wars, but when no mention was made of them by Gulamendis's brother, that fear vanished. But now, suddenly, that fear returned, yet it was tempered by the fact the Demon Master was bringing greetings.

"Tell me of him," whispered the Regent Lord, and at that

moment, Gulamendis knew his life was safe for the moment. Gulamendis told of Tomas, changing the story of the boy lost in the cave—omitting any mention of the Dwarf King—to one of a brave lad seeking to destroy an evil demon; that resonated well with the Meet.

After Gulamendis finished, the Regent Lord asked, "This human turned Ancient One, he seeks not to rule?"

"It is most strange," said Gulamendis carefully, "but he seems content to protect Elvandar and leave rule to his wife, the Queen." The Demon Master slightly emphasized her title, again reminding the Regent Lord there were old ties that need never be forgotten. The elves of Elvandar might be rustics in the sight of the Taredhel, but they were blood kin, and after the losses suffered against the demons, as many kin as could be mustered was a necessity. After the Demon Legion had been confronted, then the Regent Lord could worry about ruling this world.

The Regent Lord asked questions about Tomas and the Elf Queen for nearly a half-hour after, but then dismissed Gulamendis. As he and Tanderae left the Meet, the Lorekeeper said, "You acquitted yourself well, my friend."

Saying nothing, Gulamendis thought, *Friend now, but only so long as it suits you.*

Two days later, the assembled members of the Regent's Meet stood in the central plaza of the newly christened city of E'bar, awaiting the arrival of the Queen's Consort. Gulamendis had been invited to attend, given his role, but had been relegated to one side by those of higher rank. From a short distance away, Tanderae nodded greeting to the Demon Master, a faint acknowledgment of his usefulness in this coming negotiation between the Regent Lord and his titular Queen.

Gulamendis had purposely neglected to mention Tomas's likely mode of travel, thinking it might serve the Regent's Meet to be awed slightly. They stood waiting for a signal from the outer garrisons that riders were approaching.

Instead a large shadow suddenly covered them as a massive flying figure appeared above, looming over them. Most of the members of the Regent's Meet stood motionless, though Gulamendis noticed a few flinching until they recognized nothing was dropping down on them precipitously. Then he saw the reaction as recognition set in: a gigantic golden dragon was descending into the central plaza.

With a thunderous beat of its wings, the dragon halted its descent, then landed gently. The size of a building, the enormous creature nevertheless was a thing of grace and beauty in its movement. A head the size of a freight wagon lowered on a surprisingly sinuous neck to allow two figures to dismount.

Gulamendis's eyes widened as he recognized the second figure as his brother. Laromendis nodded ever so slightly in his brother's direction, acknowledging his presence, but stayed close to the Dragon Lord.

Gulamendis was delighted. Arriving with Tomas was guaranteed to prevent any rash punishment the Regent Lord might mete out for Laromendis's absence. Gulamendis had inquired about his brother after having parted company with Tanderae, and no one had seen him since his being posted to the defense of Tarendamar, which meant either he was dead or had deserted his post. Gulamendis had been certain it was the latter, unless his brother had been terribly unlucky, as Laromendis wasn't the kind to stand defiantly and be overwhelmed by the Demon Legion.

If Tomas had shown restraint when confronting Gulamendis outside the Holy Grove, he withheld nothing as he dismounted the dragon. He used his mystic arts to unleash the full power of his Valheru aura. Gulamendis, who had experienced this in part before, and Laromendis, who had ridden with the Dragon Lord from Elvandar, both were rocked.

The members of the Regent's Meet were stunned. Several fell to their knees reflexively, some with wailing and weeping. Others stood trembling, unable to move. Only the Regent Lord and two of the most senior among his advisors stood silently, waiting.

Tomas strode toward them, exuding power in every step, his left hand on the hilt of his sword. He wore golden armor, with a helm set with a dragon crest, as if a miniature golden dragon had lain upon his helm, down-sweeping wings forming the cheek-guards of his helmet. His tabard and shield were both white, with a golden dragon emblazoned on both, and every movement was fluid and graceful.

He was beautiful and fearsome and a legend come to life before their eyes. Whatever arrogance the Taredhel possessed, whatever certainty of their own supremacy, fled before the magnificent power that was Tomas in the guise of a Valheru.

He came to stand before the Regent Lord and said, "My lord," and then waited.

Almost whispering, the Regent Lord said, "How should I address you?"

Tomas smiled and it was as if a huge cloud passed away, and he said simply, "My name is Tomas. And before anything more is said between us, I must tell you this:

"In ages past, when war raged across the heavens, the wearer of this armor sat astride a dragon like this, my friend Sarduna, and he proclaimed to the world that all who had once served, all among the Edhel, were now a free people." With a slightly wry smile, he said, "Your ancestors fled this world before that voice was raised, so I say to you now, you are a free people.

"Let it be clear I have no claim upon you nor are you obliged in any fashion because I wear this armor and this mantle. I come to you in the hope of friendship, on behalf of my lady, Queen Aglaranna, who also bids you welcome to your ancestral home and wishes nothing but friendship and peace."

There was silence for a moment, then the Regent Lord said, "Fairly spoken . . . Tomas. You are welcome."

Quick introductions were made and the Meet retired to the council chamber, where Tomas would discuss two things with them: the prospects of the Demon Legion following the Taredhel to Midkemia and an alliance with the established inhabitants of Midkemia, should that occur.

Tanderae lingered a moment as the brothers were reunited. "You both did well," he said quickly. "I must attend our masters and see to soothing things should tempers flare."

Gulamendis said, "Do you think they might?"

With as close to a grin as the Lorekeeper could allow himself, he said, "Given Lord Tomas's presence, not until after he
departs. He is . . . impressive." He glanced at the retreating
back in gold and white, who, while shorter than every elf in
the meeting, still somehow seemed to tower over them. "Stunning, even." Looking back at the two brothers, he said, "I have
work to do, but consider that whatever sanctions have been
placed against you are currently abated." He pointed to the
north and said, "Find housing. There will be a magistrate up
on that hillside who will ask you many stupid questions; give
him this." He handed them a token with the Regent's seal on
it, and turned away.

As the Lorekeeper hurried to overtake the Regent and his
guest, Gulamendis said, "You made quite the entrance."

His brother replied, "Yes, I expect."

"How did you manage?"

"Come, I'll tell you as we go find ourselves a nice set of
rooms." They left the central plaza, and as they walked, Laromendis said, "I managed to win free of the battle at Tarendamar
early—my command was obliterated and as we fell back, I was
ushered into a company of refugees who were being escorted
to the portal. As I was not in uniform, I expect everyone who
knew I was detailed to serve on the wall and might recognize
me was already dead. And as my new superior officer was or-
dering me to go through the portal 'with all haste,' who was I
to argue?"

"You weren't disguised as an old woman, by any chance?"
asked the Demon Master dryly.

"No, I swear. No illusion. I didn't even get a chance to
argue." He smiled. "Of course, I was disinclined to argue."

"How goes the battle?"

"It's over, but for the closing of the portal." He glanced up
to the hillside to the west where refugees were still arriving and
said, "They'll close that soon, and whoever is on the other side
will die."

Changing the topic, Gulamendis said, "How did you contrive to arrive on the back of a dragon?"

"I went looking for you, and after a few days wandering around to the west, I decided that no matter whatever else you were doing, you were going to see the Elf Queen in her court, so that's where I went. As I didn't wander around all that much, I managed to get there in fairly quick order." He slapped his brother on the back. "Lord Tomas and the Queen said you had been there, and said you'd most likely be waiting here when he came to call, so he offered me a ride and I said yes. Riding on the back of a dragon! Can you imagine?"

Laughing, very glad to see his brother, Gulamendis said, "Actually, I've ridden on one."

"You!"

"Yes, and it's a story. The locals have some very fine wine, and if I can secure us a skin or bottle, we'll find a place to sit, drink, and I'll tell you a story of my visit to a very special island." Lowering his voice, he said, "I think it's a place you'll wish to visit, and very soon."

As they walked northward, seeking the magistrate who would supply them with quarters, Laromendis said, "I just realized; you and I, the two outcast brothers, we are the only Taredhel in history to ride a dragon!"

Gulamendis said, "Ironic, in its way, especially if you consider how much the Regent Lord would likely want one for a pet."

Both brothers laughed and began looking for a bottle of wine and a place to live.


A bitter wind blew across the plateau. Pug and Magnus stood motionless, accompanied by two other magicians. Randolph, a middle-aged man from a village near Tulan, was Magnus's best student of battle magic, and looked it. He was a bull-necked, broad-shouldered brawler with a balding head and a barrel chest. If it wasn't for his ability to conjure spells of stunning power very swiftly, Pug would have judged him as unlikely-looking a magician as he had ever encountered.

The other magician, Simon from Krondor, was Randolph's exact opposite in appearance: tall, ascetic-looking, late in years, and his blond hair now prematurely white, matching Magnus in outward appearance. He was a master of the far more subtle craft of detection. He and Pug both stood silently, attempting to sense any arcane presence.

"Nothing," said Simon. "If there has been any magic used in this area, it's been years."

"I as well get nothing," said Pug. He pointed to the north-west. "There, that's where we'll find Ahsart, the City of Priests."

It had taken Pug the better part of a day to recalculate cre-ating a rift to Shila. He had forgotten how difficult it was to redefine an ancient rift if there hadn't been constant contact. His efforts had resulted in two failed attempts and a serious headache, before he succeeded. He was thankful he had become rigorous about taking notes over the years and could find every-thing he had recorded about Shila and how to get there.

Once the four magic-users had arrived, it had taken another few hours for Pug to get oriented. They had begun a slow pro-cess of using Magnus's exceptional ability to transport them magically to distant locations to move in jumps across the planet, seeking any sign of demon activity.

There had been none.

Pug's thesis was if the portal from the demon realm was still closed, there would be no life on Shila. If this was, indeed, the planet where the Taredhel explorers had encountered the de-mons, there would be some movement between the original gate and wherever the rift to the Taredhel hub world was located. There should have been a steady stream of demons flying and running out of Ahsart.

All was quiet.

Magnus used his arts and took them to a hillside overlooking the City of Priests.

The city had been an immense metropolis in its time, a sprawling home to millions. The ancient city that had been the heart of Ahsart was surrounded by a high wall, but the foulburg spread out five times the distance, indicating that this region had been peaceful for centuries after the original city had been founded. Broad streets crisscrossed throughout and tall towers rose here and there. Pug indicated a path downward and they began walking.

"In ancient times, a gate had been created between the demon realm and this world, before recorded history. It had been sealed and protected, which is how this place came to be in the first place. This was where the Saaur shamans and priests who had sealed the gate lived. Others came to study, and it became a holy place," said Pug. "The Saaur were a race of noble warriors, and they counted in the millions. They rode across endless plains of grassland and hunted." Pug motioned for them to walk toward one particular avenue. "Then something changed."

"This must have been a remarkable place," said Simon. "In size it rivals the City of Kesh." He glanced at Pug and said, "What changed?"

"A mad priest, so the story goes," said Pug, "opened the seal, admitting the first demon, and for his troubles was devoured. But before the other priests could reseal the breach, they were overwhelmed."

Randolph said, "Sounds like the demons were ready to launch an offensive through the breach when it was opened."

"Yes, it does, doesn't it?" agreed Pug.

As they entered the now-deserted ruins, the only sound in their ears was wind. In the hours they had been on this world, there was no hint of life. As far as they could tell, this planet was completely devoid of even the tiniest insect. At one point they had passed through a region just after a rain. Pug had remarked that the scent of wetness lacked something familiar. Simon had replied that life was abundant in the soil, moss, lichen, and spoors of all sort, and water caused their scent to rise. None of that existed here.

They walked down desolate boulevards, immense by human standards. The Saaur were a huge race, and the scale of their city reflected that. Their horses were twenty-five hands at the withers. These were a nomadic people whose concessions to city life were few. No rider of the Saaur would ever be caught far from his mount.

Pug paused, trying to get his bearings. He pointed. "That way lies the main temple." As they walked, he said, "As I understand it, the great hordes of the Sha-shahan, or Ultimate Ruler, rode throughout this world. It has smaller oceans than Midkemia and, save for a few big islands, it's possible to visit every part of the globe on horse.

"This city originally was a holy place, and the hordes left it alone. Some of their own shamans came here to study, I was told. But for some reason, the hordes changed their attitude—after centuries of this city being holy and respected, the hordes decided it was time to be paid tribute. When the hordes arrived here to demand tribute, the priests and shamans of this city were divided on what to do. Some wished to continue their work in peace and were willing to submit, but others refused and before a consensus was reached, war erupted." Looking at Randolph, he said, "You're the battle-magic expert here. Imagine five thousand magic-using priests and shamans confronting a hundred thousand mounted warriors."

"Messy," said the bull-necked man. "If the magic-users were really good, they might hold them outside those walls for a week or so. Then the attrition and fatigue would win out for those still outside the walls." He pointed at all four corners of the compass. "Somewhere the perimeter would be breached, and the slaughter would begin."

"Which is precisely what happened," answered Pug. He pointed. "Over there, somewhere, a gate was battered off its hinges, and the defenders overrun. Mostly priests with temple guards, they were no match in hand-to-hand combat with the horde.

"Had they surrendered then, it would have ended well enough, for after a few public executions to demonstrate the iron rule of the Sha-shahan, Jarwa by name, who would then have pardoned the rest to demonstrate his leniency, the horde would have ridden on, leaving little more than a garrison and tax collector behind.

"Instead, a highly placed priest unsealed the Demon Gate, in the mad hope that the demons would repulse the horde, and that

he could seal up the gate after." Pug shook his head. "He was
the first one devoured." He sighed as they mounted steps leading up into the great temple. There were fifty steps in the flight
leading upward, a broad expanse of carved stone, and on each
end a pillar rose up, atop which sat empty stone cauldrons where
offerings to the gods and ancestors could be burned. "Of course
the demons drove back the horde, but they destroyed the only
possibility of repulsing them as well, the now-exhausted priests
and shamans of the Saaur.

"A very courageous and intelligent shaman, by name Hanam,
seized control of a demon through a brilliant ruse, and used that
control to infiltrate the demons and get to your mother and me,"
he said to Magnus. "He was instrumental in defeating the demon
captain Tugor, as Macros, your mother, and I battled Maarg,
keeping him on the other side of the rift."

"Tugor was defeated?" asked Magnus. "I thought one of
those imps mentioned him . . . perhaps I was mistaken."

"We'll ask Amirantha when we return. I have the impression
that demons are more difficult to kill than we thought," said
Pug. He led them across a large pavilion, into an antechamber.
Looking around, he said, "It looks so different."

The stones of the city themselves were now free of the soot
and ash that had coated them the last time Pug had been there.
Fires had still raged across the landscape, but a century of wind
and rain had effectively rid of any stain the stone everywhere but
in the deepest recesses.

Pug recognized a few hallmarks, a massive stone bas-relief
showing some legend of the Saaur, and moved toward a deep
vault. Once they were inside, the gloom swallowed them; Magnus moved his hand reflexively and light sprang up around them
in a comforting cocoon.

For reasons he couldn't explain, Pug felt the urge to whisper.
He resisted it and said, "Over there." He pointed to a cavern-
ous doorway leading into the Seal Chamber, where the Demon
Gate had been located. When last he had visited, Pug along with
Miranda, Macros, and the Saaur shaman Hanam in the form of
a demon, the alien race Shangri had been trying to move a rift to

Midkemia directly before the entrance from the demon realm. They had disrupted that and fled, after Macros and Hanam had given their lives to stop the demon invasion. Pug had slain the Shangri who had created the rift and assumed the portal to the demon realm had been closed as well.

When they reached the site of the Demon Gate, all four men froze in astonishment. A body lay sprawled out before the wall that had housed the gate. It was emaciated, barely larger than a human, but Pug instantly recognized it. Now he whispered, "It's Maarg."

When he had last seen the Demon King, he had been this mammoth, gross creature rearing up, nearly thirty-five feet in height. Massive jowls hung down from his cheekbones, giving him almost a bulldog-like expression. Eyes of burning fire had regarded Pug with a hatred that came in waves; his mere presence was an extant heralding of evil.

"Everything is so much smaller now," said Pug softly. He turned Maarg over and the body weighed almost nothing. His face looked like a parchment drawn in on hollow bones and still showed the pattern of being fashioned from the skins of living beings. When Pug had last seen him, every inch of his visage moved and twitched, as if those souls he had devoured were attempting to escape somehow. His nude body was likewise a thing of tattered skins that now looked sewn together like patchwork.

Pug stood up. "He had wings to spread across this chamber, and . . ." He looked at the wall. "Unbelievable."

The stone was gouged with deep talon marks, as if once the Demon Gate had closed, Maarg had tried to claw his way back into his own realm.

"How?" asked Magnus.

"When your grandfather died, I thought the gate closed, but Maarg must have somehow slipped back into this realm moments before it closed. Your mother and I were already on Midkemia, with that gate closed." He shrugged. "He must have devoured every life on this world and when hunger drove him even madder than before, he returned here and tried to get back . . ." Pug shook his head. "I can hardly feel sympathy for a thing like this, but it must have been a terrible way to die."

"There's one thing, Father," said Magnus.

"What?"

"Amirantha's imp was terrified of Maarg. If Maarg lies here dead, who is pretending to be Maarg, enough so to convince other demons he's their king?"

Pug looked stunned by the question.

# CHAPTER 19

## ONSLAUGHT

Miranda signaled.

She could manage to bring six people with her—Sandreena, Amirantha, Brandos, Jommy, Kaspar, and Father-Bishop Creegan. The moment they appeared at the mouth of the passage leading up into the clearing where the summoning would occur, they were under instructions to remain silent.

Kaspar said, "I don't care how many times I do that, I'll never find the experience pleasant."

Miranda smiled slightly. "It is, however, efficient."

Kaspar glanced at her and smiled back. "This is true."

Sandreena looked around, to see if there was any sign remaining of the Black Caps. All appeared quiet.

She relaxed and considered this undertaking. She was pleased the Father-Bishop was with them, for while he had never been a warrior like the Knight-Adamants of her Order, he was a magic-user of significant power, especially in the area of banishing demons. Brandos she knew from her first encounter with Amirantha, years before in the village of Yellow Mule. Kaspar and Jommy were also brawlers, if she could judge men, and she could, and would be useful to stand at her side if they needed to protect the spellcasters.

Sandreena also found herself wondering about Miranda. At first the woman annoyed her, and Sandreena couldn't quite understand why. Then it dawned on her: she had the same expectation of obedience—the woman liked to give orders—that was the hallmark of the High Priestess of her Order in Krondor. The difference was, Sandreena suspected, Miranda had earned that attitude, whereas the High Priestess considered it her birthright.

Miranda looked around, as if saying, *If everyone's ready, let's begin.*

They had fashioned the plan over the last four days. If possible, they were going to try to gain some sense of what was taking place, who these Black Caps, these Servants of Dahun, were in reality, before the mayhem was completely under way. The agreement was they would all observe as best they could from hiding and no one was to launch any assault unless discovered or upon Miranda's command. Getting some knowledge of the enemy was vital.

Too many times in the past Miranda and Pug had discovered forces at play behind the apparent forces they were facing. Banath, the God of Thieves and Liars, had a hand in everything so far, and they were horrified to discover the so-called Dark God of the Dasati was actually a Dreadlord who had managed over centuries to insinuate himself into the Dasati culture, usurping the allegiance of the Dasati race, twisting and warping them into a wholesale tool of evil.

Miranda had tried to pry as much information out of Amirantha as she could, but he had not had contact with his brother in any meaningful fashion in over a century, and had no notion of what had brought him to this current position, the apparent leader of these Black Caps. After several long discussions, Miranda was convinced of only one thing about Amirantha: he wanted to see his brother dead and now was none too soon.

Miranda's own childhood had been anything but conventional. Her father, the legendary Macros the Black, had vanished when she was still a child. Her mother, known by several names over the years—Lady Clovis, the Emerald Queen, and others— had been alternately loving and remote. After Miranda matured, the only thing they had in common was their love of magic. But Miranda had inherited, perhaps from her father, a fundamental distaste for the very things that drew her mother deeper into darkness: power and a fear of aging. Ironically, Miranda never seemed to age, though in part it was due to her aging very slowly, and also because of her exposure to the released energies of an artifact called the Lifestone.

All of which gave her a unique perspective: she understood how two brothers could end up being so un-alike, and why Amirantha would show no hesitation in killing Belasco.

Belasco was the mystery. He was unknown to any of them, save Amirantha and Brandos, and in the second case, by reputation only. What the old fighter knew about Belasco came from Amirantha.

It wasn't so much that Miranda warned about trusting the Warlock; she didn't. Nor was she particularly fearful of him. If Miranda had something close to a critical flaw, it was her own estimation of her ability. Should the demon-summoner prove to be a danger, she felt certain she could handle him. She was more uncertain what his motives were, beyond dealing with a murderous brother. He said he was envious of the community on Sorcerer's Isle, and wished to return after this encounter to spend time learning from Pug and the others. Miranda half-believed that. She just didn't know what he was hiding, and she knew he was hiding something.

Miranda also didn't care for the fact Sandreena and Amirantha had a past relationship. One that was far from happy, by all appearances. One of the reasons she agreed to have Creegan accompany them was he might be a calming influence on the Knight-Adamant. Like most of those of her Order, Sandreena was used to working alone, unsupervised. She might be a powerful fighter, but she also might be as dangerous as loose cargo on the deck of a ship during a storm.

Jommy and Kaspar were people whom she trusted with her life, and Kaspar had worked hard to gain that trust.

Creegan she had reservations about. Not his character, though she tended to mistrust the politically ambitious, and he clearly intended to be the head of the Church of Dala someday. It wasn't even a case of his dedication; Pug never would have recruited him for the Conclave had there been any doubt of that. It was his ability. He was not a brawler, not someone who had been tested in battle, in her opinion, though he claimed to have faced demons before in his youth.

And there was always the complication that the Conclave could encounter some serious issues with the Temple if she managed to get one of their Father-Bishops killed along the way. Pug would have forbidden his coming, she knew. But then Pug wasn't here. He was on another godsforsaken planet who knew where, doing whatever it was he and her son did when they were off on another godsforsaken planet.

She tried not to worry, but couldn't help it; she was a wife and a mother.

Miranda signaled again and Sandreena, Jommy, and Kaspar took the lead, moving in a roughly V formation, with Sandreena in the van. As the heaviest-armored of the three, she was the most likely to survive any unexpected surprises. Miranda and Amirantha came close behind, with Brandos serving as a rear guard.

Slowly, they made their way along the narrow trail, into the cleft that led up into the clearing where the sacrifices had occurred before. As expected, they encountered another sentry, but this time they weren't concerned about being subtle. Kaspar threw a dagger that took the man in the throat and he died before he could utter a sound.

From that point on, they walked in a crouch, moving slowly to avoid alerting any second sentry by sound or sight. As Miranda anticipated, with a special ceremony planned, two additional sentries were stationed—ironically, on the very ridge they had planned to watch from.

Miranda motioned to Jommy and Sandreena to follow Kaspar's lead. He was the most experienced soldier in the group. He knelt and whispered, "Can you get them over here without alerting those on the other side of that ridge?"

"I have a 'trick,'" she said, thinking instantly of Nakor. How that funny little man would have loved this sort of madness. It was exactly the sort of insanity that seemed to bring out the very best in him.

She whispered, "I'm going to get them over here in a hurry, so you need to subdue them before they can alert anyone. Now, we need to wait until their attentions wander for a moment."

Time passed slowly, and the air was suddenly filled with chanting, more rhythmic and lower than the sound they heard four nights earlier. Miranda waited, patiently, watching as the two guards stood their post. She would occasionally glance at Kaspar and the others, and they all waited, poised to act. Miranda was gratified to see not one of them was losing focus or letting the tedium dull their readiness. Too much was at stake to grow lax even for a moment.

Then a scream of absolute horror and agony caused the two sentries to look for a moment toward the source of the sound. Instantly, Miranda was on her feet, and with a short incantation she mystically reached out and seized both men as a cat would grab kittens by the scruff of the neck, and had them flying backward in a high arc, to land at her feet. At once, Kaspar, Jommy, Brandos, and Sandreena were upon the men, and they died without a sound.

"Now we go!" said Miranda and she led the way to the ridge from where she had plucked the two sentries.

They hurried, less mindful of the noise they made as the chanting reached a crescendo of screams and chants. They breasted the rise at the same moment, and right away Miranda knew they faced obliteration.

There was no ceremony. Rather, two hundred armed warriors stood ready, poised to charge, and behind them, on a large rock, stood Belasco. The chanting was an illusion, cast by a robed magician at his side, and at his other side was the nude figure of Darthea, clutching Belasco as she would her love. She looked at Amirantha with contempt as Belasco shouted, "Brother! You've brought friends! How considerate!" To his mob of warriors, he shouted, "Kill them!"

"Hold!" shouted Miranda to Sandreena and Brandos, who readied themselves for a charge.

With a sweeping gesture, Miranda sent a wave of flame rolling toward the attackers. Men screamed as flames rolled over them, several falling to the ground, only to trip others or be trampled on. Amirantha began to conjure and Sandreena shouted, "Don't!"

He paused and shouted back, "Why?"

"Isn't that your lady love over there with your brother?"

Amirantha suddenly realized exactly what Sandreena meant: no demon he conjured could be trusted. They were all in thrall to whomever was behind his brother's plan.

Amirantha acted as much out of pique as self-preservation. He sent a punishing spell toward Darthea. The demon recoiled, almost pulling Belasco off his feet before he let go of her. The agony she felt was passed along to him for a moment, until contact was broken. He staggered, while she fell and writhed on the stones. She contorted in agony and her body shifted, smoke roiling off her skin. Her features changed, becoming more demonic by the second, as her illusion of human beauty faded. She stopped thrashing and lay quivering and twitching. The thing that lay at Belasco's feet had the torso of a woman and her face was still beautiful, in an otherworldly fashion, but her legs were those of a black-furred goat. From her forehead two long horns swept back, and her fingers ended in black claws. Suddenly, a burst of green flame consumed her, as Belasco scuttled backward to avoid being burned.

The magician at Belasco's side began a conjuration, and San-dreena pointed her mace at him. A blast of energy, clear and col-orless, but rippling the air as it shot out from her weapon, sped across the clearing and took the magician in the chest. He was slammed backward in an explosion of white and yellow lights, to lie stunned on the rocks behind Belasco.

"Close your eyes!" shouted Miranda, and those warriors not consumed by her wall of flame were greeted with an explosion of blinding lights.

"Now!" shouted Miranda. "Fall back!"

"Back!" shouted Kaspar, lashing out to skewer one blinking Black Cap who came too close.

All around them burning, screaming men lay, while others tried to see through eyes blinded by a white-hot flash so bril-liant some feared they would be blind for what remained of their lives. A few cried out in fear, and suddenly the angry resolve of a moment before was replaced by a rising panic. The stench of burning bodies and the screams of the dying only added to the growing terror.

Jommy saw an opportunity and shouted, "We've been be-trayed! Belasco lied to us! We're all going to die!"

No one among the Black Caps could see who shouted that, but, as he hoped, the warning was repeated.

Miranda almost pulled him off his feet by grabbing his collar and hauling him away. "Now!" she hissed.

They moved back, seeking enough room from potential at-tackers so that Miranda could transport them away. Across the sea of writhing bodies and smoking chaos, Belasco rose to his feet and shouted, "No you don't!" He reached back and flung his arm forward, as if throwing a rock, and they all saw a flaming ball of orange ripping toward them.

It was Creegan who reacted first, throwing up a mystic barrier that caused the flames to spread up and around the intended targets. It was still hot, and Jommy yelped as his hair was singed. Brandos drew out his dagger and with an impres-sive heave sent it speeding across the gap between themselves and Belasco.

With a maniacal laugh, the magician dove to one side, shout-ing, "That was too close! Time for me to bid you all farewell!"

He vanished.

"Damn!" shouted Miranda as she sent a bolt of searing red energy into the midst of a clump of warriors attempting to get organized, sending most of them into the air as if thrown up-ward by some giant's hand. "Back!"

Most of the warriors serving Dahun were dead or blinded, or confused and trying to get away from the struggle, but enough of them were gathering their wits that soon Miranda and her companions risked being overwhelmed. "Back!" she repeated.

They hurried up the draw into the narrow path that even-tually led down toward the sea. Brandos, Kaspar, and Jommy backed along the path, swords ready, but those few Black Caps who followed seemed less than eager to engage. They had seen the damage the magicians behind those three fighters had done, and their own magicians were nowhere to be seen.

When Miranda felt safe to conjure, she said, "We were led into this trap. Somehow they knew we were coming."

"We can sort all that out when we get back to Sorcerer's Isle," said Kaspar.

Miranda's eyes widened. "We must go there now!" She reached out and grabbed Amirantha and Creegan and shouted, "Hang on!" When everyone was holding on, she willed herself to the island.

And they arrived in the middle of a holocaust.

Pug and Magnus finished examining what was left of the Saaur library at Ahsart. As the shamans and priests of the city had gath-ered their writings over the years, most had perished with them, but a few older clay tablets and a handful of bound books locked away in a vault had endured. The language was unknown to them. Simon said, "Had I the time, I have a spell which would allow me to decipher these within a week, two at the outside."

"We don't have the time," said Pug. The discovery that Maarg was dead and someone or something else was using his name to mask his identity was troubling. This was not the first time in his life he had discovered that much of what he assumed to be true was half-truth, inaccurate, lies, or just wrong. "With no one here, we can arrange for some students to come and gather this up, and return with it to Sorcerer's Isle. Then," he said with a weak smile, "you can study them at leisure."

Magnus came to stand next to his father and spoke softly. "What is it?"

"Something is terribly wrong," said Pug, not caring if the other two magicians overheard him. "Every bit of information we received about the Demon Legion led us to believe that things were much as they had been when we battled the Emerald Queen." That one demon captain, Jakan, in the guise of the Emerald Queen, the Lady Clovis, had engineered a war that had engulfed half of Midkemia. "But now we see that Maarg lies dead, a victim of his own gluttony, stranded here . . ." His eyes widened. "Is it possible?"

"What?" asked Magnus.

"Everything that has happened to me from the day I was captured by the Tsurani, all of it was part of a much larger plan. Your grandfather said so, Ban-ath said so, and I've always seen myself as a player in a larger drama. But like a player, I've only been concerned with my part. Oh, I'm aware of the parts of those around me, your mother, Tomas, Nakor when he was with us, even to a lesser extent Ban-ath's.

"But because I know my role, or think I do, and because I know something of the others' roles, doesn't mean I understand the complete drama." He visibly winced. "I am such a fool!"

"What?" asked Magnus, obviously not following his father's deductions.

"At first I blamed the Nameless, because I was told he was at the heart of every evil thing that befell Midkemia. It was logical, even obvious, given he is the God of Evil.

"But what if there's another agency, another cause of evil that is creeping into our realm using the Nameless's own acts as a cover, to prevent us from seeing his hand behind things?"

"The Dasati Dark God?"

"Perhaps he was a tool as well. For all his power, did he strike you as particularly subtle?"

"He gulled the Dasati into thinking he was their Death God," reminded Magnus.

"True, but that is a simple deception compared to what I'm imagining."

"What are you imagining, Father?"

"I assumed that Jakan, the demon playing the role of the Emerald Queen, wanted to reach the Lifestone, to seize its power for his own use. I was unclear whether that was to fortify his own role in our universe, to return and battle Maarg for supremacy of the Fifth Circle of Hell, or for some other motive. I was so intent on stopping him, I almost got myself killed, and I really didn't care why he wanted the Lifestone." He looked at Magnus and a rueful smile crossed his face. "What if he was bait?"

"For what?"

"To lure Maarg here to die of starvation, while someone, or something, else gained domination of the Fifth Circle. Jakan was on Midkemia; Tugor died fighting Hanam; and Maarg was left here to die.

"Someone else is ruling the Fifth Circle, but doesn't want us to know his identity."

"Why?"

"Because understanding that identity might be key to defeating him. Else why guard it so jealously with all this misdirection?"

"Perhaps Amirantha might shed some light on this, or maybe the elf, Gulamendis?"

"We certainly will need to speak with both of them." To the other two magicians he said, "Come here and stand close." To Magnus he said, "Take us back to the rift, please."

The four magicians stood near enough to grip hands, and Magnus used his arts to take them to a position before the rift, a short distance from the edge of the plateau overlooking the city of Ahsart. Pug started to step through and halted.

Instantly, Magnus said, "What is it?"

"We're being blocked!"

"What?" asked Randolph.

"We cannot go through this rift."

"How is that possible?" asked Simon.

Pug looked around the hillside and saw a large rock. He threw it at the portal, and when it touched the shimmering grey void that marked the rift, it bounced back. "At least you wouldn't have been killed, but you'd have gotten a fair bloody nose from walking face-first into that."

"Who could do this?" asked Magnus.

Pug took a deep breath and said, "The same evil bastard who's able to subvert Amirantha's summonings and use them against him, I think."

"Belasco?" asked Magnus.

"Or whoever his master really is," answered Pug. He looked around and pointed to another clear area. "Come, let us begin. We're not going to waste time trying to overcome that barrier. I know enough rift lore to know that I can make another that will follow this one to our home. It should only take an hour or so, faster with your help."

Randolph said, "Tell us what to do."

They began.


The heat rolled off the burning building like a wave, sweeping over Miranda and her companions as they appeared in the garden. "Grab hold!" she shouted, choking from the heavy smoke. As no one had stepped away when they appeared, it took mere seconds for them to resume their previous positions, and Miranda willed them a short distance away, on a low hillock overlooking the rear of the main building.

Everything was on fire.

Below, the main house burned like a bonfire, and the outer buildings were reduced to either flaming skeletons of wood framing or little boxes with flames shooting out their windows and doors. The ground around the compound was littered with the bodies of students and instructors, and Miranda could barely contain her rage.

Then the first demon came into view, running around the corner as he chased one of the students. Miranda pulled back her arm and let fly with a bolt of energy that should have reduced the creature to ash. Instead, the spell stunned him long enough for the student to put more distance between herself and the demon, as the infernal creature stood reeling for a minute. Then he shook his head and looked to find the author of the insult.

Spying Miranda on the top of the hill, the demon lowered his shoulders and charged. He was roughly human in the torso, but with shoulders far broader than any human's. The head looked like a cat's skull, devoid of flesh, with exaggerated fangs. The legs looked like the back end of a horse, and while it appeared to be at risk of falling over at any step, it moved with uncanny speed.

Miranda's eyes widened in surprise that the demon weathered the blast she had sent and she began another attack. Then her mind locked up, and suddenly she couldn't remember anything.

Amirantha incanted a spell and unleashed it at the charging demon, who stumbled, then stood motionless, trembling as if seized by a monstrous hand that shook it. "If one of you would please kill this horror," he said to Sandreena and Father-Bishop Creegan.

Both hurled their most powerful spells of destruction, especially crafted for demons, and the creature let out a howl of agony as it fell to its knees and was consumed by bursting orange flames.

Miranda said, "Thank you. I thought . . ."

"Demons are not like mortal creatures," said Sandreena. "Sometimes, brute force works—"

"Sometimes it doesn't," finished Brandos. "Look out!"

A flying horror, all wings and talons, came swooping in, apparently intent on ripping someone's head off. Creegan shouted a single word as he stuck out his hand, and a black shape, looking like nothing so much as a shimmering blanket of silk, suddenly enveloped the demon, smothering it. As it fell to the ground, the wrapped demon grew smaller and smaller, until it vanished completely.

Sandreena said, "Look!" and pointed at a knot of demons who were gathered together, surrounded by some of the island's magicians. The magic-users were using a variety of spells and enchantments to keep the monsters at bay, and it appeared to be working.

"We've got to help them!" shouted Miranda, charging down the hillside.

"Oh, mercy," said Brandos as he was a half-stride behind her.

Miranda pulled up short and began to cast a spell, but Brandos dove from behind and dragged her down, just as the demons unleashed a blast of blackness pulsing with purple lights. Each magician was consumed by the clinging, pulsing energy that wrapped around them like a shroud. They fell to the ground, screams muffled as if their faces were covered in cloth.

"When they gather like that in a knot, they're going to pull something like that," shouted the old fighter. He leaped to his feet and helped her up, as a demon in that small group charged.

Amirantha, Sandreena, and Creegan all caught up, and Sandreena intercepted the charging demon, bashing it in the face with her shield and swinging her mace in a wicked arc, crushing the creature's skull.

Miranda allowed herself to be pulled over by Creegan and Amirantha, as Jommy took up position beside Brandos. "What do I do?" asked the young noble.

"Keep these bastards off the spellcasters so they can do their work," he said, slashing out at a demon who got too close.

"What about Sandreena?" asked Jommy as he backed off another demon with a wicked cut of his blade that took the creature on an unprotected forearm.

"Don't worry about that girl," said Brandos, backing off another demon, who was leaping toward Amirantha, as if he recognized where the real threat was coming from. "She knows how to take care of herself."

Sandreena was expert in avoiding the animal-like claws of the demons. This bunch was something like those she had encountered before, mostly sinew and fangs, little intelligence, though they were cunning, as demonstrated by the trap they had unleashed on the young magicians.

Miranda tried to pull the smothering fabric off one young magician that she could reach, but the stuff resisted her every attempt to remove it, whether through spells designed to dispel enchantment or by physically trying to claw it off. She felt her heart sink and she went cold inside as the young magician, a bright young man from Yabon named Patrick, died as she was helpless to save him. "Do something!" she shouted at Amirantha out of frustration.

He recognized and ignored her frustration, concentrating as much as he could on dealing with the threat right before him. He could easily have gated in a half-dozen demons of his own in this period of time, but now he realized he could not trust one of them to do his bidding. Instead he focused on the spells at his disposal that would either destroy them outright or banish them back to the demon realm. But it took time. Each target had to be in his line of sight for nearly a minute as he enchanted it, and sometimes the break in his concentration forced him to start over.

Father-Bishop Creegan seemed to have different abilities at his disposal, more effective but slower. He would single out a demon, chant, and, after a minute, a bright light would envelope the target and it would freeze motionless. Then, after a few more minutes, it would simply vanish. Unfortunately, from Amirantha's point of view, he could only manage one at a time.

The wind shifted and suddenly they were choking from the smoke, as it billowed off the flaming buildings and swept over them, a blinding wall of darkness that filled the lungs and caused the eyes to water. "This way!" shouted Miranda, coughing as she tried to lead them around to a point upwind of the flames.

Sandreena crouched as another demon tried to claw at her, its claws scraping harmlessly off her helm, and then she stood, bringing her helmet up under its chin as she held up her shield to block a second demon to the right of the first. Then she spun to the right, her mace held out, so that when she finished the circle, the mace's head slammed into the demon's side. It doubled over and fell atop the stunned first demon, and Sandreena retreated after the others.

As they moved back, regrouping, before them unfolded a scene of horror. Of the hundreds of students and instructors in residence on Sorcerer's Isle, most lay dead on the ground. Many of those had been maimed or mutilated, or partially devoured. Scattered around the area were demon corpses, mute testimony to the courage of the young magicians.

From their vantage point, they could see scampering figures in the fire as the main house went up in a tower of flames. Then they saw it.

In the middle of the flames, where they reached highest into the sky, stood a figure of undiluted terror. Monstrous in size, it was nearly twenty feet tall. The head was like that of a bull, but with an elongated snout, and the horns were impossibly wide, spanning eight feet. Massive shoulders and enormous arms with muscles looking like heavy cable under a black-silk skin. The eyes were red flame, and steam or smoke blew out of flaring nostrils. As if challenging heaven, the creature threw back his head and bellowed a call that was painful to hear.

Confusion and panic were mounting on all sides, and Miranda struggled to make sense out of what she could see through the blinding smoke. "Amirantha! What is that?" she demanded.

"If I were to guess," said the Warlock, coughing from the smoke, "it's a demon captain, perhaps the Dahun those Black Caps were summoning. Right now—" he exploded into a fit of coughing, then swallowed hard—"I don't know if I understand anything about demons." His tone left no doubt he was shaken by the day's revelations.

"Everything we saw over by the Peaks was a distraction," said Father-Bishop Creegan. "To lure us away so they could destroy the Conclave."

"As long as I'm standing and Pug and my sons are alive," said Miranda, "so is the Conclave." Her tone left no doubt of her anger. And she shot forth a bolt of searing energies that should have withered the demon where he stood. Instead, he turned and looked at the source of the attack.

Sandreena, Amirantha, and Creegan all reacted within moments, unleashing three spells of banishment. The creature seemed stunned, staggering back, but didn't vanish as intended.

"It's tethered!" shouted Amirantha.

"Tethered?" asked Jommy.

It was Brandos who answered. "Something's anchoring it here, in this realm. You do it to keep a demon from going home if it's unhappy with what you want it to do!"

"Look for anything over there that's out of place," shouted Amirantha. "An icon, a pole, something that's not burning. That will be the tether. Destroy it, and we can banish that horror."

Miranda said, "I can't see a thing with all this smoke and flame."

Then the monstrous demon recovered from their attack. With a bovine grin, it advanced on their position, a band of scampering, running, and hopping smaller demons in its wake.

Brandos shouted to Jommy and Kaspar, "Don't try to attack it directly. Kaspar, break to the left! Jommy, break right with me, when I give the word! Keep those smaller devils in front of you! Don't let any of them get behind you!

"Amirantha, you have to protect Creegan and Miranda as best you can!"

"Understood," shouted the Warlock. He shouted to the Father-Bishop and Miranda, "Don't act until I give the word!" He reached into his belt pouch and pulled a large gem out of it. Crushing it in his hand, he shouted a single word, and suddenly they were engulfed in red smoke.

"Now!" shouted Brandos and he and Jommy ran right, while Kaspar took off in the other direction.

The large demon bellowed again and swung a massive claw through the space occupied a moment before by the three fighters, and then backhanded the cloud of red smoke. He shouted in pain and anger when his hand came away with red smoldering sores, as if he had touched acid. The unexpected wound distracted the creature for a moment, while the smaller demons rushed the fighters.

Inside the smoke cloud, Amirantha said, "Back up slowly!"

His two companions did as they were told and moved back, until they could see the befuddled demon captain standing over the roiling cloud of caustic gas. "Whatever you have, Miranda," said the Warlock, "now's the time."

Her eyes were wide with anger and frustration, and she reached down to the depth of her power, using her will to focus the most destructive spell she could muster. A line of blinding light extended from her outstretched palm to strike the creature, and down it flowed a brilliant white light. The demon captain stood stunned for a moment, then bellowed in pain and began to writhe.

"I see it!" shouted Jommy to Brandos. He pointed to a strange object, a black post with alien runes carved on the surface. It sat in the midst of the flames, untouched.

He took a step toward it, but Brandos grabbed him from behind and yanked him back just as a demon leaped to the spot he had vacated. The old fighter swung hard with his sword, severing the creature's head from shoulders. The body lay flopping on the ground while the head's features contorted and it tried to scream. "Unless you're fireproof, that's not going to work. And look out!"

Another pair of demons leaped at them, each about the size of a large monkey. Jommy extended his sword point and allowed the creature to impale itself. The shock that ran up Jommy's arm almost cost him his sword. He lifted his boot and kicked hard, as he pulled back, sending the demon tumbling backward. Brandos beheaded the other one in efficient fashion. "Point's useful, but not that way," he said as he struggled to breathe in all the choking smoke.

Jommy was forced to agree and began slashing at anything that tried to approach. "What do we do about that anchor?"

"Wait," said Brandos, looking around, as if seeking inspiration. The large demon seemed to be coming out of the shock induced by the three spells hitting it and stood still, slightly shaking its head, as if clearing it.

"Miranda!" shouted Brandos. "If you can destroy that totem over there, Amirantha and Creegan can banish—"

He stopped as he saw a figure in white and silver dash through the flames toward the carved pole. "Oh, girl, no!" he shouted.

Sandreena had worked her way around to the other side of the fire and now was making a mad dash for the totem. She obviously understood as much as Brandos and Amirantha did the significance of the device. Her tabard was stained with soot and char, and was smoking along one side of the back. Mindless of the scorching heat, she raised her mace above her head, then brought it down in an underhanded sweep, all the while not stopping. She threw her complete weight into the blow, and when her mace struck the wood, the shock reverberated throughout her body, but the wooden icon shattered, bursting into fragments that instantly went up in flames. She kept running, and her tabard was alight.

"To me, girl!" shouted Brandos. "To me!"

She turned toward the sound of a familiar voice, and Jommy slashed at a demon who turned to see what was coming up behind him. The blow cut the demon's throat and black, smoking blood gushed from the wound. Sandreena was blind from the smoke and started to run past Brandos, who reached out and grabbed her arm, shouting, "Fall down!"

She did as she was told, and he lay atop of her, putting out the flames with his own body. Jommy kept his blade slashing in all directions as demons sought to swarm over the fallen Knight-Adamant and the old fighter.

A sizzling bolt of green fire sped out of nowhere to strike two demons from behind, causing them to fall to their knees then convulse, their red leather hides smoking and blistering as they writhed then vanished in a blinding white flash.

Jommy looked to see the origin of the bolt and saw Pug, Magnus, and two other magicians floating above the fray. Randolph and Simon were not the masters of destructive magic Pug and Magnus were, but knew enough of the more violent side of magic to inflict harm on the demons below.

"Pug!" shouted Jommy, and he felt reinvigorated as he hacked at the demons in front of him, allowing Sandreena and Brandos to regain their feet. Whatever damage the young woman warrior endured, she ignored as she joined in the fray, using her mace to good effect and driving the demons back so the older fighter could get his wind and join the fight.

The massive demon was stunned by Sandreena's attack, and Amirantha and Creegan both began complicated banishing rituals. They were almost in harmony with their chants, though both were speaking different words. Then, as one, they finished, and the large demon simply faded from view.

The tide of battle changed for with their captain gone, demons sought a means of escape. Several had the arts to will themselves back to their own realm, but others appeared to be abandoned to the less-than-tender care of those they attacked. Other magicians, many gravely injured, began to appear around the edges of the fire, and they did what they could to keep the demons surrounded.

"Remember that nasty trick of letting us surround them!" shouted Brandos.

Pug threw a massive energy bolt, but instead of striking the assembled demons, now down to about a dozen of them, it caused a huge compression of the air above them. The thunderclap caused everyone's ears to pop, and, as if blowing out a massive candle, the flames dispersed and suddenly the fire was mostly out. A few hotspots still burned, but mostly the building was now smoking char.

Miranda ran down the hill to help finish the fight, when suddenly a prone demon leaped to his feet, then onto Miranda's back.

Pug shouted, "No!" as the creature set his fangs to her neck, faster than she could react, and tore out the side of her throat. Miranda's legs gave out and she collapsed, a fountain of blood pumping out of her neck.

Magnus's cry echoed his father's, and he extended his hand and the demon withered to ash in a moment. The rage he displayed was incredible, and every demon who saw him turned to flee, only to be cut down by those nearby. Pug ignored everything but cutting a charred path through demonic bodies as he struggled to reach his wife.

In less than a minute it was over. Pug and the others reached Miranda, and he knelt next to his wife. No one needed to be told she was dead. The lifeless pose and her fixed gaze made it abundantly clear. The attack had been so sudden, the damage to her neck so severe, only the most powerful healing magic used instantaneously might have saved her. In the scant moments it took for Pug to reach her, she had bled to death.

Pug was motionless. Magnus came to kneel next to his father and both were still.

The struggle was over, and silence fell, only punctuated by the occasional crackle of flame and pop of cooling embers. Slowly, they all gathered around Miranda, save for a few who were trying to tend to the other wounded.

Nothing was said for a long time. Pug reached under his wife's prone body and lifted her with the help of his son. His features were set, but wetness ran down his cheeks, as he softly said, "I will see to my wife." He glanced at Magnus and said, "You must be strong. There's work still to be done."

Magnus looked around and nodded. His face was ashen, but his features showed resolve. He looked at one of the injured students and asked, "My brother?"

Unable to speak, the student merely shook his head in the negative, then pointed at the heart of the house, where the office used by Pug and his son had stood. Only smoking rubble remained, and throughout that part of the building charred bodies lay in contorted positions.

Magnus hung his head a long moment, then, with tears running down his cheeks, said, "Come, we have much before us." He led the others away from where his father stood motionless, holding his mother.

And in the end, Pug remained alone with his wife amid the smoking ruin of what had been their home for decades.

# EPILOGUE

## EPITAPH

The crowd was silent.

Father-Bishop Creegan, sporting bandages from burns received during the fight the day before, stood in front of a single stone marker as the sun rose and lit the landscape with golden and rose hues. Up on a hill a pyre stood ready, and Miranda's body, wrapped in white linen, lay prepared for cremation. Other bodies were also ready for final rites, but most were burned beyond recognition, so they were receiving group rites.

Caleb and Marie were somewhere in that group. Over sixty bodies had been recovered and four more were missing, assumed completely devoured in the heart of the fire; the community at Sorcerer's Isle was now reduced by two-thirds. Of the three score teachers, only a dozen were left, and of the hundred students, not quite twice that number survived.

The entire population of the island was stunned from the events of the day before, and all duties and tasks had been carried out quietly, as if most of the populace was too numb to speak. Pug and Magnus had spent the entire night sitting with Miranda's body as it was prepared for this morning's funeral. Pug had let no one else help him carry her to the top of the hill, where he placed her gently atop the piled wood.

Magnus's face had been set in a fixed expression all night, and he and his father barely spoke.

Creegan said: "Our time on this world is short. Even those like Miranda, who lived longer than most, her days were brief. Some will count her life a full one, replete with achievements enough for a dozen others, yet we feel her time with us was too short."

He fell silent for a moment, then said, "It is not the usual duty of my Order to conduct services like this for an outsider, but Miranda was not an outsider to me. Our work together for the greater good made her my sister." He looked at Pug and Magnus. "Everyone here shares in your loss, even if we can only claim a small portion of the grief you feel, Pug, Magnus. We know a great injury has been done to you, and we mourn with you. We know that it seems as if something profoundly unfair has happened.

"We in the Service of Dala believe in achieving balance, seeking the equitable outcome. The universe doesn't always permit that, and the ways of the gods are manifold and difficult to comprehend. I offer no comfort in saying this, but rather seek to allow that comfort may be out there, somewhere, beyond our ability to find it today, but with the hope it may come to us in time.

"Miranda served others and put herself at risk many times, and endured hardship and privation for the sake of others. There is no higher calling in life than service such as hers, and I believe at this moment she is standing before Lims-Kragma and being judged as worthy and being offered a better place on the Wheel of Life. I believe our Goddess, Dala, is standing at her side and recommending her to her Sister Goddess."

He took a breath, fighting back emotion. "Caleb stands on her other side, I'm certain, with Marie, his wife, and so many others who served the good here at the island. They are all to be praised and they will be missed, for they were our brothers and sisters in struggle. Good men and women all, may the Goddess bless them, each and every one." He turned and looked up at the top of the hill, and signaled. A torchbearer began the blaze, moving around the edges of the pyre, setting the kindling at the bottom alight. Quickly, the flames spread and the bodies atop the wood were eventually consumed.

Magnus spoke quietly, "There's been too much fire, Father."

Pug could only nod.

Without another word, Creegan came to stand before Pug and took his hands in his own, held them for a moment, nodded once, then moved down the hill toward the remains of the villa. Others followed suit, and when it was over, the remaining community of Sorcerer's Isle waited some distance away while the father and son said their good-byes to Miranda and Caleb.

Time passed, then, finally, in a whisper, Pug said, "We have work to do."

"What first, Father?" said Magnus. "I need to keep busy for a while."

"You will," said Pug, turning toward those waiting below. "Your mother and I discussed many things, including what we must do should such a terrible day visit us.

"We move to the castle, and we shall stay there for a while. Let those who did this think us in tatters and running and hiding. We shall send out messages to all our agents around this world and the struggle shall continue.

"We will find Belasco, Dahun, whoever else is involved, and uncover who is truly behind this madness. We will also find the Demon Gate, wherever it is, and we shall close it down."

He continued down the hill, determination in his step, and his son followed, swallowing his grief for his mother and brother. If his father could endure such a loss and press on with the work that needed to be done, Magnus was determined he could as well. If only the pain would fade, even just a little.

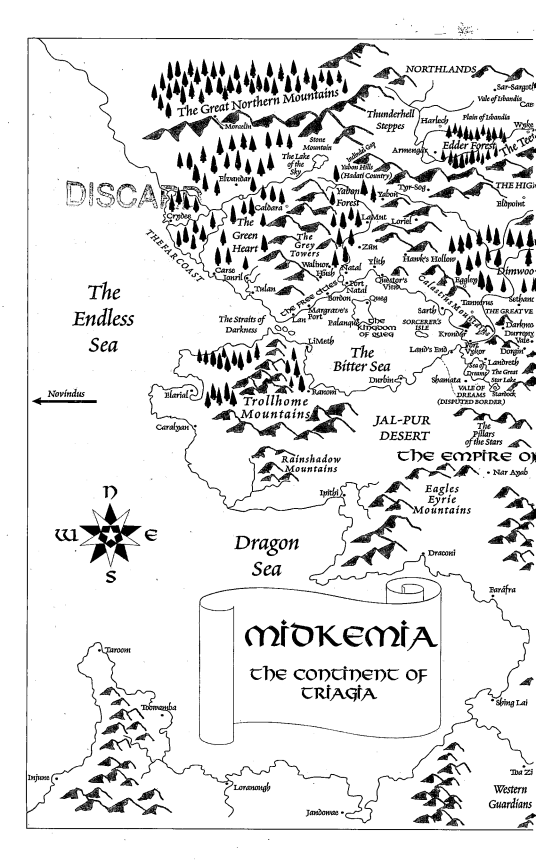